Kingdom of Briars and Roses

Cursed Fae Courts

Book One

Heather Hildenbrand

Cursed Fae Courts
Pronunciation Guide

Aurelia Valeen – Aur-el-ee-ya Vuh-leen (Princess of Summer)
Sonoma Eko – Suh-no-muh Ek-oh (Aine warrior)
Tyrion Valeen – Teer-ee-on Vuh-leen (King of Summer)
Celeste Valeen – Suh-lest Vuh-leen (Queen of Summer)
Heliconia Kucera – Hel-ihh-cone-ya Cue-seer-uh (Conqueror of the north, self-declared Queen of Winter
Rydian Nytherra – Rid-ee-in Nigh-terra (Second son of Duron)
Callan Ashfall – Call-en Ash-fall (Autumn prince)
Duron Ashfall – Der-on Ash-fall (Autumn King)
Lesha – Lee-sha (Aine warrior)
Amanti – Uh-mon-tee (Aine warrior)
Daegel – Day-gull (Rydian's friend & confidante)
Meerdra – Meer-druh (Oracle in Grey Oak)
Koraz – Core-azz (Duron's top advisor)
Lemuel – Lem-yule (Duron's advisor)
Vanya – Vah-n-yuh (Aurelia's first maid at Grey Oak)
Beryl – Bear-uhl (Aurelia's second maid at Grey Oak)
Talthis – Tuhl-th-iss Lightshore emissary

Naliadne/Nali – Nal-ee-ad-nee (Princess of the Osphanis/River People)
Patamoi – Pa-tuh-moy (King of the Osphanis/River People)
Dorcha – Dor-cha (Aurelia's sword)
Latha – La-thuh (Sonoma's sword)
Verdant – Verd-ant (Healer tribe with powerful magic that lived a thousand years ago
Moriori – Mor-ee-or-ee (Pacifist people from an island in the northwest sea)
Rada – Rah-dah (Sea fae people)
Naiad – Nigh-add (Mermaid fae)
Menryth – Men-rith (Name of the planet/world)
Calidium Empire – Cuh-lid-ee-um (Once a great southern empire before it fell during the Great War)
Alorica – Al-or-ee-kuh (Western continent across the sea)
Vorinthia – Vor-in-thee-uh (The last kingdom to wield strong magic before it fell in the Great War)

THE
MOON

Chapter One
Aurelia

The day before my life went to Hel, the world outside Sunspire Castle appeared deceivingly serene. From my bedroom window, I surveyed the view. Our capital city of Rosewood sprawled northward, vibrant with the hum of merchants and the laughter of children. To the west, the Osphanis River sparkled in the afternoon sunlight as it wound lazily toward the forest. But beneath the peace, I couldn't shake the feeling that my destiny lay beyond these walls—waiting, dangerous, and inescapable.

As always, my thoughts drifted to the monster who lurked out there too.

Heliconia.

She was a powerful threat that loomed ever greater with each passing day. One the king and queen of the Summer Court would do anything to defeat.

Even sacrifice their firstborn daughter.

I looked down at the empty finger where my mate's ring would go and rubbed absently at my palms. As if I could wash my hands of this whole damned mess. As if I hadn't spent the last eight months trying and failing to do just that.

A soft knock interrupted my thoughts, and I turned as my bedroom door swung open.

My younger sister Lilah skipped in, her honey-blonde hair bouncing with each step. At eight years old, she was pure light and joy, untouched by the burdens of politics and arranged alliances. It made my heart squeeze to think what kind of world might await her when she reached her own twentieth birthday.

"Aurelia," she sang, her blue eyes bright.

I tugged on her pointed fae ear. "Hey, rascal."

She stuck out her tongue. "I'm not a rascal. I'm a princess."

"Why can't you be both?" I countered.

She frowned, clearly undecided, then changed the subject. "Mother is waiting for you," she scolded. Ugh. She was our mother reincarnate when she used that voice. "She said you were due an hour ago to discuss final arrangements."

"I know," I said, ruffling her hair. She wrinkled her nose in mock protest but didn't bother straightening the mess. Her royal mannerisms might've come from our mother, but her willingness to forego the perfection of styled hair and fancy gowns was all me. "I just needed a moment."

"They shooed me out, which means they're probably talking about Heliconia again. Why does she hate us so much anyway?" Her innocent gaze as she asked the question was enough to make my heart ache.

"I don't think it's about us," I told her.

"Then what's it about?"

I gave her a pointed look. "Nothing you need to worry about."

She scowled. "No one tells me anything important."

"That's because you're supposed to be enjoying the perks of being a kid."

"Mother says ignorance is the mark of a terrible leader."

I rolled my eyes. "I don't think that applies to eight-year-olds."

She shrugged. "I don't make the rules."

I grinned at that. "All right, fine. Heliconia once competed to become one of the Aine."

"But the Aine are so *good*," Lilah protested.

She was right.

The Aine were an elite caste of warriors among the fae. A sacred dozen selected by the Fates to protect the realm from any threat. The selection was a practice that dated back a thousand years and was one of the few traditions honored by every single court. The female warriors were chosen for their lethal strength but also their pure hearts. Heliconia had proven one but not the other.

Her heart was much more like the Furiosities.

If the Fates were the light, the Furiosities were pure darkness. Kings of Hel whose shadow gifts fed off the black-hearted and the corrupt. They were the demons of nightmares and the bedtime stories used to keep children from being naughty.

"Probably why Heliconia wasn't chosen," I pointed out.

"Yeah," Lilah muttered. Her expression sharpened. "Then what happened?"

"When Heliconia lost her place among the Aine, she became bitter. She blamed the Fates and the Aine they'd chosen—specifically the Summer Court's warriors—for shutting her out unfairly. Her heart twisted with darkness, and she vowed revenge."

"What was her revenge?" Lilah asked in a hushed voice.

"One night, she trapped a demon in the forest and forced him to give her some of his dark magic. Then she used it to kill one of the Aine and took its power inside herself. She's been using that power to kill the Aine and end the practice of making more ever since."

Lilah stared at me with wide eyes until I'd finished the story. Then, she blinked, and her expression cleared to something so matter-of-fact that it caught me off guard.

"I know, but why us?" she pressed. "*We're* not Aine. And we didn't do anything to her."

"She's power-hungry and bloodthirsty. And instead of taking one life at a time, she craves the realm itself."

"That's why she attacked Concordia," Lilah said.

"Yes." And why she'd vowed to come for the rest of us.

"She's a meany-head," Lilah declared.

"A complete meany-head," I agreed.

I braced myself for more questions, but my sister was apparently satisfied enough to change the subject—back to the one she undoubtedly cared about most right now.

"I asked Mother if I could go to your party, and she said no. It's not fair." She pouted.

"It will be way past your bedtime," I reminded her.

"And yours," she shot back. There was a dreamy sigh in her voice as she added, "I just want to meet Prince Callan."

Callan.

His name was spoken more often than I cared to hear it. My future husband, the heir to the Autumn Court. The fae male I was meant to marry to secure an alliance strong enough to protect Sevanwinds from the growing threat of Heliconia. To ensure we didn't share Concordia's fate.

Lilah looked back at me, stars shining in her eyes. "Do you think he's handsome?"

"I think that matters a lot less than if he's good or fair or kind."

Lilah shrugged, still too young to understand the gravity of our world. "I bet he's handsome. You're lucky. By the end of the week, you'll have a prince for a husband. Mother says maybe someday I'll get one, too. And then we can both have our own castles."

Her innocence, her joy... It made me smile, though there was a heaviness beneath it all. I envied her. To be that carefree, untouched by duty. I couldn't remember the last time I'd felt that way. If ever.

"I'm sure you will," I said softly. "But for now, you're too young to be thinking about princes and husbands."

Lilah laughed and twirled, her blue dress spinning around her ankles. I spotted dirt along the hemline and shook my head. Before I could warn her about letting Mother see it, she conjured a fistful of wildflowers and held them to her chest like a bridal bouquet.

"One day," Lilah said as she twirled, "I'll have a big wedding just like you, with flowers and music and dancing—"

"Lilah," I interrupted gently, catching her mid-spin. "Marriage is not just about parties. It's hard work."

"How do you know?" she teased. "Have you ever been married?"

I shook my head. "Have you?"

Lilah tilted her head, but before she could say whatever was on her mind, a bell tolled from the temple tower across the courtyard. It was past time. And now I was late for more than just the meeting with my parents.

Hels.

I gave Lilah a quick hug and sent her off with a playful nudge. "Go find Maelis," I told her. "You're late for your afternoon lessons."

Lilah ran off, still clutching the flowers, singing to herself as she disappeared around the corner, her footsteps echoing down the hall. I watched her go, affection tightening my chest. The marriage alliance stipulated I'd spend half the year in Grey Oak with my husband and half the year here in the Summer Court. I wasn't sure what I'd do without Lilah's light in my days for the half-year I was gone.

I hoped she never lost that light.

Or that Heliconia never found a way to snuff it out.

To ensure it, I would give myself to Prince Callan even if he wasn't any of the things I'd told Lilah I wanted. Even if all I'd ever wanted was to be a warrior, mateless and free like the Aine.

~

Sunspire's throne room was grand, all high ceilings and sun-drenched whitestone walls with the banners of Sevanwinds hanging proudly from the ceiling. At the far end, two ornate thrones, also made of whitestone, sat on a dais, beautiful glittering jewels embedded along their plated gold backing. On another platform high above it all stood a whitestone sculpture of the Fates. The curved, singular body portrayed three faces in one; Maiden, Mother, Crone. The goddesses who bestowed their favor—or their disfavor—upon all creatures who walked Menryth. A similar likeness stood inside every temple across the realm, but this one was special.

Mother had once told me the whitestone sculpture and matching thrones had been gifted by the Fates themselves at my royal dedication ceremony. The sculpture had never held much interest for me, but the thrones always drew my attention for some reason.

Lilah and I had sat in them once while our parents were at a dinner—her idea, not mine. The porous surface was meant to absorb power, thus imbuing the stone with strength. They were even more uncomfortable than they looked. Cold and unforgiving with sharp angles and hard edges.

We never bothered to sit in them again.

Currently, they were empty as the king and queen of the Summer Court stood over a long table draped in an emerald silk cloth. Several maps of the fae realms lay spread before them, scattered with markers showing the kingdoms, the courts, and the fae who ruled them.

After years of trying to forge alliances with the courts, the only one that had entertained our request was Autumn. According to my father, the river people had spent the one and only meeting they'd attended arguing with the representatives of the Midnight Court—a conflict that had nearly devolved into a physical altercation. The Moriori, though they dutifully attended each meeting, were pacifists and didn't possess an army large enough. Spring had sent word that they'd consider pledging their support only when we had the allegiance of enough others for theirs to matter. I couldn't understand the fae's unwillingness to unite, especially after watching Concordia destroyed in its isolation.

That last meeting had been almost a year ago now. I'd begged my father to let me attend with him, but he refused, telling me to enjoy the months I had left as a blissfully unaware young adult. I'd done exactly that by using my free time to make out with a handsome stable hand. He'd been wrong about my being unaware though. I'd overheard enough conversations to know things were bad for the realm.

Heliconia's power had grown, as had the frequency of her attacks along our border villages. Our time was running out— I could feel it. Why couldn't they?

With Grey Oak our only option—and me our only bargaining tool—it had come down to this: a marriage that would join Summer and Autumn into one court. My parents were sacrificing their entire empire to ensure we survived Heliconia's hatred.

Every time I thought of it, my stomach roiled.

Bracing myself for the conversation that awaited me, I approached them quietly, my footsteps soft against the cool stone beneath me. Father looked up first, his golden crown gleaming in the sunlight. His blue eyes filled with warmth as they settled on me, though an edge of concern remained in his expression.

My mother took one look at the pants and tunic I wore and frowned. "What are you wearing?"

"Training gear," I reminded her.

She sent a death glare to the sword I'd strapped to my hip. But I refused to have this argument with her—again. My mother liked to believe a princess was meant to fight her battles through verbal sparring alone.

My father, as usual, broke the tension.

"Aurelia," he said, motioning for me to sit. "We need to speak about final wedding arrangements."

I tensed, trying to bite back my usual argument against the idea. "Mother and I have nearly finished planning everything."

"Except for your dress," my mother said sternly. Her strawberry blonde hair had fallen over her shoulder in waves, softening her austere features. "I'm told you still haven't made a final decision on the lace samples I sent you."

I took a seat across from them, smoothing my tunic as I sat. The stone beneath me felt cold, but I kept my posture straight, my expression composed. Normally, I would have thoroughly enjoyed the fittings and fabric choices and all the trappings that went with a party like this one. But considering this wedding ceremony felt a lot more like a prison than a partnership, I'd been less than enthusiastic about the process.

"I'll send my choice to the seamstress before the end of the day," I told her.

She waved me off. "Don't bother. I already did. I went with the single layer as I think the simplicity is best."

I nodded, not bothering to argue. The dress was the least of my problems, anyway. I was much more worried about what would happen when I came out of it. Not that sex was a mystery. But the idea of offering myself to someone I hadn't chosen sent waves of disgust through me.

Mother's voice was quiet but firm as she added, "Callan's emissary arrived this morning. Callan will be here by nightfall, and we're expecting you to greet him."

My heart squeezed, but I ignored it, keeping my voice even as I said, "I'll be here."

Callan's arrival would signal the official start of the three-day Solstice celebration, beginning with the lamplight party tomorrow night. My father had started the tradition years ago as a surprise birthday party for me. I'd always loved seeing the floating lights glowing against the night sky, but I wasn't sure I'd feel the same after tomorrow when the occasion became my engagement party too. And then, three days from now, the Solstice celebration would end with my wedding.

"We'll also need you present day after tomorrow to sign the marriage contract," my father added.

"Of course." I nodded at them both, though my throat felt tight. At their wary expressions, I added, shoving the words out, "I won't let you down. I know how important this alliance is for us."

Father leaned forward, his brow furrowed. "More than important, Aurelia. It's essential. With Concordia fallen, and no one willing to ally with us, we are vulnerable. Heliconia's power grows by the day. If—no, *when*—she moves against us, we'll need Grey Oak's strength to hold her back."

Concordia, the Winter Court, had once been a bastion of strength. Now, it lay in ruins, overtaken by Heliconia's dark forces. Rumors said she'd torn Queen Valfina's broken body from her ice throne and tossed it off a mountain before proclaiming herself the new Winter Court queen. The news had sent shockwaves through the fae realms where peace had ruled for a thousand years—until now.

The stories of Concordia's invasion had already grown to hideous legends, the kind told to scare children and soldiers alike—how Heliconia's creatures, twisted by her dark magic, had swept through Concordia like a plague, consuming everything in their path. Some they'd killed. Some they'd imprisoned and forced to fight each other for sport.

It was horrible to even think about. All those small villages tucked into the mountains. Traders. Farmers. Peaceful fae. So many innocents caught in the crossfire.

"I still can't believe the Midnight Court sat by and watched," I said, unable to keep the hardness from my voice. "Heliconia's invasion happened practically on their doorstep, and they don't even care."

"The Midnight Court claims to have their reasons, though they haven't bothered to share what those might be," my father said, his eyes flashing with a fury I rarely saw him display. "But we're past pointing fingers. We must look to our own survival."

"Grey Oak is the stronger ally anyway." Mother's voice sharpened. "Their army is vast, and the prince has a reputation for ruthlessness, which we will need if we're to beat Heliconia."

"He sounds like the perfect husband," I said wryly.

She sighed, softening a little. "Like it or not, you are the key to this alliance, Aurelia. Your union with Callan will ensure that our armies are strong enough to resist whatever Heliconia brings. And when the time comes, you will lead Sevanwinds to victory."

My chest tightened at the words. *Lead Sevanwinds to victory.* As if it were all but guaranteed. As if there was no chance of failure. As if placing a male's ring on my finger somehow transformed me into a weapon.

"I know what's at stake," I said, keeping my voice steady. "I'll do what's necessary."

Mother's gaze lingered on me, searching for cracks in my resolve. But she said nothing more, simply nodding in approval.

Father reached across the table, his hand warm as it rested on mine. Some of that was thanks to his magic. The Summer Court ruler wielded the power of a solstice sun. Or that's what the summer fae claimed about their king. For decades now, fae magic had been waning so that each new generation wielded less than the last. The sad truth was that, if my father could truly wield the power of the sun, we wouldn't need to marry me off to gain an army.

Then again, if I had magic at all, maybe I'd be useful beyond the benefits of a marriage contract.

"You are our future, Aurelia," he said softly. "Someday, you will be queen of a vast kingdom, one twice as big as it is now—"

"I know," I said, unwilling to let him convince me this was a good thing.

Once, I'd looked forward to my future as queen. A fair and just ruler beloved by her people. Like my parents.

But not anymore.

No matter how hard they tried to spin it, this marriage would still be something forced on me. A cage I would be locked inside—all to preserve our freedom and our lives.

I rose from the table. "I'm late for training."

"Aurelia, wait." My father's voice softened. Our eyes met, and I watched as duty gave way to affection. "We're so proud of you. And so grateful."

A rush of emotion tugged at my heart. Frustration. Resentment—and love. It was a tangle of feelings. But at the root, I found myself unwilling to stay angry with them. Not when they were giving up so much in this arrangement too.

My mother rose and came around the table, holding her arms out to both of us. The three of us embraced, silent and still for just this moment.

"Make me proud," she whispered in my ear.

Her display was much rarer than my father's, which only

served to drive home how much was at stake. But for the span of a breath, I shoved it all away and let their arms envelop me. For just a moment, they weren't the king and queen. They were parents. Good ones with kind hearts and a love for their people. A love for me.

Standing in the circle of that love, I prayed to the Fates and the Aine warriors who served them that the horrible feeling in my gut wasn't an omen that this might be the last time we ever stood this way again.

THE
MOON

Chapter Two
Aurelia

The trees of the Emerald Forest whispered as I wove through them, my steps soundless on the familiar path. The sunlight streaming overhead was warm, but down here, under the dense leaves, the air was cooler, laced with the damp scent of earth. After the meeting with my parents, I felt lighter inhaling that scent. The forest had always been my refuge, a place where I could breathe, away from the watchful eyes of the court.

Here, the trees were sentient and long-lived, their consciousness a sort of comfort. I listened to their whispers, trying to discern what messages they carried, but their language was too old and obscure to decipher. Druids rarely bothered with mortals anymore anyway, not even the fae who were longer-lived than most.

I pulled the hood of my cloak over my head, grateful for the cover as I ducked beneath a low branch. If anyone saw me out here, if they knew what I was about to do… It would mean the end of afternoons like this one forever.

Heliconia's wrath had come for nearly every Aine warrior across the realm. Four years ago, she'd slaughtered an entire camp of recruits in one night. After that, the Fates decreed that no more Aine would be chosen to compete.

From that moment on, training with the Aine was forbidden.

A princess of Sevanwinds doing so was beyond dangerous, but these training sessions with Sonoma were my lifeline. And despite the weight of my future bearing down on my shoulders, learning to fight and hunt had never added to that burden.

My pulse quickened as I neared the clearing where Sonoma and I met in secret. The trees were thicker surrounding it—part of the wards Sonoma had erected to keep curious eyes from wandering too close. And not just Summer Court citizens either. Some of the hunters and merchants who traveled these woods had reported sightings of Heliconia's creatures as far south as the Broadlands—a territory dangerously close to Rosewood's borders.

Our best soldiers patrolled the forest in defense.

The last thing I needed was one of them stumbling onto a training session between Sevanwinds's most powerful Aine and the heir to the Summer throne.

As I drew closer, the tang of powerful magic hit my tongue—Sonoma's shield, which muted our voices from curious ears and kept us invisible to any errant visitors. I stepped easily through the barrier, my skin buzzing. There was no magic left on Menryth as powerful as the Aine's magic. Except for maybe the dark queen herself.

Sonoma stood in the center of the clearing, her back to me, her silver hair braided and hanging over her shoulder. A pair of wings—a gift the Fates bestowed on all the Aine—were tucked in, their translucent surface reflecting what light filtered through the trees. In her hand, she held her sword, Latha, the names of the Fates etched into the blade in a language long lost to our people. She spun it idly in slow, practiced arcs, and I found myself distracted by the power that practically shimmered along its surface.

Turning away, I let my cloak slip from my shoulders. Sonoma didn't turn, but her voice carried through the space, steady and sure. "You're late."

"Mother says a princess is never late. Everyone else is early."

"The queen's rules apply to everything except training," she replied, her gaze still focused on the movement of her wrists, though I could feel her attention shifting to me. "You're distracted."

I scowled. "I have a wedding to plan."

Sonoma's brow rose as I pulled my own sword free from its sheath. It had been handed down to me from my father. A gift on my twelfth birthday—the day I graduated from a wooden sword to a real one. I'd been so proud of myself until Sonoma had swung out with hers and I could've sworn the impact broke my arm.

Thank the Fates, it had become much less painful over the years.

Sonoma finally turned to face me, her silver eyes sharp as she noted my expression. "Today, you meet your betrothed."

I couldn't help but wince. "Apparently."

Sonoma's eyes narrowed slightly, and for a moment, I thought I saw the same turmoil reflected in her gaze. She lifted her sword, motioning for me to attack. "Begin."

My sword cut through the air, and Sonoma met it with a smooth, effortless parry. The clash of metal echoed against the stillness of the forest, the flurry and rush of it grounding me. We moved in a familiar dance, Dorcha and Latha singing with each strike and deflection.

Sonoma was better than me. Much better. Even without the use of her wings to aid her speed, she was faster than any fighter I'd ever seen. Some said it was due to the Fates' gifts, but I'd heard enough stories from her and the other Aine to know most of their talents had to be inborn to make it through the recruitment process. The Fates only chose the strongest and most skilled warriors—and then they honed them to lethal points.

But I'd learned to hold my own—mostly.

As my body grew tired, my form slipped. Sonoma's sword ripped past my defenses and tore a hole in my tunic.

I scowled.

Sonoma looked smug. "You could have stopped me."

"You have decades of experience on me," I groused.

"I meant with your magic."

My scowl deepened. "Am I supposed to smother you in rosebushes like my mother or give you a hot flash like my father?"

Sonoma only bit back a smile. "If those are the gifts you have at the ready, why not?"

"I have no *gifts*, remember?" I ground out between heavy breaths.

Sonoma said nothing as her sword clanged against mine.

My muscles screamed at me, but I kept going. I refused to think about my lack of magic or all the possible—weakened— abilities I might yet develop. Most fae discovered their magic between sixteen and eighteen. But more and more often, fae were coming of age without a single drop of power at all. While the fae of Menryth grew weaker, Heliconia grew stronger.

I refused to think about that either.

Twirling her sword, Sonoma barely looked winded. "A good warrior embraces what she has available rather than dwelling on what she doesn't."

I resisted the urge to roll my eyes—mostly because taking my gaze off her for even a second would only lead to defeat. But her familiar words grated. After my conversation about the wedding earlier, I was already feeling sorry for myself. And the reminder that my magic was nearly nonexistent wasn't helping.

Our swords rang out as they clashed, the only sound between us for several minutes. Taking her advice, I drew on the small kernel of power inside me and brought forth one of the tree roots at our feet. Sonoma stumbled but quickly righted herself again.

She smirked.

I glared.

"How can I protect my people if my worth is no more than a marriage contract?" I finally blurted, lowering my blade.

Sonoma's eyes softened. "You're more than you believe, Aurelia. You'll see."

I shook my head, frustration bubbling up inside me. "Are you sure? Because it feels like every choice is being made for me. What if I don't want to do it this way? What if— What if I *can't* do it?"

Her hand came to rest on my shoulder, the grip firm. "Your kingdom may not know what I've done in training you, but that doesn't erase what you've become. You are a warrior, Aurelia. And warriors fight even when the battle is fought with something other than a sword."

I stared at her, suddenly overcome with emotion.

"Will you be there?" I asked quietly. "At the wedding?"

Sonoma's expression flickered with regret, just for a moment, before she turned away. "Lesha, Amanti, and I will be on duty," she said, her voice back to its usual composed tone.

"On whose orders?" I couldn't help but ask. Anger rose in me, swift and hot. "The queen?"

But Sonoma shook her head. "I volunteered."

My anger drained away. Hurt bloomed in its place. "Why?"

"We will be guarding the court against potential threats throughout the celebrations."

Guarding the court. Always the warrior. Even when I needed her to be a friend. Sonoma's dedication to her oath both filled me with admiration and carved me hollow with loneliness.

"There've been reports of dark magic felt as far south as Rosewood's northern boundary," she added.

I waited for more, but she didn't say anything else. I didn't push. I knew better.

Suddenly, Sonoma froze, her hand darting out in a warning signal. Her silver eyes flickered with sharp awareness as she stared into the thick trees.

Beyond the safety of our shield, the forest felt charged with an unnatural energy, dark and malicious.

"Raise your weapon," Sonoma said, her voice low, scanning the shadows.

"What is it?"

Sonoma's expression was grim. "An Obsidian."

THE
MOON

Chapter Three
Aurelia

My pulse quickened as my own senses finally identified the scent and movement of something creeping through the trees. Just outside the barrier but crawling closer as if it could see right through to where we stood. I strained for a glimpse of whatever it was but didn't have to wait long. A second later, a flash of black-as-death eyes confirmed Sonoma's words, and my breath caught at the sight of it.

At first glance, it looked like nothing more than a pale-skinned fae male with haunting, obsidian eyes—but I knew pure evil lurked inside that form.

The Obsidians had been fae until Heliconia twisted them into something else with her dark magic. I'd heard stories about children and parents alike being taken from their beds and painfully transformed. I ached with empathy at the way my people's lives—and souls—had been stolen from them in such a horrible way. To be remade into a mindless monster enslaved to a wicked queen was a fate worse than death. But now, facing one in the flesh, my only emotion was fear.

Even from where it still huddled in the brush, the foul

signature of its dark magic was stronger than anything I'd felt before.

Sonoma gestured at me to fall into a formation familiar from our practice sessions. But this was no practice, and for a moment, I stood frozen. She gestured again, never taking her eyes off the creature yet somehow managing to project her impatience and irritation.

Move.

Out of sheer will and muscle memory, I got into my fighting stance. Sonoma stood beside me with an unyielding stare that had felled enemies much worse than this one. Then she lowered the barrier.

"Is that wise?" I hissed. "It can't reach us inside the wards."

"It can see us," she said grimly. "The damage is done."

We watched as the Obsidian crawled toward us on all fours, its movements more animal than fae.

A shudder went through me that wasn't fear. Anticipation. Or maybe a reaction to the immense power that rippled out of the elder Aine warrior. In Sonoma's hand, Latha gleamed as if it, too, relished the idea of a fight.

But the Obsidian was mindless enough to ignore the warning. Almost too fast for me to see, the creature lunged from the undergrowth. Not at Sonoma. At me.

Large onyx eyes glinted with unnatural hunger before it was nearly on me, its mouth open and sharpened teeth aimed for my throat. I brought my sword up just in time to crash the hilt against the creature's jaw. It stumbled sideways as Sonoma whirled, her footwork flawless as she brought her body around to shield me.

The Obsidian hissed, the sound thick with malice. Its pale fingers, sharp as claws, stretched toward Sonoma as it advanced.

She lifted her blade to meet it. Latha sliced clean through

the creature's wrist. Its hand fell to the ground with a thump. Blood poured from the severed limb, and the creature screeched, making me cringe.

With renewed determination, it lunged with its remaining hand outstretched, but Sonoma was quicker. She dodged, spinning out of the way and slashing her blade across its chest. The creature stumbled, its dark blood spilling onto the forest floor, rotting the ground where it touched the earth. When it straightened, Sonoma no longer stood between us.

The Obsidian realized it too.

"Keep your blade up," Sonoma snapped at me.

I lifted Dorcha higher, my heart thudding so hard I thought it might crack my ribs. My breaths came in short gasps.

I had trained for this.

Trained.

It felt like pretending compared to standing before the wretched thing now. My blood crawled with distaste—but also with something that felt like recognition. Whatever this Obsidian was made from, it called to me.

It sang inside me.

That scared me more than the fact that it wanted to kill me.

As I stared, its face began to change shape. Instead of a male fae with a shock of chestnut hair and dead, obsidian eyes, it was a woman. She was beautiful with long dark hair that fell straight down her back. Her eyes were depthless and, unlike the hollow obsidian gaze, held a vastness of secrets—and rage.

The smile that curled her lips was cruel and knowing. "Hello, Aurelia."

"Who are you?" I asked.

Sonoma screamed and brought her sword down, but the creature danced out of reach.

The woman's eyes glittered. "Sonoma. Is that any way to greet a sister?"

"I am not your sister," Sonoma spat.

I stared in confusion while Sonoma shoved me aside to plant herself between me and our attacker.

"What is going on—?" I began.

"Get out of my kingdom," Sonoma spat at the strange female.

"Nothing's changed, I see. Still wearing your heart on your sleeve. It always did make you reckless, you know."

Sonoma snarled.

I blinked, confused at the intimacy between them. No one had ever called Sonoma reckless, but this creature said it like she knew from personal experience.

"Who are you?" I demanded.

The woman smiled at me. "My name is Heliconia."

Shock rippled through me, though deep down, I'd known no one else could've pulled off the kind of magic she was using now.

"I take it you've heard of me," Heliconia added smugly.

"What do you want?" Sonoma demanded through clenched teeth.

"Confirmation," Heliconia said. Her voice was deceivingly light, but the look in her eyes was pure malice. "You did a good job of hiding her, I'll give you that," she added, her gaze flicking to me.

Sonoma seethed, but I jolted.

"What are you talking about?" I asked.

"You're the one they think will stop me," Heliconia said.

I blinked. Was my marriage to Callan that intimidating to her?

"The Fates do not make mistakes," Sonoma said, and I whipped my head toward her, my stomach churning.

Whatever Sonoma meant by that, one thing was clear: This wasn't about my marriage.

Heliconia smirked. "Is that so?"

"What do the Fates have to do with me?" I demanded.

"Ah, you haven't told her about her destiny." Her amusement made it clear she didn't remotely consider me a threat. Nor even worth addressing as she looked at Sonoma again. "Imagine the disgrace when I show up here and watch her cower like a novice at the sight of one of my soldiers." She snorted. "This is the best the Fates have for me? It won't even be a fair fight when I cut her down."

"There is an army waiting for you to try," Sonoma said coldly.

I couldn't help the pang of embarrassment that she hadn't bothered to stand up for me directly. But I kept my chin high, refusing to react to the slight.

Heliconia merely narrowed her gaze. "You've gone to great lengths to stop me, old friend. But in the end, it won't matter. I will come for you and take the Summer Court for myself."

"The only thing waiting for you here is your destruction," Sonoma snapped, raising her sword. "If you've come for it now, stop hiding behind spells and shadows, and fight me."

"And what about your young trainee? You'd steal her chance to be a hero?" Heliconia *tsk*ed. "Not very Aine of you at all."

"I *am* Aine, and I will destroy you," I said with as much confidence as I could muster. It sounded weak even to me, but I couldn't stand by and watch her dismiss me like a trifling inconvenience.

Heliconia snorted, but her dismissal only urged me on.

"I will not let you harm my people," I added.

Something inside me whispered encouragement, a magic I'd never felt before stirring at last. It gave me the confidence to stand straighter—even when Heliconia sent tendrils of power toward me.

Shadows—nothing more.

And still, it took everything I had not to react as they poked and prodded at my ankles, snaking up my legs.

When I refused to cower, she smiled that catlike smile again.

With a battle cry, Sonoma swung out her sword, cutting through the shadows until they broke apart.

"If you touch her," Sonoma snarled, "I won't wait until you decide to march to these gates. I will come and slaughter you myself."

Heliconia's eyes narrowed.

I gripped my sword, ready for an attack.

"Your fear is unbecoming," Heliconia snapped at Sonoma. She whipped her gaze to me. "If you want a fight, you shall have it. Let's see what you're really made of."

Her face vanished, replaced once again by the Obsidian's. His form solidified—I knew it somehow in my bones, thanks to whatever strange, new magic surged through my veins.

Sonoma knew it too.

She whirled, racing around with her sword already swinging.

The creature managed a single step in my direction before it lurched forward awkwardly, arching its back. Its mouth opened in what promised to be a scream but came out as a gargling hiss. Blood leaked from its open mouth before it fell, shoved face-first into the dirt by the force of Sonoma ripping her blade free from its back.

She hadn't even bothered to let me fight it.

The creature moaned, the sound rattling and wet as it rolled onto its back and stared up at the sky. That strange call in my own blood returned as I looked down at it.

Magic whispered, sinking beneath my skin.

A forbidden song in my veins.

I couldn't look away.

More blood leaked from the Obsidian, and I found myself fisting my hand to keep from reaching out and touching the liquid that pulsed with the creature's ebbing life force.

"Aurelia." Sonoma's voice held a question—and a warning.

"I can feel it," I murmured, stepping closer to the fallen monster.

The creature's head jerked up, its once-fierce eyes now glazed with terror as if it could sense the end. Its lips curled in a silent snarl, more black blood bubbling up through its mouth.

I knelt beside it, my boots squishing in the wetness.

Sonoma's words cut through the stillness. "Aurelia, don't."

But I couldn't stop.

The magic rose inside me, dark tendrils of power curling through my body like smoke. My hand extended, my fingers trembling.

The dying creature's life force unraveled before my eyes—twisting, writhing tendrils of magic lifted from its body, drawn toward me. The energy surged into my outstretched hand, a dark and intoxicating force that burned as it entered.

The creature screamed—its final sound a haunting echo—before it fell limp, collapsing into itself as if drained of every last drop of vitality.

My pulse thundered in my ears.

The magic was cold, searing through my veins, but beneath the chill, there was something else—something alive. Not summer's warmth. Not light or heat or any of the things a Summer fae princess should possess. It was power born of death, drawn from the last remnants of a dying thing.

And now it was mine.

I staggered, my heart racing at the implication of what I'd just done—what I'd just become. I tried to resist it, to remove it somehow, but it was too late for that. I could feel the darkness feeding me, strengthening me.

My surroundings sharpened, the colors of the forest becoming more vivid. The ground beneath my feet seemed to hum as if the forest, too, could sense the shift in my magic.

"Aurelia!" Sonoma broke through the haze, and I gasped, drinking in the last of the creature's energy with a shudder.

Sonoma was at my side, her face pale. "Are you all right?"

"I... What happened?"

"Your power awakened."

My power... I had magic. Finally. Relief coursed through me for a split second until I realized how stricken Sonoma looked.

"What's wrong?" I asked.

"How long have you known you had death magic?" she asked in a strange voice.

Death magic?

I blinked, trembling as her words sank in. "I...I don't. That's impossible. It's—"

Death magic belonged to the Furiosities. It belonged to Hel. To demons. To darkness. Not to summer fae like me.

But Sonoma was grabbing my shoulders, shaking them. "Look at me. Has this happened before?"

"No," I said quickly. "It just came over me, and I took some of it in— Am I going to become like that thing?"

She shook her head. "I don't think so."

Her certainty broke through the fog of my fear, and I realized with startling clarity that, while Sonoma looked unhappy, she didn't look surprised.

"How do you know so much about this?" I asked.

"Because I've seen your kind of magic before, and I know where it comes from."

"Where does it come from?" I asked, dread coiling in my gut.

"Hel," she said.

Despite those exact suspicions, I gaped at her. It was one thing to know it and another to have it confirmed. But it made no sense. Magic was bestowed through bloodlines. I'd seen our lineage as part of my studies. Both of my parents were very decidedly summer fae. There wasn't a trace of demon in the entire royal line.

"How do I have it?" I asked.

And then, somewhere in the distance, I heard it.

Trumpets. From the castle.

The sound was faint, carried by the breeze through the trees, but unmistakable. Sonoma's expression shuttered, and the moment was over. Callan was here. And I was already late.

THE
MOON

Chapter Four
Aurelia

My heart pounded to the beat of my hurried footsteps as I raced through Sunspire's halls to the grand foyer below. Servants scurried aside to let me pass. I took the stairs as fast as I dared in my heels and gown. My blonde hair trailed out behind me, cascading down my shoulders in loose, messy waves. After returning from the debacle in the forest, I'd only had time to hastily comb it out though it undoubtedly needed a wash—or two, thanks to the musty, dead smell I swore still clung to me. But there'd been time for no more than a cursory attempt at taming it before I pulled on a fresh gown and shoved my feet into these awful heels. My mother was going to be furious that I hadn't made more of an effort. Hopefully, the knowledge that I'd been attacked by an Obsidian—possessed by Heliconia, no less—would soften her irritation toward me.

As long as that knowledge didn't include the story of my death magic. Sonoma had made me swear not to mention it—not even to my parents. I'd agreed immediately. Mostly because the idea of telling them I possessed the same magic as the Furiosities left my stomach in knots.

Death magic was the mark of evil.

What did that make me?

There'd been no time to ask before Sonoma and I had split ways. She'd gone deeper into the forest to hunt for any more of them while I'd raced here to greet the prince.

My future husband.

Who was currently about to walk through the front entrance, I realized as I reached the bottom of the stairs.

No, scratch that.

His entourage came first.

I noted the half-dozen footmen and even more Autumn soldiers who hurried into the grand foyer ahead of him before my mother's tongue clicked with judgment. Bracing myself, I glanced at her. She glared at my dress and then my hair, her disapproval a darkening storm cloud in her normally bright green eyes.

"What have you done with your hair?" she whispered in horror as she grabbed my arm and pulled me close. "And you were supposed to wear the new dress I sent up."

"Too many laces. There was no time. Sonoma and I had an ... encounter," I said quietly, though my words drew my father's sharp stare.

"What kind of encounter?" he asked.

"She asked that she be the one to tell you," I said just as the trumpet sounded again—this time so close that I flinched at its sudden harsh notes.

A signal that the prince himself was crossing the threshold.

The trumpet call was an outdated tradition and a little ostentatious in my book, but apparently Callan had requested the full extent of royal formality.

My mother adjusted her grip, holding my arm with a lighter touch, one meant to offer affection—and I was grateful for it. But even with her silent reassurance, my heart lurched as I looked at our guest.

Prince Callan, heir to the Autumn Court throne.

His chestnut hair hung just long enough to brush his forehead and cover the tips of his pointed ears. His russet jacket lined with gold buttons shone in the sunlight that framed him in the doorway. As if even nature herself had been consulted in the planning and perfecting of such a moment. But it wasn't his impeccable clothing or immaculately styled hair that caught my attention. It was those golden, gleaming eyes.

With one swift glance, his sharp eyes took the measure of every fae in this room, including the king and queen—and me.

I fought the urge to squirm.

He was handsome with his tousled brown hair that shone like auburn in the light. But his eyes glimmered with something that felt too pointed to be genuine warmth. And his smile—a charming curve of lips—was just the right amount of friendly and just the right amount of controlled. He wielded that smile like a weapon; I knew that instinctively.

He strode into the room with ease, his presence commanding the attention of everyone as though he'd been born for this sort of thing—because he had. The only son of widowed King Duron, Callan Ashfall had built a reputation as the ruthless and unyielding commander of Grey Oak's vast armies. Armies that Sevanwinds desperately needed if we were going to escape the Winter Court's fate.

My thoughts drifted to my encounter from earlier, and I shuddered.

Callan's gaze marked it as he drifted closer to where I stood.

"Prince Callan," my father greeted. "Welcome to Sevanwinds."

"Your Majesties." His voice had a rich, smooth timbre that could've been mistaken for sincerity if I hadn't already been on edge. Instead, it reeked of false tribute. "King Tyrion and Queen Celeste, your hospitality is appreciated." He bowed deeply, perfectly, before straightening to face me. His golden eyes locked onto mine, assessing me with a mixture of intrigue and calculation. "And you must be the beautiful Princess Aurelia. I've heard so much about you, but none of it did justice to your loveliness."

Even if I hadn't heard the rumors of his many conquests, his flattery wouldn't have found its mark.

"Prince Callan," I said. "Your reputation precedes you as well. Welcome." I offered a quick dip of my chin that was almost insulting when paired with my backhanded words.

But his smile never faltered.

His gaze lingered, and I fought the urge to shift uncomfortably under his scrutiny. "I hope I don't disappoint." He winked, startling me, then turned away as my cheeks flushed with surprise.

"And Queen Celeste, you are a vision of summer's beauty." Callan took her hand and brought it to his lips.

My mother peered down her nose at him, not unfriendly but certainly not impressed. If only he'd realized a compliment to her sharp, strategic mind would've gone so much farther. "Your Highness," she said simply. "Welcome to our home."

"It's truly an honor," he told her.

She sniffed, apparently satisfied by his gratitude. "It's a shame your father couldn't make the journey."

"He is immensely disappointed to miss it, but our borders remain as threatened as yours, I'm afraid. We couldn't risk both of us so far from home."

"I understand completely. Send him our best."

"Of course. I hear you enjoy a good hunt, Your Highness," he said, turning to my father.

"Indeed. We've scheduled a day of it in honor of your visit," the king replied, and I listened politely while they spoke of their plans for a pheasant hunt at dawn.

"And will the princess be joining us?" Callan asked, glancing at me.

"On the hunt?" My father lifted a brow in my direction, clearly letting me make the call. But spending an entire day trekking through the forest with the Autumn prince—before I was legally required to do so—wasn't my idea of a good time.

"I'm afraid I'll have to pass," I said.

"You do hunt, don't you?" Callan glanced from me to my father, forehead creasing as if in concern. "Surely you allow your females to learn a warrior's skill. You do have three surviving Aine still in your service, after all."

I nearly winced. The Autumn Court had lost all three of their Aine last year to Heliconia's attacks on their borders. And with the selection process currently forbidden, it left them without such a safeguard for the future.

"The Aine protect against threats to the realm," I said, not sure why I felt the need to defend them—he hadn't outright compared Sonoma, Amanti, and Lesha to pheasant hunters, but it felt close. "That's not quite the same thing as hunting game for supper."

"Of course. I merely meant that you are to be protector of Sevanwinds. Surely you see the value in a warrior's training."

His voice was light, but suspicion pricked at me. Did he know about my training somehow? Had he seen me in the woods today with the Obsidian? My heart beat faster, but I forced it to slow again.

"I reserve my hunting for securing political alliances," I said with a smirk.

My mother stiffened, and I knew she was mentally chastising me for such a provocative answer. But I held my ground.

The prince's eyes gleamed with amusement. "A worthy endeavor, especially in these dark times." He paused before adding, "I'm sure we'll make a formidable team."

I remained silent, refusing to take the bait.

"Your engagement party is scheduled for tomorrow evening," my mother said, clearly trying to fill the silence. "After that, you'll have a couple of days of excursions so you can become acquainted with our lands, and then the wedding itself will be held on the Solstice." She caught the eye of the maid lingering at the edges and added, "As I'm sure you're tired from your journey, a maid will show you to your rooms so you can rest."

"Tomorrow then." Callan looked at me. "I imagine we have much to discuss about the future of our courts." He gave a small, almost conspiratorial smile before bowing slightly. "Good night."

Before I could respond, he turned and strode away, leaving a trail of courtly charm in his wake. My parents' faces mirrored one another's: a mix of unease and resignation.

Play nice, my mother's expression seemed to say. My father gave me a grim nod as if to remind me of the stakes.

As if I could possibly forget.

Walking slowly back to my room, I swallowed hard, trying to unwind the knot of anxiety forming in my chest. Callan was handsome, yes. Charming, undeniably. But something about him felt too calculated. Like a game was already being played and I was the piece he intended to move next. Except, instead of being his queen, I had the distinct impression that, if I wasn't careful, I'd be nothing more than his pawn.

THE
MOON

Chapter Five
Aurelia

I stood at the window in my bedroom, gazing at the city of Rosewood stretched out before me. Rows of tiled rooftops were interrupted by patches of yards dotted with gardens. In between, wide streets cut through it all, teeming with fae and humans alike making their way home before the Solstice celebrations started tomorrow. Here and there, a mage or shifter darted among them. Above, the pink and orange hues of twilight had begun to fade into the soft purple of night, casting long shadows.

The air was warm through the open window, but a chill settled over my skin anyway. I'd been standing here since the meeting with Callan ended, his arrival putting me out of one misery and into another. Because now that I'd met him, my impending marriage was much more real than it had been before.

I was brooding, Sonoma would say.

But she hadn't said it. She hadn't even come to check on me.

I couldn't help replaying that moment in the forest. When

Heliconia had demanded I fight to prove myself and Sonoma had stolen my chance by slaying the Obsidian herself.

It stung, knowing she hadn't believed I could do it myself.

Underneath my churning emotions, my new magic swam inside me. It pressed against the edges of my skin, whispering at me to release it. Curious, I opened my hand and concentrated on the center of my palm.

Heat rose to the surface.

Sparks shot out, fizzling across the room.

With a surprised yelp, I shut my hand and snatched it behind my back. But not before I'd seen the color of the flame.

Black.

Like the fires of Hel.

Sonoma had said so, but I hadn't wanted to really believe it. Now, my heart raced as the truth settled over me like a cloud of dread.

All these years of frustration and fear that I had no magic at all—and here it was. Not like anything I'd expected. And definitely not something I could tell a soul.

Summer magic was sunshine and roses and rain showers and sometimes lightning flickering across the skies. This was fire and brimstone and death. A nod to the demons descended from the Furiosities themselves.

I thought of the priestesses who worshipped the Fates in the temples across the city. Who dedicated themselves to the light and condemned anyone who bore the mark of Hel. What would they say about me when they learned I contained such darkness inside me?

What would the Autumn prince think when he knew?

It would be a scandal to rival all others.

I might even lose my crown.

The longer I stood, weighing the danger, the more my stomach churned with my secrets.

A quiet knock on my door broke through the tumult.

I turned as my mother entered, her gown trailing softly behind her. She didn't come to my chambers unless something weighed on her mind, and from the look in her eyes, this visit was no exception.

"Is everything okay?"

Her presence filled the room as it always did, regal and composed, but there was something softer in her tonight. Rather than comfort me, it put me on edge. I tucked my hands safely behind my back, clasping them tight.

She crossed the room, her steps slow and deliberate, and came to stand beside me by the window. For a long moment, she said nothing, simply looking out at the view as I had been doing.

I waited, hating myself for hoping she was here to change her mind about this ridiculous wedding.

Finally, she sighed.

"Sonoma told us what happened," she said quietly, her voice barely more than a whisper in the fading light. "About the Obsidian who attacked you. And Heliconia appearing."

I tensed.

Had she told them what I did? What I'd become?

"Where is she now?"

"She and Amanti are meeting with your father to discuss how to respond to the threat."

"Did they find any other Obsidians?" I asked.

"No." My exhale of relief was short-lived as she added, "There were traces of dark magic at the city's northern border, however. Signs that she'd come that far herself before using some kind of spell work to project through the Obsidian."

I swallowed hard, trying not to think the worst. But if Heliconia herself had come to our borders... how long until she attacked our lands?

"I don't understand. We have soldiers there."

"She evaded them." She shook her head, frustration shining in her hard gaze. "She's clearly grown more powerful since seizing Concordia."

I stared at her. "This changes everything. The wedding, the party—we don't have time. We need to act. Send more soldiers to the border, organize our army, prepare for war—"

"Aurelia." My mother's voice was sharp.

I fell silent.

"Your father and I decided," my mother said, turning to face me now, "that we must move forward with the wedding."

"What?" I stared at her. "Even after what happened today?"

She nodded, her expression unwavering. "The alliance between us and Autumn is more important than ever. If Heliconia has truly turned her sights on our lands, gaining Grey Oak's army is imperative to our defense. We cannot afford to falter."

I turned away from her, looking back out over the city, trying to let her words sink in. She was right, of course. The alliance with Grey Oak was crucial. Without their numbers added to our own, we wouldn't stand a chance against what was coming. But that didn't make it any easier to accept.

"The prince doesn't know," she said after a moment, her voice quieter now. More careful. "And we've decided not to tell him. There's no need to burden him with this yet. Let him enjoy the party tomorrow. Let him focus on the wedding."

"You're afraid that, if we tell him, we might lose him," I said.

"Yes," she said simply, not even bothering to deny it.

I grimaced.

"Aurelia," she said, stepping closer. Her hand found mine, warm and steady. "I know this isn't easy. None of this is. But you must remember why we're doing this."

I looked up at her, my throat tight with emotions I couldn't quite name.

"For Sevanwinds," she continued, her voice soft but firm. "For our people. You've been raised to protect this kingdom, to lead them one day. This marriage, this alliance—it's the best way to ensure that."

I blinked back the sting of tears that threatened to surface. My mother wasn't one for displays of tenderness, but in this moment, the warmth in her eyes and the soft strength of her hand on mine made me want to collapse into her arms like I had when I was a child.

I nodded, swallowing hard. "I just... Sometimes I wonder if I'm ready for all of this. To do what's necessary."

Her hand moved to my cheek, cupping it gently as she tilted my face toward hers. "You were born for this, my love."

Her words struck something inside me that had been brewing ever since Heliconia had shown herself yesterday. "Can I ask you something?"

"What is it?"

"In the forest, Heliconia made it sound like I was meant to be some kind of threat against her. Like she'd come here for me."

My mother's expression clouded, and dread clanged inside me.

"Is it true?" I asked.

She stepped back. Something like regret swam in her eyes —and maybe a little shame. It was a look I'd never seen her wear before. "I think you should let Sonoma explain. Or your father should be here. I—"

"I see," I cut her off, angry at the truth she held back. "Whatever this is, I'm the last to know."

"You've been protected by those who love you," she said. "Whatever you feel about what's to come, remember that."

"What exactly is coming?" Impatience leaked into my words, making me sound more desperate than angry.

"You are so much more than you think you are," she said softly. "And I promise to explain it all first thing tomorrow. Deal?"

Duty warred with emotion. She was right; this wasn't the time to get into it.

"Deal," I muttered.

"You have the heart of a queen—and a warrior, even if you don't see it yet."

"I feel like a prize horse being sold as a broodmare," I blurted.

Rather than being angry, she nodded grimly, understanding shining in her green eyes. "I know. But this alliance is only the first of many maneuvers you'll make on the battlefield. I believe in you. I always have. And I love you. Not for what you'll do for us. For who you are."

I closed my eyes for a moment, letting her words wash over me. When I opened them again, I found a renewed sense of determination settling in my chest. I wasn't just doing this for myself. I was doing it for Sevanwinds—for Lilah, for the people who lived behind our castle walls and in Rosewood beyond, for everyone who depended on us to protect them.

"You can count on me," I said quietly, more to myself than her. "I'll do what it takes to keep us safe."

My mother smiled, the lines of worry around her eyes softening until the only thing I saw there was sadness. "I know you will."

She leaned in, pressing a soft kiss to my forehead. It was such a rare display of affection from her that it took me by surprise. When she pulled back, her eyes were full of pride, and for a moment, I felt like the future queen she believed in so fiercely.

The dutiful ruler she needed me to be.

As she turned to leave, she paused at the door. "Tomorrow, at the party... don't let your doubts show. Nor your knowledge of what happened in the forest today. The court will be watching. And so will Callan."

I nodded, the stakes of my task settling deep within me. The mask of a princess, of an heir, was one I'd learned to wear long ago. Tomorrow, I would wear it ruthlessly—death magic or not. The people I loved deserved nothing less.

THE
MOON

Chapter Six
Aurelia

Sunspire's rooftop had been transformed by the time I arrived to the party. Lanterns, glowing with soft golden light, floated above the courtyard like fireflies, casting a romantic haze over the night. The scent of roses, jasmine, and moonflower drifted through the air, carried by the cool night breeze. The stars glittered like jewels in the inky sky above us, and the sound of music—the soft strum of harps and lilting voices—filled the space with a dreamlike quality.

All around me, guests moved in a swirling mass of gowns and laughter, wine glasses in hand as they exchanged pleasantries. It was a scene straight from the bedtime stories Lilah loved—where everything appeared perfect.

Except I was standing at the center of it all, about to promise myself to my future mate. And I was dreading every step along the way.

Callan had kept his distance so far, though his presence lingered in every glance sent my way and in the hushed whispers between courtiers who tracked his every move. They were eager for the future our marriage would bring. Or, more accurately, eager to mingle with Autumn fae courtiers.

The other courts had been out of touch for years. Our borders were open but rarely traveled as the roads along the way became more and more prone to bandits and thieves. And in recent years, Obsidians. As Heliconia's power grew, the darkness in the realm spread until travel between courts had become almost non-existent.

Callan's arrival, though he'd been accompanied by enough soldiers to fight a small war, was evidence that we might one day travel between our borders safely again. The only thing Summer fae loved more than a loud party was one with new friends.

I might've agreed if I weren't being forced to wed a male I barely knew while keeping a secret that might well get me imprisoned—or worse. Now that it had wakened, the magic inside me refused to rest. It churned and coiled, begging to be freed.

I couldn't let it.

Adrenaline coursed through me as, across the space, Callan tipped his head back and laughed at something a courtier said.

Not for the first time, I wished for a friend beside me. But Lilah had gone to bed hours ago on Mother's orders—much to my sister's disappointment. And Sonoma was off guarding the borders. Even Lesha and Amanti, the other two Aine who lived in Sevanwinds and served the crown, were absent tonight, patrolling and keeping watch from the skies.

The only other person I spent time with was Maelis, Lilah's tutor. She'd come down with a cold this morning, opting for rest at home tonight.

Sadly, that was the extent of my list of friends, and even they were either family or servants of the crown. I wasn't sure that qualified them as true friends, but they were all I had.

Growing up, I'd become friendly with a few of the daughters who came to court, whose fathers were mostly military leaders or advisors to the king. But as I'd grown older, Sonoma had demanded I put in more training time, and my parents had required my attendance at dinners with guests and dignitaries. We'd quickly grown apart, and I'd clung instead to my family and the Aine for support. I wasn't lonely, but sometimes I wondered if that was only because I had no idea what I was missing.

Either way, in this moment, I was on my own.

I lifted my glass of wine to my lips—liquid courage—but the taste was bitter. My thoughts kept drifting to that moment in the foyer yesterday; the way Callan's smile hadn't quite reached his eyes, the way his words had felt more like well-placed moves than genuine conversation.

"Enjoying yourself, Princess?" asked a deep voice, ripe with condescension.

Caught off guard, I blinked at the stranger who'd spoken.

Our eyes met, and my breath caught as the world seemed to tilt.

He was the most handsome male I'd ever seen, with dark hair that hung carelessly over his forehead and stormy gray eyes that seemed to see right through me to the secrets I guarded from the world.

"I am," I finally managed to stammer.

His mouth quirked in amusement. "Careful with the wine. You'll want your wits about you when your announcement's made."

His reference to my engagement along with his rude tone cleared my head instantly. I did a quick scan of his clothing, but there was nothing to suggest whether he belonged to Summer or Autumn. His tunic was charcoal with no emblem or identification anywhere on it. His pointed ears gave him away as fae, though I felt no power coming from him at all.

Maybe a soldier or special guest of my father's?

The king had rewarded the unit who'd most recently

returned from the front lines with an extensive leave period. Maybe this was one of his men who didn't understand the formal dress requirements for an event such as this. Out of his depth, clearly. And overstepping his bounds.

"My wits are just fine, thank you." I turned back to the crowd, silently dismissing him.

But he only shifted himself so we stood shoulder to shoulder.

It was a bit easier to think without him looking at me, but his shoulder nearly brushed mine, and my body hummed at our closeness. His scent, some heady blend of smoke and spice, clouded my senses.

"Do you enjoy parties, Princess?" His deep voice slid over my skin, sending a shudder through me.

I forced myself to breathe evenly, shocked at my body's reaction to a simple conversation. And an annoying one at that. "Excuse me?"

"Do you enjoy spending your time waltzing in pretty dresses and drinking until you forget who you've danced with?"

I turned to him, glaring. "Who the Hel do you think you are, talking to me like that?"

He shrugged. "It's a simple question."

"It's insulting. You don't know anything about me."

His brow lifted, transforming his handsome features into something I wanted to slap. Or at least touch. "Is that a no?"

To counteract the heat flushing through me, I gave him an icy look. "It's none of your business what I like. I don't even know your name."

"My name is Rydian."

"And who exactly let you into this party, Rydian?" My voice twisted with disdain on his name.

Something dangerous flashed in his eyes, and all amusement vanished. "I go where I please."

"Actually, this is my kingdom. You go where *I* please."

"In that case, tell me, where would I please you, Princess?"

His words scraped over me, igniting me with a need I'd never felt before.

I licked my lips, trying to form the response his impertinence warranted. His gaze darted to my mouth, tracking the movement. Suddenly, I was aware of how close we stood. Somewhere along the way, he'd turned back to face me. Or I him.

And now I was staring up at him like he was the only male in the room. Probably not a good thing considering this male wasn't my fiancé.

"You don't," I managed to say lamely.

"Don't what?"

"Please me," I said.

"Not yet. But we're just getting started." He made the words sound threatening.

Still, my breaths shortened. I found myself studying his mouth. That full, sensuous mouth looked like it might do a fantastic job of pleasing me.

"Maybe you just need some time to think about it," he murmured, leaning closer.

I froze, horrified he was going to kiss me in front of all these people. In front of my parents. And Callan.

Seven Hels, Callan.

I blinked and took a step back, forcing the heat inside me to turn to ice. "My time is already spoken for. As is my pleasure."

He frowned, but I looked away, dismissing him—this time for good.

"Enjoy the party," he murmured, and then he was gone, and I was alone.

I refused to let my shoulders sag under the relief I felt. Or the disappointment that registered—as ridiculous as it was—now that he was gone.

He was no one.

A soldier favored for one night.

A rake, from the way he spoke to me.

I was positive I'd never see him again.

And yet... that last thought bothered me.

Before I could do something stupid like search the crowd for him, Callan's voice, smooth as silk, pulled me from my thoughts.

"There you are."

He stood before me, looking as effortlessly handsome as ever. His auburn hair was perfectly tousled, his golden eyes gleaming beneath the lantern light. He wore a deep green jacket embroidered with a stag head, its antlers wrapped in a strand of goldleaf, the official crest of his court. Every inch of him screamed "royalty." The sight of him made my pulse quicken—though not in the way Rydian had.

"Are you all right?" he asked, scrutinizing me more closely than I liked.

"Of course," I said with a tight smile. "The party is lovely."

"As it should be," he said, his voice a rich hum. "This is a celebration of the future, after all. *Our* future." He tilted his head, a charming smile curving his lips. "And yet, I sense you're not entirely enjoying yourself. Is it me?"

I fluttered my lashes. "How could it be you when I've barely spent a moment with you all night?"

Rather than act offended, he winked. "An error I intend to rectify immediately. Shall we dance?" He offered his hand.

I had no choice but to take it.

Setting aside my wine, I let him lead me to the dance floor. A hush swept through the crowd, and I felt more than saw my parents' eyes on me from their place on the dais. I didn't dare look over at them. Not while Callan's eyes were fastened firmly on mine and the rest of the guests drank it in.

In this moment, we weren't two people dancing. We were a symbol. A hope for our future. A promise that the realm would endure.

Even I felt the buzz in the air like a change on the wind.

Then the music began. Callan was a good dancer, though I'd expected nothing less, and I found myself relaxing in his arms bit by bit as we twirled around the lamplit dance floor. The scent of blue vervain wafted faintly as we spun, and my mouth quirked. It was a party after all. I couldn't blame anyone for wanting to partake in the "party herb."

When the third song ended, Callan gestured to a quiet corner. "Shall we take a break for refreshment?"

"Please," I said, grateful for the invitation to catch my breath.

He led me to a space less crowded, and while it only offered the illusion of privacy in an open space full of creatures with impeccable hearing, it was better than nothing. By the time we stood side by side near the potted rosebushes lining the balcony, he held a drink in each hand, no doubt swiped from a server we'd passed.

"For you," he said, handing me a glass of something pink and bubbly.

"Thank you." I drank generously, earning me a raised brow from Callan. His reaction reminded me of Rydian's warning, and irritation flickered.

"Have you never seen a princess drink?" I challenged.

"Considering yours is the only court with an eligible female royal, the answer would have to be no. In fact, you're the first heir I've met who hasn't tried to eat me for dinner."

I shoved aside my temper in favor of curiosity. "You're saying others have?"

He winked, but it lacked his previous teasing as he said,

"Let's just say the Midnight Court makes Heliconia look well-mannered."

I gaped at him. "You went to the Midnight Court?"

"Someone had to try to secure alliances."

"Was it as dangerous and awful as they say?"

"Worse." He shuddered, and it looked genuine. "Creatures who would drain your blood for a snack. Dark-winged monsters with razor-sharp teeth. And a court full of barbarians who call themselves royals. I don't recommend it."

Horror swept through me. "My father asked to meet with them, but they refused."

"Ah. I suspect that had something to do with the river people being involved."

"Why do those two courts dislike each other so much, anyway?"

I braced myself for a dismissal, knowing full well what my mother would have to say about talking politics at a party. And when I'd asked her about it at the last strategy meeting, she'd simply told me, "The Midnight Court hates everyone, darling." But Callan didn't seem to mind, nor did he seem impatient with my questions.

"They're both very serious about their grudges."

I gave him a dubious look. "What does that mean?"

"For them, the Calidium Empire is gone but not forgotten."

"That kingdom was destroyed a thousand years ago," I scoffed.

"Do you know how?" he challenged.

I frowned, straining to remember from my history lessons.

But Callan went on to explain. "The Calidium Empire was the most united to exist in this realm before or since. Fae, faery, humans, and countless other creatures all led by a single beloved queen who ruled from her Marble Throne. Under her rule, there was peace across Menryth."

"Then the moon split," I put in, recalling bits and pieces from the reading I'd done. The astrological event had been unprecedented. Scholars said a large rock called an asteroid collided with our moon—breaking it in two.

The addition of a second moon created a pull on our oceans and water levels. New rivers formed on the continent. Old ones overflowed. Mer and sea monsters and kelpies and sirens emerged from the ocean's depths. They fought for their own stronghold in the region, and war broke out. It waged for many years until Calidium was finally overtaken.

He nodded. "When the empire fell, the tribes were scattered. The dark fae escaped, but not before the river people chased them north all the way to the edge of the eastern mountains where they remain."

"The Midnight Court is the remnant of the dark fae who escaped the war?" I tried to remember if I'd learned that in my history lessons. If I had, it hadn't seemed important.

He nodded. "And the Midnight Court blames the river people for that destruction."

"It was a millennia ago," I said, disgusted with them all over again. "They'd throw away maintaining peace now for a war they lost a thousand years ago?"

"Fae magic has been waning ever since. And the fae have very long memories. Just look at Heliconia. Her grudge against the Aine is already more than twenty years old, and she's as determined as ever to destroy them—and the rest of us along with them."

I sighed. "Heliconia is the reason we should all be working together." But I would've been lying if I said the history didn't intrigue me. Maybe there were answers in the past—some way to get through to the other courts, to make them want to ally and fight. "What other stories do you know?"

"Is that what you intend to use me for?" His eyes glimmered—the teasing was back. "Not a dance or a smile or anything else we could enjoy on a night like this one?"

I decided to ignore the anything else part. But his flirting was shameless enough that I said, "I wasn't aware you were willing to allow yourself to be used at all."

He gave a dramatic sigh. "Such is the life of a royal, I'm afraid. We're all being used. The only thing we can control is how."

His tone was light, but his words hit close to home. I found myself empathizing and then softening. "You're not as bad as I expected," I admitted.

His eyes lit. "Is that your version of a compliment?"

"I'm just being honest. Besides, you can't tell me you didn't have expectations of me in return."

"Expectation seems like a strong word. I will say I'd hoped you and I could be friends."

"Friends," I repeated.

He lifted a brow. "Is that too far-fetched for an engaged couple?"

I shook my head, not buying into his charm for a single second. "Friends seems like a strong word," I said, tossing his words back at him.

His smile widened, a gleam of mischief entering his eyes. "Is it? I'm told most find my company rather... delightful." He leaned forward, and I caught a minty scent on his breath. Not altogether unpleasant.

Still, I eyed him coolly. "Most probably do."

Callan's laugh was deep and warm, and for a moment, it disarmed me. "So, you're immune to my charms."

"Not immune. Just... aware." I took a sip of my pink wine, watching him over the rim of my glass. "You're a flirt, Callan. You say what people want to hear. It's impressive, really."

He chuckled again, clearly not offended. In fact, he looked

even more amused. "Ah, now we're getting somewhere. So, you think I'm all smooth talk?"

"I think you're very good at playing your role."

"And what role is that?" he asked, stepping closer, his voice lowering to a near-whisper. "Future husband? Charming prince? Something else?"

"All of the above," I said.

He tilted his head, his smile shifting into something softer, almost thoughtful. "Is that so terrible? That I'm good at courtly games? We both know how much rests on this alliance. And now you know why the Midnight Court and the river people will likely never fight together. Surely, you can understand the need to be... persuasive."

My body buzzed where he hovered close. It was the wine, I told myself. Especially since it was nothing like what I'd felt when standing beside Rydian.

Before I could respond, he held out his hand.

"One more dance before we get down to business?"

I knew what business he meant. Announcing our engagement to the people of my court. And he was right. That was exactly what this was: business. A transaction. A trade. For some reason, knowing he saw it that way too helped me regain my balance.

With a smile that no longer felt quite so forced, I placed my hand in his.

He led me to the center of the rooftop where the other couples danced, his grip firm but not forceful. With a smooth motion, he pulled me against him, our hands clasped as he guided me in time with the rhythm of the music.

I found myself searching as I spun, trying to find Rydian in the crowd. But he was gone. And I was stupid for even thinking of him again. Instead, I focused on Callan—on my future.

"You're good at this too," I said after a moment. He spun

me around gently, and I couldn't help but feel like I was being led in more ways than one.

"Dancing?" His breath was warm against my cheek. "I've had plenty of practice."

"Of course you have."

He laughed softly, a low rumble. "You make me sound like some sort of scoundrel."

"Well, are you?"

"Maybe," he mused. "Or maybe I just enjoy beating others at their own games."

That, I understood.

Wasn't I doing the same thing right now? Keeping Heliconia's visit from him so he wouldn't realize the danger until we'd sworn the oath to fight beside each other no matter what?

I shoved away the thought that I was somehow betraying him.

This was necessary for the survival of my people.

And maybe Callan was right, and we'd be friends. He would understand why I'd kept the truth from him for a few more days.

We both wanted the same things in the end.

Our steps fell into sync, and the world around us faded into the background. It was just me and Callan, the future hanging over us like one of the floating lanterns above. Except, for the first time since agreeing to this alliance, I wondered if the future might be brighter than I'd imagined. If maybe a life with Callan wouldn't trap me after all. If maybe it could even offer—if not the freedom I longed for—some measure of happiness.

"Tell me," I said, needing to shift the conversation and my own dangerous thoughts, "What was it like fighting at Staghall? I read the reports of the attack and how you'd laid out the whole thing as a trap. I hear the Autumn Court's soldiers are unmatched even against Obsidians."

The word almost stuck in my throat, but I managed to get it out.

There was a flicker of something in his expression—hesitation, maybe even discomfort—before he quickly recovered, his smile returning. "Staghall was... intense, I suppose."

"You suppose?"

He twirled me gently, deflecting. "War is never pleasant, even when you win."

"True. But that's not really an answer." I studied his face, noting the subtle tension that had crept into his features.

Callan shrugged lightly, his voice losing some of its earlier charm. "The details aren't important. What matters is that we won, and we'll continue to win, especially with Sevanwinds' armies by our side."

I frowned, sensing there was more to his reluctance than he was letting on. "For someone with your reputation for battle, I thought you would be more willing to share what it's like on the battlefield." And a little more willing to brag.

Maybe even out his magic. I still had no idea what his power was. And for someone with his obvious arrogance, his secrecy surprised me.

His jaw tightened. He looked away, the charming prince slipping just enough for me to see the cracks beneath. "Let's just say... Autumn shows no mercy."

Before I could press further, the music stopped abruptly, and a ripple of unease swept through the crowd. Callan paused, his hand still on my waist, as we both looked to identify what had made the musicians stop in the middle of the song.

Another ripple—this one of magic, heavy and dark and ancient from the way it made my blood sing. Just like it had done with the Obsidian.

I tensed, dread filling me as swiftly as breath.

"Get back," Callan said, tugging my hand.

I went with him, straining to see where my parents had gone, but black smoke erupted, filling the space until I couldn't see past my own nose. All I knew was the scent of dark magic and Callan's hand squeezing my own as we stumbled back.

People coughed and cried out as we passed them, everyone blinded by the thick smoke.

Someone screamed.

Panic gripped me, but I shoved it back. I wouldn't freeze again. Not like I'd done with the Obsidian. If another one had managed to find its way here, I would face it.

Hels, I needed a weapon.

Something like thunder boomed, rending the air. I flinched, ducking my head instinctively.

A second later, the smoke cleared all at once, like a veil being lifted.

Callan halted.

Our eyes met, and I reminded myself he was the realm's most formidable fighter. Surely he would have a weapon or a plan. But in the next blink, I registered his fear right alongside my own. Then his gaze shifted to something over my shoulder, and he froze. I turned, scanning the gathering, trying to understand what had caused the sudden shift.

And then I saw her.

She stood at the edge of the rooftop, her dark eyes glittering like the night sky above us. There was something fierce and wild in her gaze, a dangerous glint that sent a chill down my spine. Her presence was enough to silence the entire party, every fae in sight turning to stare at her with stark fear reflected in their faces.

"Heliconia," I whispered, my heart racing.

The dark queen had finally come. And her attention was focused entirely on me.

THE
MOON

Chapter Seven
Aurelia

Breaking our stare, Heliconia's dark gaze swept over the crowd like a predator sizing up prey. Her beautiful face was twisted with hate, her lips curled into a smile that chilled me to the bone. The Summer Court's roses, always in bloom, seemed to wither in her presence. Even the lamplight had gone dim.

My knees trembled, but I stood straight as I faced her.

Some of the guests tried to flee for the exits, but an invisible wall had been conjured, preventing anyone from leaving. Or getting in.

I glanced at the skies, searching for the Aine, but saw only a veil of shadows. The stars were no longer visible through it.

Over the sound of wails and tears, Heliconia's voice rose. "I see my invitation was lost for this special occasion."

The king, my father, rose from his throne, his face hard as stone. "Heliconia," he called, voice sharp. "You are not welcome here. Leave now, or I will see you thrown into the dungeons." He lifted his hand, and heat flushed his skin, spreading up his arm as he called on his magic.

Heliconia's shadows thrashed at his words, her power

pulsing with rage. No one else seemed to feel it but me. A gathering... as if she were pulling it in so she could unleash it on us all.

"Father—" I tried to speak, to warn him, but Callan yanked me back, hissing at me to shut up.

Power shot from Heliconia's hand. A dark arrow that speared through my father's palm. He made a sound of pain as soldiers rushed to his aid. A few other guests attempted to use their own magic. A small streak of lightning flew from Elyn, my mother's advisor and best friend. A gust of wind from Cruve, the commander of my father's guard. And snarling at full speed ahead with claws outstretched, Norley, a panther shifter closed the distance.

None of them reached their target before some dark artifice of Heliconia's making snuffed them out or stopped them in their tracks. The wind died. The lightning winked out. And Norley fell with a black blade buried in her heart.

Ignoring the commotion that followed, Heliconia took another step, a slow, deliberate movement, her eyes sweeping the room once more before re-settling on me. "It's nice to see you again, *Princess*."

People gasped, and fury flushed my cheeks. She was insinuating I'd met with her willingly.

"There's nothing nice about you," I spat. "Which is why I tried to kill you the last time."

"You froze like a coward," the dark queen scoffed. "Just like you're doing now."

"Enough!" My mother's voice cut through the tension, her golden gown shimmering in the lantern light. "We will not tolerate your intrusion. Guards!"

The handful of royal guards stationed nearby surged forward, placing themselves between Heliconia and the dais where my parents stood. The soldiers pointed their swords at the dark fae queen.

She rolled her eyes.

"Be gone from my court, demon witch," my father demanded.

He stepped out from behind his guards as power shot from his unharmed hand—a burst of heat with enough power behind it to spark as it flew. It struck out with lethal precision at Heliconia's chest, only to sizzle away like steam before it could pierce her flesh.

"I'll come and go at my will, old man, not yours," Heliconia said coldly. "My business is not yet finished here. And you will address me as a queen."

"We have no business with you," my father said. His voice was steel, but his eyes... his eyes betrayed his fear. "And you have done nothing to earn that title except to steal it. This court doesn't recognize thieves."

My stomach roiled. If King Tyrion was afraid...everyone should be.

"Not you," Heliconia said. Her gaze swung back to mine. "Her."

The guests standing nearby seemed to shrink away from me. I couldn't blame them. Callan remained, but I felt him tremble as Heliconia's attention settled on me.

"I have nothing to say to you," I told her.

"The Fates think they can stop me, but they are wrong," Heliconia said, hatred dripping from her voice. "It took me a long time to learn what they'd done with you. Mostly because I wasn't bothering to look. Silly me thought the Aine would never betray their sacred laws." She snorted. "My mistake. Although, I'm not sure it matters now that I've seen what you are—and what you're not. Yours is a foolish destiny, girl."

She strode forward, and I braced for whatever attack she would launch. More guards would be coming, but it wouldn't be enough.

The worst part was that I wouldn't be enough, either.

I had no idea what she meant about my destiny being foolish, but I knew for sure, standing in her presence, that I would die for it before I'd had a chance to live.

"If I'm not a threat to you, why bother hunting me down?" I asked, buying time—for what, I didn't know. Prolonging the inevitable maybe.

Heliconia's eyes flashed with pure fury. She didn't like being challenged. "Why does a cat hunt a mouse?" she shot back. "The fun of the kill, I suppose." She lifted her hand, dark magic sparking from it—

"Heliconia, stop this," my mother commanded, her voice trembling now as she was nudged back behind her guards. "You've made your point. Leave. There's no need for violence."

But Heliconia only laughed. Low. Cold. Her eyes glittered with cruel amusement. "You're the ones who bred a weapon for my destruction. And for that treachery, violence is precisely what you'll get." She spread her hands wide, and power shimmered around her. Dark, ancient magic. It radiated through the thick air, sending shivers down my spine.

Unlike with the Obsidian, there was nothing about this dark force that appealed to my strange hunger.

The smoke veil over our heads began to descend again, clogging my throat. I choked on it, my eyes watering as I bent over to try to breathe.

"Aurelia!" Sonoma's voice came from somewhere above me.

Hope speared through me, and I straightened, straining to see her and the other Aine through the swirling blackness.

"Come and fight us, bitch!" Amanti's voice rang out.

I felt the pulse of their magic as the Aine desperately attempted to break through the wards Heliconia had used to seal them out.

Desperate to do something, I picked up a broken plate and

hurled it upward. It bounced off the barrier and slammed to the ground at my feet, shattering into tiny pieces.

Callan flinched.

The great and terrible general, the warrior of Autumn, stood and simply cowered.

"The Aine will save us," someone uttered behind me.

"The Aine are weak. They cannot save you now," Heliconia hissed.

I turned slowly, dread pooling in my gut. Around me, several fae had begun whispering prayers to the Fates, pleading and begging for their help.

"The Fates will not intervene," Heliconia declared. "Their time ruling this realm is finished. Mine is only beginning."

People gasped at that. Some began to sob.

Heliconia's words thundered inside me. If she were telling the truth—if the Fates had abandoned us—even the Aine couldn't stop her now.

"Take me," I blurted. "Leave them alone. I will go willingly or do whatever you want. Just leave them be."

"Princess Aurelia," she said, her voice dripping with venom. "The girl who was never supposed to be. The warrior meant to destroy me. I'll happily take your life, but it won't spare theirs."

"She is not a threat to you," Sonoma's voice rang out through the veil. And I felt the cut of her words slice all the way through me.

Heliconia glared up through the shadowy ward she'd erected against the sky. "Did you think I wouldn't know?" she demanded. "That the forest wouldn't whisper what you'd done behind my back? Concordia spilled all your secrets to me." Sonoma snarled, but Heliconia only seemed more pleased by it. "I found your cabin. The scent of your little family is still there, you know."

She waved her hand, and another layer of shadows

appeared. It thickened like smoke in my lungs. I struggled to breathe through it, my eyes burning. Somewhere above me, Sonoma shouted again, but her voice was muffled now, as if the barrier between us had solidified, swallowing the sound.

I needed a weapon. Some hope of defending myself—but there was nothing. And then a figure moved beside me.

Callan.

He stepped forward, jaw clenched. I spotted a jeweled dagger in his hands. It was clearly only meant to be decorative; an accessory to his tailored party clothes. But he raised it anyway, and my heart squeezed at the way he stood ready to defend me. Or at least try. But then he moved again, and I realized he wasn't defending me at all—he was backing away.

Toward the exit.

Heliconia's laugh was sharp, cutting through the tension like a blade. "Going so soon?" she sneered. "The Autumn Court's perfect little prince deserting his new friends. How disappointing."

Callan had almost made it to the door.

Magic slammed into Callan, lifting him off his feet and sending him crashing into the stone wall on the far side of the roof. His dagger clattered uselessly to the floor, and he slumped down, unmoving.

"Callan!" I screamed, but he didn't stir.

"Marriage is such a waste of a vow," Heliconia murmured, almost amused, her eyes flicking back to me. "But don't worry, Princess. Your turn is next."

Power crackled around her.

"Why are you doing this? I'm no threat to you."

"Not yet," she agreed. "But someday, you might have been." She lifted her hand. "There's only room for one of us in this realm."

"No!" I tried to move toward her, to stop her, but the

power was already building—twisting like a storm, violent and out of control.

She raised her hands to the sky. "Die screaming, daughter of darkness."

Black smoke spilled from her fingers. She lowered her hands, pointing the smoke at the crowd. Fae and human alike screamed, trying to run from it, but they didn't get far before they fell.

In a horrific wave, it brought down everyone standing.

Scrambling back, I tried to call up my flame as I'd done before, but it barely had time to spark to life before her magic snuffed it out—and sank right through my skin.

Pain seared me, worse than any wound I'd ever known. My vision blurred. My legs gave out. A scream built and then died in my throat. The magic inside me stirred, attempting to turn the poison into something it could feed on. But it spread too fast.

The world burned hot and bright—and then blurred.

The ground rushed up to meet me, and all I could think was, *This is it.* A last breath caught in my chest.

Around me, the Summer Court lay still, unmoving. Silent.

My heart broke for them just before oblivion swallowed me whole.

THE
MOON

Chapter Eight
Rydian

The princess didn't bother to watch me walk away. I would've known if she had—because every sense in my body was attuned to her awareness. Not that I welcomed such a reaction. She was entitled and haughty and irritating as Hel. Exactly what I'd expected of the pampered heir. But worse than all of that, she seemed clueless about her destiny. Unfortunately, meeting her confirmed my fear; that her kingdom wasn't likely to win in a war against Heliconia. Even now, they seemed to have no idea how close that war was to their doorstep. Talking to the princess had been incredibly reckless. I hadn't planned to get so close tonight. The objective had been recon. Nothing more. And yet, something about her had drawn me in.

Now, it was all I could do to make myself leave.

Callan had nearly spotted me. I wasn't ready to let my half-brother discover I'd found a way out of the cage our father had put me in so many years ago.

No one stopped me as I descended the stairs and strode out of the castle. Guards had been stationed at regular checkpoints, but they barely glanced at me as I left, wrapped in shadows.

Outside, torchlight lit the path through the castle grounds. I followed it only as long as the guards could see me then veered off into the gardens, shoving straight through hedges to make up time.

I pulled my own shadows in tight around me, using them for cover and as a shield against the thorns from the queen's favorite rose bushes.

"There you are," came a male voice in the darkness. "What the fuck were you doing in there? Moving in?"

"I got caught up," I said in a clipped tone that hopefully wouldn't invite more questions.

Slade, my second, snorted as his shadow-wrapped form peeled away from moonflower bushes that stood taller than any I'd ever seen. He fell into step beside me as we made our way toward the eastern corner. Our footsteps made no sound on the soft grass, but even so, I pulled my shadows in more tightly around us. We were almost done; best not to get careless now.

"Well?" he prompted when I didn't speak. "How'd it go?"

"She's a piece of fucking work," I said darkly.

"What the Hel does that mean?" Amusement laced his voice.

I shot him a glare, and his smile vanished. "If she's the Chosen One, we're all fucking doomed."

"That bad, huh?"

"Pampered, entitled, naïve. Completely unaware of her destiny or the extent of her power—"

"Well, did you tell her?"

"Tell her what?"

"About Heliconia's plans to attack? Our scouts say they have less than two months—"

"Our objective was recon," I said. "Why would I tell her anything?"

A boom thundered across the sky. I whirled, drawing my sword as I looked for the source of the noise. Magic—dark and rotten—filled my nostrils, and I tensed as understanding dawned. I knew that scent. Heliconia. She'd come early.

"What was that?" Slade whispered.

"Magic."

A beat of silence passed.

"I don't see anything," Slade finally hissed.

He'd drawn his own sword and looked ready to tear something to ribbons. But after a long moment of scanning the empty courtyard, I realized the threat wasn't on the ground.

In the night sky, smoke roiled as three winged Aine tried and failed to penetrate a large shield that smelled of brimstone straight from Hel. And on the edge of the castle rooftop, among the lights and the fae and the princess's party guests, stood the dark fae queen herself.

I tightened my grip on my sword, warring with myself.

Another figure shoved through the hedge line. Daegel, my third, was a broad-shouldered fae male with a thick beard and a softer heart than most realized. His eyes were wide as he stared up at Heliconia.

"Seven Hels," he breathed. "I know I was supposed to wait for you, but..." He stared at the sight of the chaos above us.

People screamed and scattered as Heliconia shot a bolt of magic from her hands.

"We have to help them," Daegel finished, taking a step forward.

"No," I said grimly, hating myself more than I'd ever thought possible.

They both turned to look at me, fury and determination in their eyes. "Ryd—" Slade began, his stubbly jaw hardening.

"If she's not enough to save herself, we need to stay hidden until we find the one who is," I snapped.

"The prophecy named her," Daegel argued. His cheeks had flushed red. He was angry at me. I didn't blame him.

More screams sounded.

I gritted my teeth and stared my men down. "The Fates named her," I corrected. "That's not who we serve." It wasn't entirely true. Even the one I served agreed she was the key to stopping what was coming—if that's what she chose to do. The fact that he'd insisted she should have a choice in the matter kind of negated the whole prophecy thing.

"Did you forget your brother is up there?" Slade demanded.

Something hot boiled up inside me. "Half-brother. He's not my concern."

Slade stared at me then shook his head.

Daegel, however, continued to push. "You can't just expect us to stand by while—"

A scream rent the air. Her scream. I wasn't sure how I knew it, but I did. And then my feet were moving, and my entire being was focused on getting to her.

I raced back through the gardens, vaulting over low hedges and ripping through the middle of the taller ones. My chest tightened with the knowledge I'd never make it in time. Not to mention I was outing myself by even trying. But I didn't care. All that mattered was the spoiled princess. The beautiful, sharp-tongued, possibly Chosen princess I'd taken one look at and hated on sight.

The thunder boomed a second time, this one powerful enough to shake the earth. My feet came out from under me as magic split the air with a force unlike anything I'd ever felt before.

My body absorbed the blow like a hammer strike. My

breath whooshed out, and pain exploded in my ribs. I groaned, or tried to, but sound proved impossible.

The last thing I saw before my eyes slid shut were three winged Aine, their eyes alight with the Fates' fury, descending over the rooftop. No one moved but them, and a sense of utter loss sank into me, bone deep. The princess had fallen. And now we would too.

THE
MOON

Chapter Nine
Aurelia

I jolted upright, the sheets tangled around my legs, my breath coming in shallow bursts. My heart pounded, a frantic rhythm against my ribs, and I blinked at the sight of my bedroom.

Sunlight streamed in through the windows, curtains fluttering in the breeze. It looked like any other morning. But somehow, I knew it wasn't.

Then I remembered: the party. Heliconia. Her killing blow.

What came after was harder to recall.

I tried to piece together how I'd gotten here. How I was alive at all. I looked down. A nightgown clung to my skin, itchy against the layer of sweat that slicked my back. My face felt hot and flushed like I'd been fighting a fever. I pressed a trembling palm to my chest, trying to calm the wild panic bubbling inside me.

Was it a dream?

Heliconia's dark magic. My people falling, their bodies crumpling to the ground. I had fallen too—hadn't I? That horrible darkness had swallowed me whole, and I was sure... I was sure I'd died.

But here I was. Alive. In my bed. Dressed in a nightgown.

The faint scent of roses drifted through the window, the same scent that always lingered in the halls of Sunspire. Birds called outside, their song happy and bright.

It all felt so... normal. As if nothing had happened.

I swallowed hard, pushing the covers aside. My legs were weak as I stood, but I forced myself to move, padding barefoot across the cool floor. There was no breakfast waiting on the side table. No dress hanging on the armoire signaling what I should wear for the day. No evidence anyone had been in this room but me.

Except I couldn't remember putting this nightgown on. Or climbing into this bed. Or peeling myself off that rooftop.

I opened the door to my room and stepped into the corridor, the familiar sight of the arched windows and soft rug comforting me. But something was off. The usual bustle—the life that always hummed through the castle—was gone.

Everything was quiet. Too quiet.

"Hello?" I called softly.

No answer.

The hallway stretched ahead of me, empty, the light through the curtains casting long, eerie shadows across the floor.

"Hello?" I tried again. "Anyone there?" My voice echoed in the silence, bouncing off the high walls, but still, no one answered.

I walked faster, the soft sound of my bare footsteps unnerving in the stillness. The emptiness followed me, pressing in on all sides.

The castle felt like a tomb.

I passed through the main hall, my eyes darting around for any sign of life, but there was nothing.

Only me.

Fear coiled tighter in my chest as I changed course and climbed the stairs to the royal wing, my hand trailing along the banister. The smooth wood felt cold beneath my fingers, lifeless. The deeper I went, the more the stillness sank into me, heavy and oppressive.

Finally, I reached my parents' chambers. The door was slightly ajar. My heart lurched.

"Mother?" I whispered as I stepped inside.

Shadows greeted me. I tensed, remembering Heliconia's shadows and the darkness within them, but this was only thick curtains pulled tightly closed across the windows, obscuring most of the light.

It took my eyes a couple of blinks to adjust and then—

I halted.

Lying together in their grand, canopied bed, the covers pulled up to their chests, my parents slept. Their faces were peaceful, serene even. But everything about it felt wrong.

I stepped closer, my breath catching in my throat.

"Mother?" I reached out, my fingers trembling as I touched her hand. Her skin was warm. Too warm to be—

"They're not dead," a familiar voice said softly from the shadows.

I spun around, heart racing.

Sonoma stood against the wall, her silver hair and sheer wings glowing faintly in the dim light. She looked exhausted, her shoulders heavy. I replayed her words just to be sure I'd heard them right because I saw only grief reflected at me.

"What's wrong with them?" I asked.

"They're asleep," she said. "Everyone is."

"What do you mean everyone?"

"I mean the entire kingdom of Sevanwinds is under its effect."

"The effect of what?" My voice cracked, panic rising again. "Sonoma, what happened?"

"The curse," she said, stepping forward, her face tight with tension. "It didn't kill them like she'd apparently intended, thank the Fates. But no one has woken, nor will they until we can figure out how to break this wretched curse."

My knees gave out, and I sank onto the edge of the bed. The room swayed, the weight of her words crashing down on me like a wave.

"They're... cursed to sleep without waking—forever?" I breathed. "All of them?"

Sonoma nodded grimly. "Every Summer Court citizen inside Rosewood—and most of the outlying farms," she said grimly.

I shot to my feet, horrified. "Lilah!"

I was already running, tearing down the hall to her room. My pulse pounded in my ears, my bare feet slapping against the cold stone floor. I reached Lilah's door, throwing it open.

She was there.

My sweet, bright-eyed sister, curled up in her bed, her flaxen hair spread across the pillow, her small hands tucked beneath her cheek. She looked so peaceful. So utterly oblivious to the horror that had trapped her. I stumbled toward her, my heart breaking at the sight.

"Lilah," I whispered, dropping to my knees beside the bed. I shook her gently, my voice thick with desperation. "Lilah, please, wake up."

Nothing. She didn't stir. Her chest rose and fell with steady, even breaths, but there was no response. No flicker of recognition. Just deep, unending slumber.

A sob caught in my throat, and I pressed a kiss to her forehead.

Footsteps sounded behind me. I turned to see Lesha and

Amanti standing in the doorway, their faces pale and drawn. Their wings, usually stretched tall and gossamer, bore scratches and small tears in the webbed linings. They looked as weary as Sonoma, who lurked behind them like a ghost. At the sight of them all here, tears spilled over, running down my cheeks.

"Aurelia." Lesha held open her arms, and I went to her, letting her pull me into a hug. I stepped away, too desperate for answers to accept comfort.

Amanti pressed her forehead to mine before quickly straightening. Relief flashed in her dark eyes, and then she was back to business. "How are you feeling?" she asked me.

"I'm fine," I assured her. "Why?"

She and Lesha exchanged a look.

"What is it?" I asked, but they remained silent.

"Just tell her," Sonoma said, resigned.

Lesha swallowed hard. "Come and see." She tugged my hand, leading me to the mirror beside Lilah's armoire. When she nudged me and I caught sight of my reflection, I gasped.

A symbol was inked into the side of my neck just below my ear. I pulled my hair out of the way, leaning in to see it better. A tiny black moon with three stars etched above it, painted in black ink so dark it seemed to suck the light from the space around it.

"How did I get it?" I asked, leaning in to get a better look.

I traced a finger over the symbol. At my touch, magic, strong enough to steal my breath, rippled inside me. I opened my hand, letting some of my power slip through my control. The sparks I'd managed to conjure before shot to life in my palm, along with a black flame that felt ready to ignite everything in this room at my command.

All three Aine gasped.

I glanced up to see them staring at the flame I'd made,

shock on all their faces. Sonoma was the first to recover. She blinked at me, something like awe shining in her eyes. It felt as if she were seeing me for the first time.

"Furyfire," Lesha whispered.

Fury. Like the Furiosities of Hel and the demons they ruled. Like my death magic.

"Is it...bad?" I managed.

"It's powerful," Lesha said firmly.

"Powerful like demons of Hel or like a new kind of summer gift?" I asked with what I already knew was a naïve amount of hope for the latter.

Lesha started to answer, but Amanti nudged her. Hard. Lesha pressed her lips together and looked away.

"It's rare," Amanti told me.

I looked at Sonoma. "You said my magic comes from Hel," I said, my voice wavering on the last word. I glanced at the stone-faced Aine, but she refused to meet my eyes. "Is that true?"

Again, it was Amanti who spoke. "Furyfire is a gift only the Furiosities have ever possessed, yes. But you're not evil," she added firmly.

Her certainty was the only thing that kept me from losing it.

"How is it possible that I would have it?" I asked.

Amanti cleared her throat. "The Fates imbue certain ... gifts to all the fae."

"But how would the Fates be able to offer something that wasn't theirs to begin with?" I pressed.

Sonoma was frustratingly silent.

Amanti shook her head. "We're not sure why you were given these gifts."

Lesha stepped forward, breaking her silence. "But they don't change who you are, Aurelia. Only you get to do that."

The others nodded.

I let the flame wink out and glanced again at my reflection, trying to understand what it all meant. How the strange tattoo had gotten there. Why my magic was suddenly so much more accessible? What had made me immune to this curse?

"I remember so much pain when her magic struck me," I said, running my hand over my chest absently.

Amanti spoke up. "After you fell, the wards keeping us out finally broke. I suspect Heliconia had exhausted her magic, casting that wretched spell to kill you." I flinched at that. "Heliconia vanished before we could get to her. By then, the mark had already appeared on your skin."

I had no idea why I'd been spared, but the fate of the kingdom was far more pressing than a strange tattoo and the power of furyfire. Or that's what I told myself. Maybe it was just a distraction so I didn't have to face what I'd woken inside me.

I turned from the mirror, unwilling to look at myself any longer.

"What happened to Callan?" I asked, bracing myself for the worst. "He went down before me. He tried to get away, and she— He wasn't moving."

"The Autumn prince and his people are fine," Sonoma said in a clipped voice.

I tried to gauge whether her sharpness was directed at me, but Lesha's soft rebuke came before I could ask.

"It's not their fault Heliconia's spell excluded them," Lesha told her friend.

"Lesha's right," Amanti said wryly. "You can't be angry at the guy for not being cursed."

"I'm not angry about his being unharmed," Sonoma said. "I'm angry that he fled like a coward." At her words, I stiffened, remembering how Callan had tried to run.

He'd deserted me when I'd needed him most.

"Where is Callan now?" I asked, looking back and forth between them.

Amanti sighed. "We … removed him and his people."

"Define removed," I said warily.

Amanti huffed. "They are unharmed and remember nothing. Lesha wiped their memories of the attack. They'll go home, thinking the marriage contract was rescinded. The only harm done will be to his precious ego."

Sonoma snorted, but unease coiled inside me. Something told me a cut to Callan's ego was not a wound to be made lightly.

"Callan can help us," I protested. "We should've asked him to bring his best healers here to—"

"Absolutely not," Sonoma snapped.

I glared at her.

But Amanti cut in. "Sonoma is right. We have no sitting queen or king. No one ruling this land. Our people are asleep in their beds—exposed to any threat that walks through their door. Heliconia will figure it out soon enough, but if Autumn knew it, they'd likely seize their opportunity to claim this kingdom for themselves."

"You don't know that," I argued.

"And you do?" Sonoma challenged. "You spent one evening with the male. Will you vouch for him? Would you swear it on Lilah's life?"

I didn't answer.

"Lesha's magic will hold well enough," Amanti told her. "They won't remember anything beyond what she planted in their minds."

"We'll see that it does," Sonoma agreed, a glint in her eye.

"We have to break the curse," I said, urgency lacing my veins as powerful as any magic.

Sonoma's expression softened with sorrow. "We'll find a way. But it'll take time. Heliconia's magic isn't entirely from this realm, and it's not something we fully understand. We don't even know where to start."

Lesha voiced her question reluctantly. "What if the only one who can undo it is Heliconia herself?"

"Actually," Sonoma said slowly, "there is one other whom the Fates gifted with the power to undo Heliconia's damage."

My heart hammered in my chest as she looked at me.

The comments Heliconia had made in the forest, the accusations she'd aimed at me during the party, the way my mother had insisted I hear the truth from Sonoma...

"It's me," I said bleakly. "Isn't it? I'm some sort of chosen one meant to save the realm."

Sonoma's expression was pained. "Yes."

"I knew it. Mother refused to answer my questions last night. Said we should wait for you and Father to be there." I glared at her. "All this time, you've kept this from me."

"I was going to tell you," she said quietly. "We all were."

"When?" I demanded, the word whipping out like a blade.

Lesha flinched, but Amanti and Sonoma stood their ground. I studied their faces, noting that Amanti and Lesha didn't look surprised. Everyone knew but me. And keeping it from me had very nearly gotten us all killed.

"Let me guess? You were waiting for the right time," I snapped.

"Something like that," Sonoma said quietly.

I snorted. "And look at where we ended up while you waited for the perfect moment." I shook my head, wishing for boots and a sword rather than this stupid, flimsy nightgown.

"I hope you're proud of your lies," I snapped, hot betrayal rising and roiling inside me.

All three of them, powerful warriors stronger than any the realm had ever seen, hung their heads.

None of them answered.

The truth of it—known too late—only fanned the flames of my temper.

"Is this why you trained me as one of the Aine?" I nearly yelled. "So I'd have a fighting chance when my time came to challenge her?"

My hands curled into fists at my sides. When Sonoma wanted to train me, I'd thought it was a compliment to my skills. Some special talent she saw inside me. But no. It was a duty borne of knowing my destiny before I did. Just like with the stupid wedding, I was no more than a tool, a weapon. One they hadn't even bothered to consult before sharpening me into points.

My mother's words of encouragement. About believing in me. That I was a warrior. It was all based on this hidden destiny. This secret. That somehow, without any memory of it on my part, the Fates had looked upon me and decided I would be the one to deliver us from Heliconia.

How in the seven Hels I would do that, especially when I had no idea they'd chosen me in the first place, was beyond me. But the Fates were goddesses from a realm beyond our own. Strangers to me. Ethereal ideas of beings. The warriors who stood before me were my family. And that hurt worst of all. Standing among the women I most respected and admired in the entire realm, I'd never felt more alone.

Hot tears burned my eyes, but I blinked them back, refusing to give in to them.

"You are done keeping things from me, all of you," I said, my voice trembling with rage. "And no one gets to make decisions for me ever again. From this moment forward, I'm in charge of my own life. Do you understand?"

They exchanged a look then Lesha and Amanti lowered their heads as if to defer to Sonoma.

"All right," Sonoma said, and the others nodded with her.

I looked back at the three of them, heart aching with the

knowledge that, if we were going to survive whatever came next, I'd have to find a way to forgive them eventually. But not today.

Today was for mourning.

I took a deep breath that felt as if it might break me into a million pieces if I let it. "Never lie to me again."

THE
MOON

CHAPTER TEN
AURELIA

Seven years later...

The castle library felt as hollow as my own heart. In my childhood, I'd avoided this room, dreading the boring lessons I'd been forced to take here. The ancient history tomes I'd been made to read and report on to my tutors. I would have much rather been outside in the forest, training with a sword or exploring on my horse. In the last seven years, however, this library had become a retreat from the threats that lurked beyond the walls. And in a twist of irony that I didn't find the least bit funny, I'd spent countless hours poring over those same history books, searching for answers—with little to none to show for it.

Now, more often than not, I drank whiskey here instead and practiced my furyfire until the alcohol dulled my magic or snuffed it out entirely. Conjuring fire was a reckless thing to do among all these books. But maybe that was what made me do it. All these precious accounts of Menryth's greatest magic-wielders, and none explained how or why Sevanwinds remained cursed. Or how I possessed the magic of Hel inside me.

Tonight, I wasn't alone. Though none of us bothered with the haphazard piles of discarded volumes.

That wasn't why we were here.

The great hearth crackled with fire, but no one spoke as the three of us gathered around it. My fingers dug into the armrest of my chair, knuckles turning white as I stared at the flames I'd conjured to light the kindling. Inside, my magic writhed and wriggled against the leash I'd learned to keep it on. Not from books but from practice—sweaty, tearful, raging practice. And even now, after such careful mastery, it wanted out. To fight. To rage. To curse every obstacle and horror we'd faced in the last few years.

I had too much control to let it.

But today, the temptation alone left me gritting my teeth.

Sonoma sat across from me, her silver hair glinting in the firelight, the same stern expression she always wore fastened in place—guarded but tired. The circles beneath her eyes were dark, suggesting sleepless nights and worrisome days. They were deeper ever since Amanti left.

No, since Amanti hadn't returned.

Lesha stood by the window, her curvy silhouette framed by the dark sky. Her translucent wings were tucked in tight against her back; a sign of her tension. Outside, the world looked quiet, untouched. But we knew better. The curse was suffocating us, inch by inch. Year by year. Failure after failure. And now... Amanti had been gone for six months with no word.

In the past seven years, she'd made many trips across the continent to search for answers, and while none had yielded a cure, she'd always returned in one piece. This last one had been to follow a lead into the southern territories to a place called Vorinthia. The southernmost part of the continent where the remote and mostly uninhabited lands had once held a powerful tribe of magic-wielders now lost to the eons. According to our research, Vorinthia had been the last kingdom to wield magic as strong as Heliconia's.

But Amanti hadn't returned.

Her absence felt like a blow to the hope we'd managed to hang onto these last years. Hope for answers. For a way to end this purgatory.

Lesha's voice broke the heavy quiet. "I've made a decision."

I tore my gaze from the fire and looked at the dark-haired Aine who was like an aunt to me.

Her expression was pinched as she said, "I'm leaving tomorrow."

My breath hitched in my chest. I'd known this was coming, had seen it in the determination that had hardened her normally soft features over the last few weeks. But hearing it still sent a wave of dread through me.

"Where do you intend to go?" I asked.

"South."

To search for Amanti—and whatever kept her away.

"Is that safe?" I asked.

Lesha hadn't left on her own for quite some time. Amanti had always been the stealthier of the two—and the one most willing and ready to sacrifice herself for us all. I tried not to think about that part. "If anyone finds you, they'll know we're here—"

"No one will find me."

Neither of us pointed out that someone had likely found Amanti already.

Besides, maybe she was right, and no one would notice her. The realm had bigger problems these days than an Aine no one had seen for seven years, even one presumed dead at the hands of Heliconia's death curse.

Years ago, Amanti and Lesha had spread rumors to the other kingdoms that the Summer Court had succumbed to a dark enchantment that still hung over the entire city like a poisoned cloud. Fear had kept out all but the bravest—or most reckless—and any who dared try to come anyway were met with impenetrable wards thanks to the Aine's magic.

After that, word spread that everyone inside these walls had fallen that night at the solstice party. Treasure hunters arrived in droves at first, but none managed to get through. Soldiers and mercenaries sent their recruits to test their strength and bravery against the magic that kept everyone out. Over time, they all stopped trying. It had been a year since a single soul had triggered the security traps Sonoma put in place. The loneliness that came with the solitude of surviving was enough to hollow me out. Some days, I pretended the rest of Menryth had died with us. It was easier than knowing they were out there somewhere.

It was a devastating thing to be thought dead—and then forgotten. But it was our best chance at surviving long enough to end this nightmare.

And we were running out of time.

Seven years later, Menryth was once again living on the brink of invasion.

A collective breath hold. That's what Amanti had called it. Lesha claimed that was dramatic, but Amanti wasn't one for subtlety.

For seven years, Heliconia had reigned from her stolen throne in the north. According to Amanti's sources, the power Heliconia had used on me that night had drained her nearly to death, which meant that, instead of invading the other courts after she'd cursed ours, she'd been forced into hiding to recover.

While the dark queen licked her wounds, her Obsidians had continued threatening the other courts with war unless they bowed to the self-proclaimed queen. But even though no one had officially given in to her demands, she hadn't called them on it.

Yet.

It was only a matter of time until she was strong enough to come down from her mountain and take her vengeance on them. At least, she hadn't been able to look too closely at the Summer Court. Amanti claimed Heliconia still thought she'd succeeded in killing us all that night.

I had no idea if that was true—we couldn't take the risk of infiltrating her northern camps to find out. Instead, we concentrated on searching for others who could help heal our people and break their curse.

The barrier Sonoma constructed had kept us hidden from prying eyes and given the citizens of Rosewood a place to rest. It had taken us weeks to get them all into the castle, and a few more still to organize them so they weren't lying piled in the halls. But we'd done it.

My people were safe. And alive. Even if they weren't really living.

If Heliconia found out that we'd deceived her—that we'd found a way to save ourselves—she'd come for us. And she wouldn't fail a second time. Not even my furyfire, honed and sharpened over these last years, would be enough to take on Heliconia at her full strength.

It was plenty, however, to protect Lesha's back.

"You don't have to do this alone," I said to her now, the words rushing out too quickly to be anything but desperate. "I'll go with you. We can search together—"

"No." Lesha turned from the window, her eyes fierce with determination. "We can't risk you being discovered, Aurelia. You know that."

I sighed, unwilling to rehash old arguments.

"This is for me to do alone," she added. "Besides, there's something you can do while I'm gone."

I sat up straighter, eager to have a mission. "What is it?"

"I have a lead on a healer hiding out in the Broadlands, near the Trolech Forest. She studied under the Verdant, which means she knows about the old magic. She might know something that can help."

The Broadlands was the only thing that stood between Summer's borders and the foothills of the Concordian Mountains. It was ruled by no court and filled with deadly things. Out there, lawlessness reigned, and there were worse things that prowled than Heliconia's Obsidian scouts. But we couldn't afford to ignore the ancient magic the Verdant had possessed. It was the one lead we'd managed to uncover these last years. The one place where the magic to save us might still exist. It's why Amanti had gone to Vorinthia, a lost kingdom thought to be deserted for nearly a thousand years now. If someone in the Broadlands knew something, I had to try to find them.

Sonoma was already frowning at me when I caught her eye, but I nodded at Lesha. "I'll do my best."

"This is a fool's errand," Sonoma said, and it took me a minute to realize she was speaking to Lesha and not me.

Lesha stood her ground. "I have to find her, Sonoma. We need her magic to keep the wards strong. Besides... Vorinthia is the one place where the veil could still be thin enough."

I looked between them. "Thin enough for what?" I asked.

Sonoma looked away, scowling.

Lesha said softly, "To make contact with the Fates."

Sonoma and I shared a look of irritation at the reference to the missing goddesses. In this, we agreed.

"They don't want to help us," I grumbled.

Lesha's chin lifted. "If they won't speak willingly, I'll make them."

"Make them?" Sonoma echoed from across the room. "They've been silent for seven years. What makes you think they'll listen to you now?"

"I don't have a choice." Lesha stepped closer, the thin lines in her translucent wings reflecting the firelight. "We're running out of time. You feel it, don't you? The way the curse is changing—tightening its hold on the land. On us."

I felt it.

It was in every breath I took, the heaviness settling deeper in my chest as the months and years stretched on. It was in the way the trees in the Emerald Forest, once sentient enough to whisper to me, had grown quieter, the river slower. The kingdom itself was suffocating under Heliconia's curse, and we were powerless against it. My magic had strengthened since that horrible night seven years ago, but none of my gifts could stop the curse from spreading.

"She's right," I said quietly.

Sonoma's mouth was a thin slash. "We'll fight it. Like we always have."

"We're draining ourselves," Lesha said, and though her words were gentle, Sonoma flinched.

"We've tried everything," I whispered bleakly, the words barely audible. "All of it—useless. And now Amanti..." Her name cracked in my throat, a wound too fresh even after six months. "She should've been back by now."

Lesha's lips pressed into a tight line. "That's why I'm going after her. She might have found something—an answer, a lead. Something we've missed."

My chest tightened with every word. "What if she didn't? What if—"

"I have to try," Lesha snapped, her voice rising before she sighed, dragging a hand through her hair. "And if the Fates won't come to us, I'll find a way to get to them. We were faithful to them for years. I won't allow them to turn their backs."

"Maybe they can't help," Sonoma muttered, her gaze darkening as she leaned forward. "Maybe that's why they're silent."

Lesha's expression hardened. "You could try *him*, you know."

"Absolutely not," Sonoma hissed.

I studied them, confused. "Him who?"

Lesha opened her mouth, but Sonoma cut her off with a vicious look. "No one."

Her tone was angry enough that I let it drop.

Seven years ago, I'd gotten the truth out of them. The secret my parents had kept from me since birth: that I was Chosen by the Fates to save the kingdom. Learning about their lie had hurt me deeply; a wound that had taken a long time to mend.

Believing in my own destiny took even longer.

I still had no idea how I could possibly be the one the Fates had chosen. Especially when they'd refused to answer our summons. But where faith failed, training took over. After years of practicing with the most formidable warriors to walk the realm, I'd honed myself into the weapon they'd bred me to be.

In all the ways that counted, I'd gotten my wish and become one of the Aine. We'd become equals, the four of us. Warriors fighting side by side for the same tenuous future. Until Amanti hadn't returned.

Her absence had broken something in us all.

Lesha shook her head. "Fine, but the Fates know something—they always know something."

"The temples are empty," Sonoma said, her voice brittle. She was angry at the goddesses. I didn't blame her. "Not even the whitestone is enough to summon them."

"Then I'll find another temple," Lesha insisted stubbornly. "I'll visit every temple from here to Vorinthia if I have to."

Sonoma and I exchanged a glance.

Lesha was the last of us who still believed the Fates could be bargained with, that there was still some divine intervention left for us in this cursed world. Her steadfast faith—as naïve as it was—reminded me of Lilah. My sister's innocence and sweet belief in the good this world had to offer were two of the things I loved most about her. About both of them. I refused to be the one to tell Lesha all the good in the realm was gone.

"Come home," I whispered to her instead, my throat tight.

She smiled—a small, brittle thing. "I'll do my best."

THE
MOON

Chapter Eleven
Aurelia

Trapped in a stranger's bedroom, I accepted the fact that I would have to commit murder if I wanted to make it home. Venturing this far into the Broadlands had been a risk, but I'd had little choice. Apparently, the monsters that prowled here were counting on that.

I paused just inside the doorway of what had once been a very modest bedroom—probably belonging to a farmer if the adjacent barn was any indication. On the other side of the small room, the wooden frame of the bed had rotted so that it rested unevenly on two legs instead of four. The mattress had already disintegrated and was now nothing more than a pile of stuffing. And there was a dampness in the air that didn't bode well for the stability of the place.

It was old and unkempt.

Forgotten.

Just like me.

But I much preferred being forgotten to being found by one of *her* creatures.

I stood perfectly still and listened for signs someone else was with me inside the tiny, rotting cabin. Well, someone other than the dead healer I'd come to find. I glanced again at her fae body slumped in the corner opposite the bed, throat cut and drained of blood. For what, I was sure I didn't want to know.

Dark magic. Rituals.

Pleas for more magic to be imbued upon the petitioner.

Every fae in Menryth wanted more magic. I couldn't blame them when its waning presence only left them more defenseless.

Then again, the Broadlands and the Trolech Forest that bordered it were full of nightmarish creatures. Any one of them might've wanted her blood for nourishment or enjoyment just as easily as for a sacrifice. Either way, I'd been too late.

And I wasn't the only one who'd been drawn to the scent of her spilled blood.

For a moment, there was only the complete stillness that had been the hallmark of my world for the last seven years. At first, that stillness had been a reprieve from the constant demands of royal life. I'd dreaded my marriage and the war that would follow, and while it shamed me to admit it, that first year had been a gift in some ways. A clemency. But then I'd come to realize that stillness was its own kind of prison.

After seven years, the silence grew to a roar when I concentrated on it—like now.

Most days, I tried very hard to ignore that roar—and the nightmare it represented—but in this moment, ignoring it could very well kill me. And all of them along with me.

I would never let anything happen to my family.

I focused on the small changes in the air just like Sonoma had taught me and listened harder. The abandoned farmhouse creaked on its rotting foundation, settling around me. Outside the window, the grass rustled softly in the slight breeze.

It was all so natural. Nothing ominous.

But my sensitive ears caught another sound. No more than a shift of the air, but I knew what it was.

Outside the cabin, someone approached.

A moment later, the front door opened, creaking on loose hinges.

Footsteps clunked as the visitor stepped into the sagging main room.

I braced myself, surprised to find hope rising at the sound. Maybe the visitor was another fae. Or something friendly. The Autumn prince's face flashed in my mind. Callan was nothing more than a daydream. A remembrance that I'd once not be so isolated and alone. That parties and laughter and dancing had been real. And in this moment, I wondered what it might be like to have that daydream back again.

Before I could temper my longing, the scent hit me. I wrinkled my nose, the foul odor confirming what I already knew: it wasn't friendly.

In fact, it wasn't someone at all; it was some*thing*.

An Obsidian.

My hand tightened around the hilt of my sword. I couldn't risk using magic on it. Not when that magic would give me away to any other Obsidians that might be lurking close by.

The air shifted again as the *thing* crept toward the bedroom. My muscles tensed as I gathered my strength to strike. If my instincts were right, it stood directly on the other side of the flimsy wall between us.

I pictured the soulless creature, calculating its next move —and mine.

Onyx eyes. White teeth sharpened to points. Pale skin, so white it was almost translucent. And the worst breath I'd ever encountered in anyone—dead, alive, or in between. Sonoma claimed their smell was from the dark magic running through their veins—the very magic that kept them animated long after their humanity had been stolen. But my coin was on morning breath.

Either way, the creature would kill me without a shred of hesitation if I let it.

I didn't bother rounding the open doorway to face it. The monster was counting on that. Instead, I drew my sword and jammed it forward—slicing clean through the sagging wall. The sharpened blade slid easily through the rotting wood, the years of age and neglect softening any resistance. I felt its tip pierce the body on the other side, sinking through flesh and muscle and bone in one powerful thrust.

The creature screamed, tearing itself off my sword in a panic.

Grunting, I stepped back, pulling Dorcha with me. The metal came away stained with blood.

I wrenched the bedroom door open and stepped into the hall in time to see the Obsidian fall. It landed on its knees, clutching at its chest where blood seeped through to stain its worn jacket. As more spilled, it darkened, turning from burgundy to black within seconds. My power thrummed at the sight of it.

The creature balked at me, and I knew its reaction was about more than just laying eyes on its killer. More than being bested by a female, even. By now, I understood very well what the cursed monster saw in me. What its mind didn't want to accept as it struggled against the pain.

I was Summer Court fae.

No, more than that. I was its lost princess. Valuable above anything else it might've found while scavenging this deserted slip of land.

"You're... her," the creature rasped as it fell onto its back with a grunt. "Princess Aurelia of Sevanwinds, the forgotten one."

I knelt beside it, ignoring its sputtering, and snatched the crooked blade out of its limp hand. The scent of a long-dead animal wafted from the dried blood coating the steel. Gross. Setting the weapon aside, I ripped a section of its tunic free and pressed it to the wound in its stomach. Blood immediately saturated the fabric.

Shit.

"How does it work?" I demanded.

Blood leaked from its mouth as it stared up at me from its back.

I pressed harder, knowing it was futile to try and prolong the inevitable. But I needed information. And I wouldn't get another chance like this again. "Tell me how it works, and I'll find you a healer," I said.

"How does what work?"

The creature had the voice and look of a fae male. But he was much more than that. A cloying sense of magic, dark and twisty, clung to him. It leaked out along with his black blood, calling out to the death magic inside me. The darkness inside me was hungry—and impatient.

"Her magic. Her control over you," I snarled, leaning harder on the wound as blood continued to leak out around my hands. "Tell me how to break her spells."

He paled, and I knew he was bleeding out—faster than I liked, considering all the questions I wanted to ask. That wall had been softer than I'd anticipated.

"You cannot defeat her."

"Tell me," I hissed. "Or tell me how to break her wards in the north. How to get to her."

"She is ... untouchable," he said, his words no more than a gurgle as more blood ran from his mouth and leaked out onto his chin.

Seven Hels.

"Tell me anyway."

"She sees things," he said, his voice strained from the

obvious pain. "Things the darkness is afraid of." The Obsidian gagged.

"What else does she see?" I demanded, urgency driving me to shake his shoulders. To keep him alive long enough to hear his answers.

"She sees you ... allied with the prince—and she sees her own destruction."

My mouth went dry. "What? How? What do you mean?"

His eyes rolled backward as he gasped for air through lungs now drowning in fluid.

"Wait. I'll find a healer," I said.

"Just...let me go." His eyes turned pleading. "Please. Let it be over."

The life force leaking out of him clawed at my ankles.

My power whispered to take what was offered like I'd done so many years ago in that forest. Before I could stop myself, I inhaled, drinking it in.

My power thrummed, expanding as it fed.

My vision sharpened. My awareness amplified. Every cell in my body was focused on my meal.

"What does the prince have to do with Heliconia's destruction?" I asked, breathless with the effects of the power I'd consumed.

The Obsidian sputtered, but no words came. Only blood. And its leaking, fraying life force. Frustration gripped me.

"By the Fates. What good are you when you speak in fucking riddles?" I dropped my sword and grabbed his collar, yanking his head off the floor. "Tell me how to break this damned curse!"

But he was already dead, his onyx eyes lifeless and staring emptily past me. Muttering curses, I released him and watched his head thud against the floor.

The remnants of his life force ribboned through the air,

weaker now, slower. No longer a temptation. Just like he was no longer a source of information.

Sonoma was going to lecture me again.

Another Obsidian dead without the information we so desperately needed.

"Do you not understand the meaning of interrogation?" she'd demanded of me last time.

"Dammit," I muttered and grabbed my sword as I climbed slowly to my feet.

Outside the farmhouse, leaves rustled.

I almost believed it to be nothing more than a breeze, but something in my chest tightened. My heightened senses went on high alert. I crept toward the still-open front door and raised my sword. No other sound came, but I knew I wasn't alone as certainly as I'd known when the Obsidian arrived. My heart pounded at the thought of another one lurking.

Good because it gave me another shot at answers. Bad because the more Obsidians that found me, the higher the chance that one would escape and report to *her*.

Outside, the land seemed to hold its breath.

The trees had stilled unnaturally, and a shiver crept up my spine.

I didn't let myself overthink it. Gripping my sword, I whirled onto the sagging front porch, careful to avoid the rotted wood I'd seen earlier.

A male stood in the grass near the barn.

Broad shoulders. Long cloak, its hem flapping in the crisp wind. Hair tousled. Wild. Eyes dark but not like the onyx of the enemy.

Not an Obsidian.

Fae.

His eyes roiled as if a storm raged inside them. Recognition slammed into me.

Rydian.

The male from the lamplight party. The one who'd insulted me then flirted with me shamelessly right in front of my parents. And my fiancé.

I'd never forgotten him. Couldn't have even if I'd wanted to, thanks to the dreams that haunted me still. His ruggedly handsome face. His wild eyes full of secrets. And that voice that seemed to burrow beneath my skin, touching me everywhere. He'd infuriated me and then slipped away as if he'd never been there at all.

In my loneliest moments—and my drunkest—all my fantasies were full of him.

And now he was here.

Despite the time that had passed since that night, he looked the same, right down to the charcoal tunic that gave no hint of the court he belonged to and the same angry set of his jaw.

The wind rustled, the hissing of the tall grass pulling me from my inspection. I blinked, scowling at myself for focusing on his good looks rather than assessing him as a threat. Whatever he was doing out here, it couldn't be a coincidence. The area was too remote.

Sure enough, he shifted his body, and I caught sight of a blade in his hand. He'd tucked it behind him earlier but now let it flash into sight as he took a step toward me.

"You killed it," he said, his deep voice scraping over my skin like it had all those years ago.

Despite his accusation, pleasure rippled through me at the sound of his voice. I shoved it aside. He didn't seem surprised to find me alive. I needed to tread carefully. "Killed what?"

His eyes narrowed. "What are you doing out here, Princess?"

I made myself shrug. "Passing through. Like you."

He studied me. My heart hammered so loudly I was sure he could hear it from where he stood.

"The Broadlands are dangerous," he said, and the tone made it clear which danger I should be focused on just now.

My gaze flicked to the blade he held. "I can handle myself," I said, tightening my grip on my sword.

He snorted. "There are worse things than Obsidians in the Broadlands."

"Things like you?" I taunted.

His brow lifted. "Did you kill the female too?"

"What?" It took me a moment to understand who he meant. Then confusion became outrage. The healer. Did he really think me capable of such a thing? "Of course not. She was an innocent." After a beat, I demanded, "Did you?"

He snorted as if the idea were preposterous. "He thinks you're dead, you know."

The way he flitted from subject to subject was exhausting. Or maybe I was out of practice when it came to conversation. "Who?"

"You know who. Tell me, what's it like to be a coward and a liar?"

Indignation rose swift and hot inside me. "Excuse me?"

"I will not excuse any of it. Nor will I be the one to explain how you're alive and wandering around, killing Obsidians, while your broken alliance with Autumn causes their suffering."

I stiffened. "I'm not sure what you think you know about me, but—"

"Spare me," he said wryly—and then in a hard voice, "I'm not the one who deserves an explanation, Princess. But don't worry, you can tell him yourself soon enough."

"I'll pass," I said flatly.

My heart raced, though. Who did he mean? Callan? The Autumn king himself? Or some other male who felt entitled to an explanation of my survival?

"Where have you been all this time?" he asked, sounding truly mystified.

For reasons I couldn't explain, even to myself, some part of me was actually tempted to tell him the truth. The words rose to my lips, ready and almost willing, but I shoved them back down my throat and instead bit out, "Surviving."

"And is that all you intend to do with your life, Princess? Survive?"

"What I do with my life is none of your business," I snapped.

"That's where you're wrong. This choice you're hiding from is the business of every fae in this realm. And I, for one, am tired of waiting around for you to make up your mind." Rydian flashed his teeth—a warning, not a smile—then pushed me back a step with a burst of power. My breath whooshed out of me at the force of it.

I gasped, struggling to refill my lungs.

When I straightened, he stood in the same spot as before, but the power was gone, tucked away where I couldn't sense it at all. Just like that night at the party.

Once, I'd thought him a simple soldier. One of my father's warriors.

But his comments made it clear he was loyal to Callan. And that single shove had spoken volumes about what he was capable of.

"You refuse to fight back?" he taunted, eyes glittering in an expression hardened to stone.

Dark flames licked at my palms. I curled my hands shut to keep from giving myself away. Instead, I retreated a step, not stupid enough to turn my back on him but also ready to get the Hel out of this place.

"What are you?" I asked, backing toward the trees.

He smirked. "I'm the thing nightmares fear."

The moment I reached the cover of the forest, I turned and ran.

THE
MOON

Chapter Twelve
Rydian

Wind whipped at my cloak as I watched the princess slip away. When she was out of sight, I started slowly forward. Her scent would be easy to follow; there was no point hurrying. A moment later, Slade emerged from the trees and fell into step beside me. I felt his eyes on me.

"Amanti was right," he said finally, which wasn't a question.

"I never doubted her."

"But you didn't tell the princess about the Aine we rescued."

"She didn't ask," I tossed back.

"And she killed that Obsidian without magic," he said. "Even though she has plenty of it."

I didn't bother commenting.

"Those flames in her hands were something else."

I gritted my teeth. I'd seen them. She'd refused to use them though. On me or the creature. Despite my attempt to bait her into it. Doing so was a violation of the vow I'd made but hopefully a gray area. And if it prompted her to admit what she was —to finally make her own choice—all the better.

"Aren't you going to say something?" he demanded.

"You weren't asking a question," I told him.

"Do you think she's the Chosen One now?" he asked in a wry voice.

I shot him a look, but Slade wasn't intimidated. Not by me. Not anymore.

"She smells like one of us," he said, and even though he wasn't wrong, I snarled.

"She's hiding," I said through gritted teeth. "I want nothing to do with a coward, chosen or not."

"I don't recall you having a choice in the matter." Slade was way too fucking cheerful for words that provoked me so close to violence.

"Bastard," I muttered.

"Aren't we all?" Again with the cheery tone.

I considered smashing my fist into his face. One look at his smirk, and I knew he'd seen my intention.

"It wouldn't make you feel any better," he said.

"I disagree," I said.

Slade laughed darkly, and we trudged on. An hour later, we slowed when we nearly overtook her progress. Masking our presence with my shadows, Slade and I watched as the princess released a rabbit from a trap and slit its throat with a short blade she pulled from her boot. She bled it then cleaned her weapon. She didn't bother to skin the animal before tossing it over her shoulder and resuming her trek.

Slade and I followed, still wrapped in shadows as we closed the distance. Her scent hung thicker here, making it harder to follow from a distance, so I kept her in sight. It was the only reason I knew she'd crossed a ward line—there one second and gone the next.

"What the fuck?" Slade said as we both stopped.

"Wards," I reminded him quietly, unsure if they muted sight and sound. We'd scouted these borders too many times to count over the years. The fact that there were wards here had become obvious. How to get through them less so. Some said they contained a layer of poison that would kill anyone who tried.

A few years ago, Slade and I had camped in what was once the neighboring city of Rosewood for a week. We'd sent all sorts of small game scurrying to the ward line, only for every one of them to be shoved back or turned away. Not even birds had been able to penetrate what was apparently a completely enclosed bubble of protection over the entire castle grounds.

"How the Hel did she get through them?" Slade wondered.

"They're clearly spelled to allow her access."

"No way she created them herself. They're too powerful. I can't even feel them," he said.

"They're made from strong magic," I said, my senses straining to find the invisible ward line where iron-clad magic guarded whatever was on the other side. But even with my shadows cast out, I couldn't recognize the signature.

I'd never been able to get anywhere with them.

It was frustrating as Hel.

Whoever had created them had to be powerful. Even Heliconia hadn't been able to breach them. Nor had any of her Obsidians. But if Amanti had known the princess lived, something told me the Aine herself had ventured to the other side of these wards. She'd been too injured to tell me anything when we'd found her and handed her off to healers. Now, I wondered if we should have stayed nearby long enough for her to offer some answers.

"They're clearly made with something not from this world," Slade said.

"The Aine," I said with certainty.

I'd always suspected it. The memory of Amanti and her friends barreling through Heliconia's smokescreen seven years ago came to mind.

Protecting her, I realized now.

Somehow, Amanti and the other Aine had saved the princess from that killing blow. And then they'd cast these wards to keep the world out.

"It makes sense." Slade turned back to the spot where the princess had vanished. "You think she's been right here all this time?"

Anger rose inside me, and I nodded. "Like I said, a coward."

"What do you think will happen if I try to go through?" Slade took a step forward then another.

He slammed into an invisible wall, his forehead taking the brunt of it. He stumbled back, rubbing his face and wincing. "Well, shit," he grumbled. "I guess I have my answer."

"Come on," I said, shaking my head. "We need to meet Daegel and the others."

We headed back the way we'd come, careful not to leave tracks.

Slade was quiet for once, and I knew we were both thinking over everything we'd witnessed. The princess I'd seen today was nothing like the one I'd met on that rooftop. That girl had been naïve. Clever but completely unaware of who and what she was. This one was secretive and ruthless. This one had power and wasn't afraid to use it.

The way she'd taken out that Obsidian, demanding answers, was proof of how far she'd come. And those answers had stung more than I cared to admit. Her destiny remained tied to Callan's. It was a bitter truth, knowing my spoiled half-brother remained the key to saving the realm. Or that she would end up at his side before it was done. But who she chose for a mate wasn't my concern. Nor did I have any interest in such things for myself.

I had a job to do. A blood vow to fulfill. And a kingdom to inherit. So why did I care so much about one long-lost princess—even if she did haunt my dreams to this very day?

THE
MOON

Chapter Thirteen
Aurelia

Two hours later, I felt the magic in the air that marked the powerful wards encircling the castle. Stepping through, I shuddered as the magic clung to my skin, prodding at me until it determined I was welcome inside its boundaries. I exhaled, glancing behind me one last time to be sure Rydian hadn't followed—but the way was clear. I was safe now, even if it meant spending yet another night in the tomb I called home.

The carcass of the rabbit I'd trapped was slung over my shoulder. My sword—wiped clean of Obsidian blood—and the dagger I'd taken from the Obsidian were both tucked away.

Hopefully, I looked none the worse for wear. With any luck, I could convince Sonoma I'd never even stumbled into one of the monsters. Or Rydian.

He was just as handsome as I remembered. And just as mean.

Gods, what had he been doing out there?

It couldn't have been a coincidence. Was he tracking me? How could he have known I'd be there when I hadn't?

Then there was the dead healer.

Had Rydian killed her to keep her from talking to me? I'd come home empty-handed, and that stung. Well, not entirely empty. The Obsidian's confession rang in my head, rattling me. An alliance with Callan that ensured Heliconia's destruction. I had no idea how to feel about that.

No, that was a lie.

I'd considered it several times over the years and rejected it every time. Callan had been a coward that night. He'd tried to run rather than stand beside me like the brave general he claimed to be.

I wanted nothing to do with that arrogant bastard.

Hearing I'd need Callan's help against Heliconia only made me hate him that much more. And if Rydian was on his side...

"What happened?"

I pulled up short. Sonoma stood in the doorway of the castle's staff entrance, her eyes sharp and discerning.

I tried to smooth out my expression as I closed the distance. "How do you know something happened?"

"Your boots are stained, and I can smell the Obsidian blood from here." She propped a hand on her slender hip. "Now, what happened?"

My shoulders sagged as I gave up my lie. "It was a dead end."

"The healer was gone then?"

"Killed before I got there," I said bleakly.

She said nothing to that. I knew we both wondered if it had all been a trap, though until Lesha returned, we wouldn't know anything for sure.

If she returned at all.

I shoved that last thought away.

"And the Obsidian?" Sonoma asked.

I sighed. "The contact was unavoidable."

"Please tell me you at least used the opportunity to get intel."

"I tried," I said tightly.

"And?"

"My initial contact didn't leave much room for lengthy conversation."

Her expression didn't alter an inch, but I could feel her disapproval from here. "I told you, Aurelia, self-restraint is harder than self-defense."

"I know, all right?" I huffed, her tone making me feel like a kid all over again. "I tried to make it talk. The thing spoke in riddles."

"What riddles?"

I dropped my voice low in a dramatic—and admittedly terrible—impression. "Heliconia sees what she fears most. You and the prince united—to her destruction." I blinked and said in my own frustrated voice, "Even after seven years, the most I have to offer my kingdom is to become a bride?"

She frowned, looking pensive. "I don't know."

I waited, hoping she'd dismiss it as nonsense. When she didn't, I looked away and fought the urge to let my thoughts wander to Rydian again. No way was I mentioning him to Sonoma. She'd only worry needlessly. We had the wards to protect us, so what did it matter, anyway?

"Anything from Lesha?" I prompted.

"No."

"Didn't she promise to send updates weekly?" I asked, knowing full well she had.

The Aine had a secret code for communication, and the three warriors I knew were fond of using ravens to do it. Amanti had sent a raven with a small scroll tied to its leg every two weeks. Her updates had stopped coming months ago, which was the only reason we knew something had gone wrong. Lesha, so far, had sent nothing.

"I'm sure she just lost track of time."

The words were her way of softening things for my sake, but I could hear the worry beneath them. Still, I couldn't let myself think the worst. Not yet.

Her attention shifted to the rabbit slung over my shoulder. A brow lifted. "Dinner?"

I shrugged. "Only the best for us."

Her lips twitched, her frustration giving way to an easygoing nature few others had witnessed. "A princess deserves nothing less," she teased. "Come on. I'll help you dress it."

I rolled my eyes and let her lead the way into the royal kitchens.

The space was vast with enough ovens and countertops to feed the entire royal court. Once upon a time, that was exactly what they'd done here. Lavish dinners and fancy balls catered by the best fae chefs in the realm. Pastries and spiced meats one would've sworn had been infused with magic itself. Then there was the wine... Fermented on these very grounds in greenhouses that were now planted with potatoes, lettuce greens, and other fresh foods we could harvest even when the weather tried to freeze everything to stone.

I hadn't been born into a world where winter existed inside our borders, but ever since the curse, it grew colder and more brittle every year. Proof Summer's magic was fading. And when it was gone, I wasn't sure what would become of us.

Over dinner, Sonoma talked about the coming harvest, droning on about soil nutrients, but I only half-listened, distracted by the empty chair beside me. Lesha's absence was a stark reminder of how precarious things were. How easily this could all end. If something happened to Sonoma, the wards around this castle would disappear. Seven years of determined effort gone, just like that, leaving the sleeping fae vulnerable to any threat.

I couldn't let that happen.

We ate until we were stuffed, thanks to the rabbit along with potatoes from the garden. When we were finished, the sun had nearly set, plunging the room into shadows. The days had grown shorter already.

Candlelight flickered against our empty plates, casting a happy glow over the absolute mess we'd made. Teaching myself to cook had been one thing. Learning how to do it without turning the kitchen upside down was a work-in-progress.

"I should clean up," I said, pushing to my feet. "Tomorrow, I'll search again, farther west maybe. See if Lesha's intel on the healer might've been off somehow—"

"Aurelia, wait."

Sonoma remained in her chair.

It wasn't her words but the look she wore that had me sinking back into my seat. Dread crawled up my spine as she stared down at her hands, shoulders hunched. Sonoma never hunched. Willowy and straight-backed, her posture was that of a warrior imbued with the magic of the Fates themselves.

Or it had been—once.

Seven years of expending powerful magic to maintain the wards around this place had taken its toll. I could see it in the way her white-blonde hair had dulled and small lines crept in around the corners of her eyes. Even her faery wings—a gift given only to the Aine—were dim and sagging.

Sonoma was aging.

"What is it?" I asked, concern for her softening my tone.

She hesitated before meeting my eyes. "The wards are failing."

I frowned. "They're a bit frayed in places, but it's nothing we can't—"

"I'm afraid it's more than that." She cleared her throat. "A month ago, two Aetherfox came through the northern border."

My brows pinched as I recalled that day. "You said you called them through and trapped them—for making pelts."

"And last week, a glimfang slipped through and nearly got one of the chickens," she went on.

I frowned. "But—"

"I killed it and buried it behind the greenhouse." Her jaw hardened as if she were steeling herself. "Aurelia, I'm dying."

I stared at her, lost and overcome. "But... you're immortal."

Sonoma was the leader of the Aine, the strongest of them all. A goddess in her own right. Even Lesha and Amanti were no match for her.

Sonoma shook her head. "I'm not. Longer-lived, maybe, but with the amount of power I've had to maintain, I'm afraid it's drained me faster." Her eyes were mournful now. In them, I saw regret. Sadness.

"But Aine magic works differently," I said, willing her to be wrong about this. "The Fates themselves supply it, and they're... It's not possible."

"Under normal circumstances, it wouldn't be," she agreed slowly. "If this kingdom were full of fae actively using magic, I could draw from them. Or from Menryth's magic constantly being replenished by the exchange."

She wasn't wrong. Fae magic and earth magic were so intertwined, you couldn't have one without the other. Fae magic fed the land which, in turn, fed the fae. I'd always considered it a beautiful cycle—until our kingdom's magic disappeared and the land itself began to wither.

Even so, I hadn't worried for her. Not when the Aine's magic came from the Fates themselves. But now the Fates had vanished—apparently taking their unending source of power with them. And I hadn't even realized it was happening.

"Now the only magic user here is me," I realized. "Wait. Can you use me? Draw from me?"

"No." Her tone was biting—and final. "I will not take your birthright, Aurelia. Don't ask me again."

My throat closed. "My birthright," I repeated, a brittle laugh escaping. "All I have is a prophecy that's never even come to pass. And a magic that feeds on darkness and death. My *birthright* is nothing but empty words."

"It's more than that," she said quietly, but hearing her defend it only made me angrier.

"What good is it when everyone I love is about to be lost forever? This whole kingdom will die if you..." I couldn't bring myself to say the words.

Sonoma ignored the implication. "The fact is, every time you go in and out or any time someone or something else tries to break through, I am forced to strengthen the barrier. Reinforcing it draws on my power faster than it can be replenished."

I wanted to tell her to forget it then. To drop the wards and be done with it. Except those wards were the only thing protecting the others. Because if Heliconia learned what had happened here—that the Summer Court had only gone to sleep that night seven years ago... If she knew I was alive and unharmed... If that happened, the kingdom of Sevanwinds would truly be lost, not just forgotten.

"What if I use more magic," I said, desperation leaking in. "To give you something to draw on. You wouldn't be taking the magic inside me, only the magic I've spent." Even as I said it, I drew my power to the surface, bringing a small black flame to life in my palm, but Sonoma shook her head.

"We're past that point, I'm afraid."

Sadness shone in her blue eyes, and I felt my own emotions welling, drenching me in fear, grief, despair. The flames winked out. "But... you can't leave me."

Some of her stoicism slipped, and she reached for my hand across the table. "Please don't mourn for me, Aurelia. I've lived a long life. I've served my kingdom proudly, and I've watched you grow up into a strong, beautiful warrior. It's exactly what I asked for."

I gaped at her. At how she seemed to have already decided. "You can't just give up."

"Of course not," she agreed. "I'm still here, still fighting."

But I could see the truth in her shimmering eyes. She was nearly done fighting now. And that terrified me.

"You're a warrior," I told her as if she needed reminding.

"I am. But so are you. And soon, you will need to think about fighting for yourself."

Her words cut at me, but I refused to give in to the pain. It felt too much like accepting the inevitable. "What can I do?" I choked out. "There has to be something."

She shook her head as if to say "nothing," but I gripped her hand tighter, unwilling to believe that.

"You stop using magic then," I said. "We drop the wards."

"The entire kingdom would be at risk—"

"Maybe we can move them. There's a network of caves by the river. We can bring everyone there, and when the Obsidians come to the castle, it'll be empty. Then we bring everyone back again when it's safe."

"Aurelia."

In that one word was a gentle rebuke. It was a stupid plan. Logistically impossible. There were far too many sleeping fae for the two of us to carry them without detection. But I couldn't lose her. I wouldn't.

"We have to do something," I whispered as a single, traitorous tear slipped down my cheek.

"We don't have to find the answers tonight," she said, her voice heavy with exhaustion. "I have some time yet."

I let those words reassure me. "Lesha will know what to do when she returns," I said with more confidence than I felt.

But Lesha was already late returning, and I had a feeling I knew what that meant. We were alone.

I was alone.

"Maybe," she allowed. "In the meantime, venturing outside the wards is probably not a good idea. Each time you pass through, my magic drains."

The reality hit me then, what she was asking. What she required.

"You're saying I have to stay here. No more looking for a way to break the curse."

"Unfortunately."

I sat back, letting that sink in. If I couldn't leave the wards, it meant being trapped inside the castle walls. No more missions or following leads, no more looking for a way to end this blasted curse. It meant accepting my fate and living my life as a prisoner to this wretched fucking spell. Because if I did leave, Sonoma would die. And as much as it pained me to accept my prison, I'd do anything to save the one giving her very life to protect me.

"In that case," I said, forcing a smile onto my face, "I guess the dishes can wait after all. I've got all the time in the world to do them."

According to the curse, I had forever.

THE
MOON

Chapter Fourteen
Rydian

My boots were heavy against the stone floor of the throne room. Or maybe it was the fact that I would rather have been anywhere but this gods-damned castle. The dim light from the iron chandeliers above did nothing to combat the coldness of this place. Only the heat in my own veins chased away the perpetual chill. The fact that I had to come when summoned and not a moment later set my blood boiling. It was nothing more than a tug of the leash. One I endured for the sake of those I would die to protect. And Duron knew it. He never let me forget what he'd done for me, even as he squeezed every inch of use from the oath I'd sworn to him.

Across the cavernous space, he sat on his gilded throne, surrounded by advisors who looked down their aristocratic noses at me. I ignored them, my attention fixed on the way Duron's tunic strained against his ample physique. Between his lack of physical strength and his waning magic, I would kill him easily in a fight. It was little comfort, though, knowing his loyal advisors would never let me get that close.

As if he'd read my violent thoughts, Koraz loosed a quick

zap that struck the floor just ahead of me. I stopped short, snarling at him where he stood tucked beside the king's shoulder. "Come out from your hiding place, and do that again."

Duron raised his hand.

"Koraz, he's no threat," Duron crooned.

It took everything in me not to prove him wrong, but I forced myself not to reach for my sword.

"He disrespects you with his existence," Koraz spat.

"Yes, well, no one is perfect," Duron said dismissively.

Koraz continued to glare at me, as did the other advisors. Sorcerers, the lot of them. None had any true wisdom or diplomacy skills. But that wasn't why Duron kept them close. The old bastard wasn't interested in diplomacy anyway. He needed protectors—powerful ones. His own magic was failing him, though he went to great lengths to ensure no one outside his inner circle knew it.

"Will you not bow to your king?" Koraz demanded.

After a hesitation that bordered on treason, I bowed low, the movement precise, measured. Even as I promised to kill every single one of them someday. "Your Majesty," I forced myself to mutter.

"What news?" Duron's voice cut through the tension, already moving on from this ridiculous display.

Rising, I met his gaze, my tone steady. "Princess Aurelia of the Summer Court is alive."

The advisors went silent.

The King of Autumn leaned forward, his interest unmistakable. "Alive?" His voice was a mixture of disbelief and calculation.

I'd known I couldn't keep this from him. Not if I wanted to keep Amanti's part of it quiet. Not to mention keeping his belief in my loyalty intact. If he thought for one moment this vow wasn't forcing my obedience, he'd find a much worse way to bring me to heel. So, I'd made a choice and could only hope it would prove to be the right one.

"And where has she been hiding?" he asked.

"Inside Sevanwinds borders," I said.

"Impossible," Koraz sniped. "No one has managed to breach those borders in years."

"I watched her walk right through the wards," I said, daring him to challenge my claim.

"He lies," Koraz declared. "He wants to trap you so he can take your throne."

"The oath prevents him from deceiving me," Duron said wearily. For once, I didn't blame him. This was an old and tired argument. One I was more than happy to end with the tip of my sword.

Koraz huffed and lapsed into silence.

"I believe the wards may have been cast by one of the Aine," I said.

"Yes, I've heard your theories." Duron waved me off, clearly uninterested in the origin of the magic that had hidden her for so long. Once, he'd ordered me to identify and nullify it. But when years had passed without result, he'd given up and turned his focus to other methods of gathering power.

His eyes gleamed as he asked, "Do you believe she's the Chosen One now?"

I hesitated, not because I doubted my answer but because I knew what it would ignite in the old man. Once I opened this door, I could never close it again.

Duron's eyes flashed with impatience. "Answer me, boy. The oath demands it."

"Yes," I said. "She survived Heliconia's attack seven years ago. That in itself should've been impossible. But more than that, while I observed her in the Broadlands recently, she killed an Obsidian without the use of magic."

"That proves nothing," Lemuel, another of the advisors, muttered.

"She's become a capable warrior," I said, my temper and patience both straining. "And I sense power in her. Enough to make her a formidable foe if honed correctly."

Duron's lips curled into something resembling a smile. "And a dangerous weapon." He stood, his thick body wrapped in a velvet cloak. He descended the steps slowly, approaching me with a faraway look in his eyes. "Find her. Bring her to me. If she is the Chosen One, she will be of great use to us."

"The wards are impenetrable," I reminded him.

"You will find a way," he bellowed, his temper snapping.

I didn't bother trying to explain that an Aine's ward was unbreakable by anything less than the Fates themselves. Not even Heliconia had breached it these last seven years. Something told me reminding him of that would not end well.

I tried a different tactic. "She won't come willingly," I said, keeping my tone flat. "She made it clear she didn't want to be found."

His laughter was a jagged thing. "Why should that matter? Free will doesn't factor into destiny. Didn't you tell me that once?"

I didn't answer, but he waved a dismissive hand, clearly uninterested in a response anyway.

"Go," he said simply. "Use whatever resources you must. But don't return without her."

I bowed again, leaving the throne room as the weight of his command settled heavily on my shoulders.

Heading straight for the rear doors that would take me to the stables, I thought only of getting out of here. Getting home. Or the closest thing I had to a home anyway. Across the city, a quiet townhouse waited for me, bought and paid for using the name of a laborer who had died ten years prior. Slade and Daegel were there along with a ward line of my own that kept Duron's spies out, and that was what mattered.

I'd nearly made it outside when a familiar voice called out behind me. "Rydian, wait."

I stifled a groan as Callan rounded the corner. Behind him, the hallway was dark and empty. No torchlight shone in that direction, and he was completely alone, which was unusual for him. Even inside the castle, the prick usually had an escort.

He hurried up to me, his golden eyes full of arrogance and that perpetual amusement that suggested he saw life as a joke.

"I have somewhere to be," I said.

"Is it true?" he asked. "Is Aurelia alive?"

My jaw tightened as I thought of the Obsidian's last words. That Aurelia and Callan were destined for one another. "Yes."

"Heliconia failed then," he mused, almost to himself.

There was something in his tone, a flicker of emotion I couldn't place. It was undoubtedly self-serving and made me suddenly oddly protective of the spoiled warrior princess.

"You're going to get her?" he asked.

I didn't bother to mask my irritation. "If you eavesdropped on the entire conversation, why bother asking me?"

"I'm going with you," he said.

"No." I strode for the door.

Callan hurried to catch up. "She won't come willingly."

I bit back a snarl at the way he tossed my words back at me.

"I can make her want to come," he said.

I winced at the innuendo of that statement. But Callan merely blinked, his expression hopeful as he waited for me to respond.

"She'll want to see me," he added confidently.

"She broke your engagement then hid for seven years," I said. "Why would you want to see *her*?"

His confidence melted away until desperation burned in his golden gaze. "Heliconia sent a message to Father."

I frowned. "What kind of message?"

"She proposed marriage," he huffed disgustedly.

I stopped walking and stared at him. "To whom?"

"To me, asshat. Who do you think?" Callan managed to look both offended and revolted.

"Why would she do that?"

"Father says it's because she knows the courts don't recognize her as a true queen, no matter how much blood she spills. He thinks she's attempting to marry a crown for the recognition it would bring."

My brows rose because it made sense. "She'd kill you before the end of the first night."

"No shit." He shuddered. "She's insane."

"Don't tell me the old man is considering it."

"He thinks he could eliminate her first and take Concordia for himself."

Of course he did. He was too cocky to realize Heliconia was ten times more powerful than all his sorcerers combined. He'd be dead before he realized what had happened.

Callan, at least, understood—and had the fear in his eyes to prove it.

"The princess is your way out," I said.

"We were engaged once. If she'll honor that agreement, she'll come willingly. Marry me willingly. And save our kingdom in the process."

I shook my head at his selfishness. He would sacrifice the princess if it meant saving himself. "If you do this, Heliconia will come for us. Come for her."

"She'll come anyway," he said, and I didn't see a point in disagreeing.

Still, the protectiveness I felt for the Summer Court heir

wasn't something I could extinguish at this point. "If you bring her here, the old man will use her," I warned.

"I'll protect her." The confidence was back. So was the naïveté. But I had my orders, and there was no point pretending I'd do anything else. The lifeblood oath demanded its fulfillment. Duron had given me an order, and I had no choice but to follow it.

"She might refuse you. Or fight us," I said.

Callan's smirk returned. "I like my chances."

The urge to cut the smirk off his face rose in me, sharp and hot. I'd never been jealous of Callan in my life. When we were kids, I'd pitied him. Especially knowing he bore the brunt of Duron's attention—and cruelty. But in this moment, I might've killed him just to take his place in the stupid prophecy. Let the princess be destined for me. Not him. Anyone but him.

The thought disgusted me. I wanted nothing to do with his crown. Besides, the part of me that remembered the boy he was—before Duron shaped him into this—hoped he'd be better than the old man someday.

The citizens of Grey Oak deserved that much.

"Fine," I said at last. "We leave at dawn."

THE
MOON

Chapter Fifteen
Aurelia

Two weeks passed. I went through the motions of my days with a growing sense of suffocation. Training each morning with Sonoma had become nearly unbearable as she began to show more and more signs of weakness. I realized now that those signs had been there all along; I just hadn't seen them. Or hadn't wanted to. But I couldn't deny that she was deteriorating.

Lesha still hadn't returned, but we didn't talk about it. I didn't dare venture out to look for her, either. I couldn't imagine what Sonoma's condition would become if I used the wards now.

I shook off a chill at the thought.

Together, Sonoma and I harvested the crops inside the greenhouses then turned the soil for the next planting. The manual labor did little for my mood but helped burn off the worst of my anxious energy.

I spent my evenings in the library, warming myself with my own furyfire and getting lost in the novels Lesha had found on a scouting mission a couple of years ago. We'd gone looking for books about spells and curses. Instead, we'd found love stories with scenes so scandalous I'd had to read them alone under the blankets. I'd never cared for reading growing up, but it was the only escape I had left.

The season slid fast toward winter. But more than that, there was a strangeness to the crisp air that set me on edge. It felt like we were running out of time. Like the end of this curse was approaching—one way or another.

My thoughts drifted again and again to the Obsidian's last words. Heliconia feared me. It was ridiculous. Clearly a lie. Or the insane rambling of a dying creature with neither soul nor brain. I thought of Callan too. Our alliance. Of what my life would've been like without the curse—which only left me in a sour mood.

And even though I hated myself for it, I thought of Rydian. *I'm the thing nightmares fear.* I didn't know what he meant exactly, but that glimpse of his power suggested he wasn't bluffing. He was the only other fae I'd ever met who possessed power as big as my own. What could his power do against the dark queen?

What would it taste like if I let myself drink it in?

I shoved that thought away and glanced up at the gray sky.

The wind had picked up, plucking the leaves off the trees. They fell in large clumps, still green. There was no autumn here. Only summer—and then, abruptly, and harshly, winter.

With my hair blowing wildly, I collected the last of the clean sheets from where I'd hung them to dry in the courtyard this morning. In a desperate attempt to distract myself, I'd thrown myself into the work of keeping up the castle.

Sonoma had tucked herself away in the study for the afternoon. Lately, she'd resorted to searching the old texts from the royal temple's collection for some clue about what we might do to turn things around. I'd spent the curse's first year doing the same thing, scouring the royal library and looting every home in this city that contained books, and turned up nothing at all. I wasn't going to punish myself twice. Instead, I planned to spend the days wearing myself out until my brain could no longer torture me with the reality of my situation. And when that failed, I'd lose myself in someone else's story. One where the heroine always found her own happy ending.

With the clean linens piled into one overflowing basket, I hefted it onto my hip and aimed for the east entrance. From there, it was a short walk and then a climb to the royal bedroom.

I let myself in and set the basket of sheets on the floor before approaching where the king and queen rested on the large four-poster bed.

"Hello, Mother." I leaned down and pressed a kiss to her cheek. Her skin was warm. Vibrant, even. She hadn't aged a day in over seven years of slumber.

"Father." I kissed his chin, the course salt-and-pepper hair of his beard tickling my cheek. It wasn't my favorite, the bearded look, but it was his. Letting him keep it was the least I could do.

"And how are we today?" I asked, forcing my voice toward chipper.

Neither stirred as I replaced their bed linens, rolling each of them carefully left then right. It was a chore that took a considerable amount of skill and strength to perfect, but in just a few minutes, I'd stripped the old sheet and tucked the new one in without anyone getting tossed onto the floor in the process.

That had happened a lot in the beginning, giving a whole new meaning to the idea of "heavy sleepers." At least, none of them snored. A castle full of snorers would've driven me crazier than the silence already had.

"The wind's picked up," I commented as I worked. "Winter's coming faster than last year. This one might be colder, too. There's something in the air."

I didn't voice my fears: that Sonoma's death was being heralded on the wind. That it was all happening too fast. And that the Fates, the goddesses who'd created the Aine in the first place, had abandoned her.

Abandoned us all.

Lesha once told me there was a chance the sleeping could hear us. Ever since then, I was careful not to burden them with things they were helpless to do anything about. It was my responsibility to save them. Even if remaining here to guard their sleeping forms meant never fulfilling the prophecy I'd been destined for.

Maybe I was doomed to fail them all.

Maybe Heliconia's greatest victory would be forcing me to watch them all die slowly and realize there was nothing I could do to stop it.

"Sleep well," I said as I finished up.

Then I made my way to Lilah's room.

"Hey, you," I said, dropping a kiss on my sister's forehead.

The lump in my throat had lessened over the years, but it was still hard to look at her and know she wasn't going to sit up or answer me.

"I have fresh sheets for you," I told her. "The lavender ones you like best."

Lilah's honey-colored hair was still braided from Lesha's last visit with her, and a blue ribbon had been woven in; a perfect match for her eyes—if they ever opened.

I worked on changing her sheets, careful not to look too hard at the ribbon or think too much about what would happen when Sonoma's magic finally failed.

When I was done, I lingered, talking about my trip to the Broadlands. I left out the parts about the Obsidian I'd killed or my run-in with Rydian and focused instead on the sights of the countryside. The Broadlands had proven beautiful, despite the dangers. Lilah would've loved the adventure of it all.

"And before you ask," I said playfully, "there were no handsome princes your age along my way." I sighed, remembering Lilah's daydreaming. She'd dreamt of a fancy party of her own, complete with ball gowns and dancing. I refused to believe she'd never get her wish. "I'll ask Lesha to bring a new ribbon the next time she does your hair," I added as I tucked the blankets in tight. "She's supposed to be back soon."

The lie tightened my throat, and I paused, listening to the distant roll of thunder. Through the window, the fading daylight had already turned to shadows cast by swiftly approaching storm clouds.

Already, the temperature in the room had dropped, and a draft slipped through the castle.

It would be cold tonight.

At Lilah's door, I paused and aimed my magic at the logs stacked inside the hearth. Black flames shot from my hands. The logs caught in a bright reddish-orange glow, the heat slowly warming the room.

I looked back at Lilah, double-checking the blankets I'd tucked beneath her chin. She didn't need them, nor the fire. The curse kept them from succumbing to the elements; we'd learned that the third year when winter came to the kingdom.

No, the fire, the blankets...those were for my own comfort.

Slipping out, I moved on to the other rooms. Twenty-two bedrooms in all. Then there were the parlors, drawing rooms, meeting rooms, throne room, and finally, the ballroom. It was a monstrous undertaking—caring for the comatose. Lesha had cast a spell that first year preventing sheets from becoming dusty or in need of washing. But I couldn't just ignore them entirely. So, I walked the rows of cots and beds, squeezing hands and murmuring comforting words to the sleeping Summer fae.

When the sun began to set, I went in search of Sonoma. In the study, reference books were piled high on the worktable below the window, strewn haphazardly and lying open to whatever page had caught her attention. But she wasn't there. I glimpsed a drawing of a Vorinthian rune before turning for the door.

Retracing my steps through the castle halls, I aimed for her workshop instead. In the early years, she'd disappeared frequently. Sonoma was a solitary creature who valued privacy and hated crowds. All of the Aine were that way. What she and Lesha and the others did for me, staying here to protect Sevanwinds, wasn't something I took lightly.

If she needed space, I gave it.

Usually.

Today, however, felt different.

I searched everywhere. The kitchen, the dining hall, the Great Room. I even retraced my steps and checked the royal bedchambers—sometimes she looked in on the king and queen when she thought I wouldn't notice—but they were all empty.

I shoved panic aside and headed for the stables, which housed chickens Lesha had managed to bring through the wards a few years ago.

I hadn't gone far when movement caught my eye.

Along the low garden wall, a black tunic blurred past as someone sprinted away.

"Hey," I called, my voice ringing out in the silence.

When they looked back, I sucked in a breath at the sight of onyx eyes in a pale face.

Dread curled inside me.

An Obsidian.

Here.

Inside the wards.

For a moment, I stood there, stunned. Then it snarled, and my brain screamed at me to move.

I took off after it.

The rain clouds had grown thicker overhead, blotting out what little sunlight remained. The air smelled of a storm, and I could only hope it would hold off long enough to track the creature before the rain washed its scent away.

By the time I scaled the garden wall, the Obsidian had disappeared. I spun in a frantic circle, searching with my full senses. It couldn't have gotten far.

Rosewood was a mile north where houses and shops sat in utter stillness—too many places for me to search before I inevitably lost the trail. On my right, abandoned fields lay overgrown with grass and wild corn that had sprung up in the absence of anything else planted. On my left, the Emerald Forest beckoned, as dangerous as it was majestic.

Near the woods' edge, the black tunic flashed again, and my jaw tightened as I sprinted for where the creature had just vanished into the trees.

I followed, urged onward by desperation. Inside the forest, I slowed only a little, careful not to trip over tree roots and stray branches. Trees flashed by me in a blur of greens and browns.

Magic hummed inside me, begging to be loosed.

My stomach tightened as I thought about the creature running back to tell its master that it had finally breached our wards. Would it bring hordes of Obsidians, or would it bring *her*?

Up ahead, a loud crack sounded, followed by a vicious snarl that could only belong to an Obsidian monster.

I pushed harder, and a moment later, I cleared enough of the trees to see it. The creature writhed on the ground, its ankle caught in a rabbit trap. The thing rolled side to side, howling in pain. Even from here, I could see its burnt, boiled flesh. The wards hadn't let him through unscathed.

It was a mild comfort; not nearly enough.

I slowed to a walk, approaching carefully. My empty hands

tingled with magic. I ground my teeth as I thought of Dorcha —hanging just inside the door to the kitchen. Useless now.

I'd have to rely on my magic alone.

Don't get carried away. Interrogation doesn't work if he's dead, I reminded myself. *Self-restraint is harder than self-defense.*

I opened my palm, and a black spark erupted into a small flame that danced harmlessly along my skin. It might not hurt me, but it would melt him.

The Obsidian jerked its head up, eyes wide but not from fear. Fury, cold and determined, shone in the creature's onyx gaze. A fae male's eyes, once. And beneath all that determination and rage was victory. Smug bastard thought he was going to get away.

Despite the trap mangling his ankle, he climbed to his feet. "Hello, forgotten one."

"You can wipe that smirk off your face because you aren't going to live long enough to tell anyone what you just found," I said.

His eyes gleamed, and he raised his chin. "Your defenses are failing. It won't be long."

"Those defenses nearly killed you." I smirked, eyeing his blisters.

Not enough.

My magic whispered at me, singing through my blood. With one gesture, I could ignite him like the fire in Lilah's room. I could drink his sorry life force in one gulp—

"She comes for you. When the last of your fair friends are dead, she will arrive. And you will have nothing left to keep her out."

My mouth went dry, but I did my best to keep my fear hidden. Heliconia knew I was alive.

"You tell that bitch to bring it," I snarled. The flame in my hand flared brightly.

His eyes narrowed as he glanced from it back to me, but he didn't move. "You would speak of the queen in that way?"

"She's not a queen," I nearly spat. "Besides, I survived one of her curses already. I'm not afraid of another."

His eyes glimmered with something I didn't understand. "That is your mistake. You should be afraid. You should be very afraid of what comes."

Despite the magic roiling inside me, I suppressed a shudder.

Something brushed against my leg.

I looked down and found dark, thick shadows winding up my legs. I could feel them running over my skin like fingers. These were not a life force to drink. This was Heliconia's twisted darkness—looking for a new host.

Urgency speared through me.

I lashed out with my flames, burning through the thick tendrils until I could wrench myself free. My eyes narrowed again on the Obsidian watching it all with smug satisfaction.

Screw interrogation.

This bastard was going down.

With a sharp cry, I conjured a ball of furyfire and prepared to burn him to ash. Before I could ignite him, a cloud of smoke erupted where the Obsidian stood. I doubled over, coughing as the smoke enveloped me and snaked down my throat.

From somewhere inside the dark cloud, the Obsidian laughed.

Bitter residue coated my tongue. I spat it out. More laughter echoed around me, and I jerked my head up, straightening and whirling toward the sound that came from everywhere and nowhere at once.

I hurled my furyfire.

It burned a narrow tunnel through the smog and landed in the grass, charring it to ash.

"Show yourself, asshole," I demanded, but there was no answer.

I blinked, my eyes burning from the gray vapor that was finally beginning to clear. When it did, I could only turn in quick circles, searching for where the creature had gone.

The clearing was empty.

The rabbit trap was empty too.

I was alone.

The relief was quickly overshadowed by alarm.

The dark magic that flowed in the Obsidian's veins was nothing more than a life force, a way to animate them from corpse to monster. In all my years hunting them or being hunted by them, not one of them had ever shown any sign they knew how to use that magic. But this one had done just that—and somehow disappeared in the process. Gone to tell his mistress he'd found a way in.

She'd waste no time sending more of them. Or coming here herself. Which only proved one thing: Even after seven years of a bleaker life than I could've ever imagined, things could absolutely get worse. In fact, they just had.

THE
MOON

Chapter Sixteen
Aurelia

The rain began as I emerged from the forest, a sprinkle that became a downpour almost immediately. Halfway across the lawn, I spotted Sonoma striding toward me. Her gait was uneven, and her left arm was bleeding.

My heart lurched as I hurried toward her. "Seven Hels, you're hurt."

"It's nothing serious."

But her frown only deepened as I took her uninjured arm and slung it over my shoulder, offering her my support as we made our way back. She didn't refuse the aid, and that alone spoke volumes.

By the time we reached the castle, we were both soaked through. With a trail of puddles in our wake, I led us into the kitchen and helped her into a chair.

While I made tea, I darted glances at where she sat cleaning and bandaging the wound on her arm. It was a clean slice, probably a short blade. No poisons or infections from the looks of it—but that shouldn't have been enough to slow her down like this. It should've healed by now.

Out of the corner of my eye, I noted her holding a small vial to the wound, capturing a few drops of the blood that still leaked from it. Then she tucked it into her pocket and began dressing her wound again.

I carried tea over for us and set it in place; then I slid into the chair beside hers. When her gaze lifted to mine, I could see the questions written there as easily as if she'd asked them aloud.

"You first," I said.

"I came down to make dinner, and the creature surprised me." She scowled, and I knew it grated on her to admit. "It got a lucky slice in before I drove it back and out the door. Then I went to find you."

"I must've just missed you," I told her then recapped my own story for her, including the trick with the smoke.

"Are you sure the smoke didn't come from you?" she asked.

I shot her a look. "I know my own power."

"Yes," she agreed on a sigh, "you do."

"It doesn't make sense, though. Since when do those things know how to wield magic?"

"It could have been a glamour he purchased. A vial of fae blood might—"

"It came from him. I felt it." I shuddered, remembering how it had crawled over my skin. "The magic coming from that smoke was strong—and dark. I almost..."

"Almost what?"

I shook my head. "It distracted me. I wasn't expecting it."

She looked grim. "Neither was I. The wards have begun to fail. I..." She didn't finish the sentence, and that, more than anything, broke my heart. To see the great Aine warrior brought so low...

"What can I do?" I whispered, pain lacing my words. "Tell me. I'll do anything to stop this."

Her own expression twisted in pain.

I didn't expect her to answer, so when she suddenly straightened and said, "There's only one thing left to try," it took me a moment to process it. When it did, hope surged.

"What?" I asked quickly.

"Come with me." Her voice was suddenly stronger than it had been in days. She stood, and her eyes gleamed with something other than pain—resolve.

"Where are we going?" I asked.

"I think the library will be best for this."

I wanted to ask what that meant, but she was already moving, steadying herself on the edge of the table. Biting back my questions, I followed her through the castle's winding corridors. Her pace was determined, and I found myself rushing to keep up. Outside, the rain pounded against the windows, the wind groaning through the trees.

In the library, Sonoma closed the door behind us with a heavy thud, the sound echoing through the space. She pointed to the hearth where hot coals still glowed from earlier.

Above the fireplace, a tapestry with the royal crest—a golden sun over a laurel wreath—hung on the wall. I glanced at it and back to Sonoma.

"Stoke the fire, would you?"

I tossed on a couple more logs from the box against the wall then used my magic to light them, not wanting to waste time waiting for them to catch. In seconds, the fire was burning brightly, casting dancing shadows over the rows of books and ancient scrolls Sonoma had left on the table.

"Why are we here?" I repeated.

"Hotter." Her silver eyes locked with mine. "Use your magic. Make it burn as bright and hot as you possibly can."

"Why?" I asked warily.

Maybe this was a test—

"We're going to do a summoning."

I stilled. "Who are we summoning?"

Sonoma didn't look up as she gathered stones from where Lesha had dumped them in the corner after the last time she'd tried—and failed—to contact the Fates. Vorinthian runes had been carved into the flat sides of each one. Amanti had brought them back from a scouting mission. Just before she'd left for Vorinthia.

"The Fates?" I pressed when she didn't answer.

"No," Sonoma said, moving toward the hearth with the stones. Her silhouette slanted across the rug as she bent down, placing the stones in a half-circle.

A line of protection between the fire and us.

Despite the heat of the flames, a chill crept up my spine. "Sonoma, who exactly are we calling?"

She stood, turning to face me, her face set in grim determination. "The Furiosities."

My blood turned to ice. "What?"

"The Furiosities," she repeated, her voice steady.

"The Princes of Hel?" My voice rose in disbelief, a wild edge creeping into it. "You—you're talking about summoning pure darkness."

"Kings, actually. And yes, they are the only ones who can help now," Sonoma said, her voice softer but no less firm.

"How can they possibly help us?"

"They are the only beings who know the truth of the magic Heliconia used against us in that curse."

Heliconia's dark magic. I wasn't surprised it had its origins in the Furiosities' realm. But still... calling them here?

I shook my head, stepping back. "You can't be serious about this. They're *demons*. Pure evil. They don't help anyone."

"They'll help me," she countered, meeting my eyes with a look so fierce it pinned me to the spot. "They owe me a debt, one they will answer."

"How could they possibly owe you anything?"

None of this made sense.

Sonoma served the Fates—the light. What business could she possibly have with the enemy?

Sonoma stood, raising her hands, and I felt the first stirring of magic.

Panic leaped inside me. "Wait. What if they demand payment... something we can't give?" I asked, still struggling to understand this reckless plan.

Her gaze softened, and it wasn't fear or even desperation in her eyes when she looked at me. It was sadness. "I know the risks. And the reason I know them is a story longer than we have time for. But the Furiosities won't hurt us. I need you to trust me on this."

I looked at her, uncertain. But I trusted no one more than Sonoma.

"You're sure they'll help?" I asked quietly.

Sonoma nodded. "To survive what's coming, you'll need their aid."

You.

Not *us.*

I shoved that aside, forcing myself to focus. "What do you want me to do?"

"Make the fire burn as bright and hot as you can. I'll do the rest."

The flames flickered again, and I glanced into them. Summoning demons—who thrived on chaos, who ruled Hel and were the very definition of evil—was a line I never thought we'd cross.

But then again, the world I knew was already unraveling.

Sonoma was right. I had to do whatever it took to survive.

With a deep breath, I stepped forward, raising my hand toward the hearth. My magic stirred, the familiar warmth tingling through my fingertips as I whispered a word of power to it, coaxing it to the surface. Flames shot from my hand. The fire leapt higher, crackling and roaring with renewed energy, casting the room in bright, orange light.

Sonoma watched the fire flare then turned to me, her face grave but resolute. "Are you ready?"

I swallowed hard. "Yes."

No.

Together, we stood before the fire, the heat pressing in on us as Sonoma reached for her blade.

"Blood of the bride," she said quietly, slicing her palm and letting her blood drip into the fire. "The first offering."

With a hiss, the fire turned black, curling with dark smoke.

I shot her a look. "Bride?"

She handed the blade to me. "Your turn."

Whatever this magic was—whatever these words meant—she'd never mentioned it before. Not in all years' worth of research and reading had I ever read anything about summoning the Furiosities. But Sonoma did it like this wasn't her first time.

I sliced my palm and offered my blood to the flames.

"Blood of the heir. The second offering," Sonoma called out.

The hissing grew louder as the flames expanded, licking up the chimney in bright bursts.

"And the third," she said, pulling a vial from her cloak. "Blood of the darkness."

Taking out the small vial of blood she'd gathered earlier, she poured it onto the fire, and it crackled, blazing so brightly it hurt my eyes.

I gasped as, within the flames, two figures appeared. They were nothing more than an outline at first. Then, almost as if made from the flames themselves, the forms solidified until two males stepped out of the hearth and into the room.

They passed right over the circle of protection stones.

Useless, even the ones etched with runes, apparently.

The one on the left was middle-aged with brown hair and a cruel snarl. The one on the right was an old man with a nasty glint in his murky eyes. Power, ancient and terrible, radiated from them both.

They blinked at Sonoma and then at me. The younger of the two sniffed at me like he was taking my measure. The older one just gave Sonoma a look that could've melted steel and said, "You have some nerve summoning us like this."

My bones trembled at the furious power in his eyes.

Sonoma met his stare unflinchingly. "We need to talk," she told them coldly.

"Two decades of the cold shoulder, and now you suddenly have something to say?" the older one demanded.

The younger one snorted.

"What's wrong, Age?" Sonoma said, taunting in a way I'd never heard from her before. "Did you miss me?"

The younger one grinned. "He's missed bickering with you, I'll tell you that."

"Shut up, Eld," the one called Age snapped—and then to Sonoma, "Is this what you called us here for? To argue and taunt?"

"No." The light in Sonoma's eyes winked out. "I am ready to come home."

I stared at her, stunned, but she didn't meet my eyes.

"You are finally prepared to relinquish your Menrythian power," Age said with a sniff.

"You're the one who told me the power in this realm was inferior to yours," she said.

The old man just grinned, though there was nothing pleased about the expression.

"We agreed you would remain here as long as possible," the younger one—Eld—said. "To use the magic of this realm against that little thief."

Sonoma looked pained. "My Aine magic has failed me, and I... I need to take my rightful place if I'm to remain useful."

Age and Eld said nothing, but I couldn't hold my tongue any longer.

"What the Hel is going on?" I demanded.

Both Furiosities turned to me, and I recoiled at the power that came with those stares. The sheer weight of it against my shoulders threatened to send me to my knees. But I refused to cower—at least until I had some answers.

Eld gave me a once-over and turned back to Sonoma. "You haven't told her?" he demanded.

She shook her head. "Too many would kill for this truth. It was safer that she not know—or don't you remember this discussion?"

I ignored Age still studying me and turned to Sonoma. "What else haven't you told me?" I demanded. When she didn't answer, I looked back at Age. "Do you know me?"

His expression was unflinching. "I know you as surely as I know all who share my blood."

"Your... what?" It felt as if the breath had been knocked out of me.

"You're one of us," Eld said almost gently compared to his brother. Almost.

My heart slammed against my chest. One of them? Dread crawled up my spine, and a strange and sickly sort of anticipation came over me. Like whatever they had just said—and whatever they were about to say next—was going to change my entire life.

"What are they talking about?" I asked Sonoma.

"Your father is Ire," she said quietly. "The third ruler of Hel. Their brother."

My mouth fell open. Neither of the Furiosities contradicted her. I wasn't sure why I'd expected them to. Except that this was madness. Complete and utter nonsense. It had to be. My father was lying in his bed next to my mother—sleeping a cursed sleep.

And yet... didn't it make sense of my power if I'd been sired by Hel itself?

My mouth went dry. Already, I could feel reality shifting on its axis to accommodate this new truth. No, not truth. Possibility. I couldn't make that leap yet.

"This is where my death magic comes from?"

Sonoma watched me as if I were some wounded animal. "Yes."

She met my eyes, and I saw pain—so much pain. Regret. Sorrow. Longing. It was heartbreaking, but I couldn't let myself feel it. Not now, in front of them.

I looked back at the dark demons who looked more like a couple of grumpy grandfathers than rulers of an underworld. "I want to see my father."

Age merely grinned. "Such entitlement. She's got his personality, hasn't she?"

Eld sniffed. "That's impossible," he told me.

"Why?" I shot back. "You're here. Why isn't he?"

"A deal was made," he said simply. "If you want to know what it was, ask your mother. We're done here."

They stepped back toward the flames.

"You owe me a debt," Sonoma said. "I didn't give up your secrets. And your brother stayed away. Now it's time to do your part. Protect this place until she can free them."

Both males looked at me again, assessing.

"If we help you," Age said to me, "do you swear to take back what that bitch stole from our brother?"

I swallowed hard, my heart thudding wildly. I knew exactly who they meant. Heliconia. "Why can't you do it yourselves?"

Eld snarled at that, but Age merely grinned. "A bargain

was made, niece. Neither the Fates nor the Furiosities have true power in this realm until the darkness is extinguished. It's up to you now. Will you accept your duty?"

I nodded, worry carving a hole in my chest at the thought of going against Heliconia alone. But if it meant protecting Sevanwinds until I could free them, there was no question. "Yes."

Eld turned back to Sonoma, nodding as if satisfied at what he'd found in me. "You'll have what you need," he told her.

"And the heir?" Sonoma pressed. "Will you provide a way for her when it's time?"

Age scowled at me. "Our reach into this realm is limited to the bargain owed. There has been a certain measure put in place for aid, but... she'll have to find her own way home."

And then they were gone.

Sonoma sagged, reaching for the back of the chair to steady herself. I stared at her, shocked and reeling from everything that had just happened.

She didn't look at me as she said, "I know you have questions."

"Damn right I do."

"I promise to answer them, but first, I could use a whiskey."

She looked at me expectantly.

With a snarl, I stalked over to the bottle I'd left out and poured her a glass. The contents sloshed over the edges as I shoved it at her. She drank, draining the entire thing.

It might have been impressive if I hadn't still been reeling.

When she was done, she took a ragged breath and said, "We'll start with the biggest one, I guess. Go ahead. Ask me."

I hesitated only a second before demanding, "How could my mother possibly cheat on my father—with a prince of Hel?"

Her expression was grim, her mouth set in a hard line as she said, "She didn't cheat."

"But you just said Tyrion wasn't my father—"

"And Celeste isn't your mother."

I blinked, stunned.

Without a word, I reached for the bottle of whiskey I still held in one hand and drank deeply. The alcohol burned my throat, searing through the shock roiling inside me.

Sonoma simply watched and waited.

When I could breathe again, I rasped, "Then who is?"

Her mask of stoicism slipped, her eyes brimming with pain and regret and sorrow as she said, "Me."

THE
MOON

Chapter Seventeen
Aurelia

I shook my head, unable to find my voice. Learning my father was a king of Hel was one thing. Shocking, yes. But I'd never met the male. Had no picture in my mind of what sort of evil creature he might be. I'd known Sonoma my whole life. Grown up with her. Trained with her. Considered her my friend. It was that closeness that made her last admission so much more painful than the first.

So, I stood there, speechless. Reeling. Wanting to cry but not able to summon the strength to do so.

Sonoma was the first to break the silence. "When I was newly chosen Aine, I became pregnant," she said quietly.

Her voice, those words, shattered all my control. My temper snapped. "Let me guess. I would have screwed up your plan to remain emotionally unattached, so you handed me off."

"You were my greatest joy, but you didn't belong only to me." Her voice remained even. As if I hadn't just practically screamed at her.

"What does that even mean? Either you wanted me or you didn't." Furyfire seared my veins, but I fisted my left hand, refusing to let it ignite. Then I remembered the whiskey bottle I still gripped with my right. I barely managed to set it aside without lighting it on fire.

"The Aine are forbidden from bearing children. We take a vow of—"

"Celibacy, yes, I know." It was one of the few reasons I'd been okay with not being able to officially compete to be one of them. Even being one of the Aine couldn't make up for never having sex again. "It seems you weren't able to hold up on that promise."

I was being cruel.

I knew it, and yet I couldn't seem to stop the comments from flying out of my mouth. It was all I could do not to light this entire library full of furyfire.

She'd lied.

Seven years ago, she'd sworn never to lie to me again. But it seems she'd never stopped.

"I thought the Fates would strip my magic or worse when they found out about you. But they blessed you instead. Before you were ever born, they imbued you with gifts and a prophecy. You became their Chosen One. The great Aine warrior who would defeat Heliconia and bring peace back to the realm."

"Why me?" I asked, my voice barely above a whisper.

"You come from two great bloodlines. Light and dark." Her expression hardened. "Though I've always suspected it was their punishment against me."

"Whose punishment? The Fates?" I knew I sounded skeptical, but I'd only ever heard the mystical goddesses described as being benevolent.

But Sonoma shook her head ruefully. "Even goddesses have a temper. And I couldn't refuse their gifts or your destiny in case they decided to do something worse instead."

Anger and hurt and disappointment tangled inside me.

Sonoma was my mother. Sonoma was my *mother*. *Sonoma* was my mother.

"How did I get here?" I asked, my voice finally losing its sharpest edge. My temper was quickly becoming heavy—like an exhaustion. I had no idea which was heavier: the truth or the lies still between us. "How did I come to be adopted by ... Celeste and Tyrion?"

I stopped myself from calling them my parents, suddenly unsure what the rules were for something like this.

"After the Fates declared you as theirs, we knew you were in danger. We wanted to keep Heliconia from learning the truth as long as possible," Sonoma said. The words were spoken quietly, as if she were trying to be gentle.

"Is that why you chose not to tell me who my parents really were?" I shot her an accusing glare. "You really thought so little of me that you couldn't trust me with my own fate?"

"That's not—" Sonoma began.

"You don't believe I can do this."

Sonoma frowned. "Of course I do."

"Is that why you killed the Obsidian yourself without giving me a chance?" I demanded.

"What are you talking about?"

"The Obsidian in the Emerald Forest. The day Heliconia came and spoke through it. You killed it, knowing it was meant as a test for me. You didn't even give me a chance to fight."

"I was protecting you. Like I've always done."

"And my father? The male"—I couldn't bring myself to say demon "—whose magic I wield? Where is he now? Does he not care enough about me—or you—to help us fight?"

Sonoma stepped forward, gaze burning. "Everything I've ever done is because I love you," she said firmly. "More than I can ever offer in words."

"Except that words are exactly what I'm asking you to give

me," I hissed. "Seven years ago, you promised you wouldn't lie to me ever again. And now you tell me this? That *everything* I knew about myself is a lie."

"I'm sorry—"

"Don't," I snapped. "I don't want your apologies. I want only answers. From him, not just you. Where can I find him?"

"Your father cannot come to us. Not yet." My anger rose, but she added quickly, "This is not my choice. Or his. The sacrifices we've made are many, Aurelia. And I am sorry they are hurting you. But there is much more at work here than what you can see or know today."

I had no idea what that meant, but it was clear she'd told me as much as she was going to about him.

I told myself I didn't want to know. If he couldn't be bothered to meet me all these years, he could go to Hel. "And the favor you asked of the other two? For protection?"

"I promised I wouldn't speak of what happened to anyone in this realm. Including you. They protect their own realm as fervently as I have protected you in this one. I kept up my end, and now they owe me a favor. They'll ward the castle when I can no longer do it myself. You will have the time you need to search for a way to end this curse."

Me.

Not her. Not us.

Just me.

The weight of it landed on my shoulders like a whitestone boulder.

I wanted to argue. To scream and rail at her about the lies. The omissions. What else had she kept from me all these years? Why had she bothered to stay here, to practically help raise me, all the while, watching me call another female Mother? Hadn't that been painful for her? Hadn't she wanted to tell me the truth? If not for herself, then for me?

All the times I struggled with my magic—or lack of it. All

the times I worried that I was so different from the summer fae. Wielding furyfire and feeding off souls rather than conjuring rainstorms or coaxing roses to bloom. And the entire time, she'd known the truth of what I was. Where I'd come from. And what I had always been meant to do.

I still had endless questions. But I wasn't sure I could handle anything more. Knowing I was the child of a King of Hel and that my parents were no longer my parents was hard enough to wrap my head around.

So, when Sonoma finally walked past me, murmuring about giving me time to adjust, I let her go, and when the door clicked shut behind her, I slumped into the nearest chair, pressed a pillow to my face, and screamed.

THE
MOON

Chapter Eighteen
Aurelia

A crash woke me. I straightened, disoriented, taking in my surroundings. I was still in the library, slumped over in the chair where I'd fallen asleep. The fire had burned down to nothing but embers. Now, there was no trace of the Furiosities who'd appeared from within it. Sonoma's discarded glass was on the table beside me, and next to it, the bottle of whiskey stood nearly empty.

My mind felt hazy, both from sleep and the drink. Memories returned slowly. The fire, the blood offerings. The Furiosities who'd named me their niece.

The heir, Sonoma had called me.

A title that had nothing to do with the Summer Court throne.

Because I was the daughter of a Furiosity. And Sonoma was my mother.

I shoved those things aside, trying to place what had woken me. Another crash echoed through the castle, louder this time. I shoved to my feet, fast enough to send the empty glass thumping to the rug. I left it where it fell and ran, heart hammering in my chest.

The sounds were coming from inside the castle, which was alarming enough, but worse—they came from the floor above me. My heart dropped. My entire family was up there. Lilah. I forced my legs to move faster, breath sharp in my lungs as I raced up.

By the time I reached the top of the stairs, the crashing noises had stopped, replaced by the low murmur of male voices. I couldn't make out what they were saying, but the shattered vase was evidence they'd come this way.

I crept silently after them, trying not to imagine all the horrible creatures that might have somehow gotten through the wards. Obsidians weren't the only monsters to worry about. Nor were they the hardest to kill.

Voices reached me, too low to make out but a clear sign that the intruders were not the beasts my worst fears conjured.

Still, I tensed, my worry growing with each step. Doors had been opened along the hall, but I ignored them and kept moving, aiming for the room at the end where the voices were coming from.

I slowed, moving with soundless precision as I counted. Two, both male. They didn't smell or sound like Obsidians, but that did little to settle my nerves.

I pressed my back to the wall beside the door and listened.

"Seven Hels," one of them muttered in awe. "Look at them. Tyrion and Celeste. The king and queen of the Summer Court. Asleep, just like the legend."

I sucked in a sharp breath at the wonder in his voice. And the small speck of magic that radiated from him. Not Furiosities or Obsidians. Fae males.

The fact that fae were standing here, in this castle, felt like a dream. It was also a nightmare.

"Enchanted, maybe. Cursed. Don't touch anything," the second voice warned, sharper than the first. "We don't know how far the curse extends."

"Yeah, yeah," the first male said, excitement creeping into his voice. "You think *she's* here somewhere too?"

I stiffened.

"I don't know, but we need to be cautious," said the second voice, firmer now. "We don't know who or what else might be lurking."

"Good point." The first male's voice held a shudder.

There was a beat of silence, and I bit my lip, trying to weigh the risk of an ambush. I had no weapon, but I'd have the element of surprise, at least.

"Fletcher!" the second male called sharply. "What did I say about touching anything? That goes for people."

That was all I needed to hear.

In one swift motion, I shoved the door wide and raced toward the intruders. They whirled toward me, startled. Soldiers, based on their uniforms. A stag head, its antlers wrapped in goldleaf, was stitched onto the breast.

The room glowed softly, thanks to the moonlight streaming in through the window. But I clung to the shadows and hoped my expression was fierce enough to make them hesitate.

The one closest to me did just that, eyes wide as he began to lift his sword then stalled. I closed the distance between us in the blink of an eye, ducking low and sweeping my leg out the moment I was inside his reach. He went down on his back with a thud.

I grabbed his sword from his hand and spun to face the other one, crouching to keep my balance. The new blade was heavy, foreign. But I ignored the protest of my muscles and raised it high.

He stared at me like he'd seen a ghost. "W-wait."

"You're trespassing," I snarled. "Get out."

The one I'd laid out groaned. I could hear him getting to his feet behind me and knew I was almost out of time to take them both on. Not without using my magic, which wasn't remotely an option.

With a guttural yell that I could only hope would spook them, I raised my stolen sword and swung out. The second soldier managed to block me—barely. But the clang of our blades seemed to snap him out of his shock. He fought with renewed ferocity.

"Keep her busy," the first male said then raced out of the room.

I snorted.

A coward then.

If the second soldier—the one called Fletcher—was upset by being abandoned, he didn't show it. His expression merely hardened with determination as I came again.

Our blades clashed, the sound of steel meeting steel ringing in my ears. I pressed the attack, relentless, forcing him toward the wall as far away from my parents' bed as I could manage.

"Holt," he shouted, but there was no answer.

He glanced past my shoulder to the empty doorway, and I saw my opening.

With a practiced movement, I brought my sword around in a vicious arc, aiming for his exposed side. He tried to dodge, but I was faster. My blade grazed his ribs, a thin line of blood appearing where my sword made contact.

He grunted, falling back to recover, and I readjusted my stance to finish him—but the sound of footsteps behind me made me hesitate.

Two sets of heavy boots approached from the hall.

A moment later, I felt them behind me. The soldier who'd fled —and another with him. I hoped it was Sonoma, but the voice that spoke wasn't hers. It was male, charming, and deceivingly confident. The familiarity of it cut through the silence like a knife.

"Hello, Aurelia."

My blood froze. I spun around, my sword still raised, and there he was.

Callan.

The fair-haired Autumn prince stood in the doorway, looking untouched by time and circumstance. His golden eyes gleamed in the moonlight as if the night itself had conspired to bring him back here—finally.

For a heartbeat, I couldn't move.

"I'd heard you were alive but didn't quite believe it," he said, a faint smile touching his lips. His eyes swept over me slowly, taking me in, like he couldn't believe what he was seeing.

I stayed silent, my breath coming in sharp, shallow bursts. My pulse roared in my ears. Rydian was to blame for this. He had to be. He'd accused me of not honoring my alliance. Like I'd hidden away for all these years just to get out of a stupid marriage.

The thought of the dark male sent rage coursing through my veins. Gods, if I ever saw him again, I would kill him for this alone.

"Fletcher." Callan took his eyes off me only long enough to jerk his chin at the soldier I'd cornered. "You all right?"

"I'm fine." The male slipped out and took up a position directly behind the prince. The other soldier was already there, hovering, watching.

My hand tightened around the hilt of my stolen sword, my knuckles taut with the effort of bearing its weight. I adjusted my grip so that the sharp end was aimed at the cowardly prince.

"What are you doing here?" I asked, my voice strained.

Callan's brows creased as he took in the sword I'd pointed at him. "Searching for you. What are you doing?" He took a step forward, and I took a step back, waving my blade at his face.

His smile faltered. "I thought you'd be happier to see me." The warmth in his eyes flickered with something else. Hurt, maybe, which was ludicrous. Except...

He didn't remember.

The last time I'd seen him, he had fled like a coward rather than stand and face Heliconia's wrath. If the curse hadn't thwarted our future together, that act alone would have changed my mind. But his memories were gone, thanks to the Aine, wiped clean like the cowardice he'd shown never happened.

Not to him, anyway.

Now, the arrogant prince who'd once been my fiancé—who'd abandoned me and my people when we needed him most—was standing in my home, acting as though I should be overjoyed to see him again.

It was the worst kind of insult, and I couldn't even tell him why. Not without admitting what the Aine had done to him. I also couldn't very well kill him for it. Not with the wards obviously down and his father undoubtedly vengeful enough to send his armies after me in retribution.

All that mattered was protecting my people.

I didn't let myself look over at my parents asleep in their bed as I lowered my sword, but my voice was sharp as a blade when I spoke. "Why have you come here, Callan?"

His smile faltered. "To save you, of course. The legends have proven true."

"What legends?"

"That you and your kingdom were trapped here by Heliconia shortly after I left. I've spent years searching for a way back to you—a way that was blocked over and over by some kind of magical boundary line. But now that boundary seems to be gone, and here I am."

He paused expectantly, as if waiting for me to declare him the hero. I decided to ignore his blatant lie about searching for me and instead focused on the rest.

"The legends say all that?"

He shrugged. "They say other things too. That you were all turned into Obsidians or torn apart by the Aqras Heliconia keeps locked in her dungeons."

Aqras? I shuddered as I pictured the monsters from stories. With the lower body of a scorpion and the torso and head of a male, they were beyond lethal. But no one had ever seen one in the flesh. "Aqras are a myth."

"That's what they said about you being alive. Anyway, I didn't believe those versions of the story."

"Why not?" I couldn't help but ask. After seven years, I'm not sure I would have held out such hope.

"I wouldn't have gotten to swoop in and save you in those scenarios." He winked. *Winked.*

Unbelievable. Amanti had done all that work, planting stories of our demise, and Callan had clung to the one version that would've brought him back to my doorstep as confident and cocky as ever.

He cleared his throat, glancing at the bed and the sleeping royals on it.

"They do not wake?" he asked when I remained silent.

"No," I admitted, cringing.

"But they are... alive?"

"Yes."

And I would do anything to keep it that way.

His expression flashed with pity, which was almost worse than the heroism. "What can I do to free you all from this wretched fate?"

I searched for some spark of power emanating from him, but just like the first time we met, there was no trace of magic in him.

"There is nothing you can do," I said quietly. "Except leave me in peace and never return. And never tell another soul you saw me."

His smile faded entirely. I braced myself for more questions, but instead, he glanced at the sleeping king and queen as if they were the intruders in this conversation.

"Is there somewhere we can speak?" he asked.

I sighed. He wasn't going to leave without some explanation. That would've been too easy.

Resigned, I stalked past him and out the door. The two soldiers parted quickly to let me pass.

"This way," I called. "Shut the door behind you. And bring your men with us. If they try to enter this room again, I'll cut their throats."

Sonoma was nowhere in sight as I led the way to the library. I couldn't decide if her absence was good or bad. But one thing was for sure: Her wards had officially failed.

And that left a pit of worry in my stomach.

I had to get rid of Callan as quickly as possible so I could find her.

We reached the library, and I was relieved to find it still empty. I'm not sure what I expected—Sonoma or the Furiosities were equally terrible options for company. I hoped Callan wouldn't stay long enough to find out about either one.

"Your soldiers can wait in the hall. But I'll know if they wander off." I pointed my stolen sword at them, and they nodded.

"They'll stay put," Callan said before following me inside and closing the door with a click.

I strode to the fire and used the iron poker to stoke the coals. Lighting it with furyfire wasn't an option, but the cold had begun to leech through my tunic. Or maybe it was the shock of this visit.

When I turned to face him, Callan lifted a brow. "What have I done to earn your ire?"

I stiffened at the truth on my tongue. "You try being stuck in the house as the only one awake for seven years and see if it doesn't make you grumpy."

He didn't look convinced, and I braced myself for more prodding. But he said gravely, "I can't imagine it. They truly never wake then? Not for all this time?"

My eyes burned as I shoved out the word, "No."

His expression softened, and I bit my tongue to keep from breaking. Sympathy wasn't something I was prepared to brush off.

"We thought you'd all been killed, you know. After you ended our—" He cleared his throat and started again. "After I returned home, we learned of Heliconia's attack. The scouts all said the castle had been destroyed, along with everyone in it. We assembled soldiers and returned, but...we were unable to enter the castle grounds. We tried. For a very long time, we tried."

I frowned, thinking back. Sonoma hadn't mentioned any attempts by Callan to breach the wards. I'd waited, silently hoping he'd try. Back then, I'd half-believed Callan would somehow find a way to save us all. That his reputation as formidable general and skilled warrior would prove true. I'd given that hope up after the first year. And replaced it with faith in myself instead.

"There are wards keeping our enemies out," I said, my throat tight.

Fear stabbed through me as I thought again of Sonoma. The fact that she hadn't come to investigate all the noise was a bad sign.

"And I am your enemy?" he asked.

I didn't answer.

"Tell me what I can do for you, Aurelia."

"I told you already. Leave and never return. And never speak of what you saw here."

He frowned. "That's not going to stop others. Legends have circulated for years. And if these wards are down, as you say—"

"That's not your concern."

"It could be. If you let it."

"What's that supposed to mean?"

"We were allies once. Is it so far-fetched to consider the idea we might renew that alliance now?"

The Obsidian's words came back to me. *She sees you. Allied with the prince. She sees her own destruction.*

"That was for mutual benefit, Callan. I have no army to offer you anymore. No kingdom to rule. The land is dying. In a couple of decades, it will be barren and devoid of the magic that once flowed here. There is nothing in it for you to ally with me."

"Nothing except you."

I shook my head, refusing to be flattered. "That's a stupid strategy. I'm not useful to you. Not without soldiers."

"What if I could help you break the curse? Free your soldiers?"

Again, I searched for some trace of power on him. Again, I came up empty.

"How?"

He shrugged. "What do you know about it?"

That the magic Heliconia had used sprung from a well of darkness so deep and ancient that no other living creature could access it—or reverse it. That the only magic strong enough to compare sprung from a tribe that had vanished from the continent hundreds of years ago. That the last fae queen who'd ruled with that kind of magic had lost her kingdom and her life. And if anyone found out I possessed that same dark power, they'd likely do to me what they all wanted to do to Heliconia: Kill first; ask questions later.

"Not enough," I admitted grudgingly. "I need access to more resources than I've been able to locate. Whatever this is, it's old magic. Dark. No one I've met these last years has been able to explain it."

"Then let me help you find someone who does know."

"Like who?"

"There's a fae in Grey Oak. An ... oracle of sorts. She is long-lived and well-versed in obscure magics. I can bring you to her."

"Why? Why are you offering these things when I can't give you anything in return? What's in it for you?"

He sighed. "Things are a bit bleaker than when we last saw each other."

"Heliconia hasn't attacked anyone else," I said.

"It's true, Heliconia hasn't marched on the other courts. But she's been slowly killing us in other ways. Her soldiers poison crops and destroy harvests so villages starve. They steal fae from their beds so she can turn them into Obsidians with her dark magic. They say the north is now filled with monsters she's conjured from the pits of Hel. They slip into our northern cities at night to hunt and eat. People won't even leave their homes after dark because of it. At this rate, when she invades, we'll be too weak and full of fear to fight back."

Empathy panged in my chest. The idea of so many living in fear. Children stolen from their beds—made into monsters... it was horrific. But I couldn't do anything to stop it. Not without leaving my own people defenseless.

"How does an engagement help any of that?" I asked.

"The realm needs a spark of hope, Aurelia. I think bringing home the lost princess of Sevanwinds could be that hope for them."

"What are you saying?"

"Marry me. Unite our kingdoms, and inspire the fae to fight for their own families as you've fought for yours. In exchange, I will help you break the curse."

THE
MOON

Chapter Nineteen
Aurelia

The earnest vulnerability in his expression was the only thing that kept me from laughing in his face. Still, there was no trace of hesitation in my voice as I said with absolute finality, "No."

Callan blinked. He looked...stunned. Like he'd never even considered the possibility I might refuse.

I did my best not to roll my eyes at the entitlement in that. "You can stay tonight," I added. "But if you're not gone by the time the sun is over the trees, I will finish what I started with this sword."

"Aurelia, can we please talk—"

I stepped back. "My answer is final."

His eyes hardened enough that I knew he at least understood there would be no more discussion.

"You can sleep in here. There's wood for a fire and chairs enough for you and your men." I strode to the door and pulled it open. The soldier called Fletcher nearly fell from where he'd been leaning against it but managed to catch himself.

I gestured for them both to enter.

They did, watching me warily as they passed.

"Good night," I said stiffly and started to leave.

"Uh, excuse me," the one called Holt said. I turned and found him glancing down at the sword I still carried. His sword. "Can I have my weapon back?"

I frowned. "It'll be outside the door in the morning."

The door clicked shut behind me. I tapped my hand on the knob, using the locking ward Lesha had shown me. The click was soft but final as the magic sealed them safely inside. Then I propped the stolen sword against the wall.

I couldn't let Callan just leave. Not without swearing to keep his mouth shut, and even then... Wiping his memory would be wiser. Which reminded me...

Sonoma.

The urgency in my chest propelled me forward, each step faster than the last, until I was nearly running.

Something was wrong. I could feel it in my bones.

The knot in my chest twisted tighter as I turned the knob, bursting into her small bedroom in the servant's quarters.

And stopped short.

Sonoma lay on the bed, her body unnaturally still, her face too pale. Dark circles ringed her eyes, and her wings lay folded and frail at her back.

"Sonoma?" My voice cracked.

Her eyelids fluttered, and she forced them open just enough to meet my gaze. "I'd hoped you'd come," she whispered, her voice barely audible over the roaring in my ears.

I rushed to her side. "I should've been down here sooner, but—"

"I know you're angry with me. For not telling you what you are. Where you come from."

"No," I hurried to say.

"Liar." She tried to smile, but the effort was too much, and it faltered halfway. "Listen to me. Your uncles... they'll reinstate the wards once I'm gone. Stronger ones. Impenetrable by anything in this realm."

Her words hit me like a punch to the gut, and I swallowed hard. "I can't do this alone. I need you—"

"My time here is done, my darling. But you can do this. The prophecy—"

"I don't care about the stupid fucking prophecy." I nearly screamed the words, but Sonoma merely blinked, waiting for me to calm. It infuriated me—the way she was acting like this was all normal and fine. So I said the one thing I thought might rattle her now. "Callan is here."

Her calm slipped, but she only looked confused. "The Autumn Prince? How?"

"The wards are down, and he and a couple of soldiers found their way in. I caught them in the royal bedroom."

She closed her eyes, exhaling, and I instantly regretted upsetting her. But she merely opened her eyes again, unruffled, and asked, "What does he say?"

"He wants to marry me," I said bitterly. "To rekindle our alliance. He doesn't seem to care that I have no army to offer him. He's an idiot, as always."

"Say yes."

"No." I jerked back, horrified. "Absolutely not. He's arrogant and entitled and—I won't be used like that."

"You have to leave this place, Aurelia." Her silver eyes pierced mine, pleading. "There's no going in or out once they seal the wards again. You'll be locked out until you can find a way to break the curse."

"So what?" I scoffed. "You taught me to defend myself. I'll figure it out. The Broadlands—"

"You and I both know Heliconia will find you. That Obsidian would've told her about us by now. You must accept Callan's offer. Use him for protection. He has resources. Access. Find out what kept Lesha and Amanti from coming back. Find out what the Obsidian meant about your alliance being the key to Heliconia's destruction."

I shook my head, but my resolve was crumbling. Sonoma was right, and I hated that in this moment. Hated everything including the Fates and the Furiosities. Especially them. "There has to be another way."

Sonoma's smile was sad. "You're stronger than you know."

Tears blurred my vision. I couldn't stop them anymore. I leaned down, my forehead pressed against her hand. My voice was no more than a whisper, but I couldn't hold back the one word I'd kept secret all these years. Just once, I had to say it. Out loud. Just for the two of us. "Don't leave me, Momma. Please."

But when I sat up, Sonoma only smiled faintly as she brought her hand up to cup my cheek. "My daughter," she murmured. "I'll still be watching over you." A strange calm settled over her features, and she closed her eyes. "I'll see your father soon."

My heart clenched. "I want to meet him too."

"He loves you very much, you know." I bit back a sob at the longing on her face. "He sacrificed knowing you to protect you. Being apart from him was the hardest choice I ever made. But choosing you was the easiest."

I took her hand, holding tight as if my grip could keep her here.

A shudder passed through her body, and for a moment, I thought she was already gone. But then, with a sudden gasp, her eyes flew open, wide and glassy and full of wonder. "Finally."

I looked up, my breath catching in my throat.

In the corner of the room, a figure stepped out of the shadows. Tall, dark-haired, and with an unmistakable aura of power that clung to him like shadows.

Ire.

The third Furiosity—and demon king of Hel.

My father.

I scrambled to my feet, my body trembling with shock. But he wasn't looking at me. With an expression of longing and pure, radiant love, he crossed the room in a single fluid movement and knelt beside Sonoma. His touch was gentle as he cupped her face, his gaze softening in a way I'd never imagined possible for a being like him.

"You fought well, my little warrior," he whispered, his voice deep and reverent.

Sonoma's lips twitched into the faintest of smiles. "I've missed you, darling. Is it time?"

Ire nodded. "At last."

I stood frozen, my mind spinning, watching helplessly as Ire bent and pressed a kiss to Sonoma's forehead. Her body relaxed instantly, the tension melting away as she exhaled her last breath in a soft sigh.

"No." The word broke from my lips before I could stop it, raw and filled with grief.

But Sonoma didn't stir.

She was gone.

Tears spilled down my cheeks as I stared at her still form, my heart aching with the loss of the memories we'd never make together. Time we'd never get back.

Ire turned to me then, his dark gaze locking with mine. "You'll see her again."

Hope bloomed painfully in my chest. "When?"

"Time is a hard thing to know from one realm to the next. But have faith." He studied me, and a lump formed in my throat at the pride reflected in his soft smile. "You have her eyes."

Did I? I'd never noticed it before. Maybe I hadn't been looking for it.

"I have your magic," I blurted.

"And my personality from what I hear," he added with a smirk. But then his humor vanished as he said, "You are a miracle, Aurelia. Born with the blood of two realms inside you. Blessed by a third. You are the best of me. And I'm sorry —" His voice cracked. "I'm sorry I couldn't be here with you. It was a necessary part of the deal we made with the Fates."

"What deal?" I asked.

"When your mother became pregnant, the Fates intervened. They tried to dictate terms, but your mother negotiated ruthlessly for her own interests—and yours." His smile turned wistful. "Don't bother trying to talk that woman into anything."

I smiled ruefully through my tears. "Yeah, I learned that the hard way."

He grinned.

"What did she negotiate?" I asked.

"The Fates wanted Tyrion and Celeste to raise you as their own. To protect your identity—and ours as your parents."

"But isn't that what happened?"

"We asked to wait until you were eighteen. To live together as a family first. But in the end, it became necessary to bring you here sooner."

"I don't remember," I said.

He nodded. "You were young. We spent your first two years in the mountains of Concordia. It was the happiest two years of my existence."

Heliconia's words came back to me from that day in the woods, and my stomach tightened. "I found your cabin," she'd told Sonoma. "The scent of your little family is still there, you know." She'd been taunting her with the truth.

"What changed?" I asked, my voice turning sharp. "Why couldn't we stay?"

"Heliconia," he said grimly.

"She got her power from you," I said, accusation creeping into my tone.

But the demon king remained unruffled. "She found your mother and me together one evening in the forest. She threatened to tell the Fates. To have your mother stripped of her Aine status for breaking her vow to them. So, I offered her a spark of what I have in exchange for her silence."

My jaw dropped. "That's why you gave her your power? To keep your girlfriend a secret?"

His brow arched as if he somehow still had his sense of humor about the whole thing. "Very romantic, isn't it? I take it your mother never told you?"

"She never told me a lot of things."

He sighed. "Yes, that was an unfortunate part of the deal, I'm afraid." He managed to look sorry for it.

"I don't understand. You said you negotiated with the Fates to keep me until I was eighteen. But you brought me here anyway. Why keep the secret in the end?"

"When I gave my power to Heliconia, I broke the treaty my brothers and I had with the Fates. Up until that moment, the Furiosities ruled over the dark souls of Menryth, and the Fates watched over the light. For a millennium, we maintained a balance that way. But with Heliconia, the scales had tipped in our favor. According to our treaty, I should have paid for that in my own blood, and Menryth would have suffered the consequences. Instead, the Fates blessed you. It was their way of rebalancing things. But it didn't come free."

"What do you mean?"

"I was no longer allowed to step foot in this realm. And I was forbidden from contacting you."

"That's harsh."

He smirked. "The Fates are not as gentle as the priestesses have led you to believe."

"And you're not as evil?" I couldn't help but ask.

His smirk widened. "Your mother sought a balance of her own," was all he said. "She would put aside her crown and her access to Hel in exchange for being in your life."

"She let me believe I was someone else's daughter."

"She was forbidden from speaking the truth, same as me."

I didn't know what to say to that. I'd been so angry that Sonoma had kept the truth from me. But if she'd been bound by magic... Did that change the betrayal?

The damage had still been done.

"Why now?" I asked. "I thought you weren't allowed to contact me."

"I'm here to collect my bride." He winked. "I would think Hel's daughter recognizes a loophole when she sees one."

I scowled.

"It didn't work," I pointed out, needing to change the subject. "Giving up your power for Heliconia's silence. The Fates found out anyway."

"They did," he agreed.

"And now she has more power than anyone in Menryth."

His dark gaze held no apology as he said, "I would've done that and more for your mother." His expression was somehow both sad and full of love.

For a fleeting moment, I was happy they would be reunited at last. Even though it meant I had to lose her. Lose both of them. Tears burned at that, but I blinked them back, desperate to soak up my father's company for as long as he was here. "You both gave up everything for me."

He took a step closer. "And we would do it again in a heartbeat."

I remained still, my breath frozen as he closed the distance between us. Father or no, he was the ruler of Hel, after all. But he only brushed a warm hand over my cheek. Power sparked at the contact, and he grinned.

"Will I see you again?" I asked.

"Someday, we shall be united at last. Until then, I am always watching over you, daughter."

Daughter.

It was the one word I'd always dreamed of hearing from my true parents. And it was the one word Sonoma had waited to give me until the very end. Hearing it from him, spoken with so much love, tugged something loose in my chest. It felt as if I were unraveling—desperate to bind myself to some sort of anchor.

"How do I contact you again?" I blurted.

But he didn't answer.

Instead, his form shimmered, and a thick plume of smoke rose, curling around him like a living shadow. Sonoma's body vanished from the bed. A second later, she reappeared in those same shadows where Ire stood, her form ethereal and radiant —and alive. She smiled at me, an open expression full of joy. One I hadn't seen her wear in a very long time. Ire slid his arm around her waist, and they both stepped backward into the shadows.

"Wait!" I cried, lurching forward.

But it was too late. With one final swirl of smoke, they were gone.

And I was truly and utterly alone.

THE
MOON

Chapter Twenty
Aurelia

I sat in Sonoma's room until my tears dried. At some point, I'd climbed into her bed and inhaled the scent of her until my senses were dull with the effort. There was no body to bury. No grave to mark. Only emptiness. I'd once thought loneliness couldn't get worse than the kind the curse had brought me, but the clanging emptiness surrounding me now was more painful than anything I could've imagined.

Finally, my tears were gone, and the numbness that came after slid slowly into resolve. I had to leave. And soon. The Furiosities would handle the wards but not until I was gone. As long as those assholes Eld and Age didn't fuck it up on purpose.

My uncles seemed the type to do that.

But I had a feeling my father wouldn't let them.

I felt a strange sort of comfort in suddenly having family—even if they were the rulers of Hel.

Then again, meeting my father had challenged everything I thought I knew about the Underworld. I'd been raised to believe Hel was evil. Dark and deadly and devoted to suffering.

And while their power could be used for darkness—Heliconia was an example of that—it wasn't all bad.

It couldn't be. Not with the amount of love that existed between Sonoma and Ire—my mother and father. Anyone could see that what they felt for one another was pure and good.

I wasn't sure where that left me on the spectrum of evil, but by the time I sat up and dusted myself off, I almost didn't care. As long as the power I'd been gifted was enough to save my people.

The blankets rustled as I slipped to the edge of the bed. Shoving them aside, I started to rise then stopped at the sound of something crinkling. I looked down to find a slip of paper sticking out from beneath the pillow.

Yanking it free, I read the words scrawled in Sonoma's handwriting with widening eyes.

Aurelia,

The bargain I made kept you safe, but it also kept you in the dark about what you're capable of. For that, I'm sorry. Heliconia is strong, but you are stronger. The Fates' blessings are the key. Unlock those and you'll have what you need to stop her. Your uncles will seal the wards as soon as you leave. Let Callan protect you while you search. And stop fighting your furyfire. Darkness doesn't always equal evil. Light isn't always good. We love you.

Mom

I re-read it three times, committing each word to memory. Then, I took Sonoma's sword and left the rest behind.

I went to my bedroom first. It took me a scant few minutes to pack, but I forced myself to bathe first and put on fresh clothes. I dressed in the clothing of an Aine warrior. Armor made of scaled rubidium, lightweight and breathable. A cloak embroidered with a sun wrapped in roses, the crest of Sevanwinds. And both Sonoma's sword and my own strapped across my back. I braided my hair to one side, covering my tattoo.

The only two gowns I owned that weren't falling apart from disuse went into my suitcase along with a pendant Lesha had given me for my birthday three years ago.

Far too quickly, it was done.

My entire life—all my belongings—bagged and ready.

I paused at the window, staring out over the city of Rosewood one last time. The tiled rooftops, fenced yards, and wide, empty streets were like an old friend. But the overgrown gardens covered in my mother's favorite rosebushes, all of them gnarled and overgrown with thorns, shattered the sense of home. The vibrant red roses had once been a true symbol of eternal summer. Now, black petals—rotted and scented with decay—were all that grew here.

This was Heliconia's mark—and I'd be glad to leave it behind.

Even if it felt like I'd cut my own heart out and leave it here too.

I went to the royal bedroom next. The king and queen were undisturbed despite the soldiers I'd fought here earlier. I kissed each of their cheeks and pulled the covers up, tucking them in one last time. I didn't dare speak out loud like I usually did. Partly out of fear Callan or his soldiers would hear me, but mostly because I knew I would break down if I did.

On my way out, I slipped a handful of royal jewels into my bag along with the gold coins kept in the armoire.

I saved Lilah's room for last.

She was innocent and beautiful nestled in her cozy sheets.

My eyes watered at the thought of not seeing her like this every day, but I reminded myself she could be listening. I wouldn't let fear be the last thing I gave her.

"I have to leave for a while," I whispered as I knelt beside her. "But I don't want you to worry about that. You are safe here. And when I return to wake you, the first thing we'll do is throw a party. And you can stay up as late as you want, dancing and eating all the delicious food."

The answering silence pressed down around me.

I sniffled.

"Stay out of trouble," I said, hating this moment. This day. This life. "I'll be back soon. I love you."

The castle had never been quieter as I made my way to the library. The Silent Kingdom at last—with me the only one left here to make a sound. I wanted to leave a note for Lesha in case she made it back. But with the wards up and impenetrable, she would have no way to get it. I couldn't risk leaving one outside the wards where anyone could find it. The thought of her returning here only to find herself locked out left a pit in my stomach. But I'd do whatever I could to find her the moment Callan's resources offered me the chance.

Callan.

He was going to be my savior after all.

Each step closer to him seemed to echo with loss—the goodbye I'd said to Sonoma and the others, the father I'd never gotten to know, the future I was giving up by marrying the Autumn prince.

When I finally reached the library, I paused outside the door and swallowed the ache in my throat, wiping away the last of my tears before I unlocked and entered the room.

Outside the windows, dawn had broken, casting a gray-hued light over the room. Callan stood near the fire, talking in low tones with Fletcher and Holt. The Autumn Prince was just as handsome as I remembered. Somehow, seeing him so unchanged only served to remind me of how little I resembled the girl he'd met seven years ago. And how much I'd lost in those years since.

The three of them quieted when they saw me, the soldiers' eyes narrowing with something akin to suspicion—or maybe unease.

I didn't blame them. Besides, the feeling was mutual.

Callan's gaze met mine, and his brow furrowed with concern at whatever he saw in my expression. Then he glanced down, noting my armor, weapons, and the bag dangling in my hand. "Aurelia?"

I cleared my throat and shoved the words out before I could talk myself out of it. "I'll marry you."

His expression shifted quickly—surprise and then a small flicker of something I couldn't name. He approached me, stopping a safe distance away as if he thought he might spook me. "You're sure?"

The question nearly undid me. Was I sure? Of course not. I wasn't sure of anything anymore, but that didn't matter.

"Yes," I replied, my voice steady even as the ground beneath me felt like it was crumbling. "On one condition."

"Name it."

"You will help me find the information I need to break this curse—to free my people."

"Done."

I blinked. "Just like that?"

He shrugged. "It's the right thing to do, isn't it?"

I couldn't bring myself to point out that he'd never once done the right thing as far as I was concerned. Instead, I said, "Then I accept your proposal. You have my alliance."

Callan's expression softened with relief. "You're making the right choice, Aurelia. For both of us."

He took another step, so close now I could feel the warmth of his body seeping into the cold space between us. His gaze held mine as if searching for something—an invitation, maybe, or a sign. But he didn't wait for either. Instead, he leaned down, brushing his lips over mine before I could react.

The kiss was...soft, hesitant. He tasted of mint and, beneath it, the barest hint of blue vervain. It wasn't terrible, but it wasn't what I'd expected either. I froze for a moment, too shocked to move, but then—

I shoved him back.

"What was that for?" I asked, glaring up at him as I wiped my mouth.

Either Holt or Fletcher snickered.

Callan frowned, looking more disappointed than sorry. "I thought—" He straightened, his cheeks flushing faintly. "It's what the stories claimed. The legends tell of the Sleeping Beauty curse, and—"

My eyes narrowed. "And what?"

He glanced away, suddenly unwilling to meet my eyes. "It's said that only true love's kiss can break the curse of eternal sleep."

I stared at him, dumbfounded, waiting for him to laugh or smirk or show some sign that this was a joke. But he didn't. He just stood there, straight-faced and unapologetic.

"That," I said slowly, "is the dumbest thing I've ever heard."

Callan blinked, clearly taken aback. "Excuse me?"

I threw up my hands. "What fairytale are you living in? Do you really believe that a kiss will magically solve all our problems? A curse doesn't break because someone's lips touch mine, Callan."

His jaw tightened, a muscle ticking beneath his skin.

"Let's go." I hitched my bag onto my shoulder and turned on my heel, heading for the door without waiting for his reply. "We need to get out of here before the wards are remade."

For a moment, I thought he might protest—might stop me and demand we talk more about whatever nonsense he'd heard about kissing being the answer to anything. But then he sighed behind me, the sound heavy with resignation.

He followed, his soldiers trailing behind.

Neither of us spoke as we made our way down the torchlit corridors toward the exit.

What could he possibly say?

That kiss had been a mistake. It wasn't love. Wasn't anything close to it. This alliance was nothing more than a necessary evil, and I had no room in my heart for anything else. Not after what I'd just lost.

Sonoma's absence was a jagged wound, her happiness at reuniting with my father both a comfort and a knife twisting in it. And Ire—gods, Ire. That look he'd given her before they'd disappeared into the shadows was one of blinding affection. And love. And yet, he was gone now too, slipping from my grasp like smoke through my fingers.

Prophecy or not, I was alone in this—truly.

There would be no fairytale ending for me.

My only purpose was to save this land, and I'd do that if it killed me.

We reached the doors where Callan had once made his grand entrance into my life. I stopped, overcome with memories. Callan paused beside me, his hand briefly brushing my arm.

I glanced up, meeting his golden eyes.

"Aurelia," he said softly.

I knew what he wanted to say—that we could make this work. That there was still something between us, some sliver of hope for more than just a cold political marriage. But I didn't want to hear it.

"We do this for my kingdom," I said quietly. "And yours. We do this to destroy Heliconia. Nothing more."

Callan didn't argue.

I placed my palms on the doors and shoved. They swung open, and brittle dawn spilled over us. The wind bit at my nose, promising to only grow worse the farther I ventured into it.

Once, I'd dreamt of being an Aine. A warrior nomad who traveled far and wide to defend crown and country. Today, I'd gotten my wish—and it had broken every last piece of my heart.

THE
MOON

The sound of hooves echoed off the cobblestone courtyard as the horses were readied for the journey. Before me, two dozen soldiers busied themselves with preparations, talking and laughing as they did so. The noise set my teeth on edge. I hadn't expected so many after only seeing Holt and Fletcher inside, but the rest of Callan's unit had apparently camped out in the barn overnight.

The prince had failed to mention them to me.

An entire unit of men on my doorstep, and I hadn't known. It was a stark reminder that, without the wards, the Summer Court didn't stand a chance. I was doing the right thing by accepting Callan's offer, though that didn't make it any easier.

I listened as the whispers began. Word was spreading among them about the sleeping fae inside the castle's walls. Fletcher and Holt had obviously been busy with their stories. I could feel their eyes on me already. Hear their speculation about what sort of magic had made them sleep—and left me awake.

I pretended not to notice.

A moment later, Callan appeared beside me. "Ready?"

I nodded.

My bag had been strapped to a cart that made up part of our caravan, but I was to ride as there was no carriage in their party. I was glad I wouldn't be cooped up inside a box for the journey to Grey Oak, but I also couldn't bring myself to admit how many years it had been since I'd ridden horseback.

The chickens we'd housed in the barn now roamed the grass nearby.

"We should bring them," I said. "They won't have anyone to feed them."

"And how do you propose we do that?" Callan asked.

"There are a few cages in the storage shed," I said. "I used them for trapping game, but they're empty now and could fit about four or five each."

Callan snapped his fingers at one of the soldiers nearby. "Pack them up," Callan told him.

The soldier handed his reins to another then hurried toward the shed.

"Done. Anything else?" Callan asked.

I hesitated, almost trying to come up with something to delay the inevitable. But in the end, I shook my head. "That's it."

I took Callan's offered hand and swung myself up into the saddle.

The horse stomped its feet, spinning in a tight circle. Nervous, I pulled at the reins, earning a side-step from the horse that startled me. The beast beneath me was as restless as I was, its breath coming in short bursts of agitation.

I watched as Callan mounted his own horse with ease. He'd slid a silver breastplate on and buckled a sword at his hip. What sort of warrior could he possibly be if he'd left his blade outside while he'd attempted his grand rescue last night? Then again, he'd apparently assumed his kiss would be the most effective weapon.

The symbol etched into the center of his breastplate caught my eye—a great stag with a crown of leaves adorning its horns. The Autumn Court crest. It was missing the words that went with it, or at least the words I remembered from my life before.

Through Cunning, We Endure had been the Autumn Court's motto. *Ku ryeko, wa ciro* in the old tongue.

I hoped like Hel that last part was still true.

For seven years, I'd endured here alone. Now that I was leaving this place, the world outside felt more dangerous than ever.

Callan's sharp golden eyes scanned his men—two dozen, maybe more, all armed to the teeth. It felt like we were preparing for war, not a trip across the Autumn countryside.

"We'll head straight for the Emerald Forest," he said, "You know the drill. Slow. Quiet. Stay alert. We're probably not the only things in this land anymore."

The men grunted in response, and then we were moving —a long, slow line marching away from the only home I'd never known. As we passed through the courtyard gates and onto the road beyond, Callan jerked his chin at me to join him at the front. I pressed my heels into the horse's side, and it obeyed readily, speeding up to close the distance.

"Do they make you nervous?" Callan asked, guiding his horse closer to mine. "The soldiers, I mean."

I shot him a sharp look. "You didn't tell me you'd brought so many."

"You didn't ask."

I rolled my eyes. "Is an entire unit really necessary?"

His brow rose. "Have you not traveled beyond the walls of this place in all this time?"

"Of course I have. But I make it a point not to draw attention while I do it."

Callan's mouth curved into a faint smile that didn't reach his eyes. "Noted."

My fingers tightened on the reins as I glanced back at the castle—my home. Its beautiful whitestone towers stood pale against the horizon, forlorn and forgotten, like a promise I couldn't keep. Memories washed over me until my vision blurred. I blinked, and the towers wavered.

It took a few more blinks to realize it wasn't my eyes blurring.

A glamour rippled over the castle grounds, casting a haze over everything it touched.

"What is it?" Callan asked; then his breath caught in a quiet gasp.

Magic shoved at me so hard I wobbled in the saddle. One of the soldiers behind me doubled over. The rest grunted in response to whatever force had knocked into them.

Behind us, powerful magic slid across the whitestone like an otherworldly pulse. Slowly, the castle faded from sight, its mighty walls vanishing against the backdrop of rolling hills and mighty trees. Farther north, the rooftops that marked the city of Rosewood flickered like a mirage until they, too, winked out of sight.

I exhaled, silently thanking the Furiosities for their help.

The Summer Court was gone. Hidden away one last time. All that was left was the earth itself—withering a bit under the effects of a fast-approaching winter.

Looking out over the landscape, it was almost as if Sevanwinds had never existed at all.

A hollow ache settled in my chest, but I shoved it aside. The Furiosities' wards would protect this place better than the Aine ever could. All it had cost me was my mother—and my freedom.

"How did you do that?" Callan's voice, laced with awe and suspicion, cut through my thoughts.

Straightening my shoulders, careful to keep any trace of the truth off my face, I said, "Explaining myself isn't part of the deal."

He frowned but let it go. "Shall we?"

I forced a nod, though everything inside me screamed *no*. "Lead the way."

With a command from Callan and a reminder to remain silent on the road, the soldiers moved out, the sound of hooves a steady rhythm as we began the journey into the Emerald Forest.

Once we entered the trees, the formation changed.

Several soldiers rode out ahead to scout the way. And the ones behind us spread themselves thinner so that we had a watchful eye on our rear. I tried not to think about what sort of creatures we might come across.

We stopped for lunch without incident, filling our bellies with cold sandwiches and water. My thoughts drifted to my birthday last year when Lesha, Amanti, Sonoma, and I had spent the day at the falls just south of Sevanwinds. We were still inside the wards but only just, and because of that relative safety, we'd been safe enough to relax. To eat and smile and swim like we'd done when I was a kid.

For that one day, we'd let ourselves forget.

It was the last happy memory I had with all of us together. Now, it was the last happy memory I'd ever have with them. Lesha and Amanti weren't coming back—because there was nothing left to come back to. Even they wouldn't be able to get past those wards now. And if they did manage to return, they wouldn't know what had become of me. Or Sonoma.

The thought soured my appetite.

Fletcher appeared before me, his eyes darting from me to the half-eaten sandwich I'd abandoned. Without a word, I handed it to him, and he took it, flashing me a grin before hurrying off.

A moment later, we were all mounted and ready to resume our trek.

By mid-afternoon, the forest had thickened.

The air grew cooler as we rode deeper, the dense canopy of trees overhead blocking out the sun. Shadows slanted across the path, and the silence that settled took on an edge that felt unnatural. The Emerald Forest had once been a welcoming place, but it didn't feel that way today.

I thought immediately of the Obsidian who'd gotten away.

My pulse quickened, but I focused on my breathing and pushed out my senses to check for any threats. The soldiers ahead of us were tense, their eyes darting toward every rustle in the trees. I could feel it too—the unease. The feeling that we were being watched. My magic stirred restlessly inside me, but I forced it down, unwilling to betray my secrets.

There was no need to use it, I told myself. Not with Callan's soldiers at our side.

Except I couldn't shake the doubt that seeped in even as I thought it.

The road narrowed as we moved deeper into the forest. A breeze rustled through the leaves, and the hair on the back of my neck stood on end. One of the soldiers let out a low whis-tle, and I tensed. Callan's gaze swept the trees, his hand resting tightly on the hilt of his sword.

Then I saw it.

A flash of movement from the shadows, too fast to track. My horse reared with a startled whinny, and I barely kept myself from falling off. Shouts rang out from the soldiers, their weapons drawn as a figure burst from the underbrush.

Pale skin, eyes like a starless midnight, and the stench of rotted souls clinging to its flesh.

An Obsidian.

My horse bucked again. This time, I felt myself slipping and leaped away before I could land beneath its hooves. I grunted at the impact then straightened and drew Dorcha.

Behind me, a soldier cried out.

I whirled in time to see the fae's throat sliced open. The Obsidian's clawed hand came away red with the soldier's blood, but it didn't stop to revel in the kill or even check that the soldier had been truly disabled.

Focused and vicious, it cut its way through Callan's warriors.

This Obsidian wasn't like the ones I'd faced before. It was larger, faster. It moved with precision, not the mindless violence I'd come to expect. Over and over again, its eyes, dark and bottomless, darted to me with a predatory gleam.

Movement to my left drew my attention. A second Obsidian cutting a path toward the rear of our line. And then a third from the middle, splitting our ranks. Where the fuck was Callan?

Probably running again, I thought disgustedly.

There was no time to check. Just across the path from where I stood, the first Obsidian cut down the last of the soldiers between it and me. A bloodied sword, swiped from Autumn soldiers, dangled from each of its hands.

Closing the distance faster than I'd ever seen, the creature lunged, and I barely managed to draw my second sword in time. The force of the steel's impact knocked me back a step, but I held my ground, deflecting its blow with a sharp clang.

Dark magic crackled in the air.

Energy pulsed deep inside me, responding to something ancient and dangerous.

The creature lifted its hand and shot a blast of pure darkness straight at me. My magic surged in defense, slipping free before I could call it back—a burst of power that erupted in furyfire. My onyx flames slammed into the Obsidian's power, shoving it back and burning holes through it that fell like ash. Furyfire caught at the Obsidian's clothing, spreading quickly until those same flames licked at the creature's flesh, burning and melting it off.

Still, it came for me.

My pulse thundered in my ears. I took a single step back to regain my posture for my next attack, and my foot caught on a body.

I stumbled, glancing down to see an Autumn soldier lying dead at my feet. The moment of hesitation cost me. My furyfire winked out. When I looked up again, the Obsidian's eyes gleamed—it had me.

Scrambling, I raised my blades, preparing to block the next strike, but I knew even as I hurried to make it that my balance was completely wrong.

And then, behind the Obsidian, something moved.

A second later, the creature staggered, a flash of steel cutting through its chest. I leaped aside as it careened face-first to the ground, dark blood pooling beneath its chest. Its waning life force seeped into the air, tendrils of it snaking toward my ankles. Before I could stop myself, I reached for it.

The power inside me sighed as it sipped.

Delicious, it seemed to whisper.

My senses sharpened. My power pulsed, renewed.

Then a blade swung out, cutting the smoke off, and I gasped as the supply abruptly ended. I coughed, my chest burning as the power spread inside me.

"Are you all right?" a male voice asked roughly.

I blinked up at the figure who'd saved me, and my heart stopped.

Rydian.

Dark, deadly, handsome as ever—and covered in Obsidian blood.

His eyes met mine, and for a moment, it felt like the world had tilted on its axis. The same stony expression hardened his face, but those eyes… I couldn't get them out of my head.

"You," I breathed.

Had he seen what I'd just done?

His eyes narrowed. "This isn't what I had in mind when I told you to make it right," he growled.

I stiffened at that, trying to decipher if he was referring to the dark magic I'd just used or the fact that I'd seemingly taken his advice to honor my vow to Callan.

Before I could respond, Callan appeared beside us, what remained of his soldiers fanning out to secure the area. His gaze flicked from the dead Obsidian to Rydian, and I watched as something like relief crossed his face.

"Nice work," he said, and it took me a moment to realize he was speaking to Rydian. "This asshole was particularly lethal. Glad you were close."

"If you'd stuck to the route I gave you, we wouldn't have needed to deal with them at all," Rydian told him, and the derision in his voice bordered on disrespect.

I blinked, stunned to hear anyone speak to a prince that way, and even more shocked when Callan merely rolled his eyes and sighed. "The day is already fucked up enough without you lecturing me."

"What's going on?" I demanded, impatient and confused and very aware of the blood spattered across the front of my clothes, not to mention the layer of sweat and grime coating my skin.

Why did I care that Rydian was seeing me like this anyway? He looked just as dirty—except the blood and battle scars only made him more alluring. Ugh.

"Aurelia," Callan said. "Meet my brother, Rydian Nytherra."

Brother.

The word rang in my ears as I fought to make sense of it. No one had ever mentioned a second prince in the Autumn Court. But here he stood—after saving my life, no less—and yet, he still stared at me like I was the worst kind of surprise.

"Rydian, this is Princess Aurelia Valeen of Sevanwinds. My fiancée."

Rydian's expression didn't change. He merely nodded, his eyes cool and distant. "Your Highness," he said as if he didn't recognize me at all. Or maybe he didn't want Callan to know he did. I couldn't imagine why he wouldn't, but I didn't feel like explaining myself either.

I swallowed hard and forced a smile, though it felt like a mask. "It's nice to meet you," I said, trying to keep my voice light. "And thank you for your help."

"Rydian's just doing his job," Callan said, waving away the fact that I might've died if not for his brother.

Rydian frowned but said nothing.

I decided to focus on Callan, as annoying as his attitude was about a battle that had just cost some of his soldiers their lives.

"What job is that?" I asked.

"Rydian leads one of our elite units," Callan said. "His team specializes in tracking and eliminating Obsidians." Callan's chest puffed up when he called Rydian's unit elite— like he was claiming their formidable skillset for himself.

I forced myself to glance at Rydian as I asked, "Have you faced other Obsidians like these before? With enhanced magic and strength?"

"A few," he said darkly, and I thought of how he'd found me just as I'd killed that one in the Broadlands. Something told me he was thinking of that too.

Callan chuckled, unaware of the storm raging beneath the surface. "Rydian's been tracking these creatures along our borders and all the way through the Broadlands to Midnight and Lightshore."

"So you do read the scouting reports I sent you," Rydian said.

"Only the exciting ones," Callan told him, grinning.

Rydian frowned, his eyes flashing with a temper that he somehow managed to keep tightly leashed as he said, "I'm not sure the men would use that word to describe such a dangerous mission."

I cocked my head. "It can't be that dangerous if a single unit of soldiers is enough to stop them."

Callan smothered a laugh.

Rydian pinned me with a look that rivaled the one he'd worn that day in the Broadlands. For a moment, whatever door he'd built to hide his power opened just enough to remind me what he was capable of. I breathed in sharply as my newly heightened senses became suddenly aware of the sheer magnitude of it. Then, just as quickly, the door slammed shut.

Rydian sheathed his sword with a smooth motion, his gaze lingering on me for only a heartbeat before turning back to Callan. "My men and I will ride ahead," he said, his voice low, clipped. "We'll make sure the road is clear since you insist on going this way."

"It's faster," Callan said.

Rydian merely shook his head then strode over to an enormous white horse and pulled himself into the saddle. I watched him, watched the way his muscles moved as he swung his large body up.

With a low whistle, he rode away, several men falling into line behind him. They all wore the same nondescript uniform as Rydian: dark tunics with no crest or court identification.

An elite unit.

Led by Callan's brother.

A male with a power unlike any I'd ever seen. And the

unique ability to mask it whenever he wanted. A male who seemed to hate me for absolutely no reason at all.

A male who haunted my dreams.

When he was gone, I found Callan watching me. My cheeks heated, and I turned away but too late. He frowned, clearly noting my reaction. I didn't say a word. Neither did he. But something had shifted. And I wasn't sure if I could ever shift it back. Or if I wanted to try.

THE
MOON

Chapter Twenty-Two
Aurelia

For the rest of the afternoon, the company rode in tight formation, eyes sharp. As we left the dead Obsidians behind, no one mentioned the furyfire I'd used or the shadows I'd taken into myself. Worry warred with logic. It was likely none of them had noticed what I'd done, especially considering they were all wrapped up in fighting for their own lives. Even with the healer's efforts, five were dead and twice that injured. And from the expressions some of them wore, the soldiers we'd lost had been friends to one another. Watching them mourn their fallen only made my own grief that much sharper.

That night, we slept in bedrolls without tents or even a fire to warm us. I woke frequently to the sounds of twigs snapping or wind rustling the trees. Even with two Aine swords propped against the tree beside me, I'd never felt more exposed.

My heart ached with grief, and more than once, silent tears tracked down my cheeks as I thought of Sonoma, Lesha, and Amanti.

By dawn, I was bleary-eyed and more than ready to move again.

We resumed our silent trek through the forest, the tension stretching my nerves thin.

I didn't see Rydian again, though I glimpsed a couple of his men reporting in before they rode ahead. Callan rode beside me, mostly silent since the attack, his face unreadable.

I didn't have it in me to ask what he was thinking.

Three days passed.

Callan didn't talk much though he rode dutifully beside me as we wound our way west. I was more than okay with the silence. It left me to my own thoughts, as churning and wild as they were.

Nothing else attacked, but instead of relief, it only set me more on edge. Something about the calm didn't feel right. Sure enough, by the time we stopped to sleep each night, one of Rydian's men appeared to report that they'd encountered Obsidians or other predators and cleared the way for us. I pretended not to care that Rydian hadn't come himself.

Callan didn't bother to thank them before sending them on their way again.

Just before sunset on the fourth day, the forest gave way to an open hillside. From here, the land rolled gently into the distance where another forest waited. Grey Oak Forest, I realized as I studied the autumn leaves that decorated the canopy in the distance.

We'd reached Autumn's borders at last.

Callan and his soldiers seemed to relax as we started down a narrow trail that wound around the hillside. But when I caught sight of a camp ahead, I tensed. "Someone else is already here."

"Relax," Callan said, noting my reaction. "I had Rydian's men set up camp for us."

I nodded, ignoring the butterflies erupting in my stomach

as we rode toward the dozen or so tents. But I couldn't keep from scanning the distant soldiers' faces—looking for *him*. When I didn't spot him among the men, I told myself I was better off. Whatever it was that drew me to the second prince, it couldn't be good. Not when I'd already promised to marry the first.

At the edge of the camp, Callan pulled his horse up short, addressing the soldiers as they rode by us in a tired procession.

"Warm yourself by the fire. Eat a hot meal. Tend to your wounds. We'll leave at dawn." He kept his voice low, which told me we weren't completely out of danger yet.

The men grunted in response.

When the last of them had passed us, Callan moved slowly back onto the path. I fell in beside him again.

"That was quite the dramatic battle you were having the other day when Rydian intervened."

I cut my gaze to his, unable to keep from glaring even as fear curled in my gut. After four days of near-silence, this was the last thing I wanted to talk about. "How do you know what kind of battle it was?"

"I saw it."

"You saw it and didn't come to help me?"

His brows pinched. "I was too far away."

I snorted. "Naturally."

He stared at me for a long moment before saying, "One of my men had a wound that was losing too much blood. I helped him wrap it to stem the bleeding until the healer arrived. When I looked up, you were trading blows with that... thing."

I didn't answer.

He cut me a look. "Do you have something to say to me?"

"Like what?" I asked, realizing too late that my responses were based on a memory he didn't have.

"You seem to think I abandoned you."

I looked away. "I only meant I didn't see you anywhere. I thought you might've been dragged off by one of them."

At that, his eyes lit with their usual flirting charm. "Were you very worried about me?"

I forced a smile. "A little."

Flirting was safer than admitting I'd been party to altering his memories—even if I was only an accessory after the fact. But I also had to know more about the sudden change in the monsters Heliconia was making.

"Those Obsidians were different than the ones I've dealt with before," I added.

"I see, and exactly how many have you dealt with before?"

His tone made it clear he wasn't taking me seriously. But I answered honestly anyway. "A few dozen at least. I've lost count."

His smile fell away, and he blinked. "You're serious. You've fought that many of them and survived it?"

"If this is some dig at how horribly I handled myself the other day, I don't want to hear it. Sonoma's lecture is still ringing in my ears—"

"Who's Sonoma?"

I kicked myself for nearly outing two important pieces of information in the same five minutes. That had to be a record. To be fair, I hadn't had a ton of practice talking to people who hadn't shared every detail of my waking nightmare these last years.

I needed to pay closer attention from now on.

"She served in my father's court."

"Ah, of course, I know that name. She was one of the Aine."

"Yes."

He glanced over at my warrior's leathers and the two blades strapped to my back. "She's the one who taught you how to use a sword."

I hesitated, but there was no point in lying. It's not like there were any Aine left in the realm to disapprove. "Yes."

"Then I owe her my gratitude. If not for your skill with a sword, you and I might never have had this second chance together. I'm just grateful you don't have to do anything like that ever again."

"What do you mean?"

"A princess wielding a sword?" His brow lifted; his mouth quirked. "I hardly think it's appropriate for your station."

"Someone has to fight," I said tightly.

"Of course. But we lead armies, we don't enlist in them."

I flashed a tight smile. "Speaking of which, tell me about Grey Oak. I never asked how the Autumn Court has been affected by Heliconia. Is it bad?"

"As a matter of fact, Grey Oak is thriving."

"Really?"

"Why do you look so surprised?"

"You said Obsidians have begun attacking with more frequency. I assumed your lands would be threatened."

He straightened in his saddle. "Our people have the greatest army in the realm. We will not be bullied by some power-hungry castoff."

I stared at him. "Is that all you think she is?"

"She's a formidable witch, thanks to the dark magic she stole, but without her army of Obsidians, she wouldn't last— not against us."

His ego was ridiculous, even for an entitled prince. This was the savvy, strategic general of legends?

"She's much more powerful than that," I said quietly.

Something about my tone must've given my thoughts away because Callan swallowed and said quickly, "Forgive me for dismissing the damage she did to your family. Tell me about her then. Any intel you have is valuable if we're going to take her down."

I cringed as I realized he meant for me to describe an event he'd been present for. An event he'd tried to run from.

I couldn't make myself do it.

"I'd rather not talk about it just yet," I said, fixing my attention on the soldiers rushing around the camp we'd nearly arrived at. Tending wounds, pouring ale, building fires and tents.

"Of course," he said with enough pity that I bit my cheek to keep from snapping at him. "I don't want to push you. Eventually, we should record everything you can remember, though. It might help us in the battle to come."

Battle.

Not war.

He thought this would be over that quickly.

I nodded absently as we reached the edge of camp, glad to have an excuse to end the conversation.

After a quick dismount, I patted my horse, lingering long enough to brush my hands over his soft mane.

"Good boy," I whispered in appreciation.

When I looked up, Callan and another fae, a blond male with thick stubble covering his cheeks and chin, were both watching me. The stranger was clearly one of Rydian's in his unmarked tunic. I'd seen him in the forest the other day while we'd fought the Obsidians—a skilled fighter.

"What's his name?" I asked.

"Shadow," the soldier answered. "Bastard can run like a shadow in the wind when he gets it into his head. But only when he decides."

I smiled at that and shared a look with the horse whose restless energy matched my own. "Shadow," I echoed. "Thank you for today."

"I'll take him for you, Your Highness," the soldier offered.

With a jolt, I realized he was aiming that title at me. "Thanks. What's your name?"

"Slade, Your Highness."

"Nice to meet you. Please call me Aurelia."

The soldier winked. "I'll do my best."

I handed off the reins and turned to find Callan waiting with a bemused smile.

"I don't remember you being shy," Callan said.

"Just rusty. It's been seven years since anyone addressed me that way."

Something passed over his face—there and gone before I could decipher it. "Come on. Let's get you some food, although I warn you these reheated beans and rice are probably only fit for a rusty princess."

Despite everything about this day, I laughed.

Like the previous nights, I lay awake while grief gripped me and my worries played on a loop. The Obsidians had grown stronger, deadlier. And they'd seemed to know me on sight. That was a problem, especially if they were acting on Heliconia's orders.

She'd know I was alive by now.

If word got back to her that I was traveling with Autumn, she'd come for me here too. Callan claimed his army could handle her, but I wasn't so sure. Not after how easily they'd torn through our ranks in the forest.

I hated to think I'd brought death down on those men.

The prophecy said I was supposed to save the fae, not get them killed for helping me. But according to that one Obsidian's claims, I was only destined to do so with Callan beside me. So far, I hadn't seen much evidence of that being true.

At least, Sevanwinds was protected. But the ward keeping danger out didn't help me bring them back to life. And now,

Sonoma was gone, taking any answers she might still hold along with her. Taking my father with her too.

A daughter of Hel.

And I'd almost given myself away in that battle. I had to be more careful, especially with so many eyes on me now. I was supposed to be the Summer heir. If my magic was exposed, there was no way Callan would believe that lie. And without my title as the princess of Sevanwinds, there would be no alliance. No help for the people I'd left behind.

Ugh.

Frustrated, I tossed my blanket aside and sat up.

Shoving my feet into my boots, I pulled on my cloak and crawled free of the canvas walls that threatened to smother me. The campfire flickered weakly against the cool night air, casting long shadows across the stones ringing it.

Most of the soldiers had turned in. Those who didn't have the luxury of a tent were wrapped in their cloaks or blankets and gathered near the fire, the quiet murmur of their breathing the only sound aside from the occasional crackle of wood.

I glanced toward Callan's tent, listening to the soft sounds of his snoring. Then I scanned the other tents, wondering if any of them belonged to Rydian. I hadn't seen a glimpse of him in days. His men came and went like shadows, protecting and patrolling our perimeter.

With silent steps, I made my way to the edge of camp where a narrow path twisted up the hillside. My senses took in the sounds of the nocturnal insects. The bite of the cool wind across my cheeks and nose. The scent of earth and air.

I climbed all the way to the overlook then stood staring out over the darkened valley below. Nothing moved within it, and I found a strange comfort in the stillness. Like an old friend who'd changed its appearance but shown up after all, however unexpected.

The stars overhead glittered like shards of glass, their cold light offering no relief to my chilled skin. My cloak did little to keep out the bite of the wind, but I welcomed it. Anything to distract me from the restlessness churning inside.

Staring up at the sky, I rubbed absently at the tattoo on my neck. The black moon. The same color as my furyfire. And three stars—just like the three kings of Hel.

"You shouldn't be out alone." Rydian's voice was quiet but hard.

I whirled, my heart leaping into my throat.

"It's not safe," he added smugly, noting my surprise.

"I can handle myself," I said, not really caring to be lectured, least of all by him.

"Like you did the other day?" His words stung more than I wanted to admit.

I stiffened as he stepped closer. His dark eyes were unreadable, but his presence—strong, steady—grated on me even as it stirred my desire. A chemical reaction, I told myself. A result of seven years with no physical outlet. But I didn't react to Callan this way. Or any of the Autumn Court soldiers, for that matter.

The fact that I reacted this way for *him*—a male who seemed to loathe me as much as I did him—was beyond irritating.

"What's your problem with me?" I demanded.

His jaw tightened.

When he didn't answer, I said, "Is it about what happened in the Broadlands? Because I'm not going to tell anyone I saw you—"

"No."

"The party then. You insulted me before even knowing anything about me."

It felt silly to bring up something that had happened so long ago, but he didn't say that. Instead, something flickered in his dark gaze. A glimpse of power. A depth of emotion. There and gone so quickly I wondered if I'd imagined it.

"Were you protecting Callan then too?" I couldn't help but ask.

"Callan doesn't know I was at that party," he said.

I frowned, waiting for some other explanation.

"How did you survive Heliconia that night?"

It wasn't the response I'd expected. "What?"

"Every citizen of Summer fell to that sleeping curse. Except for you." He cocked his head, and my insides screamed at me to walk away. Or kill him. Anything to shut him up. "How did you escape it?"

"Your guess is as good as mine." I resisted the urge to touch the mark on my neck. "Besides, I could ask you the same thing."

He shifted his weight, his gaze flicking away as if he were considering what to say. Finally, he sighed, frustration etched into the hard lines of his face. "I don't have a problem with you."

"I don't believe you." My voice softened, and despite the tense conversation, something about his nearness felt more palpable now. "You seem angry with Callan too. Why?"

At the mention of his brother, Rydian's expression darkened. "Callan is reckless. He puts convenience above safety, and it's going to get him killed."

"He's done all right so far, considering his military record," I said wryly.

His eyes narrowed. He stepped closer, close enough that I could feel the faint heat radiating from him. "Your record is provoking as well, isn't it? A lost princess back from the dead —and at the perfectly opportune moment."

Fury ignited in me. "I never claimed to be dead," I said, glaring. "And I don't have the faintest idea what you're talking about. Nothing about this arrangement is opportune."

Surprise flickered at that. Or maybe disbelief.

"If you're Callan's brother," I said, lowering my voice, "why have I never heard of you before?"

A bitter smile tugged at his lips. "Because no one has. Especially not another royal like you."

"Why not?"

"Callan likes to use the word brother when it suits him. But not at Grey Oak. Not in front of our father." His gaze flicked up to the sky, and his voice was tinged with bitterness. "We had different mothers. The bastard never lets me forget it."

The confession hung between us, his words cutting through the night air like a cold blade. I studied his profile in the dim light, trying to understand him, trying to piece together this male who seemed loyal to Callan but carried so much anger toward the prince and their father.

"What is the king like?" I asked.

Rydian didn't answer right away. His gaze remained fixed on the valley below. When he finally spoke, his voice was quiet, almost haunted. "You'll see soon enough."

I shivered at his cryptic response. It wasn't exactly what I'd wanted to hear, especially after I'd already allied myself with the male in question.

He turned back to me, his eyes catching mine, and for the briefest moment, something passed between us—something charged and heavy. I couldn't ignore the way my pulse quickened, the way the air seemed thicker with him standing so close.

"Be careful," he said, his tone suddenly softer. "At Grey Oak, things aren't always what they seem."

"Be careful of what?" I asked, a knot forming in my stomach.

Rydian's eyes held mine. "Don't let anyone know you have that kind of magic."

My breath caught in my throat. I swallowed hard, trying to appear unfazed. "I don't know what magic you mean."

"Yes, you do."

Fear twisted in my gut. I should deny it all—but the need to understand drove me. "And if I did know, why should I be careful?"

He studied me. "Because people like Duron—like Callan—they'll use it. And they'll take everything you are in the process."

I wanted to argue, but the stark concern in his expression stopped me. I'd heard stories about King Duron. His political cunning was only outshined by his ruthlessness. It was why his army was considered the most formidable in the realm.

Rydian's eyes lingered on mine for a moment longer, as if he wanted to say more, but then he stepped back, his expression hardening again.

"Get some sleep, Your Highness," he said, the bite back in his tone. "Tomorrow's going to be a long day."

THE
MOON

CHAPTER TWENTY-THREE
AURELIA

We broke camp at dawn. Rydian was nowhere in sight by the time I dressed and joined the others. Callan was the last to emerge from his tent. I noted dark circles under his eyes, but when I asked him how he'd slept, he chirped out, "Great," and flashed one of those charming smiles.

I let it go.

Slade was waiting with Shadow, the horse already saddled and stomping impatiently.

"Morning, Your Highness." Slade dipped his chin at me and handed me the reins.

Shadow snorted at the sight of me.

I mounted without help and couldn't shake the burst of pride I felt over the accomplishment. It was probably stupid, but I took it as a sign I was fitting back into the waking world. Hopefully, I could master the skills I'd need to navigate the Autumn Court just as quickly.

As we wound through the hills and into the valley, the temperature dropped. I pulled my cloak more tightly around me and kept my face angled down to counter the wind's bite on my cheeks as much as possible.

On the far side of the valley, we crossed into Grey Oak Forest, a crowded autumn wood filled with a mass of Purple-Leaf Oaks that cast long shadows over the moss-coated ground. It was enough to distract me from the nerves that were growing worse the closer we got to the Autumn Court.

Finally, we emerged on the other side.

I stared out over a landscape rich with color—copper leaves that shimmered like burnished metal and deep emerald fields stretching endlessly under a blue sky. It was beautiful in a way that made my heart ache; a beauty that felt untouched by the looming shadow of war. I was both relieved to find it so whole and resentful that Summer had suffered so greatly in comparison.

Ahead, a large stretch of farmland yielded to a road, and we aimed northwest in a procession that became louder and more carefree the farther we went. The soldiers clearly deemed the lands this far into their kingdom safe.

I hoped they were right.

Callan rode beside me, chatting easily about the landmarks we passed.

I stole glances at him while pretending to listen, unable to shake Rydian's warning last night—that Callan and the king would try to use me. It wasn't very far-fetched to think a scheming politician might have his own angle. But this warning had felt different. Darker. More nefarious.

Then again, everything about Rydian felt that way.

Still, I tucked my magic in deep and willed it to remain dormant along with the rest of my secrets. If Callan kept his word—if he helped me find a way to wake and free my people —it would be worth sharing my kingdom with him. Or that was what I told myself.

We stopped for lunch on the side of the road.

Callan led me away from the others to a fallen log where we ate in relative silence. Despite the mostly open road, I still hadn't seen Rydian or his scouts since leaving camp. Far to our left, a forest ran parallel to the road with farmland between. I studied the tree line but glimpsed nothing and no one inside it.

"Where's Rydian?" I asked.

Callan's gaze shot to mine. "I sent him on another errand. Why?"

I shrugged. "I expected him to escort us all the way to Grey Oak."

Callan shook his head, his expression tight. "That's not exactly Rydian's scene."

"What is his scene?"

His brow rose in a sort of challenge. "Why so many questions about a bastard-born son?"

I suppressed my flinch at the insult. Clearly, he was trying to remind me what Rydian was—and wasn't. "He saved my life. I'm entitled to curiosity, aren't I?"

Callan frowned but said nothing.

I decided to take the hint and change the subject. "Are you nervous about introducing me to your father?"

"Of course not. Why would I be?"

"My mistake. So, he knew you intended to rescue the long-lost Sleeping Beauty and whisk her home to live happily ever after despite having no kingdom or army to her name?"

He shook his head, refusing to take the bait. "He expects me to take a bride of royal breeding with sufficient magic so that our offspring's power benefits the kingdom."

I blinked.

Offspring?

Seven years had been enough to make me forget all that would be expected of a royal alliance. The reality came crashing down around me.

I swallowed. "Spoken like a true politician."

He grimaced, but then his gaze became almost beseeching. "We were honest with one another once. About what this was —and what it could be. Am I wrong to think we might have that honesty again?"

I ignored the way my own conscience squeezed my heart. The only thing between us was a pile of secrets—but I wasn't going to tell him that. I gave him my best vulnerable look and fluttered my lashes. "You tell me."

He sighed then admitted, "My father is not an easy man. He'll be unhappy you don't have an army to offer him."

"A fact I warned you about when you proposed," I pointed out. "You said there were other benefits to our alliance now."

"There are." A shadow passed over his features.

"Callan," I warned. "What aren't you telling me?"

"Our lands are not as untouched as you might think by Heliconia's wrath," he said quietly. "My father demanded I find a bride who would offer a solution for our people."

"What kind of solution?"

He hesitated then said quietly, "My father would see me wed to Heliconia herself."

I blinked, stunned at the ludicrousness of such an idea. "What makes him think she would ever go for that?"

"Because it was her idea."

I shook my head. "I don't understand."

"After her attack on your court, she tried to claim her victory and your father's throne. But the other courts refused to recognize her coup or her claims as the queen of Winter and Summer. Then, she vanished, and it only solidified the realm's resistance to her rule. Seven years later, every single kingdom continues to fight against her, no matter the losses her creatures inflict."

"You think she's trying to take control through diplomacy," I said. "But why would your father ever agree to it?"

He made a face. "He's as power-hungry as she is. He thinks he could lure her here for a wedding vow then kill her."

I stared at him, understanding dawning in slow horror. "Your father would try to claim everything she's conquered for himself."

He nodded grimly. "He sees himself as lord of Autumn and Winter."

I swallowed my fury as I said, "And instead, you intend to hand him Summer."

"I'm being honest with you like we agreed," he said. "I would much rather tie myself to you in a mutual alliance than risk my life and my crown with her."

"And what happens when your father decides he wants my crown for himself?"

"I won't let him hurt you, Aurelia."

The Obsidian's words came back to me. The key to Heliconia's destruction was us. Callan and me. Which meant I had no choice but to believe the steadiness in the words he'd just offered me. "And my people? Will you protect them too?"

"I told you I'd help you find a way to free them. And I will."

Yes, he'd help me free them—just in time to hand them over to Duron as the Autumn king's subjects. But it was either this or Callan married Heliconia. And if Duron failed in his coup, if she conquered Autumn, where would that leave me? What would become of the prophecy then? Could I do this without the prince? Even Sonoma had insisted I needed his help. But so far, he was proving to be the one person most capable of stabbing me in the back.

I shuddered, suddenly chilled.

Callan noted it. "We should get going. I want to reach Grey Oak by sunset."

Three hours later, rolling farmlands gave way to large estates as we reached the outskirts of Grey Oak. Traffic became heavier as we passed carriages trimmed in gold, their occupants obscured by thick curtains covering the small windows. Clusters of modest but well-kept homes lined side streets. Children played in front yards.

My chest tightened. How long had it been since I'd seen children playing? The sight was both beautiful and tragic. They waved at us as we passed. Callan waved back, grinning like we were nothing more than a friendly parade. I blinked back hot tears and did my best to keep my expression neutral.

We left the estates and traffic behind, turning onto a narrow lane that led up to a set of iron gates. Here, no more civilians roamed. Only those in military uniforms with the Autumn crest emblazoned on their breast.

Ahead, the road was bordered by a high fence topped with metal spikes. The soldiers in our procession quieted as swiftly as they had inside the Emerald Forest. It was disconcerting after a day of non-stop chatter.

Even Callan's good mood had vanished.

A few minutes later, we passed through the heavy gates. Armed sentries looked down on us from a three-story tower on either side. My skin prickled with the feeling of their heavy gazes, but I kept my eyes fastened straight ahead as I rode beside Callan.

Behind us, the gates creaked and whined as they were pushed shut again. I flinched at the sound of them clanging together and the lock engaging. The whole setup made this place feel more like a prison than a haven.

Callan glanced at me, a tight smile flashing. "You can relax. No threat can touch you here."

I didn't answer. How could I when the only threat I was worried about now was him?

The road sloped gently upward, and as we climbed, I noted the armed men positioned at regular checkpoints along the side. Some stood watch in treetop posts, barely noticeable through the copper leaves that clung to the branches. Others marched past in plain sight, their swords gleaming at their hips.

Following the road, we wound steadily through it all, up and up and up. And at the very top of the hill, impressively large and moodily gray, stood Grey Oak Castle. I'd seen pictures of this place years ago during one of many meetings with my father and our generals. But those pictures hadn't done it justice; the place was easily twice the size of Sevanwinds. I counted five separate towers from the front view alone.

Its outer walls were made of a light, smooth stone decorated with copper and burgundy banners that flew in the wind, the Autumn fae emblem emblazoned on each one. The castle rose high above the treetops, perched right on the edge of a steep cliff as if overlooking the lands beyond like a watchdog.

Something inside me wanted to turn and ride in the opposite direction at the sight of it. But after the gates I'd passed through to get here, I had a feeling that leaving would be easier said than done.

Another shudder rippled through me. My power, tucked tightly away, strained with unease.

"I hope Grey Oak pleases you," Callan said.

I glanced at him, unsure how to respond. It was beautiful, yes. A sprawling fortress of stone and glass that gleamed in the evening light, its architecture was stunning, but there was a weight to it—a cold heaviness that made me feel small, even before we'd set foot inside.

"It's... breathtaking."

He smiled, but it didn't reach his eyes. "It's the pride of the Autumn Court. We've worked hard to keep it that way."

As we reached the front, doors opened, and servants appeared, each of them bowing deeply as we dismounted.

Standing before the main entrance, I swept my gaze over the immaculate grounds. The gardens were lush, filled with autumn blooms, the scent of oak and pine heavy in the air. No one was in sight beyond the servants. No courtiers, not even a gardener.

I turned back to Callan as he rattled off instructions to the servants about preparing rooms for me and finding me a maid.

"I don't need all that," I said, waving him off, but he scoffed.

"Nonsense. You're the future queen of two kingdoms. You need all that and more."

The servant closest to me, a female, widened her eyes, but she scurried off before Callan could notice.

He glanced at the warrior leathers I still wore and frowned. "We'll get you settled and freshened up. Find something proper for you to wear. I'm sure Father will be eager to meet you." He flashed a smile and offered his arm.

I took it, though I wasn't sure Duron would be eager about anything concerning my arrangement with Callan. Especially if it meant competing with Heliconia for his son's hand.

Inside the grand hall, the opulence of Grey Oak was immediately evident. Tapestries depicting legendary battles decorated the walls, their threads glinting gold and bronze in the torchlight. Paintings hung in gilded frames above rugs thick enough to sink my feet into.

Callan led me through a maze of halls. Finally, he stopped in front of a door and pushed it open. "Your room," he said. "What do you think?"

I stepped inside and couldn't help but gasp. The room was enormous, far larger than what I'd had at home. The high ceiling was supported by carved beams in an oak stain that matched the armoire.

A large bed, draped in silks and fur blankets, dominated the space, its carved posts intricate with fae designs—leaves and vines that seemed to pulse with magic. A fire already crackled in the hearth, casting warm, flickering light over the luxurious furnishings. Plush armchairs were arranged near the fire with more furs draped over their backs. I was sure it was all meant to be very inviting but instead left me with a chill. I rubbed my arms absently.

"It's... beautiful," I murmured, still taking it all in.

Callan chuckled at my wide-eyed reaction. "You'll grow accustomed to it. After all, this is your home now."

The word clanged through me, but even with my back turned, I refused to react.

I turned to find him watching me with that same easy smile, though his eyes gleamed with something more. He stepped closer, the warmth of his body sending a ripple of awareness through me. He reached up, brushing a stray lock of hair from my face with a tenderness that caught me off guard.

On the road, he'd kept his distance so much that I'd believed our arrangement would be in name only. But now, the way he was looking at me suggested he wanted much more from me than my name.

"I'm glad you're here, Aurelia," he said, his voice low. "That our paths crossed again cannot be coincidence."

His words were soft, almost intimate, as if we were the only two people in the world. He leaned in slightly, his breath warm against my skin, and for a heartbeat, I thought he might kiss me.

My pulse quickened as the space between us dwindled.

Behind him, a brisk knock sounded on the door before it

opened. Callan stepped back as a young maid stepped in, my bag in her hands. She took one look at us and lowered her head, eyes wide in horror.

"Apologies," she mumbled. "You sent for me, Your Highness."

"Come in," Callan told her. "You will serve Princess Aurelia from Sevanwinds—whatever she needs."

"Of course, Your Highness." She took a step forward, head still lowered as if bracing for a reprimand.

But Callan ignored her, saying to me, "I'll leave you to get dressed. My father will want to see you at dinner, and I'd hate for us to keep him waiting."

I nodded.

Callan hesitated at the door, his gaze lingering on me as if he was about to say something more. Instead, he flashed another one of those charming smiles. "I'll be back soon."

And with that, he was gone, the door closing behind him with a soft click.

I stood there for a moment, my mind racing. The luxury of the room suddenly felt stifling. I glanced at the bed, the thick rugs, the tapestries that seemed to watch me with their golden threads. It was beautiful—no question—but it wasn't home.

The maid finally lifted her head, studying me nervously. "Shall we prepare for dinner, Your Highness?"

I sighed. "I'm not sure we have a choice," I said, earning a flicker of surprise.

But she nodded and carried my bag to the wardrobe, pulling out the gowns I'd brought with me. I didn't miss the concern on her face as she studied the fabric that had once been the best coin could buy. Now, it was probably outdated, though hopefully, it would work for at least one night with the king.

No matter what deal I'd struck with Callan, the truth was

I needed the king's blessing to seal it. Callan hadn't said so, but I knew enough about royal politics to understand this dinner was so much more than an introduction. It was an interview.

A single chance for acceptance.

Without Duron's blessing over our alliance, I'd be tossed out on the street, alone in the realm against a dark army and its queen who would stop at nothing to destroy me. The truth was that I needed Autumn much more than they needed me. And I was willing to do a Hel of a lot to get what I needed.

The dress had to be right.

"What's your name?"

The maid looked up, startled. "Um, Vanya, Your Highness."

"Please, call me Aurelia."

"Oh, I couldn't possibly." Her cheeks heated, and she looked down at the dress.

But I pressed on, needing at least one friend in this dreary place. "The gown is a bit older, I know. Do you think it will work for dinner with the king?"

Vanya looked up. She searched my expression in what felt like some sort of silent interrogation then finally seemed to relax. "It's not a current fashion, but... I have some ideas," she said carefully.

I smiled encouragingly. "I'd love to hear them."

THE
MOON

Chapter Twenty-Four
Aurelia

The sun had set by the time Vanya finished helping me dress. A night sky brilliant with stars pressed in against the window, leaving a chill on the glass. The fire's warmth and light chased it away.

"Vanya, you're a genius," I declared as I studied my reflection in the mirror beside the armoire.

She ducked her head, her cheeks flushing. "Thanks."

In a short time, she'd transformed the gown into something even more beautiful. The bodice was made of silk stitched into lace, fitting my torso in flattering detail. The gauzy skirt swished but in an understated way. She'd even taken a few discarded beads and placed them on a headband she'd pressed into my upswept hair.

"A tiara for the princess," she'd said.

It was perfect.

"Wow, this makes me wish I'd brought more of my clothes from home," I said.

"Are the dressmakers in your court not very skilled then?" she asked.

I swallowed hard. "My court was cursed by Heliconia." I

ground the words out, knowing I'd have to say them soon enough to the king and anyone else I met after tonight. "They are bound in perpetual sleep."

Vanya looked stricken. "They never wake?"

"Not in seven years."

"And you escaped the curse?"

Her question was tentative, clearly not meant to offend. But it twisted the knife in my chest all the same. "The Aine helped," I said—because it wasn't a lie exactly.

Her forehead crinkled. "You still have Aine in your kingdom?"

"We did." My throat closed, and I changed the subject before the memory of Sonoma and the others cost me my control. "I came here to honor my original alliance with Autumn so they might help me free the Summer fae."

"Summer. But..." Her eyes widened. "It's a miracle from the Fates. Everyone thinks you're—" She stopped herself.

"Dead?" I finished for her. She winced in silent apology, but I offered her a smile. "Heliconia can't get rid of me that easily."

Vanya's expression softened. "You are brave to come here."

I looked away, unable to handle her pity. "You've been really helpful," I said, once again facing the mirror.

She took the hint and let it drop.

I watched while Vanya cleaned up the supplies she'd used on my dress, tucking everything into the armoire where my only other gown now hung. I went back to smoothing my skirt, studying my reflection as I braced myself for tonight's dinner.

A moment later, a soft knock echoed through my room, pulling me from my thoughts. Vanya answered it, and I turned just as Callan stepped inside.

The warmth in his gaze flickered with something unreadable as he studied me in the pale blue gown.

"You look beautiful."

I blinked at the compliment, the unexpected sincerity throwing me off guard. "Thank you," I murmured, glancing away to hide the slight flush that crept up my cheeks.

I was out of practice, that was all. When was the last time I'd been complimented? Or admired?

Callan stepped forward, offering his arm. "Come. My father is eager to meet you."

I hesitated before sliding my hand into the crook of his arm. There was a tension simmering just beneath his skin, but I couldn't tell if it was nerves or something else entirely.

"Are you nervous?" I asked as he led me from the room.

Callan chuckled softly, though the sound lacked its usual humor. "I'd be crazy not to be."

I looked up at him, searching his face. His eyes were darker tonight, the usual spark of amusement dulled by something more serious. "Do you think he'll be upset about our arrangement?"

He flashed a smile. "You just let me do the talking. Everything will work out."

Just like in the entryway, the walls around us were adorned with tapestries that depicted the Autumn fae's long rule through images of battles and thrones. Even in the beautifully sewn fabrics, the images portrayed a brutality I'd never witnessed in Summer's history. Some scenes offered glimpses into various magic-wielders, but most told a story of bloodied battlefields and sharpened swords. Not a single tapestry contained a female ruler—royalty or military.

"Any advice besides being seen and not heard?" I asked as we neared a set of double doors at the end of the hall.

Callan chuckled, completely ignoring my sarcasm. "Stop worrying. You're more than enough to impress my father."

"Let's hope that's true since I don't have much else to offer," I shot back.

A tight smile tugged at his lips, but it didn't reach his eyes.

The dining hall was dimly lit, the towering oak doors ahead of us standing like sentinels guarding a secret. Callan paused before them, turning to face me fully. For a moment, the weight of his gaze was enough to make my breath hitch, and I could feel the unspoken words lingering between us.

"If things don't go well tonight…" He hesitated, his hand reaching up as if to brush a stray lock of hair from my face but stopping just short. "I hope you know that I'm glad you're here."

Before I could respond, the heavy doors swung open, revealing the cavernous dining hall beyond. The edges of the room were wreathed in shadows that held movement and whispers—evidence that we were not alone. Only the middle of the space was well-lit by a chandelier that glowed with torchlight. And in the very center, seated at the head of a polished oak table, was the king.

Duron didn't bother to rise as we entered. His gaze—piercing and sharp as a hawk's—swept over me, assessing, calculating.

"Father," Callan said, his voice transforming into a more formal tone as we approached.

"You've returned from your little adventure, I see," Duron said. "And you did not return empty-handed."

"You're correct. May I present Aurelia, heir to the Summer Court."

Duron's eyes gleamed with hunger as they settled on me, and for a moment, I felt as though I were standing naked before him. Every secret I held, every doubt, every hope—it was as if he was attempting to dig it up and snatch it into his claws for whatever use he might have for it later.

I straightened my spine, forcing myself to meet his gaze head-on. And to keep him from taking anything I didn't willingly offer.

"Princess Aurelia," he said, scanning the length of me in a frank and crude assessment. "Alive and in the flesh. We thought the Summer Court lost years ago."

"And so they are, in a manner of speaking," I said, dipping my chin and bowing before looking up again.

He frowned. "And what manner is that, exactly?"

I tensed before shoving out the words that revealed my kingdom was vulnerable. "The Summer Court has been cursed with perpetual sleep by Heliconia. They do not wake, and they do not age. They are cursed to remain frozen while the rest of the realm moves on."

"All except you," he said, and beneath those words lurked the question.

"The Aine saved me," I said, the half-truth rolling off my tongue much more smoothly this time. "They created powerful wards, a protection against anyone who might see advantage or opportunity in the kingdom's current fate."

He showed no hint of surprise. He'd known already—at least about the wards.

"You honor us with your presence." Though his words were polite, there was a chill in them, a subtle undercurrent to match my own.

"The honor is mine, Your Majesty," I replied, dipping into a curtsy as gracefully as I could manage despite the tension coursing through my veins.

The king nodded but said nothing more as Callan led me to the second chair on the king's right. Mercifully, Callan took the empty seat between us, and the meal was served.

Servants appeared, somber and silent as they brought dish after dish. Roast pheasant and chicken, garlic-crusted groun-quail, baked summer potatoes, butter-smothered beans, and corn. It was delicious—or would've been if I could taste it. But I took bite after bite without noticing a single flavor, thanks to the nerves that gripped me.

The king ate in silence—a sound I'd grown all too practiced with. Except that, this sort of quiet was full of threats. I could feel them sinking their claws into my skin—whispering their dangers in my ears.

Finally, Duron set his fork aside and picked up his wine. Over the rim of his glass, he said, "I am told my son has brought you here under the pretense of an engagement."

I started to answer, but Callan cut me off.

"No pretense, Father. I intend to honor my word."

The king's eyes narrowed. "You are making promises for your king now?"

"Of course not. But Aurelia and I once agreed on a marriage alliance, and now that she's been returned to me, that alliance stands," Callan said. His words were careful, his tone deceivingly light.

"And this alliance—does it come with an army to aid us? Or will all her subjects serve their crown from the comfort of their pillows?"

My hand tightened on my napkin.

Callan's expression was somber. "Aurelia's kingdom needs our help, Father."

"What about what we need?" Duron growled. "Or have you lost all sense of loyalty to your own crown?"

Callan frowned. "Of course not. I am doing this for our people. Once the curse is broken, we will have the strength of two kingdoms behind us."

"And who exactly is going to break this curse?"

Callan looked at me. "Aurelia and I will find a way."

I see," the king said so sharply that I nearly winced. "And does either one of you have a plan to accomplish this task?"

I met his gaze evenly, the words tumbling out vehemently. "I intend to do whatever it takes to break the curse and take my vengeance on the one who cast it. My contribution to this alliance is being willing to drain myself of everything the Fates gifted me with if that's what it takes to bring Heliconia to her knees."

The king raised an eyebrow, clearly intrigued. "And what kind of magic do those gifts include, exactly?"

I blinked, realizing too late I'd opened myself up. "I wield the same power as my father."

It wasn't a lie.

The king leaned back in his chair. "I see."

His gaze flicked to Callan beside me, some sort of silent exchange passing between them. Callan's hand rested lightly on my arm, a steady presence amid the tension swirling around us—and a gesture the king didn't miss. Duron's mouth quirked up like he was somehow pleased Callan was being so affectionate with me.

"We are sympathetic to the fate of your king and queen," Duron said, at last looking back at me. The sorrow in his eyes went just deep enough to make his words seem sincere. In this moment, I could see where Callan got his charm, false as it was.

"My son is right," Duron went on. "A promise is meant to be kept. We will aid you in whatever way we can to end this curse. And we welcome you into the Autumn Court—your new home."

Callan exhaled.

I forced a smile. "Thank you for your support."

"Of course. Callan will provide you with whatever you need." He waved a hand, offering up riches and resources as if they were nothing but air. "And we'll throw a party the likes of which the courts have never seen."

"You don't have to do that—"

"Of course we do," he snapped, silencing me. "We are the light of the realm. Our unwavering strength is our greatest defense against the blight of the Winter Queen. We'll throw a party where you will swear yourselves to one another before every court in Menryth." He looked at Callan, eyes glittering. "This will be the first of many alliances to come."

Then he signaled for more wine, and that was clearly the end of our negotiation.

"Aren't you hungry?" Callan asked a moment later.

"The chicken is particularly good," Duron said before I could answer. "You have our thanks for the contribution."

I frowned. "My contribution?"

"You brought them with you, did you not?" Duron asked, confusion marring his thick brow.

Callan's bright expression faltered.

Realization bloomed like a poison in my gut. I nodded, forcing my expression to remain neutral. "I did."

Duron grunted and went back to his food. But I caught the cruel enjoyment on his face before he lowered it for another bite.

I forced myself to eat the chicken, but I didn't let my guard down. Not an inch.

Whatever the king wanted from this alliance, it wasn't just about politics or power. There was something more, something I had yet to fully understand. Rydian's warning echoed in my mind, but I shoved it back. I had the prophecy on my side—and the power of the Fates inside me. If anyone was going to be used, it was the Autumn King.

THE
MOON

Chapter Twenty-Five
Rydian

The quiet just before dawn was a different kind of silence. The kind that didn't settle but prowled. The kind that made you feel like the world held its breath, waiting for something to break or bleed.

I'd done both for this wretched place, and I'd do both again before it was done. But for now, I'd earned a reprieve. Just as soon as I delivered this particular report to the asshole who'd sired me.

He wasn't going to be happy, but then I didn't much fucking care what made the bastard happy. No, that was a lie. I cared very much about making sure he never got his hands on the things that made him happy ever again.

Unbidden, thoughts of my mother sprang to mind. I shoved them back, reminding myself she was safe. And as long as I played my part, she would remain that way.

A life for a life.

Wasn't that what the old man had demanded? Until either his or mine ended, I was bound by blood to the monster on this throne. My only hope for a future for the people of

Autumn was my half-brother, and I'd grown weary of such hope over these last years.

Today, I was in no mood to deal with the bratty heir.

I might've put off coming at all if Duron had been content to wait. But I already knew the bastard would summon me—probably the moment my head hit the pillow. Best to get it over with and be done with him. With any luck, he'd send me on a mission that would take me far away from this place again soon. Hopefully, not before I got some decent sleep, though. After saving Callan's reckless neck on the journey here then doubling back, I was exhausted.

We all were.

I'd left Slade and Daegel at the house and come alone to give my report. Now, I moved through the castle grounds unseen, shadows shifting in my wake. Some of them were my own. Some belonged to other creatures Duron employed here.

They would alert him to my arrival soon enough. And then he'd let me wait until after he'd eaten his breakfast before summoning me to him.

The sound of steel rang out in the stable yard, yanking me from my dark musings. I tensed, changing course to follow it. Beside me stood a small barracks area that was mostly used for the duty watch. The training arena on the far side was rarely occupied at this time of morning since most of the guards were still on duty or hadn't arrived yet.

Whoever was in that ring wasn't supposed to be there.

On full alert, I clung to the shadows as I made my way toward the sound of a sword striking its target.

When I spotted the lone figure, I stopped and stared.

She stood in the center of the arena, bathed in the gray glow of pre-dawn, her sword slicing through the air in practiced arcs. The light caught on her hair, a waterfall of gold spilling over her shoulders. Her movements were sharp, precise —but not flawless. There was frustration in the way she swung, as though the blade in her hand was an argument she intended to win.

Aurelia.

I should've left her alone. She wasn't my concern. For better or worse, her destiny was her own. But my gaze stayed locked on her, drawn to the determination in her expression, the tension coiled in her slender frame. She didn't belong here, not in the politics and brutality of Grey Oak. Not in the gilded cage of royal life. But she would bind herself to it anyway, as if duty could smother the fire I saw in her now.

That sacrifice alone proved how much she'd changed since we'd first met. And I found myself hating the gods for requiring it of her.

A misstep. Her sword caught awkwardly, and she cursed under her breath.

"You're lunging too soon."

The words slipped out before I could stop them.

She spun, her blade raised, those pale blue eyes finding me in an instant. For a moment, she froze, recognition flaring then narrowing into something harder. Suspicion.

"You," she said, the word an accusation. She lowered her sword only slightly, as if she thought I might attack at any moment. "Where have you been?"

I lifted myself over the railing and into the arena. "Out."

"Out?" Her tone cut like steel. "Is that what you call running off to do Callan's bidding?"

I smirked, though the expression felt like a mask I didn't care to wear. "Did you miss me, Furious?"

She stiffened. "Don't call me that."

"Why not? It fits perfectly. Every time I see you, you look absolutely irate."

Her jaw tightened, the faintest flush rising in her cheeks. Good. She was easier to deal with when she was angry.

"You didn't come back just to criticize my technique," she said, her voice cold now.

I let my eyes flick to the sword in her hand then back to her face. "No. But it needs work."

Her grip tightened on the hilt, the faint tremor betraying the effort it took to keep herself from aiming the blade at me. I bit back a grin.

"What are you doing here?" she demanded.

"Checking on the crown's jewel. Making sure you're settling into royal life once again."

She flinched, just barely, but her glare could've set fire to the air between us. "Is that what this is? A welfare check?"

I stepped closer, watching as her stance stiffened in response. "Call it... curiosity."

"As you can see, royal life leaves me a bit bored," she said, gesturing to the sword in her hand.

I didn't tell her the sword suited her better than a crown anyway. Nor did I let myself think of her at that party so long ago. The way she'd looked in that dress...I'd hated her then. For so many reasons that no longer mattered or were even remotely true.

I hated her now—or I was desperately trying to.

"It's also made you soft," I said because it would infuriate her. Her eyes flashed as I'd known they would. I couldn't help enjoying her temper and the way it always seemed to light her up so completely. But I also knew she'd need the power that came with it.

Her lips parted in a snarl as she started to reply, but I cut her off. "Tell me, Furious, what kind of protection are you using to guard your lands now?"

"That's none of your business."

"I hope it's stronger than whatever you had before. Given what's coming."

The fire in her eyes banked to a deadly glow. Good. She

understood the weight of my words after all. "And what do you know about what's coming?"

More than I should, but I wasn't about to tell her that. Instead, I asked, "How is that alliance coming along? Has Callan proven to be the key to Heliconia's demise yet?"

Her chin lifted. "My relationship with Callan is none of your concern."

Rage streaked through me. "Is that what this is? You and he are in a relationship now?"

Her smugness slipped as she asked, "Would you care if we were?"

I frowned, refusing to admit that I cared a Hel of a lot more than I had a right to. "I care about stopping the dark queen." I made myself shrug. "If a relationship with my brother helps make that happen, so be it."

She dropped her eyes but not before I saw the disappointment that flashed.

Fuck.

"Autumn's army is the only one large enough to stand a chance," she said.

"An army won't break that curse."

"What do you know about breaking curses?" she shot back.

"I know the only way to fight fire is with fire."

She shifted uncomfortably. "I don't know what you—"

"Where did you get that mark?"

Her hand shot to her throat, covering the ink I'd just seen as she'd angled herself away from me. Even with her hand covering it, I couldn't help but stare. Knowing she'd survived that death blow seven years ago was one thing. And I'd seen enough proof since then to stop doubting what she was. But the sight of that mark left me shaken.

How had I missed it before?

"It's a private joke," she said, adjusting her hair to cover the tattoo. "Between me and my teacher." Her lie wasn't even remotely believable.

"It's a rune."

Her eyes met mine, the pale blue blazing with curiosity. "What kind of rune?"

"Vorinthian."

Something flared in her. Acknowledgment. She knew something about that damned mark. But she said only, "Vorinthia hasn't existed for a thousand years."

I hesitated, knowing if I pushed her now, it could backfire. But if she bore that mark, she deserved to know where it came from. "What do you know about the Midnight Court?"

Her laugh was bitter, humorless. "For one thing, they're cowards."

My hands clenched at my sides, anger curling in my chest. "Why would you say that?"

She made a sound of disgust. "When Heliconia invaded Concordia, they refused to help. Entire mountain villages— women, children, elderly—all slaughtered because the midnight fae couldn't be bothered to care about anything beyond their own borders."

Anger coiled tighter, but I forced it down, shoving it beneath the mask. "You know nothing about the people of that court or their reasons, and yet you judge them so absolutely."

"What reason could possibly be good enough to do nothing while innocents are killed on your own doorstep?"

I shrugged. "What reason do you have to sell your soul to Duron?"

Her breath caught before she spat, "Go to Hel."

The corner of my mouth tugged into a dark grin. I stepped closer still, closing the space between us until the faintest scent of roses reached me. It made my voice low, rough. "Sweetheart, I'm already there."

She didn't move, didn't blink. Just stared at me with those blazing eyes, daring me to say more. I had the distinct impression that, if I tried, she'd run me through with her blade and smile while doing it.

But then she turned, her sword flashing as she resumed her training, each swing more precise, more determined than before.

I stayed a moment longer, watching her, then slipped back into the shadows where I belonged.

THE
MOON

CHAPTER TWENTY-SIX
AURELIA

For the next three days, I met with the dressmaker, the royal jeweler, a stylist, a wedding planner, a party planner, and four different candidates for the position of second maid—despite my protests about even needing the latter. Vanya quickly became a welcome source of help as I navigated each appointment, especially since I barely saw Callan at all.

He'd been distant since that dinner with Duron, claiming he was busy with meetings involving the strategists and captains who guarded Autumn's borders in the north.

"Heliconia won't like being rejected," Callan told me after dinner that night. "And she's bound to learn the identity of the one I've chosen instead. We need to protect ourselves. And you," he had added hastily.

"We should go see that oracle you mentioned," I'd suggested.

"Of course," he'd assured me. "As soon as you're settled in."

And while I'd left that dinner more determined than ever

to get to work on breaking the curse, three full days of being pampered and cared for and fully entrenched in the administrative duties that came with being royal had derailed me.

I'd forgotten what it was like to be a full-time princess. And even though Rydian's accusation had gotten under my skin, I couldn't help enjoying meals I didn't have to cook myself, walks in the garden in the afternoon, and basically any day that I didn't have to worry about the wards being breached or an Obsidian jumping out at me.

My thoughts drifted constantly to Sonoma—to everything she'd told me before she'd crossed over. To Rydian's cryptic remarks about my tattoo. A rune. From the same lost and fallen kingdom Amanti had suspected held precious answers, no less. I thought of Lesha and Amanti, who'd gone to Vorinthia to look for signs of magic and maybe found their own horrible end in the process. And sometimes to Lilah, though that hurt too much to think about for long. I owed them more than sitting around playing pampered princess.

I trained alone every morning at dawn. I told myself it was out of responsibility to the people counting on me and not because I was hoping to glimpse a certain second-born prince again. I'd half-expected him to interrupt me again. Twice, I'd sworn the shadows that gathered in the pre-dawn light were his, but three days passed, and he didn't make another appearance.

Even so, I kept the door on my magic firmly shut.

At dinner the third night, which I ate alone in my room, I'd had enough sitting around. Heliconia knew I'd survived. She was out there, likely plotting her second attempt to kill me. And she was clearly getting stronger if the last batch of Obsidians were any indication.

I couldn't afford to waste any more time.

I found Callan in the council chambers, pouring over

maps with several of his advisors. Their discussion fell silent as I entered.

Callan straightened immediately, his sharp gaze flashing with impatience. He hid it away quickly. "Darling," he greeted, stepping away from the table. "Is everything all right?"

"Everything's fine. Can I speak with you privately?"

"Can it wait? I'm afraid we're in the middle of something here."

"No."

Callan blinked. Clearly, his question had been rhetorical.

"I need to make arrangements to travel," I said with all the authority I could muster.

"Travel?" Callan asked, alarmed. "Where?"

The advisors behind him scowled, one of them glaring at me with outright hostility.

"I have a lead on a place that could provide clues about my kingdom's curse," I said, refusing to give up the information to these strangers. "You said you'd help me—"

"And I will," Callan said sharply. He relaxed and tried again. "Aurelia, you can't think we'd be able to put together a trip before we've said our vows."

What he said made logical sense, but I heard the dismissiveness and bit back my own angry reply. Pasting on a smile, I said, "Of course. We'll wait to travel until after the ceremony. In the meantime, we should visit the city. I'd like to see more of Grey Oak. Get to know the people I am to rule."

The advisors frowned, and I couldn't help the satisfaction it gave me. Yes, I would be ruling them someday, and I wanted them to remember it. Even in these moments where Callan opted to treat me like a foreign visitor and a nuisance rather than his future wife and queen.

Callan's expression didn't falter, but something flashed behind his golden eyes. "It's dangerous beyond the castle walls right now. There's been unrest in the city. I wouldn't want to put you in harm's way."

"What kind of unrest?"

"Nothing for you to worry about," Callan said.

I waited for him to explain further, but he seemed content to leave it there. And to leave me to my own devices if the last three days were any indication. Something in me strained at the idea of being kept from the outside world. I thought of the heavily guarded gate that stood between me and freedom, and urgency clawed at me to get through it to the other side.

"I understand," I replied, keeping my tone naïvely simple. "But I won't be a proper queen if I don't know the realm I'm meant to rule. I need to see them—*our* people."

He glanced at his advisors, still hesitating, and I realized it was Duron holding the leash now. Callan was only enforcing it. Ugh. More cowardice.

My gaze held his, a challenge woven into my words, one I knew he wouldn't be able to resist. "I trust, as a general and a prince, you are more than capable of keeping me safe."

I watched his ego war with whatever orders he'd been given. Finally, he nodded. "We'll go after lunch tomorrow."

I exhaled softly in relief, a grateful smile masking my triumph. "Thank you." I turned to go.

"Oh, Aurelia," Callan said, and I turned back. "My father has set the date for our vow ceremony. Two weeks from today."

Alarm speared through me. "That soon?"

"We can't afford to waste time with the stakes so high, don't you think?"

I didn't answer.

Of course the stakes were high. That was the problem. Heliconia wasn't going to sit idly by and let Callan marry someone else.

"Don't you think we'll need more time to prepare for battle?" I asked.

"That's what the party is for," Callan said, brows crinkling. "We've invited every court in the realm. They'll see our alliance makes us strong, and they'll ally with us."

"You don't think Heliconia will use the party to attack?"

She'd done it with the last one. But, of course, Callan had no memory of that.

"Heliconia wouldn't dare attempt to cross our borders," one of the advisors said. He was the meanest looking of the bunch. And he made no attempt to hide his disdain for me. "She is no match for our army or the king's guard."

"She is more than a match," I said, my voice rising. "As she proved the night she attacked my people—and won."

"The Summer Court has always been weak," he spat. "Heliconia proved nothing with her destruction of the powerless. Let her try it here." Magic sparked from his hands, and I shook my head, realizing he meant for me to be intimidated.

But I'd already seen real power, and it wasn't in this room.

Neither was common sense, apparently.

I turned to Callan. "I do hope, for all our sakes, your reputation for battle strategy has not been overstated."

Callan opened his mouth to speak, but another of the advisors cut him off. "None of this is your concern, Your Highness." The way he said my title dripped with insult. I met his stare, unflinching as he added, "Why don't you leave Heliconia to us and get back to your gowns and tea."

Anger slashed through me but I refused to waste any more breaths on these fools. They'd see soon enough what Heliconia was capable of.

Even though they deserved it, the thought of her coming here and doing what she'd done to my own people made it hard to breathe. I looked at Callan, who hadn't said a word on my behalf.

Rather than apologize or give an inch, he flashed that weaponized smile at me. "I'll see you tomorrow."

"See you then." I gave myself a pat on the back for not burning them all to ash.

Thirty minutes later, Vanya showed me to the royal library but only after I convinced her Callan had approved the idea. When we arrived, I scanned the high-ceilinged room that was mostly taken up by cozy seating areas and a large writing desk. The space was twice the size of the one I'd left behind in Sunspire but with only half as many books.

I swallowed down my disappointment, determined to see this through. The Obsidian had said my alliance with the prince was the key. But if Callan himself was going to be a complete idiot, then maybe his resources would prove to be what I needed.

It was worth a shot.

"Thank you, Vanya," I said. "I can find my own way back."

With a hesitant nod, she left me alone.

On a sigh, I headed for the stacks and began my search for anything helpful. From the looks of it, Duron's collection veered mostly toward Autumn's historical accounts. Wars, births, marriages—the king was clearly more entertained by his own kingdom's chronology than that of any of the others. There was nothing on ancient runes, Vorinthian or otherwise.

I'd nearly given up when I found a small section on foreign customs in the back. It looked untouched and forgotten, judging by the layer of dust that coated the shelves. But there were texts for each court and kingdom in Menryth.

Pulling a dusty volume marked simply *Vorinth* off the shelf, I cracked the spine and inhaled the scent of old parchment. Along with the familiar scent, memories slammed into me. Nights by the fire in Sunspire, scanning book after book with Lesha, trying to find some clue about the curse's origins. The ache of loss was a physical pain. My eyes blurred with hot tears that fell too quickly to blink them away.

I wiped my cheeks and forced myself to refocus. None of that would bring Lesha back.

All I could do was look ahead.

I scanned the pages quickly as I flipped through them.

"An interesting choice," said a deep voice behind me.

I whirled, nearly dropping the book as my heart threatened to shove through my chest.

Rydian stood smirking at me.

"You scared me half to death," I snapped, taking a deep breath and willing my pulse to settle.

His expression fell, and he ate up the distance between us in three strides. "What happened?" The concern in his face bordered on violence. When I didn't answer quickly enough, he gripped my elbow, pressing me back against the bookshelf. "Tell me. Is it Callan? Or did Duron hurt you?"

"No one hurt me," I assured him.

Shadows leaped from his skin. "Don't lie to me, Furious."

"I'm not lying. I just... I was thinking of home."

The nightmare in his eyes winked out. In its wake, a softness remained that left me strangely off balance. There was nothing soft about Rydian Nytherra. Anything that suggested otherwise was not to be trusted.

"What are you doing here?" I asked before he could do something even more off-putting like be nice to me.

He gestured to the shelves around us. "I'd think that answer was obvious."

"You're here for a book?"

"Is that so hard to believe?"

"Yes," I said with enough frankness that his eyes narrowed.

But I refused to believe this beautifully deadly male wanted a good book to pass the afternoon. Besides, he didn't live here at Grey Oak Castle, and he clearly didn't hang out here voluntarily. So, if he was here, it wasn't by choice.

That left being here on purpose. Either to see Duron or Callan. Or me.

"Or maybe you snuck up on me on purpose," I said.

He didn't look the least bit sorry as he said, "Or maybe you should pay more attention to your surroundings."

All traces of that softness were officially gone. At least, I knew how to handle him this way. Hating each other felt like solid ground at this point.

I glared at him, clutching the book to my chest and stalking past him on my way to the desk. I purposely shoved my shoulder against his, planning to ignore him until he left. But he shot a hand out, wrapping it around my arm.

I stopped, breathless at his touch. When I twisted to face him, his dark eyes raged with a storm I didn't understand.

"Is this what you sold your soul for?" he asked quietly. "A library?"

I wrenched my arm out of his grasp, my eyes narrowing. I couldn't help but notice the way his hair fell over his forehead, so long it nearly covered his brow. Suddenly, I found myself fighting the urge to reach up and swipe it away.

Instead, I gripped the book harder.

"I'm looking for answers," I said in a low voice. "For a way to save my people and stop Heliconia once and for all. What are you doing besides skulking around like Autumn's little errand boy?"

"If you want answers, maybe try the volume about the Furiosities and their power."

I went perfectly still. "Why would I do that?"

His brows rose. "Isn't that where her power comes from?"

I blew out a breath. He meant Heliconia. "Right."

But that wasn't the entire reason for his comment. Not after what he'd said to me at camp the other day. He knew what magic I had. And something told me he knew where it had come from.

"Whatever you think you know about me—"

"I know more than I care to."

I gripped the book tighter. "What's that supposed to mean?"

"How exactly did you manage to ward your castle so securely?"

That question again. I was starting to think Rydian only ever asked questions he already knew the answer to. Fuck. "I told you, that's none of your business."

He studied me, and I forced myself not to look away. "For seven years," he said quietly, "I looked for a way to break through the wards the Aine held around your castle. I searched every kingdom, interrogated, hunted, bribed—and I never found a way to unseal your borders. But this new magic is something else entirely. I've never felt anything remotely as powerful. And I've encountered some pretty otherworldly beings."

He paused, waiting for me to say something.

I didn't, and he went on. "I went back and stood where the castle should be. In the very same spot, in fact, as that rooftop where we met seven years ago. But there's only grass, brown for the winter. It's like Sunspire was never there at all."

I stared at him, surprised. "Why?" I blurted. "Why did you try for so long to break through?"

Especially when no one else did.

The look in his eyes turned anguished. "Because your scream was the last thing I heard that night. I couldn't get the sound of it out of my head."

"You were still there?" I asked. "When she... I thought you'd gone."

"I was there. Just not close enough," he said bitterly.

"But you remember," I couldn't help pressing. "You have a memory of the attack. And of...leaving?"

He looked at me like I'd lost it. I couldn't blame him. "Of course." I watched as suspicion overtook confusion. "Why shouldn't I remember?"

"No reason," I said quickly. "I only thought... the magic she used that night left me disoriented for a while."

"Is that why you broke your engagement with Callan then hid away inside those walls for so long?"

So, we were back to baseless accusations then. "I did what I had to do to protect my family. What do you know about that kind of sacrifice?"

His laugh was harsh and humorless. "More than you could possibly comprehend."

"I highly doubt that," I tossed back.

His eyes narrowed to slits. He looked like he was about to unleash some tirade, but then, just as quickly, the fire winked out. "Happy reading, Furious."

He moved to leave, and my own frustration bubbled up.

Using his own move from earlier, I grabbed his arm. My skin hummed at the contact, and when he rounded on me, lightning flashed in his eyes.

Instead of pulling away, he crowded in close.

I took a step back then another until he had me backed against the bookshelf. He leaned down until his face was a breath from mine.

"Careful, Furious," he crooned. "If you put your hands on me, I expect you to make it count."

His words conjured images of doing exactly that. Pushing onto my toes and kissing him. Sliding his tunic over his head. Running my hands over the hard planes of his torso—

I blinked and refocused on the sight of his cocky smirk and challenging stare. He was baiting me. Calling my bluff.

I'd had enough.

Making a fist, I drove it into his ribs hard enough that he grunted.

"Does that count?" I asked sweetly.

Without waiting for an answer, I stalked off.

THE
MOON

Chapter Twenty-Seven
Aurelia

Callan came for me right after lunch as promised. I'd eaten in my room as I'd done every day since arriving. No one had invited me to dine elsewhere, and I wasn't exactly antsy for another chance to share a meal with Duron, so I'd accepted the tray without complaint.

Vanya was carrying it out when Callan appeared.

"Afternoon," he said with a smile that held no trace of the strain from yesterday. "How'd it go with the interviews?" he asked. "Did you find a suitable second maid?"

"I don't see why I need two," I said again.

He shrugged. "My father insisted. It's royal protocol, apparently."

I frowned. Protocol or another form of control?

He pushed off the door frame. "I'll take care of it if you don't want to bother."

"Fine," I said, stifling a yawn.

I'd stayed up late, reading the book about Vorinth—which, it turned out, had been the capital city of the Calidium Empire some fifteen hundred years ago. I hadn't found anything that seemed useful in curse-breaking, and nothing about runes, but even worse, I'd found myself re-reading entire paragraphs after my mind inevitably wandered back to Rydian.

I hated him for hating me.

And I couldn't stop thinking about touching him.

"Ready to go?" Callan asked, yanking me from my thoughts.

"Yes," I said with enough enthusiasm that I earned a wry smile.

"Eager to get out of here?" he teased.

I bit my lip, unsure how to answer that, but he just laughed. "Believe me, I know how you feel."

He led me out of the castle where I found a waiting carriage and a full entourage of armed men.

"Is this really necessary?" I asked.

"Better to be safe," he said as he helped me into the carriage.

We rode side by side, our legs pressing against one another as the carriage bumped down the road. When we passed through the gate, Callan exhaled.

I found myself doing the same.

"You look nice today," he said.

"Thank you. The dressmaker did a good job."

He winked. "She had a beautiful canvas to work with."

We hit a bump hard enough to jostle me nearly out of my seat. Callan caught me, bracing me with his hands as he laughed. "We are in sorry need of road repairs after the last rainy season."

"Maybe it would've been better on horseback after all," I said, straightening.

"If we were on horseback, I couldn't do this." Callan slid his hand down my arm and laced his fingers through mine.

I went still, too surprised to pull away. His hand was warm and not altogether terrible. More... strange. I stared at our joined hands, wondering when last I'd been touched like this.

Lesha had hugged me before she left. And Sonoma—

No. I wasn't going to think about her right now.

"We're nearly there." Callan's voice called me back, and I peered through the small window as the first glimpse of the city of Grey Oak came into view.

I drank it in, hungry for the sight of people. But then the guards pressed in tightly around our carriage, and the view was lost.

I sat back.

Callan squeezed my hand.

Finally, the carriage pulled to a stop.

The door opened, and Callan released me long enough to climb out. He reached back for my hand, and I gave it to him, stepping into the crisp sunshine. Rows of upscale shops greeted me, their window displays dripping with luxury and jewels.

The street was empty of traffic, which I found surprising, considering all the shopping choices. It took me a moment to realize our armed escorts had blocked off the road in both directions to accommodate us.

"Where are we?" I asked, noting the wariness in the soldiers' expressions. They were truly worried for us. Callan's warning about unrest must've been warranted. It made me wish I'd strapped a sword to my body, though I wasn't sure it would've been possible given all the layers of this gown. I'd forgotten how exposed it felt to travel without a weapon.

"We're in a shopping district in the heart of the city," Callan said. "Is something wrong?"

"Actually, I wondered if we could go meet the oracle you told me about."

His eyes flashed once then sparkled again. There and gone so quickly, but I was learning how to read Callan like a book.

He was angry. "Of course. We'll go there next. There's a jewelry shop nearby I thought you might like."

A jewelry shop? "I thought we were going to meet the people of your kingdom."

He lifted a brow. "Isn't the jeweler part of my kingdom?"

"Fine," I agreed grudgingly then pulled up short, the reality only just now dawning on me. "I don't have any coin."

He laughed. "Relax, darling. You have a walking treasure chest at your side."

I didn't have time to protest before he pulled me onto the sidewalk and down the street.

The city of Grey Oak reminded me, at first, of Rosewood. The streets beyond the guards' perimeter were lively enough with fae coming and going in all directions, but the vibrancy I remembered from my own city—the light, the magic—was missing. There was an air of forced cheerfulness, and the few fae I spotted beyond the blockade bowed their heads too quickly, their smiles too brief. It all felt... muted.

Callan kept a measured pace beside me, darting glances into alleyways as we passed them. Up ahead, our escorts carefully cleared the way, and more soldiers flanked us at a distance, but I could sense the tension in their movements too.

"Here we are," Callan said, gesturing to a small boutique with a window display of jewels that shone in the sunlight.

He gripped my elbow as he guided me into the shop.

Inside, the shopkeeper—a hunched old man with graying hair—greeted us from behind the glass counter with a bow so deep it seemed painful.

"Your Highnesses," he said, his voice rasping as he rose. "It's an honor. Truly."

Callan smiled that perfect, courtly smile and gestured to the displays. "We've come to see the pieces you've prepared for Princess Aurelia."

The shopkeeper nodded eagerly, moving quickly to bring

out a tray of intricate necklaces and bracelets. I stepped closer, admiring the craftsmanship, but it was the shopkeeper's pale, trembling hands that held my attention.

"These are beautiful," I said, touching one of the necklaces lightly. "How long have you been crafting jewelry?"

"Oh, nearly sixty years now, Your Highness," the shopkeeper replied, his tone polite but strained. "Though... it's not as easy as it once was."

I frowned. "What do you mean?"

The shopkeeper hesitated, his eyes darting to Callan before he looked back at me. "I used to weave enchantments into the stones, into the metal, but ever since the donations—"

"Enough," Callan said sharply, stepping forward, his hand closing around my arm with more pressure than necessary. "Why don't you wander a bit while I have him wrap something up for you? It'll be a surprise engagement gift."

I pulled my arm free, glaring.

The shopkeeper hung his head, refusing to look at either of us, and something inside me snapped.

"No, thanks," I said flatly.

The shopkeeper's head lifted just enough for me to spot the fear and regret. "I-I'm sorry, Your Highness. I meant no disrespect."

"Silence," Callan roared at him.

The male flinched back, cowering.

"Don't speak to him like that," I said just as a crash echoed from the street, followed by shouting.

The shop door flew open, and a group of cloaked strangers barged in, their faces hidden beneath baggy, black hoods.

"Free the land, free the fae!" one of them shouted, and everything descended into chaos.

"Stop the donations," a second one yelled.

Callan was in front of me instantly, shielding me with his body as the cloaked strangers surged forward. "Stay behind me," he ordered me, his voice nearly as cold and commanding as it'd been with the jeweler.

The hooded strangers drew swords, and my breath caught. "Give me a blade," I hissed at Callan.

He ignored me.

I looked around, trying to find something I could use as a weapon. Before I could find anything beyond useless baubles, the strangers attacked.

Shelves crashed over, and beads and chains went flying. The shopkeeper cried out then disappeared through a doorway behind the counter. I debated going after him to make sure he stayed safe, but Callan lunged sloppily to block one of the attackers, and I turned my attention to not getting stabbed.

I felt naked without a blade or magic to wield, relying entirely on my quick footwork to remain unharmed. Callan stumbled and grunted and stabbed his way down the narrow aisle. I watched, confused and horrified. He had the basics down, but he looked nothing like the vicious and cunning war general the stories claimed.

Twice, I shoved him aside to help him avoid being skewered.

"Stay back," he roared at me in place of thanks.

Another Autumn soldier stumbled into me, separating me from Callan. My magic strained to be unleashed, but I held it back. Through the window, I saw three more cloaked figures rushing to the shop.

Callan must've seen them too.

"Take her out the back," he yelled.

One of the soldiers grabbed me and ushered me around the counter and through the door the shopkeeper had used.

"Hurry," the soldier urged.

The voice was familiar. I glanced back.

Fletcher.

"Go!" He practically shoved to keep me moving.

I raced through a storeroom and out the back door into a narrow alley, my breath coming fast as I tried to get my bearings in a foreign place.

"Get to the—" Fletcher's order abruptly went silent.

I turned as the young soldier suddenly lurched to a stop in the open doorway. He took a breath and straightened, all the color gone from his face. A short blade was buried in his hip.

"Don't pull it out," I said when he reached for it.

He let his hand drop.

A snarl sounded behind him.

He glanced over his shoulder, expression strained.

"Find a place to hide. Wait for me," he said quickly then slammed the door shut—sealing me out, alone. Inside the storeroom, swords were clanging.

Seven Hels.

I spun around to face the alley again and saw a cloaked figure standing at its mouth. The hood had been pulled up too far to see their face, but judging from the crooked blade they held, I had a feeling they weren't here to be friends.

I took a step back, glancing around for some sort of weapon. Empty cartons littered the alley along with bags of trash that turned my stomach with their wretched smell. But nothing I could use to defend myself.

The cloaked figure stalked forward. I kept my eyes on the hood—straining to see what lay inside it. But darkness obscured the face of the stranger.

Or maybe magic.

Something *other* clung to it, though I couldn't sense what.

The figure stopped several paces in front of me. It sniffed the air between us. Then, a raspy female voice said, "You're the Summer Court heir."

"I'm not your enemy," I replied.

"You're engaged to the Autumn Prince?"

I hesitated, but lying was pointless. "Yes."

"Then you are my enemy now."

She lifted the blade. Left with no choice, I reached for my furyfire, but she suddenly jolted. Her knees seemed to buckle, and then she fell.

Behind her stood Rydian, his dark gaze glittering with depthless, burning wrath. "She is not yours to claim," he snarled at the fallen fae, for all the good it did.

She was already dead.

THE
MOON

"**A**re you hurt?" Rydian asked, more anger flashing in his dark gaze as he scanned my length.

"No."

He met my eyes again and snarled as if finding me in one piece was somehow disappointing. To be fair, I *had* punched him in the stomach the last time we were together. I was probably lucky he wasn't the one trying to do me in today.

"What are you doing here?" I demanded.

On the main road, someone screamed.

I flinched, glancing toward the mouth of the alley then back at the male before me. Something told me, if any more of those rebels found their way into this alley, Rydian would be their death.

"More will come," I said, and my words seemed to snap him from whatever rage-spiral he'd descended into.

"You can't be here," he said. "Come with me."

Before I could protest, his hand closed around mine, and despite the danger around us, a jolt of heat shot through me. My thoughts jumbled. I nearly forgot what we were doing, but another scream brought me back.

"Hurry up." Rydian tugged my hand—hard.

Instead of running for the street, he pulled me toward the back corner. I resisted, positive he was leading me into a dead end, but then he rounded the jutting corner and angled his body to slip through a narrow opening between two walls. He pulled me through behind him, and then we ran—racing through the maze of alleyways, his grip firm and steady, until we emerged onto an empty street with narrow townhomes on each side.

It was quiet here, cut off from the chaos we'd left behind. And almost charming with the tree-lined street and the leaves swirling along the pathway as the small breeze swept them up.

Finally, we stopped, and Rydian released my hand, both of us breathing hard. I had the most ridiculous urge to grab his hand again—to find a steadiness in his touch, an anchor in the middle of this fucked-up storm my life had become. I squeezed my hands together to keep from doing something so insanely stupid.

Rydian's gaze lingered on mine, and for a breath, I could swear he was fighting the same intense urge. But then that look was gone, replaced by that granite-like disgust he always aimed at me. "You shouldn't have come into the city," he said, his voice low. "It's not safe."

"Yeah, I'm starting to see that." I swallowed hard, my pulse still thundering in my ears. "Who were those people?"

"The Withered." He paused like he was waiting for recognition.

I stared at him blankly. "The what?"

His jaw tightened. "Did Callan not tell you anything about this place or its dangers?"

Before I could answer, voices echoed from down the road.

Fae males. Two hedgerows over. Coming this way. They looked nothing like the cloaked figures from before, but I tensed anyway.

"What happens if someone finds me out here?" I asked.

With you.

We both knew the unspoken ending of that question.

Rydian eyed them then glanced at me, his frown etched like a permanent fixture on his handsome face. "This way."

He didn't take my hand this time, turning and striding off without so much as looking to see if I followed.

Arrogant asshole.

The temptation to let him go almost won out. But a group of rebels called the Withered had clearly targeted me today, and I had a feeling my fiancé wasn't going to tell me much about them if I asked. On top of that, I was hopelessly lost in a foreign city—not to mention weaponless.

Seven Hels.

With a glance skyward, I hurried to catch up.

Rydian cut through yards and hopped fences. I kept pace, though if he was surprised at my agility, he didn't show it. Eventually, we ended up at the back door of a modest house on a dead-end street.

"Where are we?" I asked, breathless—though not from the workout. The movement had been welcomed after so many days of being stuck in the castle. But no, it was the look in Rydian's eyes that made it suddenly hard to breathe.

"Somewhere safe."

He didn't give me a chance to argue before he shoved the door open and strode inside.

I followed, wary.

Then again, if he was going to hurt me, he could've done it a dozen times over by now. Or simply stood by and watched someone else do it for him.

I stepped into a small, well-kept kitchen, and the scent of freshly baked bread hit my nose. Inhaling appreciatively, I looked around for the source. But Rydian rounded on me, his large body pressing in close enough to blot out the view of the kitchen behind him. There wasn't a shred of hospitality in his eyes.

"What were you really doing in the city today?" he asked roughly.

"Shopping," I said, startled.

He frowned as if that hadn't been the right answer. "What did Callan tell you about the rebels you saw?"

"Not much," I said, trying to get my bearings. "He said there was unrest in the city. He didn't want to come today, but I convinced him."

"Why?"

"To see the city. To see where I live now. To meet the Autumn people."

Because it had been his way of shutting me down about doing anything else—like actually going to look for answers to this curse.

Rydian stepped closer, his presence overwhelming in the small space. "And what did you see, Furious?"

Before I could answer, voices sounded in the other room. Heavy footsteps approached. I tensed, balling my hands into fists as I readied to fight. Angry with myself that I'd been found weaponless, yet again, when I needed one most.

Two males rounded the corner, and I recognized them both as part of Rydian's unit. They'd ridden with us from Sevanwinds and fought ruthlessly against the Obsidians who'd attacked us in the forest. The blond male had been the one to care for my horse.

Slade.

He spoke first. "Well, that was a fucking shitshow— Oh."

Both their expressions shifted at the sight of me tucked behind Rydian. Surprise then wariness then something that bordered on admiration, especially from the larger one.

"You finally decided to tell her," he said.

"I haven't told her shit," Rydian snapped at him. "And neither will you."

Slade smirked. "I'd say bringing her to the house says plenty." He winked at me.

Even though I had no idea what he was talking about, heat crept into my cheeks. Was this Rydian's house? Did he have a bedroom somewhere in these walls? Why the Hel did I care? And why did Slade seem to think Rydian bringing me here was significant?

But even as I wondered, Rydian tensed beside me. I expected him to lash out—at me or them—but he merely changed the subject, his voice controlled and clipped. "Is it done?"

"It's over," the larger male agreed.

"And the prince?" Rydian asked.

"He'll live," Slade said flatly.

The other one snorted. "That brat's like a stable cat. Endless lives."

I tried to piece together what they were saying, but it was impossible to discern whether they were happy to hear that Callan had survived the attack or not.

"Can someone please tell me what the Hel is going on? Why did those rebels try to kill me?"

For a moment, no one spoke. I glared, a slew of curses on the tip of my tongue, most of them aimed at Rydian.

The larger male broke the silence before I could unleash them. "They're Autumn fae rebels who are angry with the king," he said.

"Yes, I gathered that," I said. "What are they so angry about?"

The three males shared a look that had temper bubbling in me again.

"Taxes," the larger male answered before I could snap.

"Taxes? That's it?"

"You were expecting something else?" he asked.

"They seemed...exceptionally angry," I said.

The larger male's brow lifted at that. "You've never been stripped of all resources for survival?"

"I..." I'd been forced to hunt and grow my own food. To rely on my own instincts to keep from being found by Obsidians and other predators. But in this moment, that didn't feel like the same thing.

"I'm Daegel by the way." He spoke with no judgment as he introduced himself. "This is Slade."

"We've met." Slade winked.

Rydian let out a snarl with enough venom to wipe the amusement from Slade's expression.

"We'll be in the other room," Daegel said, shoving at Slade to get him moving.

They both turned and disappeared into another part of the house, leaving me alone with a male I was still half-sure wanted to see me dead.

Rydian turned to face me, suspicion gleaming in his dark gaze. It didn't make any sense, and irritation rose in me, blotting out everything else.

"What's your problem?" I demanded.

"Excuse me?"

"Your problem," I repeated. "With me. Why do you hate me so much?"

His glare only intensified. "What kind of question is that?"

"You tell me. You look at me as if I'm a thief who's broken into your house to steal something precious. But I've done nothing to you. I don't even know you."

"I just saved your life. Would I have done that if I hated you?"

I crossed my arms. "I'm beginning to think the answer is yes."

I could've sworn I heard a snort from the other room.

Rydian didn't answer.

I scowled, more determined than ever to understand what was happening. "Why did you save me?"

His smirk was infuriating. "You'll have to be more specific. Which time are you referring to? What is that, twice now? Or three? I can't keep track."

I kept my expression blank, refusing to react to his taunting. Instead, I asked the question that had been bothering me since the moment it happened. "The Obsidian in the Emerald Forest. You could've let it kill me. Why didn't you?"

Something gathered in his dark gaze. An intensity that held a secret—one he had no intention of sharing. Sure enough, when he spoke again, it was to change the subject entirely.

"The Withered are fae who've been drained of their magic and now seek vengeance against the crown for what's been taken from them."

"Drained how—and why? I thought Daegel said they were angry about taxes."

"Summer's land is dying, is it not? Succumbing to the seasons, its magic slowly fading."

I blinked, surprised he knew about that. But I didn't bother trying to deny it. "What does that have to do with—"

"So is Autumn's."

I shook my head. "It looks untouched."

"That's because Duron found other means to feed the land—to offset the curse Heliconia cast here."

My heart thudded as his words hit home. This place was cursed just like my home—even if I couldn't see the evidence. And Duron had found a way to stop it. Maybe he could help me after all. Hope leaped inside me.

"What has Duron found?" I asked quickly.

But Rydian's expression morphed into one of disgust. "As

Daegel said, he's enacted a tax on all the fae who live in his land."

"What kind of tax?"

"Once every turn of the season, all Autumn fae are required to report to a donation center where their magic is siphoned away."

I stared at him. "That's impossible. Fae magic is part of our soul."

"It's in our blood, actually," he said grimly. "And it's very possible if you have the right tools." I didn't know what tools existed for that, but something told me they would be brutal. "Once drained, their magic is used as an offering to feed the land so that it continues to thrive."

"But... their magic should replenish—"

"Not if it's being drained faster than they can regain their strength. When the curse first took hold, donations were once a year, and it was enough to sustain both the land and the fae. But the curse has worsened, and donations have been ordered too frequently for the fae to regain their strength between each appointment."

"What happens to them?"

"The first few donations cause a few days of weakness. Headaches, dizziness, exhaustion. Continuing beyond that, recovery becomes slower. Over time, access to one's magic wanes, and therefore, so does our ability to heal. The weakness becomes permanent. If he stopped there, they might simply become more or less human. A mortal with an average life span, fragile body, and no magic."

"But he doesn't stop there," I said, feeling sick.

"Eventually, with enough blood draining, the body depletes of its necessary nutrients and minerals. The flesh wrinkles, the bones become brittle, the body becomes frail."

I stared at him in horror as it all clicked. "They become

permanently withered." He nodded. "What happens if they refuse?"

"If they don't comply, they are imprisoned, and their magic is taken anyway. All of it. At once."

"They wouldn't survive that."

Rydian's silence was confirmation.

My chest tightened to the point of pain as I thought of all those fae being drained of life. All so Duron could maintain the illusion that his land remained untouched by Heliconia.

"And these rogues—the Withered. They're rebelling to fight the tax."

"Yes."

I swallowed hard as more pieces fell into place. "Callan knows. He condones it."

Again, Rydian said nothing. He didn't have to.

"What about the army? They can't fight if they're weakened."

"Menryth's magic has been waning for centuries already. The king thinks his soldiers can be trained to rely on their combat skills alone."

My shock turned to horror—and disgust. "Duron would drain his own people all for a show of power he doesn't actually possess?"

"Others have done far worse in the name of power."

I frowned at the hard edge in his voice. As if he spoke from experience. But I couldn't imagine anyone worse—except for Heliconia herself.

I didn't respond, my thoughts racing. Still, Rydian watched me as if this were a test. I didn't think he was lying, but he was clearly very interested in what I said or did next.

"The Withered attacked me because they think I'll stand with Callan on this," I said quietly. My stomach twisted. Of course they did. I'd agreed to marry him. The fae of this land wouldn't realize he hadn't told me the dark truth. They'd assume I was in on it.

"Won't you?" Rydian asked.

Instead of the hostility he usually displayed, there was a challenge in his eyes. What side would I choose?

I thought of Sonoma. I'd asked her—begged her, really—to take my magic, to drain me to feed the wards, and she'd said no. I'd been miserable with helplessness at the time, but now I understood. She'd known what would happen to me if I'd let her do it. Eventually, I'd become just like the Withered. And how would the prophecy have held then?

How could I possibly save our people as a mortal shell of myself?

These people didn't deserve what was being done to them.

Duron had no right.

Callan had to see that.

"What will Duron do when all his people are drained?" I asked. "He has to know this isn't a sustainable plan."

"When this kingdom is drained, he'll move on to another."

I swallowed hard, suddenly stifled in this small room. I had to get away, get some air.

Turning for the door, I made it all of three steps when Rydian closed his hand over my wrist.

I whirled around and found his face inches from my own. "What are you—"

He pressed his fingers to my neck, and I realized with a jolt my hair had fallen away from my tattoo. I tensed, waiting for him to ask about it again. But his next words had nothing to do with the mark.

"You didn't ask me why I saved you today."

I swallowed hard, completely captured by his closeness. The way he smelled, the stubble on his jaw, the intensity in his dark eyes—all of it trained on me.

"Why did you save me today?" I asked quietly.

"I couldn't stand the thought of a world without you in it."

My heart raced. "I understand. Your loyalty is to your crown, and I'm—"

"No." he moved closer, and I retreated until my back was against the door and his chest pressed against mine. I was trapped, and I never wanted to be free again. "This has nothing to do with loyalty. Or duty. Or prophecies."

I started. "I don't—"

"You do. But it doesn't matter. Because in that alley, none of those were the reason I saved you." He cupped my neck. Gentle. Reverent even.

"Then why—?"

His fingers tightened and I remembered his words from the other day. *If you put your hands on me, I expect you to make it count.* As if he could read my mind, awareness flared in his stormy gaze.

My breath hitched.

His mouth crashed onto mine, and I forgot everything else as pleasure erupted inside me. His hands found my hips, and he gripped me tight. One of his arms snaked around my waist, and he hauled me against him, my feet nearly coming off the ground as he held me flush against his body. His tongue coaxed my lips apart, and I opened willingly, caring only that he'd finally given me what I wanted.

He tasted like spice and woodsmoke—a combination that invaded my senses until there was nothing but the feel and taste of him. Nothing about the kiss was sweet, and I only wanted more of it. More of him.

I lifted my hands to his chest, running my palms up the contoured planes and hard muscles that rippled beneath his tunic. Then I gripped his collar, pulling him closer as I strained to press my body more tightly to his.

From deep in his throat, he growled, and a thrill of pleasure shot through me. I'd never felt more powerful than I did in Rydian's arms.

He broke the kiss as suddenly as he'd begun it. "Fuck," he said, his breath ragged, his eyes glazed.

I was pretty sure I was in a similar state, but I couldn't bring myself to care. His eyes found mine, and whatever hummed in their depths, it sent a shudder through me, half-pleasure, half-fear.

"I don't have room for this," he said quietly, and disappointment speared through me. "But if anyone attempts to touch you, I will kill them for it."

A thrill pulsed inside me at his declaration. Promises of violence and bloodshed on my behalf shouldn't have excited me, nor should they call to my magic so deliciously. But I couldn't deny that they did. Though, something pulsed inside him too. A darkness that felt almost like mine. Almost. Not quite.

Then he released me, the pulse vanishing with his touch, and I felt strangely alone.

"He'll be looking for you," he said. "And I can't let him find you here. As much as I want to."

Reality crashed over me like ice water. Callan. My fiancé. But just as quickly as I remembered him, I decided. "I'm not going back."

His expression hardened. "Yes, you are."

I shook my head. "Why? Callan is not the warrior he claims to be. His army is withered and dying from loss of magic—a nightmare he condones. And he has no intention of holding up his promise to help me find a cure for my people. What reason do I have to return to him?"

If I thought Rydian would be reasonable, the hard-set determination he wore now crushed that assumption. "You're in more danger than you know."

"Because of the prophecy?" I watched as his gaze slid away. "How do you know about that?"

"I've always known," he said quietly.

"How?" I demanded, but he didn't answer. I huffed, angry at the secrets. The lies. But it didn't change how I felt about remaining with Callan. "If you know about the prophecy, then you know what I'm meant to do. But I can't stay here—"

"The Obsidian said your alliance with the prince was the key to her destruction."

His words sucked the air from my lungs. I didn't want to remember that stupid prediction. Not now. Not after everything I'd learned. But I hadn't missed the emphasis he'd put on the word prince. As if to remind both of us of the reality.

Rydian and me—this was impossible. I couldn't let myself want it.

Besides, the male clearly still had secrets he wasn't interested in sharing. And if I'd taken one thing away from Sonoma's confession, it was that I had no tolerance for secrets ever again.

"I have to get back," I said, trying to put some distance between myself and everything I'd just felt when he kissed me.

"I know this is difficult, but give me some time," he began, but I cut him off.

"I don't need anything from you," I said coldly. "And I can take care of myself."

His eyes flashed with something like regret before his mask slid back into place. It was less hateful than before but just as unwelcoming.

"I'll walk you out." Rather than usher me out the back, he led the way out of the room, his boots heavy on the bare floors.

I followed stiffly.

The kitchen gave way to a small dining area then a cozy living room that was curiously empty. The space held a couch with a worn blanket draped over the back, a stack of books on an end table along with reading glasses, and a pair of muddy boots near the door. Were those Rydian's reading glasses? Just picturing him wearing them had traitorous butterflies dancing against my ribcage.

A throat cleared pointedly, and I huffed, joining him by the door. He grabbed a cloak from a peg near the door and flung it around my shoulders.

"What are you doing?" I asked as he yanked the hood up over my head. It was so large it almost completely obscured my face. Just like the ones the Withered had worn.

"Some of the neighbors are loyal to the Withered. You're safer if they don't recognize you."

He was protecting me—again. I couldn't understand why, and the fact that he refused to tell me only sparked my temper.

"My safety is not your concern. I am engaged to your brother."

"Engaged or not," he said, his eyes smoldering again, "I will not allow anyone to touch you and live. Be careful who you let put their hands on you, Furious."

I shuddered. Were we still talking about those who would do me harm—or a different kind of touch altogether?

He didn't bother waiting for my answer before steering me out into the sunlight. When he started to shut the door on my heels, I whirled.

"What are you doing?" I asked.

"You can see the city center from here," he said, pointing toward the buildings of downtown, which towered over the suburbs where we stood. "Head there. I'm sure the royal guard will be searching for you. You'll stumble on one of them soon enough."

"You could, at least, show me how to get out of your neighborhood."

"I think it's best you turn up without the bastard prince at your side."

With that, he shut the door in my face.

THE
MOON

Chapter Twenty-Nine
Rydian

The faint *click* of the door echoed in my ears as I stood there, hating myself. I told myself it was better this way. That she was safer in the castle, surrounded by servants and my own spies.

Except she wasn't.

I'd sent her back to a cage whose walls she didn't even realize were tightening around her, a trap she'd never see coming until it was too late. She might not be the shallow princess I'd once assumed, but she was still naïve about the greed and violence Duron was capable of. I clenched my fists, my nails digging into my palms as Duron's voice whispered through my memory.

"As the Chosen One, her power isn't hers to keep," he'd said, his tone casual, as if draining her of her magic was no more significant than harvesting wheat. "Whatever the Fates gave her, it belongs to Autumn now, and I'll make sure it serves its purpose."

My stomach churned.

Aurelia's magic was meant for more than some cruel transaction in Duron's endless power games. And yet, I'd sent her straight back to the monster because to do otherwise would have violated the blood oath I'd given him.

With a roar, I grabbed a chair and shoved it hard enough to send it skittering across the room, the sharp scrape of wood on stone harsh in the oppressive quiet.

What the Hel was I doing?

My blood boiled at the thought of her staying in the castle. Not just for her proximity to Duron. I couldn't stop thinking about her with Callan. His to touch. Somewhere along the way, my duty had taken second place to my desire.

I would have her eventually.

And it would cost me everything in the process.

But she hadn't made it clear if she wanted me. Only that she wanted the truth. And that was the only thing I couldn't give.

The blood oath bound me like chains. It coiled around my tongue, my thoughts, my will—tightening every time I even *thought* about warning her directly. The penalty for breaking it would be my life, and worse, my mother's freedom.

But there were ways around it. There had to be.

Daegel entered the room, his quiet steps barely audible on the stone floor. His gaze landed on the chair I'd shoved. "She's gone, then?"

I didn't answer, turning toward the desk instead, my fingers already reaching for a pen and slip of paper.

When I started for the stairs, his voice came again, disapproval already lacing the question. "Where are you going?"

"To write a message," I said, the words clipped.

"Message for who?"

I turned back, knowing full well the recklessness of my plan. "Home."

Daegel frowned. "I thought you said it was too risky—"

"We can't afford to let her remain here," I snapped, my tone harsher than I'd intended.

Daegel's frown deepened. "You don't think there's a chance she'd listen to reason? We could ask her to leave. Simply explain—"

"No." The word lashed out of me like a whip. "She won't come willingly."

I couldn't let myself imagine that possibility. Aurelia, hearing the truth, looking at me with betrayal in her eyes for the lies I'd already told her. For pushing her to come back here, all while knowing what danger waited for her in this place.

Daegel shifted his weight. "You're assuming the worst."

"Because I know Duron." And I knew her. "He won't give her a choice, so why the Hel should we?"

Daegel said nothing, his gaze heavy with something unspoken.

I ignored it, pushing past him toward the door. I needed air. I could send the message from somewhere else. It was a risk, contacting the others. Duron could have spies watching. He could intercept it, realize what I'd built against him.

But I couldn't let her be another pawn in Duron's game.

My family would protect her. They'd keep her out of his reach. Maybe she'd hate me for it, but at least she'd be alive. Her survival was all that mattered.

"Stop," Daegel said, his voice heavy with resignation.

I halted, my hand on the knob.

"Write the letter," Daegel said quietly. "I'll make sure it gets sent safely."

I cast him a sideways look, considering. He was a better option. He'd have fewer spies watching his movements than I surely did. And he could travel faster. "If you double cross me—"

"Oh, stuff it up your ass, Ryd." I blinked at Daegel's rare show of temper. "I'd never betray you. You know that."

"Even when you think I'm a fucking idiot?" I countered.

He grinned, his easy nature returning in an instant. "Even then."

I sighed, my shoulders sagging. "Okay." I stalked to the table and leaned over it as I scrawled the message. Then I folded it and handed it to my friend.

"Make sure this gets to my mother," I said.

His expression was unreadable as he took it from me. "If they take her, you'll never see her again."

"I know."

He stared at me, and I forced myself not to flinch at the truth he must've seen in my eyes. "Slade was right," he said finally. "You care about her."

I turned away, not trusting myself to answer. Caring about Aurelia wasn't the problem. It was caring too much. So much that I'd throw away her chance at saving us if it meant I could have her for myself. And if I thought about that for too long, I'd lose my resolve to let her go at all.

THE
MOON

Chapter Thirty

With my hood pulled low, I wandered alone through the narrow, twisting streets of the city of Grey Oak. Soon enough, the quaint suburbs of Rydian's neighborhood gave way to bustling downtown until I was once again swallowed up by it. I glanced up every so often to note the direction of the taller shops, adjusting my course as I continued to aim at them. It was farther than I remembered from my earlier escape. And without Rydian leading me, it was lonelier too.

The unfamiliarity of the city pressed in on me from all sides. The towering trees, their bronze bark twisted and gnarled, loomed overhead like silent sentinels. But I saw no castle guards roaming the city, looking for the lost princess. Rydian had been wrong.

Maybe Callan thought me dead.

The streets, winding and narrow, felt claustrophobic compared to the wide-open paths of Rosewood. The fae I passed kept their gazes down, their movements slow and deliberate. There was something in the air, an unease I couldn't shake, and I was acutely aware of every step I took back to that gray castle on the hill.

The things Rydian had told me—about the fae tax and Callan's hand in it—played on a loop in my thoughts and twisted in my gut. I wasn't ready to face him yet. Not when I knew I'd see the truth in his eyes the moment I confronted him about it. My breaths came in shorter bursts as I pictured that conversation. As I faced the situation I found myself in.

I'd yielded my kingdom to the Furiosities' magic. My father's magic. I'd locked my home without a key. And I'd unknowingly tied myself to a king whose atrocities were only overshadowed by Heliconia herself.

Even if I ran, there was nowhere I could hide forever. Heliconia's reach spanned the continent. Maybe I could cross the sea to Alorica or ask for asylum among the Moriori, but neither of those were permanent solutions. Not if I wanted to truly break this curse or face Heliconia someday. Besides, if I left, Callan would marry her. And then there would be no stopping the dark queen.

As crazy as it sounded, I had to stop myself from turning around and going back to Rydian for help. But I forced myself to continue onward. Going back would change nothing. Rydian had made his choice clear. He might not plan to betray who and what I was to the king, but he certainly didn't intend to help me escape him either.

My chest panged with emptiness. I'd never felt more alone.

I turned down a side street and tried to steady my breathing.

A voice, low and rough, broke through my thoughts. "Well, hello there. And aren't you a powerfully magicked little thing?"

I froze mid-step, my heart lurching in my chest. The voice came from behind me, a fae male standing in the shadows of the narrow street.

His eyes gleamed as they roamed over me. "Pretty and powerful," he added hungrily, and I realized with a jolt that I'd let my shield down enough that he'd sensed what slept inside me. He took a step forward, and a surge of panic rose in my throat.

"I... I'm just passing through," I said quickly, forcing my voice to stay even as I began to edge away from him.

He narrowed his eyes. "Where are you from?" His gaze lingered on my cloak, and I could see the calculation in his perusal. "Not from Grey Oak, that's for sure."

"I'm visiting from the coast," I lied.

"Where'd you get that mark?" He pointed at my neck.

I reached up and grabbed my hair, covering the tattoo. But too late.

"You have power in you, girl." He sniffed. "More than the rest of us." He looked jealous—and angry enough to do something about it.

He took a step toward me, and I threw my hands up. Black flames shot from my palms, igniting his boots. They melted, burning his feet. He screamed, and I stumbled back, looking around wildly for anyone who might have seen what I'd done.

"You have darkness in you," the fae wailed.

He stomped the flames out, but I could see the blisters and burns on his flesh where his boots and socks had burned away.

"You will pay for that, bitch."

Panic tightened in my chest, and without another word, I turned and hurried down the street. His footsteps echoed behind me, slow at first then quicker, matching my pace.

My heart raced as I rounded a corner and ducked into a narrow alley.

Ahead, a small, weathered shop sat tucked between two very rowdy pubs, its wooden sign creaking in the breeze. The symbol of an open eye was painted across the door—the oracle's shop. At last.

I'd made a point to search it out on the city map I'd found in the library, but after the chaos of the day, I'd begun to doubt if I'd actually make it here before being tossed back under lock and key inside that drafty castle.

I darted inside, the bells above the door jingling softly as I pushed it closed behind me.

As if the shop were warded against it, the noise from the pubs and the street suddenly went quiet. I leaned against the door, hoping the strange male hadn't seen me enter. Through the frosted window, I watched as he passed by and disappeared.

I exhaled and finally glanced at my surroundings.

The interior of the shop was dimly lit, the scent of incense heavy in the air. Shelves lined the walls, filled with strange trinkets, books and scrolls, and jars of herbs. Threads of magic, powerful and old, lingered in the dusty space.

"Running from something, are we?" a voice, soft and knowing, called from the back of the shop.

I turned as an aging fae emerged from the shadows. Her long, silver hair was braided down her back, and her bright blue eyes gleamed with an awareness that made my skin prickle. She wore a cloak of deep purple, the edges embroidered with shimmering runes that seemed to shift in the lantern light.

"No, I—" I swallowed, trying to catch my breath. "Apologies, I needed a place to... think."

The oracle's lips curved into a faint smile as she tilted her head, studying me. "Think... or hide?"

I didn't answer, but my silence must've told her enough.

She walked closer, her footsteps barely making a sound on the wooden floor. "You're not from here," she said softly, though there was no judgment in her tone. "And you carry something... heavy."

My pulse quickened, but I forced myself to stay calm. "I'm just passing through."

The oracle raised an eyebrow, her smile deepening. "Perhaps. But you're not just any visitor, are you?"

I forced an innocuous smile. "I'm no one."

Her gaze lingered on me, the intensity of it making me feel as though she could see right through the lie. She gestured to a small table near the back of the shop. "Sit. Have some tea with me."

The sight of the runes sewn into her cloak caught my eye again. I'd seen them before. First, in a text Amanti had brought home—the one that had sent her to Vorinthia in the first place. And again in the book I'd borrowed from Duron's collection. My heart slammed harder against my chest. I'd chosen correctly when I'd spotted this place.

I followed her over and took one of the empty chairs.

"The runes on your cloak—are you familiar with the Verdant?"

She shot me a knowing look before returning her attention to the tea she now poured. "I'm familiar."

I leaned forward. "Do you know anything about their methods? The old magic?"

"I've heard of it." She set a steaming mug before me and sat, not bothering with cream or sugar as she picked up her own and drank its bitter contents in gulps. It reminded me of Sonoma.

My chest ached, and I forced myself to sip my own too-hot tea, letting it scald away my grief.

"You have lost someone," she said.

Her words—the bluntness of them—unbalanced me. Tea sloshed at the edges of my cup as I set it down hard.

"I am looking for one who knows the old ways of the Verdant," I said, deciding to be blunt too. "Someone who can break a curse laced with ancient magic."

"You are looking for yourself."

I scowled. If she was just going to talk in riddles, this would be a waste of my time. "Never mind." Pushing my chair back, I started to rise.

The oracle's eyes narrowed slightly. "She said you would come. But not so soon."

I froze. "Who?"

"The Aine."

My heart thudded. "Sonoma?"

"Amanti."

My skin prickled at that. Amanti had come here? Had she lied about going to Vorinthia? "Do you know where she is now?" I asked.

"No."

I swallowed my disappointment, but when I started to leave, the oracle snapped her finger and pointed at my chair. "Sit. I will speak to you of what you ask."

Slowly, I sat again, watching the oracle warily.

"Heliconia," she murmured as if tasting the name. "The dark queen who spreads her blight across the realms. You wish to defeat her."

"Yes."

"What makes you think the Verdant can help?"

"They were the last kingdom to walk Menryth before fae magic began to wane. Their power has never been matched since. I thought—"

"You thought the Verdant's magic would be a match for hers."

"I hoped."

"And do you know who the Verdant were? Where their power came from?"

"I was hoping you could tell me."

The oracle studied me for a long moment. "The Verdant were

once considered the balance between light and dark. Servants of the gods, some called them. And they ruled with the power bestowed by those gods. At that time, there was peace in all of Menryth. Then the moon split, and destruction came for them."

"You're talking about The Great War."

"The changing tides brought more power-hungry creatures than the Verdant could handle. The Calidium queen was killed, and the fae that remained were driven out. For decades, they wandered, searching for sanctuary. During that time, the power bestowed on the land was reclaimed by those who had offered it, and the people's power faded."

"What does that have to do with Heliconia's magic?"

"Maybe the question you should be asking is what it has to do with yours?"

"Me?" I blinked, my thoughts racing. Did this oracle know I had death magic? Did she realize what kind of power ran through my veins? And did I want to know what it was truly capable of? "Okay, what does it have to do with—"

She lifted her brows. "What payment do you have for such valuable information?"

I gritted my teeth. "What do you want?"

She cocked her head as if considering. "A favor."

"What kind of favor?"

"One of my choosing in my hour of need."

Unease crawled through me. It would be beyond reckless to agree, but it wasn't like I had other options. Callan had promised to help me find answers, but instead, he'd shut me up in his drafty castle and distracted me with dresses and party plans. Rydian knew something, but he'd made it clear he wasn't going to help me either. And Amanti wouldn't have come here unless this oracle knew something.

"Fine," I said quietly. "You have a deal. Now, tell me what you know."

The oracle held out her hand, palm up. "We'll seal the bargain."

Slowly, I placed my hand in hers, and she grabbed it tight, holding on as she whispered fervently in some language I didn't know. Tingles shot up my arm, and I tried to pull away as they turned to pain. But she held on tighter than I would've thought possible for an aging fae.

Her whispered words came faster. The pain sharpened until I bit my lip to keep from crying out.

Abruptly, she let me go.

I glared at her then glanced down at my arm, which still pulsed with the heat of magic. Ink appeared on my wrist, a strange symbol etching itself into my skin.

A tattoo.

Like the one I had on my neck.

I stared until the shape was complete, and I realized what it reminded me of. A Verdant rune like the ones on her cloak.

"What does it mean?" I asked.

"To become sharpened."

I frowned, wondering whether it was a clue about the favor she'd ask of me one day. But there were more important questions to ask. "Tell me about my magic. Is it enough to stop her?"

She drained her tea then leaned back in her chair, her gaze far away. "As the Great War waged, gods of both the light and dark were drawn to Menryth. Each side desired the realm for themselves; to rule over it, to feed from it. To grow their own power using ours. They knew, if they battled for it, the realm might be destroyed in the process so they made a compromise. A treaty that kept the peace, however precarious. The terms of that treaty allowed these gods access to Menryth, which they used both for feeding and aiding their own efforts to sway the balance of power in their favor."

"What would happen if the balance ever swayed too far?" I asked, my stomach curling with dread.

"The champion would lay claim to Menryth forever."

Gods.

Heliconia had swayed the balance. Would Menryth be hers?

"What does that have to do with my magic?" I asked, throat dry at the thought of what Heliconia's rule might bring to the realm.

"According to the treaty, the gods cannot engage in battle, so they chose a champion to do so."

"How do you know I was chosen?" I couldn't help the challenge in my tone. Even after all these years, part of me wanted her to be wrong—about all of it. But especially about me.

"You are marked." Her gaze flicked to my throat. Where my mysterious tattoo was inked.

I lifted my hand and ran my fingers over the tiny black moon with three stars above it. "Do you know what it means?"

"Those symbols you wear represent blessings. And blood. It means you have great power inside you—the likes of which the realm hasn't seen since before Vorinthia fell."

Damn.

So much for being wrong. Okay then. "The gods you're talking about...The Furiosities chose Heliconia? And the Fates chose me?"

"I can't say which side you'll fight for. That is up to you."

I drew back at that. What could possibly ever make me fight for darkness?

"But you have already unlocked one of the three gifts imbued."

I straightened. "Do you mean one of the Fates' blessings? Do you know which one?"

"*Makarios.*"

Even as she said the word, my tattoo tingled strangely. I brushed my fingers over it. "What does it mean?"

"It means life eternal in the old language."

I stared at her, stunned. Life eternal? "Are you saying I'm immortal?"

"Do you not drink the elixir of eternal life into your veins?"

"I..."

Sonoma had called it death magic, but... my heightened senses. Enhanced strength. Was she saying that, every time I drank in a life force, I added to my own immortality? And that it had come from the Fates' blessing over me rather than from my father?

The oracle tilted her head, noting my expression. "You look surprised. Does a warrior not need to be hard to kill?"

A warrior. The Fates had chosen me and gifted me with this blessing. But it wasn't free. They'd given it in exchange for what I'd do for them. Who I'd kill. The three goddesses of light and peace and love had chosen me as their murderer.

"What if I don't want to fight?" I asked.

She shrugged. "Then Heliconia will destroy us all."

Before I could muster any more questions, she stood, her eyes drifting toward the door though they'd gone opaque white as if she were seeing something else entirely. "You need to go. It's not safe for you here."

I blinked, startled. "What do you see?"

"You've drawn attention," the oracle said, her voice urgent now. "The male who followed you earlier—he will return, and he won't be alone. Our time is up."

I stood, my heart pounding again. "But I still have questions—"

She shook her head, her silver braid swaying as she moved

toward the door. "You'll have your answers soon enough. But not here, not now. Go."

I hesitated then nodded, pulling my cloak tighter around me. "Thank you."

The oracle's lips curved into a faint smile as she opened the door, the soft chime of the bell echoing in the silence. "Good luck, daughter of Hel."

My breath caught in my throat. But before I could utter a word, she was shoving me outside and shutting the door behind me. I scanned the streets for any sign of the threats she'd mentioned, pulling my hood low as I started for the castle on the hill.

The oracle was right. I would have to get the rest of my answers later.

It was time to face Callan. And it was time to stop pretending I wasn't Chosen.

THE
MOON

CHAPTER THIRTY-ONE
AURELIA

I passed several soldiers patrolling downtown, but none of them stopped me as I made my way across the city and out the other side. The road sloped upward as I left behind the glittering lights and let the darkness swallow me. Still, no one came to challenge me. No guards. No Withered. No lecherous fae males chasing me down.

The oracle's words rang out in my mind. *Makarios. Life Eternal.*

So did Rydian's. *When this kingdom is drained, he'll move on to another.*

Both felt like a warning; I had no idea what to do with either one. But I knew one thing: I was done sitting around doing nothing at all.

Eventually, I reached the palace gates. The guards stopped me, demanding my name and what business I had here. I threw back my hood and watched their eyes widen.

"Your Highness," the one blocking my path said. "We thought you were lost."

"Yes, I can see you've been very worried."

He lowered his head in a bow before gesturing for me to proceed. "We'll escort you back to ensure your safety."

I didn't point out that my safety clearly hadn't been a priority before. Or that their escort felt more like an armed guard taking a prisoner back to her cell.

When we reached the castle, the doors opened, and a servant bowed his head at the sight of me. "Your Highness."

"Where's Callan?" I asked, my temper brewing hotter the farther I went without anyone to greet me.

Had he really just moved on with his life in the span of a few hours?

"He's in his study, Your Highness," the servant said, his head bowed.

My steps quickened as I made my way deeper into the halls. Two soldiers still followed me like shadows. I ignored them, or tried to, but I couldn't deny I felt trapped.

And then I heard him.

"Aurelia."

Callan stood at the end of the hallway, the buttons on his jacket gleaming in the lamplight, his golden eyes fixed on me with a mixture of concern and fury. His jaw was set, the muscles in his shoulders tense, as though he'd been waiting for me far beyond the limits of his patience. He wasn't hurt that I could see, but the tension in the air between us was unmistakable. He wasn't relieved to see me.

"You're back," he said, his voice even but laced with an unspoken accusation. His gaze swept over me, taking in my new cloak, the mud on my boots, and the disheveled state I hadn't had time to fix. Subtly, I slid my arm further inside the cloak to hide the mark the oracle's bargain had left on my skin.

"I am," I said quietly, my voice steady despite the storm of emotions inside me.

He took a step forward, the soft glow of the lanterns casting sharp shadows across his face. His eyes were slightly glazed, but his gaze locked onto mine, unyielding. "Where were you?"

I hesitated.

I could feel the lie on my tongue, ready to slip free, but I knew he wouldn't believe it. Still, I had no other choice. I couldn't tell him the truth—not about Rydian, not about what I'd learned from the oracle.

"I was chased far away from the jewelry shop before I lost them," I said, forcing my voice to stay calm. "I wandered the city, looking for you until I found my way back here."

Callan stared at me, his amber eyes searching my face. The tension in his posture never eased, and the air grew thick between us.

"Alone?" he asked, his voice soft but dangerous. He didn't believe me, not for a second.

I tucked my hand behind my back to hide the rune on my wrist. He took another step closer, his presence commanding, towering over me as if daring me to lie again.

"Yes," I said, standing my ground. "Alone."

"You smell like fae male," he said, and I tensed at the accusation.

"I probably smell like a whole city of them," I said flippantly. "The streets were crowded. I stole this cloak so I wouldn't be recognized."

For a moment, he said nothing. The silence stretched between us, his gaze burning into mine, as though he was waiting for me to crack. But I didn't flinch.

Finally, Callan exhaled, a frustrated sigh escaping his lips. His hands, clenched at his sides, loosened slightly, though the storm in his eyes remained. "I see," he said, his voice still tight with suspicion. "In that case, I'm glad you're all right."

He reached out, brushing a stray strand of hair away from my face. The touch was tender, but it carried a weight, a silent reminder of his frustration. His fingers lingered a moment too long against my cheek, and his eyes softened, just barely.

"I was worried," he murmured, his voice low, though there was an edge to it I couldn't ignore. "I thought something had happened to you."

The fury knotted tighter in my chest, but I forced myself to keep my expression calm. "I'm fine."

His gaze lingered on me, his touch slowly falling away, but the distance between us wasn't just physical. He didn't believe me—he didn't trust me. That made two of us.

"And you?" I asked. "Were you injured at all?"

"I'm unharmed."

Just like Slade and Daegel had said.

"Who were those people?" I asked. "The ones who attacked us?"

He leaned away, his expression shuttering as effectively as if he'd slammed a door between us. "Criminals whose minds have been twisted by Heliconia. They are a danger to the crown and our people. Rydian and his men followed their trail and destroyed them already."

Lie.

My chest burned with the word I let die on my lips.

"And the shop owner," I pressed.

"What about him?"

"Before the attack, he said something about his magic being weakened."

"Just an old man talking nonsense. He's also been neutralized, so you needn't worry."

I flinched, my eyes going wide. "You killed him?"

"He was possibly complicit in—"

"Possibly?" I repeated. "You don't even know for sure, and you killed him anyway?"

"None of that is your concern. All that matters is you're

safely returned to me." His tone made it clear the subject was closed.

I paused, clearing my throat and shoving aside the sorrow that pricked at me for the poor shopkeeper. When I spoke again, my tone betrayed nothing of what I felt. "It's time we discussed those resources you promised me."

"Yes, I'm told you've been spending considerable time in the library. I supposed that's better than training with a sword in the barracks. Have you found anything helpful?"

My eyes narrowed. Did he really expect the library to be sufficient? Or that I would be content to remain locked up inside this castle? To never pick up a sword again?

"I've gone as far as I can go with the historical records you have here. I think it's time to investigate the source."

"Which is?" he asked, brow lifted.

"The Verdant—"

"That tribe's been dead for centuries."

"It's possible remnants of their magic still exist there."

"Aurelia, I promised you resources, and I've given you access to the royal library, which has an extensive historical collection. I think that's more than generous, especially given that our true focus should be on sealing our alliance and using it to bring other courts to our aid."

"I don't see why we can't do both," I said. "You spoke of an oracle—"

"I'm afraid my men were unable to locate her."

I lifted my chin, fighting the urge to drive my fist into his lying mouth. "Then I will begin arrangements for the journey south—"

"You will not leave this place unless I order it," he boomed, loud and final.

I waited for him to apologize or take it back. To smooth it over like the charmer he pretended to be. But he didn't bother.

A quiet rage slipped through me. I fisted both hands then

tucked them in at my sides. "You promised to help me," I said quietly.

"And you gave your word that you'd marry me." His words were carefully chosen. A reminder of the promise I'd made. I saw that in the flash of his bright eyes. "Are you no longer a fae of your word?"

"Are you?" I countered.

He didn't answer.

I listened as the fire crackled in the hearth. Noted the rise and fall of his chest as his breaths came short and quick. The way his nostrils flared with whatever irritation he was struggling to keep hidden. And there, his magic, small and slippery, beneath his skin.

My own strained to the surface—wanting to taste his. To drink his life force like a nightcap. I'd never been so tempted to let it free in my life.

"You and I will wed in two weeks." His voice was colder than I'd ever heard it. "And you will use the occasion to help me convince the other courts to ally with us in the battle coming."

"Or what?" I tossed back.

Suddenly, magic, bright as a hot coal, shot from his hand to land on the rug at my feet. The small spark left a hole that smelled of smoke and burnt cotton. I wrenched my gaze from it back to where Callan watched me intently.

"I don't like being lied to, Aurelia," Callan said, his voice deceivingly soft. "Remember that."

THE
MOON

Chapter Thirty-Two
Aurelia

The following afternoon, I stood still as Vanya fastened the ties of my new gown, her deft fingers working in practiced silence. I hadn't seen Callan at all yet today. The only evidence of our argument last night was the sight of Fletcher standing outside my door. He hadn't offered much more than a quick hello and had simply followed me around like a shadow while I wandered the small temple located in one of the castle's towers. I hadn't encountered a single priestess, but the small reference library's door had been unlocked, so I'd helped myself to a perusal of the titles.

The oracle had only confirmed what I'd known and fought against for too long. That the key to saving the realm lay inside me. It was time I figured out how to truly unlock it. Even Sonoma's letter had prodded me to seek the Fates' gifts. I'd snagged a book called *Embodying the Fates*, but after two hours of flipping through it, I'd found only a recitation of godly characteristics all priestesses should strive to embody. Traits like faith, kindness, compassion, worship. Nothing that remotely resembled how to access the blessings the goddesses had given me.

Callan hadn't been in his study when I'd broken for lunch. He hadn't been in the dining hall either. Nor had he made an appearance when the dressmaker delivered my new wardrobe, including my dress for the vow ceremony. After sticking his nose into every detail of my life during my first few days here, his absence today felt significant.

The events of yesterday, including my meeting with the oracle and Callan's cold welcome when I'd returned, had reminded me I was completely on my own here. No allies. No resources. I might possess power to rival Heliconia's own, but even the magic inside me was useless if I didn't learn how to wield it.

First, I needed to figure out how to access the gifts I'd been given. I doubted anyone in Autumn had that kind of knowledge. But the other courts might. If not for that fact, I might have already left. But I needed to speak with the other courts just as badly as Callan and his father did.

So, I searched for whatever clues this castle might hold. And I planned. But even Vanya's quiet presence did little to calm the knot of urgency twisting in my stomach.

"Are you sure it's not too tight?" I asked, more to break the silence than out of any real concern for the fit.

Vanya smiled softly as she adjusted the laces. "You'll barely notice it once you've been wearing it for a few minutes, my lady."

I nodded, glancing at my reflection in the mirror. The heavy velvet gown, a deep autumnal green that matched the colors of the court, felt stiff against my skin, a far cry from the light silks of Sevanwinds.

Vanya finished up and stepped back. "You look lovely."

I glanced at her through the glass and smiled. "Thank you."

"I'll set out your gown for tomorrow before I leave for the day."

"Why would you do that?"

She bit her lip. I caught the worry in her eyes as she shifted from foot to foot.

"What is it?" I asked, turning to face her fully.

Her gaze dropped to the floor as she pretended to straighten the edge of my gown. "I won't be here tomorrow morning, my lady."

I frowned, surprised by the sudden announcement. "Why not? Are you ill?"

"I have to report to the donation center," Vanya said quietly, her fingers still fussing with the fabric. "For my tax payment."

The very thought of it turned my stomach. "You don't have to do this."

Vanya's lips tightened, her gaze still fixed on the floor. "Every citizen must contribute, my lady. It's why they assigned a second maid to assist you. She'll cover for me while I'm gone."

I clenched my fists, frustration bubbling beneath my skin. "It's horrific. To force you to give up your magic... It's completely barbaric."

Vanya gave me a sad smile, the kind that told me she'd long since made peace with what she saw as inevitable. "It's just the way things are, Your Highness. The donation center is... necessary. The magic collected is used to protect the realm from Heliconia and her forces."

I shook my head, anger flaring in my chest. "Protect the realm? It's draining the people. Draining you."

Her expression softened, and she reached for my hand, squeezing it lightly. "It's my duty, just as you have yours. It won't be forever."

But I couldn't ignore the way her voice wavered, the

unspoken truth hanging between us. It wouldn't be forever because each payment chipped away at her, at all of them. Slowly, silently, this tax was draining the life out of Grey Oak's people until they would all become like the Withered.

"I can't accept this," I said. "There has to be a way to stop it."

Vanya said nothing, just continued to straighten the folds of my gown, her silence speaking volumes.

A knock sounded at the door. I turned, half-expecting Callan. Instead, Fletcher entered. "Your Highness, Prince Callan has requested your presence in his study."

"Very well," I said, trying to sound composed even as a thousand possibilities ran through my mind. Had he found out about my conversation with the oracle? Or worse... had he discovered I'd been with Rydian yesterday?

I glanced at Vanya, who nodded encouragingly. "You look perfect, my lady."

I swallowed, grateful for the reassurance, and followed Fletcher into the hall. The corridors seemed colder than before; the light less forgiving as I made my way to Callan's study.

When we reached the door, Fletcher stepped aside and gestured for me to go ahead. I hesitated for a moment before pushing it open.

Callan stood by the window, his back to me, the late afternoon light framing him in a halo of warmth. But that warmth, an illusion I saw through easily now, did nothing to soften the tension in the room. My eyes flicked to the other figure waiting, and my heart nearly stopped.

Rydian.

He stood stiffly, his arms crossed over his charcoal tunic and a deep scowl on his face. His dark eyes found mine almost instantly, and heat rushed through me.

I forced myself to look away, trying to suppress the panic rising in my throat. Did Callan know? Was this a trap?

"Aurelia," Callan said, turning to face me, his expression unreadable. "There's something we need to discuss."

My heart pounded in my ears as I stepped farther into the room, careful to keep my distance from them both. "What is it?"

Callan's gaze flicked toward Rydian, and for a brief, terrifying moment, I thought the truth was about to spill from his lips. Instead, he nodded toward his half-brother. "In light of what happened yesterday—the danger you were in—I think it's wise that you have dedicated protection. From now on, Rydian will be your personal guard. He'll accompany you everywhere you go and see that you aren't lost or separated again."

I blinked, caught off guard. "Everywhere?"

"Yes," Callan said, his voice steady, but there was a tightness to it, a hint of something more beneath the surface. "With the growing unrest in the realm, I can't take any chances. Rydian is our best. He'll ensure your safety."

My gaze shifted to Rydian, who was watching me with an intensity that made my skin prickle.

"I see," I managed, trying to keep my voice steady. "I... appreciate your concern."

Callan's gaze lingered on me, his expression still unreadable, though I could sense the underlying tension between us. "That's all for now. I have a strategy meeting to attend, but I'll see you for dinner."

The brothers didn't as much as glance at each other as Callan strode out.

When we were alone, Rydian stepped forward. "Well, Furious, it looks like we're stuck together after all. What would you like to do first?"

The way he said that stupid nickname sent a shiver down my spine. I forced myself to meet his gaze, ignoring the way my heart fluttered at the sight of his mouth—and the memory of it on mine.

"Take me to the donation center."

THE
MOON

Chapter Thirty-Three
Rydian

Callan had made his choice—and I had made mine. The moment he'd summoned me, I'd known what he would order. More lies. More selfish pursuits without a care who he hurt along the way. For him, Aurelia was nothing more than an item to possess. But looking at her now, I could see what he couldn't.

He'd already lost her.

Just as I would in the end.

But this—her request...it went beyond what even I was willing to let her see.

"No," I told her firmly and started for the door.

"Wait. Where are you going?"

"I'm taking you to the library. You can hunt for answers there."

"Stop." The command in that single word stilled my feet.

I turned to her. "You do not order me."

"Last I checked, you've been instructed to babysit me." The haughtiness in her tone reminded me of my impression of her the night we'd first met. Pampered princess—naïve and spoiled. I'd thought her too much like Callan then and hated her for it.

The only one of us I hated now was myself.

"I was tasked with keeping you safe," I said. "The donation center is far from that."

She scowled, and her gaze fell, landing on a spot on the rug and lingering there. I followed, frowning at the sight of the hole burnt into it. It hadn't been there the last time I'd visited. I would've remembered since Callan had warned me over and over again not to ruin his rug with my muddy boots.

"What happened?" I asked, my eyes snapping back to hers.

"What are you talking about?"

"The mark on the rug," I said, doing my best to rein in my shadows. Nightmares swam beneath my skin, begging to be unleashed, but now was not the time.

She tensed. "Nothing."

I stalked closer. "What. Happened?"

"Callan was angry when I returned last night."

"What do you mean you returned? The soldiers didn't bring you? Callan didn't come for you?"

"No. I walked home."

I studied her, my hands curling into fists as my mind raced ahead of her words. He hadn't said anything to me today. "Angry about what?"

"I don't think he believed I was alone."

"What did he do to you?" I asked, barely able to keep my control leashed.

"Nothing," she said quickly. "He... made a point."

"Furious," I said through my teeth, "if you don't tell me exactly what happened, I will assume he put his hands on you. Do you remember what I told you would happen to anyone who did that?"

She had the sense to look nervous then. "He didn't touch

me. He used his magic to burn the rug near my feet. I think he wanted to scare me."

I blew out a breath, my body rigid with the need to hunt Callan down and make him regret his little outburst.

"Rydian." Aurelia's voice was soft.

It snapped me out of my rage.

I exhaled, closing the distance between us and sliding my hand around her neck. The fact that we were standing in her fiancé's study ceased to matter. I just needed to feel her skin against mine. To convince the animal inside me that she was, indeed, unharmed. Leaning in, I pressed my face to her throat and inhaled her scent.

Lovely.

Delicious.

So fucking tempting.

"Rydian," she whispered my name like a plea. Her hands gripped my shoulders.

Fuck, I wanted her badly enough to throw it all away.

To get us both killed.

I stepped back, releasing her, though it caused me pain to do so.

Her expression flashed with hurt, but she covered it quickly. "I'm not going to tell him," she said. "About seeing you yesterday."

"I wouldn't care if you did at this point."

Irritation flickered in her eyes. "Well, you should. Without my arrangement with Callan—"

"Heliconia wins," I spat. "Yes, I know. You and the prince. Destined to defeat her—together." The words burned my throat, the finality of them eating at me from the inside out.

She shook her head, despair crowding her gaze. "I had hoped there would be another way."

"If there is, I swear to you I'll find it." Shadows leaked

from my fingers as I spoke. I yanked them back again, tucking them away.

"What are you?" she asked suddenly.

I shut my mouth, scowling.

"You're not Autumn fae—not fully. Even if Duron is your father," she added.

I hesitated. The blood oath kept me from admitting the full truth, but that wasn't what held me silent. I'd never spoken of my power to anyone. Not even Slade or Daegel knew the full story. To tell her any of it now... it would only put her in more danger. Not to mention she'd likely hate me.

"I am a weapon aimed at your enemies, Princess. Wield me how you see fit."

I could see the questions brimming. Like a coward, I dropped my gaze, hoping she wouldn't demand answers I couldn't give. A mark on her wrist caught my attention, and I stiffened.

She quickly tucked her hand behind her back, but I grabbed it and held it up, noting the Verdant rune with a growing dread.

"What is this?" I demanded.

"None of your business," she said, trying to wrench herself free.

But I squeezed her arm, refusing to let her go. "Where did you get it?"

"In the city," she said with a shrug.

"Furious," I warned.

She glared at me. "I made a bargain."

"With whom?"

"An oracle."

I sighed. Meerdra. It had the look of her handiwork. "And what did you promise her?"

She hesitated before admitting, "A favor of her choosing."

"Seven Hels," I muttered, finally dropping her hand. "You do understand this bargain is unbreakable."

"She fulfilled her end. I'll do the same when she needs me."

"And what did you get in return for this unnamed favor?"

She squared her jaw as if ready to defend her answer. "Information."

"What kind of information?"

"I'll share if you do," she shot back.

I shook my head, pacing. Likely, the information had to do with her dormant power—light or dark, it hardly mattered at this point. Meerdra wouldn't have offered the bargain without upholding her end, but that didn't mean her explanations weren't cryptic as fuck. I knew from experience.

"Your mark—" I tried, but the words caught in my throat.

She crossed her arms, tucking away the one Meerdra had given her. "It's not a big deal."

"Not that one." I reached for her neck, brushing her hair away and running my thumb over the black moon at her throat. Power rippled between us, but I held fast, not wanting to let go of her just yet. "This."

Her gaze met mine, her lids heavy with desire. I knew if I kissed her now, she wouldn't stop me. But there was one thing I needed from her more than her mouth on mine. I released her, letting my hand drop.

Disappointment flashed in her eyes. "You know what it means, don't you?"

This was a complete disregard for the bargain I'd made. But I couldn't stop myself from trying to answer her. "It means," I said, shoving the words out through clenched teeth, "You have been blessed by the gods. What you do with those blessings is your choice."

"What exactly am I supposed to choose?" she asked, her brow pinching.

Fuck.

I wanted to reach up and smooth her concern with my fingers. To stroke her skin until all her worries and fears had melted. Instead, I searched for the words the vow would let me speak. It wasn't easy. The leash Duron's blood vow kept me on was tight. And then there was the promise I'd made to my true king. He was even harder to work around, but then he was a Hel of a lot smarter than Duron.

"Do you know why Menryth's magic waned after The Great War?" I asked in a strained voice.

Her eyes widened, and I knew Meerdra had mentioned it. At least she'd done some of my work for me. "The oracle claimed the gods drained its power for themselves."

"Do you know which—" My throat closed and I fell silent.

"Which gods?" She finished for me. "She said it was the Fates and the Furiosities."

I nodded even though it sent pain shooting through my skull. "And?" I ground out.

"And the gods fought over Menryth, but their agreement prevented them from doing direct battle. So, they chose a champion to imbue with their power."

"What else did she say?" It was the only thing I could possibly ask that wouldn't kill me right now. Even so, my breaths were labored. Sweat dotted my brow.

Suspicion slanted her gaze. "She said the champion would have to choose which side to fight for."

I nodded, and awareness flared in her icy blue eyes.

My heartbeat galloped at unsustainable speeds, and I gritted my teeth, hoping like Hel it didn't burst from my damned chest. This was beyond fucked. I shouldn't have gone this far. But if I hadn't, she might not survive this wretched place.

"Are you all right?" she asked worriedly.

Power screamed inside me, sealing my lips shut. Forced

silent, I nodded at her, urging her to make the gods-damned choice already.

She scowled. "I don't see how it's a choice at all. Heliconia's power was gifted by Hel. Why would I fight for the same side as my enemy?"

Fuck.

I blew out a breath, and with it, all my hope drained away.

The pain in my head receded, but the ache of disappointment hollowed me out to my very bones. She'd made her choice. My duty was done. But try as I might, I couldn't make myself walk away. Not even the blood vow pounding in my veins had the power to override my need to protect her.

Whatever I did next was going to be reckless and stupid and would likely get me killed. But Duron would make his move on her soon. Maybe seeing the donation center would help her understand the danger she was truly in here. She could still choose to leave Grey Oak—to save herself. I couldn't tell her what he had planned, but I could show her.

"Come on," I said, taking her elbow and starting for the door.

"Where are we going?" she asked, but her feet moved with mine.

"The donation center. But I'm telling you now, you won't like what you see."

THE
MOON

Chapter Thirty-Four
Aurelia

The air around the donation center was thick with magic, but not the kind that had filled the streets of Rosewood with life. No, this was different—stifling, suffocating, like it was draining the very breath from the fae who passed by. The constant buzzing of whatever siphoning magic they used inside grated on my ears and made it impossible to stop imagining how it might work. Not that I ever wanted to find out for myself.

Rydian was silent and stiff beside me, hovering close as if he thought I might defy his order to remain out of sight. Part of me wanted to try if only to feel his hands on me again. But he'd been acting weird since our conversation in Callan's study. I couldn't shake the feeling that I'd disappointed him with my comment earlier. And I couldn't figure out for the life of me how.

He'd been angry about the bargain I'd made. And still, he hadn't hurt me. Somehow, I knew he never would. And that made his touch all the more dangerous. Especially out here where anyone might see.

Not many pedestrians ventured by us, though. The location on the outskirts of the city meant it wasn't exactly on the way to much else. But I had a feeling most avoided it out of principle. It could've been smack in the city center, and the Autumn fae would have taken the long way around it.

I didn't blame them.

The building loomed ahead, a cold, squat thing that seemed more like a prison than a government building. The fae coming out shuffled like shadows of themselves, shoulders sagging, eyes glazed over. On the right, a line wound out of the main entrance and down the sidewalk where those waiting to make their donation huddled. They looked worn down already—as if they'd accepted their fate, and that acceptance alone had drained them of something vital even before they'd passed through the doors.

I'd thought I needed to see it for myself, to understand what Callan's kingdom had become. But all it did was break my heart in two.

"They're walking to their deaths," I said.

Rydian didn't respond, but I felt his gaze on me—the displeasure of it thrummed right alongside the magic in the air. He was upset, but I had no idea why.

A fae woman stumbled out the front doors, her skin ashen, her eyes glazed and empty. The sight of it hit me like a punch to the chest, and I barely suppressed a gasp.

This fate felt so much worse than the one my own family had been cursed with. Guilt tugged at me, raw and sharp-edged as I thought about this horror happening just across Summer's borders. All the while, I'd been crying over the Summer fae's perpetual sleep.

This was on me.

Callan and Duron might've enforced this atrocity, but I was the one the prophecy had been written for. I was the one who had the power to stop the monster who'd cursed us all.

Instead, I'd thought only of my own people's fate while the rest of the realm suffered their own nightmare.

"Aurelia." Rydian's voice was gentler than I'd ever heard it. But I didn't want to be coddled.

I clenched my fists. "This is monstrous."

His jaw tightened, but he didn't say anything, didn't agree. He didn't need to. His silence was enough, his presence beside me an echo of my own outrage.

I watched as another fae, this one barely older than sixteen, exited the building. His eyes were dim, his shoulders sagging. No one even glanced at him as he ducked his head and hurried down the street.

I turned to Rydian, the rage building inside me. "How long has it been like this?"

"Long enough," he said, his voice flat. He didn't look at me, his eyes fixed ahead, jaw clenched tight.

I shook my head, disgust curling in my stomach. "You all just... let this happen?"

His gaze snapped to mine. His temper sliced through me, cutting so deeply I winced away. "You've spent the last seven years with your head buried in the sand while the rest of us suffered. You have no idea what I let happen, nor do you have any right to judge me for it."

I blinked, shocked at the vehemence behind his words and convicted by the truth in them. I'd been naïve—and stupid— to think my suffering was worse than anyone else's.

Rydian was right that day in the Broadlands.

I'd been hiding.

Shame burned inside me.

But I wasn't going to hide anymore. I owed it to these fae to fight with everything I had.

"It has to stop," I said. "We have to stop it."

I made it one step out of the alcove before Rydian grabbed me.

Our eyes met. His own darkened as he studied me.

"Let go of me," I said.

He let out a breath, but it wasn't acquiescence—it was something bitter, almost mocking. "So you can do what exactly?" His voice dripped with skepticism, and something else—resentment? "Walk in and burn the place to the ground? That should go well."

"I'll find a way," I snapped harsher than I'd meant to, but I couldn't stop the fire burning inside me. Mostly over the fact that he'd guessed my reckless plan so easily. "These people are being drained of their magic, their lives—"

"And you're going to what? Ask them to refuse? To fight?" His voice cut through my racing thoughts. "This is the only way some of them survive. The contributions they make here keep their families safe. You would ask them to risk that safety while you sit, warm and kept, inside that castle?"

I flinched at the bite in his words, but I didn't back down. "We're supposed to protect them, not—"

"They don't need your protection," he said, his gaze dark and unreadable. "They need someone who understands how this world works."

"And you think I don't understand?" I took a step closer, my heart pounding in my chest. He was standing too close, the space between us charged, but it wasn't just with the tension of an argument. No, it was something more, something that made the air feel too thin, made me feel like I couldn't breathe.

Rydian's eyes flashed, his expression hardening. "I think you have no idea what kind of danger you're playing with."

"I'm not playing. I'm trying to help—"

"No," he cut me off, his voice low and angry. "You're trying to feel better about yourself. But you made your choice."

His words stung more than I wanted to admit, but it was the look in his eyes that hurt the most. Where he'd been open before, now there was only a wall. And that infernal mask. I'd told myself it was an act, one I was learning to see through, but in this moment, I couldn't as much as glimpse the male who'd sworn to destroy anything that touched me.

I shook my head. "Why do you care so much about my choices, anyway?" I asked, my voice trembling with the need to hear him say it.

His jaw clenched again. He glanced to the line of fae ahead of us then back to me. For a moment, I thought he might actually answer, might finally tell me what it was he really felt about me. But then, just as quickly, he shut down.

"You don't belong here," he said, stepping back, his voice colder than ever.

I felt the sting of his words deep in my chest, but I refused to let him see it. "Maybe not. But I'm here now, and I'm not going to stand by and watch these people suffer."

He stared at me for a long moment, and in his eyes, I saw the war he was fighting within himself. He didn't think I could change anything. And yet, there was something in the way he looked at me, something that made me think maybe— just maybe—he wished I would try.

THE
MOON

Chapter Thirty-Five
Aurelia

The heavy doors of Callan's study creaked open as I stepped inside, not waiting for his permission. I was too angry for niceties, and the quiet of the palace felt suffocating after what I'd just seen. The image of the fae, drained and weakened, still burned in my mind, and every step toward Callan filled me with a fury that made my magic hum beneath my skin.

Rydian's words had hurt, but I was done hiding. I would do this with or without his help. He trailed behind me now, the loyal hound watching my back as his brother had ordered.

We hadn't spoken a word since we'd left the donation center.

Callan stood by the hearth, a drink in hand, his golden eyes fastened on me as I entered. He didn't seem surprised by my arrival—maybe he'd already gotten word about where I'd been.

Rydian followed me into the room, and when Callan's gaze flicked to his half-brother, his eyes narrowed.

"We need to talk," I said, my voice sharper than usual. But I didn't care. Not anymore.

"Wait outside." Callan's voice was clipped as he waved his brother toward the door.

Rydian didn't move, and I tensed.

"Is there something else?" Callan asked, lifting a brow.

"As a matter of fact, I think I'll stay." Rydian crossed his arms and planted his feet.

Callan glared at him. "You will leave us, or I will mention to dear old Dad that your blood vow needs refreshing."

Rydian's lip curled. "Keep your fucking hands to yourself," he snarled; then he turned and stalked out.

Blood vow?

The door clicked shut, and Callan sighed, setting down his glass. "I assume this is about the donation center?"

I shoved aside all thoughts of Rydian and faced Callan.

"Of course it's about the donation center," I snapped, crossing the room in quick, angry steps. "You never told me your land was cursed like mine."

"I told you Heliconia had not left us untouched. And that we had taken steps to counter her efforts."

"These are the measures in place you mentioned? When were you going to tell me?"

"When it became relevant."

I huffed. "You spoke of honesty and then you lie—about this? Your people are dying. Their magic is being drained like they're nothing. How can you allow this?"

His jaw flexed, and for a moment, I saw something flash in his eyes—regret, guilt, maybe even shame. But it was gone just as quickly, replaced by the unaffected charm he always wore so well.

"It's not that simple."

I stopped in front of him, anger simmering just beneath the surface. "Then make it simple for me. Tell me why we're not doing something to stop this."

Callan turned away from me, running a hand through his

hair. "For what it's worth, I'm against the magic donations," he said. "I never wanted this. It's my father's decree, not mine."

"Then *challenge* him," I said, my frustration boiling over. "You're the crown prince. You have power. You're going to be king one day—*act* like it."

"You think it's that easy?" he hissed. "You think I can just walk into the throne room and tell the Autumn king what to do? My father doesn't listen to reason. He only sees what he wants to see—and right now, that's a kingdom too weak to face Heliconia without sacrifice."

"That's not sacrifice—that's slavery and murder," I said, my voice shaking with disbelief. "You're draining your people to the point of death. And for what? To pretend you're not as vulnerable as you really are?"

Callan's eyes darkened, and for a moment, I thought I saw fear there—real fear. "You don't understand. My father doesn't *ask*. He commands. And if I step out of line, he'll strip me of everything. My position, my magic, my future. And then what will happen to you, to Sevanwinds? To the alliance?"

I blinked, caught off guard by his admission. It hit me all at once—Callan wasn't just unwilling to act, he was *afraid*. Afraid of his father. Of losing the power he'd worked his whole life to secure. He was a child still yearning for his father's favor, no matter what it cost to get it.

"Callan..." My voice softened, but the anger still churned inside me. "You can't just stand by and wait for things to change. You're the future king—if you won't stop him, who will?"

His gaze met mine, hard and unyielding. "We can't afford to fight two wars. My father's methods are wrong, but right now, Heliconia is the real threat. We defeat her first; then we deal with this. We must stay focused."

"That's what I'm trying to do," I snapped, the heat of my magic rising with my frustration. "But you're not giving me the resources you promised. How am I supposed to protect my people if I don't even have the tools to break their curse?"

"Your people?" He huffed. "Is that all that matters to you then?"

"Of course not. I meant your kingdom and mine. *Our* people," I corrected.

But Callan's mouth tightened. I could practically see his ego rearing back. "I intend to help you break the curse. But you have to do something for us first."

"What?"

"We're building a weapon. Something capable of destroying Heliconia with one blast."

"What could possibly do that? The only thing powerful enough is—"

"Magic."

I exhaled. There it was. I'd been waiting for this since the moment I'd learned of the donation centers. The moment when Callan would ask—or pretend to ask—for me to contribute. And if I said no, what then? They'd forcibly escort me down and drain me of my magic too?

Did they expect me to offer Summer fae magic? Or did Duron know what I truly possessed? I swallowed hard, my throat tight with fear.

"Absolutely not," I said, as haughty as a princess should be over such a thing.

Callan's brow furrowed. "Why not? You're the heir to the Summer Court. You're supposed to have the power of the sun at your fingertips. That would be more than enough to acti-vate our weapon."

His confusion disarmed me. So I decided to try for the truth—or some version of it. "Because." I swallowed hard. "I don't have that kind of magic."

"Yes, you do." Callan grabbed my arm, pulling me close, his eyes blazing with determination. "The ward you put around Sunspire when we left. That kind of magic is beyond anything I've ever seen."

Was that jealousy flaring in his golden gaze?

My pulse raced in my ears, and I pulled away from him. "I can't give you what you're asking."

"Then we're out of options," he said coldly. "And your people will remain where they are, trapped in sleep."

I stiffened. "There has to be another way."

"I saved your life, but my help doesn't come free." He ran a hand through his hair, frustration evident in every tense movement. "You owe us something in return. If you can't give it, there's nothing I can do."

"Why bother letting us marry at all if he thinks I'm so weak?"

Callan glanced away but not before the guilt in his eyes sent the truth leaping between us.

"He plans to do to me what he would have done to Heliconia," I said, the breath sucked from my chest at the realization. He'd see me wed to Callan and then kill me before the ink was dried on our marriage contract.

Gods.

"My father wants power," Callan said, his voice distant in my ears. "He's a politician who will use whatever resources he has available to strengthen his holdings."

"And I'm a resource." Not a person. Just something to be used. I was going to be sick. "The other courts will never ally with you when they find out."

"He doesn't intend to kill you, Aurelia."

"Right. That would cut off his supply." He meant to drain me slowly. To keep me alive as long as there was magic to drain from my veins.

Callan didn't bother to argue. "He'll wait until after the

party so that you and I can woo the other courts. They'll come here and see how healthy our land is. How strong we are. And they'll join us, fight with us."

I stared at him, disappointed and angry. "That's it? You continue to beat the dead horse of alliances with the other courts? That plan failed seven years ago, and you've come up with nothing better?"

He glared at me. "You have no idea the work I've put in to win them over," he snapped. "Rumor has it, the Midnight Court has an army more than triple yours and mine put together. If we can bring them to our side, we'll have the numbers and the strength. Their magic alone—"

"The Midnight Court hates everyone," I snapped. "Out of all the courts, they're the least likely to help us. Besides, their magic is probably just as affected as ours considering their land borders Concordia. I'm sure Heliconia—"

"You know nothing!" he roared. His cheeks blew out with heavy breaths and his face flushed red.

I stared at him, stunned into silence at his outburst.

He took several steadying breaths and straightened his collar. With a quick smooth of his hair, he spoke again, his voice deceivingly calm. "I have to work within the parameters my father gives me. This strategy is our best and one we've worked hard to ensure. The Midnight Court has sent word they'll attend our wedding. As will high-ranking members of the other courts. We'll use our alliance to win them over. That is our best path forward."

I didn't bother trying to argue anymore.

He'd clearly spent years developing this weak plan. No amount of logic or sense was going to steer him away now. In fact, all he wanted from me—clearly—was to stand silently beside him like the trophy I was.

My disgust must've shown because Callan eyed me and

added, "If you want more than that for yourself—for your people—you know what you have to do."

His tone wasn't friendly, and I found that almost refreshing. No more fake charm, no more games. He'd finally let the mask drop. At least, I knew where we stood.

"I'm sorry," he said, as if he'd read my darkening thoughts. "For what it's worth, I wanted to be your friend. Maybe even more than friends if you'd let me—"

"I'll find a way," I said, unable to bear the sound of his next words. "With or without your father's help, I will save my people. And you'll regret not doing more to save yours."

His expression turned pained. "Aurelia ..."

But I was already walking toward the door, my heart pounding with determination. I couldn't wait for Callan, for Duron, for anyone.

In the hall, Rydian stood against the far wall. He met my gaze, and I knew he'd heard. Darkness flashed in his depthless gaze, a trove of shadows and secrets that seemed to reach for all the hidden parts of my own heart.

For once, I didn't bother to hide what he might find there. I also didn't look back to see what he made of his discovery.

THE
MOON

Chapter Thirty-Six

Aurelia

I woke to the sound of light footsteps shuffling across the room. My heart leaped into my throat, and I sat up, blinking against the watery dawn streaming through the tall windows. My mind was hazy with exhaustion after such a late night, but the sight of a stranger sharpened me. A woman stood near the window, her head bent as she rearranged a breakfast tray on the small table.

"Good morning, Your Highness," she said in a crisp, unfamiliar voice. "Your breakfast is served though we don't have much time."

My breath caught, and for a moment, I panicked that something had gone horribly wrong. Where was Vanya? She was always here, always fussing over me, making sure my morning tea was the perfect temperature. This woman had dark hair tied back in a severe knot, her frame tall and sharply angled. She looked up, her expression set into a tight mask.

It took me a moment to find my voice. "Who are you?"

"I'm Beryl, your new maid," she said, stepping closer and offering a polite bow.

"Where is Vanya?"

"Vanya is running an errand today."

My chest tightened, the remnants of sleep vanishing in an instant. The donation center. I swallowed against the sickening knot in my throat.

Beryl watched me with a steady, almost clinical gaze. "The king has ordered that you meet with him after breakfast. You don't have much time if you want to eat before getting dressed."

Panic shot through me. "What sort of meeting?"

"That's not my business, Your Highness."

"Right," I muttered.

There were only a handful of reasons the king might want to see me and none of them good. Even if he hadn't heard about my argument with Callan, it wasn't hard to guess he was getting tired of waiting for what he wanted from me.

I ignored the food, my nerves taut as I allowed Beryl to help me dress. She chose one of my fanciest new gowns, and I didn't argue. If there was any way to impress him without the magic he so desperately wanted, I had to try.

Maybe looking the part would help—an illusion rather than the real thing.

You are the real thing, the shadows inside me whispered. But I wasn't Summer fae. So, I shoved them down again, and they shut up.

I half-expected to find Rydian or even Callan waiting for me when I emerged from my room, but the hall was empty.

"This way." Beryl led the way, stiff-backed and silent except for the clicking of her shoes.

I swallowed hard and followed her through the castle.

A set of grand doors loomed ahead of me, the golden trim gleaming in the sunlight that streamed through the large windows. Guards stood on either side of the open doors, their hands resting casually on their swords. They didn't make eye contact as Beryl paused before them.

"Her Highness, Aurelia of Sevanwinds, for the king," Beryl informed them.

"Enter," one of them grunted.

Beryl stepped back and motioned for me to proceed.

My stomach twisted with a mixture of dread and determination.

Last night, I'd returned to my room mostly due to a lack of other options. If I'd gone anywhere else, Rydian would've followed, and despite his loathing for Callan, I wasn't sure he wouldn't report everything I did back to the king. Especially if whatever blood vow Callan had mentioned really existed. Instead, I'd lit a candle, shut the curtains, and done my best to go inward—to the quiet place between worlds, as Sonoma had taught me. The way of the Aine, she'd called it.

A quieting of the mind that had once led to a direct connection with the Fates. It had been so long since anything waited on the other side that I'd stopped the practice.

Last night was the first time I'd tried it in years.

I'd gotten no answer.

Not from the Fates and not from Sonoma. It had been stupid to hope for either one. A flimsier plan than even Callan's.

I was on my own. So, I'd made the most of it. An effort that had lasted long into the night. But it had been worth it.

The guard at the door grunted at me, a sign I had taken too long. With a deep breath, I walked inside, straightening my shoulders as I went.

The large throne room was draped in shadows, despite the late afternoon sun filtering in through tall windows. The king stood by a table, his back to me, studying a map of the fae realms spread across its surface.

I faltered at the sight of it—so familiar. The memory washed over me like a tidal wave. My father and mother poring over a map nearly identical to this one. Planning, strategizing, trying to come up with a way to stop Heliconia.

It hadn't worked then.

I could only hope it would work now, though after hearing Callan's plans last night, I wasn't confident.

Besides, there were marked differences between my memory and this moment. Duron was dressed in full regalia, from the crown on his balding head to the gold-embroidered robes that stretched over his gut. Like he never wanted anyone to forget who and what he was, even in his most private meetings.

Three other fae males were gathered on the opposite side of the table. The same advisors I'd seen in Callan's study. Two of them stood and peered over the maps. The third sat in a chair pushed back from the table, his legs crossed, a mug held casually in one hand.

At the sight of me approaching, they all looked up. Duron's golden crown caught the light, and I had the distinct impression he'd chosen exactly that place to stand for that reason.

Like father, like son, I thought with disgust.

"Princess," he said. His voice, usually so calm and composed, held a sharp edge today. "Come in."

I did as he commanded, my steps careful and measured across the stone floor. The door shut behind me with a soft thud, sealing me in the room.

Trapped.

"You wanted to see me, Your Majesty?" I kept my tone formal, neutral, though it took every bit of my self-control not to let the tension seep into my voice.

For a moment, he said nothing, just studied me. A predator sizing up its prey. "As you know, your alliance with my son was based on certain... agreements between you."

"That's true." My heartbeat quickened.

"My son, without consulting me, offered you resources to solve the Summer Court's current predicament."

His vague wording, the way it removed the emotion and horror, irritated me. But I nodded. "He did."

"And yet you have no army to provide in return for his generous offer."

I stiffened. "Not until the curse is lifted."

"If it can be lifted," he corrected.

My hands curled into fists. I forced them open again.

"Not only has my son put our resources at your disposal, but he has provided a kingdom and a home when you had none." His words were designed to stab, but I didn't let them. Not when they were all watching me closely to see what barbs hit their mark.

"He has been a male of his word," I said. "Honoring the terms of our marriage alliance of seven years ago."

"Generous when you have not honored yours."

"My army is indisposed," I said tightly. "A situation I made clear from the beginning."

"Be that as it may, an alliance requires an offering on both sides." The king's gaze sharpened. "The Summer fae are known for their connection to the land. A bottomless magic that flows from the Fates themselves and renews the earth from one life cycle to the next."

My entire body tensed at his words—at all the ones he wasn't saying yet but soon would. "The Summer fae were very lucky to have such a connection," I said carefully.

He frowned, clearly noting my use of past tense. The other three males shared looks of concern.

"That connection is your gift to this alliance," Duron said. "Before you take your vows with my son, I need to see it."

My heart kicked harder against my ribs. "See what?"

"Don't play coy, Princess," he said, stepping closer. "Your

magic. I need to see what kind of power you possess if I'm to continue offering resources."

"I am sorry to disappoint you, Your Majesty, but my magic was lost to the curse seven years ago." I kept my voice steady, though it felt like it was taking every ounce of my strength just to breathe. "I'm afraid I no longer possess what you're asking for."

The king's jaw tightened, his eyes hardening as he took another step forward. "That's not what my soldiers tell me."

Fuck.

The soldiers who'd seen me battle the Obsidian. And drink its life force as it died.

My pulse quickened. "I'm not sure what your soldiers think they saw, but I can assure you I do not possess the magic—"

"A donation center burned to the ground last night. Witnesses say a lone figure razed the entire structure with a fire the color of midnight."

I stilled. "I'm not sure what that has to do with me."

"My soldiers say that figure had hair the color of summer sunshine. And eyes of cobalt blue. They say that figure was you."

"Your soldiers are mistaken."

"Are you calling my soldiers liars?"

"No," I said. "Only that they might've been mistaken in the chaos."

His voice dropped low. "My son says you are more powerful than any fae he's ever seen. Do you call him a liar too?"

I blinked.

Callan.

He'd sold me out. Of course he had. Holding back would've meant going against his father. It would've meant having a backbone of his own, which he clearly didn't.

"You've been here for a week, and I've seen nothing. No display of power. No sign that you are the heir this realm needs. Until suddenly one of my donation centers burns to ash. And now you expect me to pour more resources into Sevanwinds without something in return?"

The heir this realm needs.

I stared at him, unsure if those words meant what I thought they did. He couldn't know about the prophecy... could he? And if he did, that meant he knew exactly what sort of magic he was asking me to hand over to imbue his weapon.

The room blurred at the edges.

All that remained in focus was the king—his eyes gleaming with triumph.

Seeing that light in his eyes, the cruelty that lay beneath it, made me think of Vanya. Of the fae on the other side of the city currently draining their magic for a king who couldn't care less about their wellbeing. A man who valued the illusion of power more than he did actual strategy.

Heliconia would eat him alive.

I wouldn't let him do the same to me.

"I don't owe you anything," I snapped before I could stop myself, anger flaring in my chest. "I offered my allegiance so that we might fight together, side by side. But I'm not a trophy on a shelf."

His eyes narrowed dangerously. "I've been generous, Aurelia," he said softly. Too softly. "But my generosity has its limits. And so does my patience."

The threat was there, coiled between his words, ready to strike. I clenched my hands into fists, nails biting into my palms as I tried to steady my breathing.

"I've told you, I'm unable to access my magic," I managed, hating how small my voice sounded compared to his. But it was necessary.

"I suggest you figure it out," he said, his voice hard as steel.

"Because if you don't, I won't be able to protect your people. And neither will you."

I swallowed the lump rising in my throat. But I refused to cower.

The king watched me for a long moment, and I could see the calculation in his eyes, weighing whether to press harder, to push me until I broke.

Finally, he stepped back, though the tension in the air didn't lift.

"Think it over," he said, turning away from me and returning to the map on the table. "We'll speak again after the wedding is done. I'm happy to do whatever it takes to access the magic you think you've lost."

I turned and left the room as quickly as I dared, feeling their eyes on my back the entire time.

THE
MOON

Chapter Thirty-Seven
Aurelia

Rydian met me in the hall. I kept my back straight as I strode past him toward my room, my heart thudding wildly as I thought through my options. Leaving this place was going to be tricky. Getting out undetected with all the soldiers who patrolled or kept watch felt nearly impossible. But even if I managed it, there was still the matter of where I'd go.

Aside from Grey Oak, Lightshore—the Spring Court—was the only realm who'd ever been remotely friendly to my kingdom. And they were clear on the other side of Sevanwinds. I'd have to pass through Rosewood or veer up into the Broadlands to get there, and I had no doubt both were crawling with Obsidians by now.

The river people might take me in, but unless I grew gills, it wasn't exactly a viable option, no matter what the mer tried to say. Half of them probably only wanted to eat me for dinner anyway, and the other half were entirely uninterested in the problems of the surface.

The Moriori Islands were a possibility, though I'd have to make it out to the western coast and find passage on a ship, all without being recognized. Still, if I could get there, I'd at least have asylum. The Moriori were pacifists, which meant I'd be safe with them. It also meant I'd be among people who would never agree to fight or become an ally in this war.

And I'd have to get past the Rada people to make it across the sea at all. From the stories I'd heard, they were ruthless and violent with ships that could travel twice the speed of any other.

The Midnight Court loomed as a last resort, though I hardly even counted it as that. As mysterious as it was dangerous, the Midnight Court was a realm unto its own. Darkness hung over it like a veil, and no fae who ventured inside uninvited ever made it out again.

Besides, they'd ignored the Concordians. Done nothing to save them. I couldn't ally with people like that.

My thoughts drifted to Vorinthia. There was nothing there, not officially. No kingdom or army or ally to help me. But Lesha had gone there. And Amanti before her—or, at least, she'd said she was. My heart tugged at me to follow.

Lost in these thoughts, I stormed through the castle, each step pounding out the frustration building inside me. Rydian kept his distance, apparently done helping me or even pretending to be my friend. His silence felt like salt in the wound, but I refused to be the one to go to him.

So, I kept walking. And thinking. A moment later, the sound of boots echoed behind me.

"Aurelia," Callan called.

I didn't bother to stop.

"Aurelia, wait." He jogged to catch up, and I forced myself to face him, keeping my temper—and magic—in check. "How did it go?"

I stared at him, noting his casual tone. Like I wasn't being kept here as a prisoner waiting to be drained of my magic. "Do you mean how did it go when your father threatened me because you told him I have powerful magic?"

Guilt flickered, along with something almost like regret in his eyes. "I shouldn't have let you face him alone."

"You shouldn't have tricked me into this to begin with," I snapped.

Callan winced, his jaw tightening. "I had no choice. I'm fighting for my people, same as you."

My people. I'd brought that on myself.

I laughed, bitter and low. "Fighting? Is that what you think you're doing?"

"You might not like my methods, but I'm only doing what I must to save us."

"Please. This isn't about saving anyone but yourself."

He stepped closer, his eyes pleading, but I held my ground. "That's not true. You're more than just a political match to me."

"Oh, I haven't forgotten. I'm your *resource*, Callan. Nothing more."

His expression faltered. "We just need to get through the party. The other courts already know you're Autumn now. When they see us united, they will pledge their armies. And my father will realize your value."

My value.

I wanted to claw his tongue out.

Instead, I offered him a tight smile, nodding as though I agreed. "Of course."

The Broadlands then. I'd go into the only place not ruled by any court. The only place where no one could try to drag me back here. I'd be gone before the gods-damned party even started. And when the day came for Callan to show the realm who stood beside him, he would find himself standing alone.

Oblivious to my plans or my dark mood, Callan left with the promise of dinner together. Ignoring Rydian, who stood down the hall, I slipped into my room only for Beryl to enter a moment later. She set a tray of tea out, but I ignored her, wandering to the balcony to look out over the grounds.

A harsh clink of porcelain had me turning back again, irritation flaring.

Beryl didn't seem to notice as she poured tea and added honey.

Without looking up, she tossed over her shoulder, "Perhaps some fresh air would do you good."

"Excuse me?"

She straightened, her expression a mask of helpfulness. "A walk in the garden, maybe? Among the trees, where you can think clearly."

A walk in the garden? The suggestion felt too perfect, too timed. I narrowed my eyes at her, suspicion curling in my gut. Beryl had been handpicked by Callan. What if she was spying for him? Nudging me along and hoping to catch me using the magic Callan was convinced I was holding back.

"No, thank you," I said coldly. "I'm fine."

Beryl hesitated, a flicker of something—nervousness, maybe—crossing her face. "Your Highness, I only want to help."

I forced a smile, though it felt like a mask slipping. "I said I'm fine. You're dismissed."

She gave a tight nod, her hands clasped in front of her, but her gaze lingered on me a second too long before she finally turned and left. The moment the door clicked shut behind her, I snarled.

The tension inside me needed an outlet. I changed as quickly as I could, cursing the laces on the dress that made it nearly impossible to get out of without help. Finally, I pulled it loose and yanked on my pants and tunic then shoved my feet into my boots.

Marching across the room, I let out a sharp breath and flung the door open.

Rydian eyed me, arms crossed like he'd been waiting for me all along.

"I need to get out of here," I blurted, my voice sharper than I'd meant it to be.

He didn't hesitate. "Come on."

I grabbed my cloak and hurried to keep up.

Rydian led the way through the quiet halls of the castle, moving swiftly. We barely passed anyone at all, and the people we did see were servants who kept their eyes averted. Rydian greeted them all with murmurs of hello, but whether fearful of him or caught unaware, none of them dared say a word to me.

Finally, we slipped outside, the cold afternoon air hitting my face like a slap. But I welcomed it.

At the stables, the scent of hay and leather filled the air. In the third stall, Shadow whinnied at the sight of me. My spirits lifted as I spotted the familiar horse.

Rydian spoke to a stable hand, who immediately began to saddle Shadow for me.

When he'd readied his own horse, Rydian led them both out and handed me Shadow's reins, his fingers brushing mine. My breath caught, but I swung myself into the saddle before he could see my reaction.

"Where to?" he asked as he mounted.

"Anywhere but here," I said, my heart pounding with the thrill of it.

I kicked the horse into a gallop, Rydian following close behind. We tore through the fields under the cloud-heavy sky, and for the first time in days and days, I felt free.

THE
MOON

Chapter Thirty-Eight

Aurelia

It didn't dawn on me until too late that it might've been incredibly reckless to end up in the middle of nowhere alone with the prince I wasn't engaged to marry. When I finally slowed to a walk, I was hyper-aware of how isolated we were. Thick, autumn woods bordered us on both sides. Far behind us, Grey Oak castle loomed, shrouded in fog. Above us, clouds muted all but the most determined of the sun's rays, leaving the landscape in a gray gloom.

Ahead, the path narrowed as it wound down the craggy hillside. Rather than fall back into single file, Rydian pulled his horse in closer beside me. So close that our boots brushed in their stirrups.

Glancing over, I found him staring into the distance with a thoughtful slant to his brow. My gaze lingered, admiring the strong curve of his jaw and the fullness of his mouth—even if it was set in a hard line.

He looked over at me suddenly, and heat rose to my cheeks.

Busted.

He didn't comment on my staring, though I wasn't sure

the subject of his question was much better. "A strange coincidence about that donation center."

I shrugged, secretly bracing myself for his reaction. "I wouldn't know."

He snorted. "Right."

When he didn't answer, I peeked at his face. But the wry humor was gone. He looked like he had earlier when I'd come out of my meeting with the king. A deadly sort of concern was etched in his brow as he asked, "What will you do about Duron?"

I wanted to tell him it was none of his damn business, but instead, the truth tumbled out. "I will refuse him."

He said nothing as we rode on.

I didn't bother with conversation, relieved to embrace silence for once. I'd lived with it for seven years, to the point of near-madness some days, but I couldn't help feeling that, since coming here with Callan, every word uttered had been a waste.

Lies.

Betrayal.

Manipulation.

I had to get away from it, even if it meant fighting for survival on my own. But I couldn't do that until I found a way to stop the donations.

"Does this lead to the Osphanis?" I asked as we finally made it to the bottom of the hillside.

Just ahead, the riverbed, though wide, had dried up so that nothing but mud and rock remained. The banks on either side were lined with dead grass and rotted brush. My nose wrinkled at the smell of dead fish.

"Yes, it's a tributary— Seven Hels," Rydian breathed.

He pressed his heels into his horse's sides, closing the distance. I hung back, watching as he dismounted and ventured all the way to the edge of the healthy grass. He stopped just short of the dead patches and bent to one knee, studying the ground.

"What is it?" I asked.

He rose and looked toward the forest in the north. "The curse," he said grimly. "It's spread to this side of the river."

"This is a new development?"

He nodded then swung back onto his horse. "Come on. We shouldn't be out this far."

He scanned the trees again, and the hairs on my neck prickled with unease. Then he turned his horse back the way we'd come. I followed reluctantly. So much for finding an escape route. At our backs, the wind felt like an invisible hand trying to grab me before I rode out of reach.

"What will the king do?" I asked, keeping an eye on the distant woods as if an Obsidian army might pour from it at any moment.

Rydian glanced at me but said nothing.

My stomach tightened as the answer dawned on me. "He'll up the donations, won't he?"

"Your engagement party is in a few days," he said grimly. "He'll want Grey Oak to look pristine for his guests. So, yes. He'll up the donations."

"Duron has to be stopped," I said, gripping the reins as we began to ascend the hillside.

"On that, we agree."

Something about the way he said it suggested an outrage that went much deeper than even my own. And for the briefest moment, I finally felt as if Rydian and I were on the same side.

"It's a shame your future husband won't allow your opinion to matter."

Or not.

I glared at him, but he didn't even bother to notice. Anger simmered inside me for the rest of the ride.

When we reached the stables, Rydian headed for the castle alongside me.

"You don't have to walk me," I snapped. "I can find my way."

"I need to speak with Callan," he said.

Of course. "You're going to tell him what we saw."

He cut me a look that probably would've made a lesser fae cringe. "Yes."

"You don't have to," I pressed, refusing to back down. "You could fail to mention it or at least wait until after the party—"

"Duron will find out," he said. "Do you really think it's worth looking like some kind of traitor over information that will come out anyway?"

"I think it's worth it to the fae you'd be protecting," I said.

I bit my lip, hoping my words would sink past that stone encasing his heart—if he even had one at all. But he merely scowled and began stalking toward the castle once again. When we reached the doors, Rydian began to veer off without as much as a goodbye.

"Your Highness!"

Vanya was pale as she hurried up to us with dark circles ringing her eyes. But more than her obvious exhaustion was the urgency radiating from her.

"What's wrong?" I asked. Had something happened at her donation today? Maybe it had taken too much from her. "Are you okay?"

"The king is looking for you," she told Rydian.

From somewhere deep in the castle, a roar sounded. The sheer volume and rage it held boomed painfully in my ears. Vanya winced, and her urgency turned to fear.

"What's happened?" Rydian asked.

"Two Obsidians were caught on the castle grounds," she said quietly. "He blames Callan and the guard for letting them get this far." She hesitated before telling him, "He blames you."

Rydian cursed. "Where's my brother?" he asked her.

"Already inside," Vanya said.

The roar came again, followed by something shattering. The sounds came from the throne room, which should've been too far away to hear it so clearly. Duron's temper was fueled by his power, though. And he was clearly unleashing both without restraint.

"Take Aurelia to her room," Rydian told Vanya.

"We'll have to pass by the throne room to get there," Vanya said, voice trembling. "If he sees her—"

"Take her through the passageway," Rydian told her. "Beneath."

Vanya nodded as if the word alone explained everything.

"Wait," I said when Rydian started to walk away. "What will he do to you?"

A range of emotions passed over Rydian's expression. Hatred. Disgust. Resignation. "His worst," he said simply. "Now, go. And don't come out until Callan comes to get you."

Callan. Right. Because it wouldn't be Rydian. It couldn't ever be Rydian.

I watched him stride, unflinching, toward the throne room.

Vanya tugged at me to follow her. "This way," she whispered urgently, her eyes darting around as if she was half-afraid the king would jump out at us. "Hurry."

She led me away from the throne room down a hallway that displayed portraits of past kings and queens. None of them looked much friendlier than Duron. Through the open doors we passed, I glimpsed a sitting room and a music room before Vanya led us through a door and into a room that seemed to be nothing but storage. Furniture covered in white cloths sat dusty and forgotten. In the light that streamed through the window, dust motes danced in the air.

Vanya led me across the room and over to another painting of a long-dead fae ruler. She reached for the gilded frame and pulled it away from the wall. It swung open like a door, and when I saw the hole cut into the wall behind it, I realized that was exactly what it was.

"Come."

She stepped through the opening, and I followed, heart pounding. I glanced back over my shoulder, half-expecting one of Duron's guards to appear at any moment, but the room behind us remained empty.

Vanya pressed a tiny button on the wall, and the painting swung shut, clicking softly as it latched.

The tunnel was cold, damp. The smell of earth hung in the air like something ancient and forgotten. My breath came too fast. I forced it to slow, trying to calm my racing heart— and the dark magic that woke inside me.

I couldn't afford to panic now.

The passageway twisted down through the bowels of the castle—narrow and winding. As we trekked our way up the other side, another roar sounded, but it was muted inside the walls of the tunnel. Still, I tensed to think what might be happening in that throne room now.

"What do you think the king will do?" I asked.

Vanya glanced back at me, her expression tight. "The king is unpredictable when he's angry."

"Will he hurt them?"

She didn't answer, but her shoulders stiffened.

I swallowed hard, my footsteps heavy on the stone steps as we climbed upward. "Where does this lead?"

"To your room," Vanya said simply. "There's a passage behind the guest quarters. Not many know about it."

I blinked. I'd been in that room for days and had no idea there was a hidden way in—or out.

"Why are you doing this?" I asked quietly as we reached the top of the stairs and entered a long, narrow tunnel. The air here was colder, the walls damp with condensation. "Why help me?"

Vanya stopped, turning to look at me. The flickering torchlight cast shadows across her face, and for a moment, I thought I saw something pass through her eyes—something like hope. "Because you're different. You care in a way that no one except—" She broke off then started again, "I know what the king is like when he doesn't get what he wants."

Her words hung between us, a clear warning.

We resumed our trek in silence.

When we reached another small door at the end of the passage, Vanya handed me the torch and pressed her hand against the stone wall, searching for something. After a moment, there was a soft click, and the door creaked open into darkness.

"This leads to a small passageway behind your room," she whispered. "You'll be able to slip back in without anyone seeing."

"You're not coming with me?" I asked.

"I'm not on duty again until tomorrow," she said. "The other maid will find it suspicious if I show up before then."

Beryl.

Hels, she'd probably be wondering where I was by now. Maybe even waiting inside my room. I'd need to make sure the room was empty before slipping in.

"How did it go today?" I asked quietly. "At your appointment." I couldn't bring myself to say the words "donation" since that was hardly what it was.

"Fine," Vanya said, not meeting my eyes.

"I'm sorry," I told her. "For what you were forced to give."

"I would've done so willingly if I thought it would actually help—" She broke off, her cheeks flushing. "Forgive me."

"Don't apologize. I know what you mean."

Relief flooded her expression.

I hesitated. My room lay just beyond this hidden corridor, but somehow the distance felt vast. "Thank you for helping me."

"Be careful," she said softly, her eyes meeting mine in the dim light.

Before I could respond, she stepped back into the shadows, letting the door slide shut between us.

I stood there for a moment, listening to the quiet. The castle seemed to press down on me from all sides, heavy and cold.

Taking a breath, I turned and started down the short passage toward my room. The sound of my footsteps felt too loud, too sharp against the stone floor, but there was no one else here. No one except me—and the creeping sense that everything was closing in.

When I reached the small panel in the wall, I pushed it open quietly, stepping into the familiar space of my room. The cold air from the hidden passageway followed me, lingering like a shadow.

THE
MOON

Chapter Thirty-Nine
Aurelia

Hours passed, and no one came. Outside my window, the sun set, and darkness overtook my room. I paced so long my feet ached. Beryl brought me dinner, but I took the tray from her at the door and sent her away, too worried to eat or even pretend everything was fine. To her credit, she didn't push. Even she seemed to sense the tension hanging over the castle.

I considered going back through the hidden passageways to search for Rydian or Callan, but I didn't want to make things worse for either of them if I was caught.

The moon had risen high, and I'd finally begun to doze off in my chair when the soft creak of my door opening brought me awake suddenly.

Callan stood in the doorway, his usually confident stance faltering. Some hidden part of me deflated at realizing it wasn't Rydian—but I shoved it away. Instead, I focused on the male I considered my true enemy now. His amber eyes, normally sharp and full of calculated intent, were glassy and bloodshot. He reeked of blue vervain.

"Callan?" I asked, taking in the disheveled state of him.

His russet jacket hung loosely like he'd pulled it on in haste, and his hair was messier than I'd ever seen. But the worst was the black eye, an ugly bruise forming beneath the skin along the tip of his cheekbone. A cut ran below it, the blood dried but not tended.

I stood, gaping. "What happened to you?"

He shut the door behind him, leaning against it for a moment as if gathering himself before pushing off and walking toward me. "It's nothing." His voice was hoarse, heavy. "Just... my father being my father."

"Duron did this?"

Callan chuckled darkly, rubbing a hand across his face. "When things go wrong, I'm always the one who takes the blame."

"Why would he hurt you like this?"

And where was Rydian? Was he hurt too?

"Come here." Rather than give me an answer, he closed the distance and tugged me into his arms. I stiffened but didn't pull away. He didn't deserve my comfort, and yet I knew whatever he'd become, his father had been the one to make him this way.

Finally, he stepped back and gazed down at me, brushing my cheek with his fingers. "You are so beautiful." His breath hit me—the scent of alcohol so strong I nearly choked on it.

"You're drunk," I said with disgust. And high. But it wasn't the first time for that.

He grinned. "Yeah."

I shook my head, but he caught my chin with his fingers and held my gaze. "So fucking beautiful," he said again. Then he brushed his lips over mine.

I shoved him off me, glaring.

But Callan didn't seem to notice or care about my reaction.

He turned almost sullen. "My father—he said I should've

known Obsidians would get in. Should've fortified our defenses better."

"How could you have known?"

"I'm the general, remember?" He sounded bitter. Resentful. "The great and victorious commander of Autumn." He snorted. "The people would love to know it was Rydian's strategy and my face on it that won us Staghall."

I stared at him, only surprised that he'd said it out loud.

"Does your father know Rydian's the strategist?" I asked carefully.

"Of course he does. Why do you think he's so angry all the time? His bastard son is the brains *and* the brawn in the family. And what am I beyond a punching bag or an errand boy?" He shook his head. "His temper's never good when I— when something like this happens. But with the engagement party coming up, it's even worse. He wants everything perfect, everything under control, and he blames me when it's not."

"He called for Rydian too. Is he okay?"

Callan's eyes narrowed. "He'll live to see another day." He pinned me with a look that was suddenly much sharper than it had been. "You seem awfully concerned with the brother who isn't your fiancé. Any particular reason?"

"He saved my life once," I reminded him.

"You're marrying *me*, Aurelia." He took a step forward so suddenly that I took one back. "Not him. Worry for me. Care about me."

"Callan, you're not yourself."

"You think I don't see how you look at him?" I remained silent, but his eyes flashed with fury. "Rydian's a bastard son. He's nothing to this kingdom. A soldier. A weapon to wield. And he always will be. Remember that."

A weapon to wield.

Except that Rydian had told me he was my weapon now.

"Where are the Obsidians?" I asked, needing to change the subject.

He shook his head, pacing now, his movements restless. "Dead, thank the Fates. The guards—" He swallowed hard, his voice dropping to a whisper. "The guards were barely alive when we found them. If more had come, if they'd reached the castle..."

My heart raced, the danger too close for comfort. Had they come for me? Did she know I was here? "But they didn't, right? Everyone here is safe."

"Not safe enough." He stopped pacing and turned to me, his eyes pleading now, desperate. "Aurelia, your magic... You could help. You could stop this from happening again."

I shook my head, heart pounding. "Callan, I told you, I don't have that kind of power."

"Yes, you do," he insisted, stepping closer, reaching out as if to convince me through touch. "You don't need to do anything grand—just... help us keep the castle safe. Maybe at the party. Use it to keep things running smoothly, make sure no Obsidians can get close. Just once."

I shook my head, pulling back from him. "I can't."

"You're lying." His voice dropped, and the sadness that had clung to him began to twist into something darker, something more dangerous. "I know about what you did to that donation center. And I know about the prophecy."

My heart stopped.

"I know that the Fates chose you to stop Heliconia," he said, his voice hardening with every word. "I know how powerful you are. You're the key to all of this. The Chosen One."

"I don't know what you're talking about." The words tumbled out of me, too fast, too defensive.

But Callan's eyes narrowed, the drunken sorrow fading entirely, replaced by cold fury. "You've been hiding it from me.

From all of us." He took another step forward, his towering presence suddenly suffocating. "All this time, pretending you're just a princess with some simple fae gifts. But it's not true, is it? You've been keeping your real magic a secret."

I backed away, my pulse hammering in my ears. "I haven't—"

"Stop lying!" he roared, his voice echoing through the room as he grabbed my shoulder, his grip bruising. "You think I'm a fool? My father told me everything. He knew from the start, but I defended you. I forced this marriage, believing we could work together. But now I see... you were lying to me all along."

My skin prickled with fear as he squeezed my shoulder, his face mere inches from mine, twisted with rage. He reached up and brushed my hair back, exposing my throat. He pressed his fingertips to my tattoo, squeezing.

"You kept this from me," he accused. "*Me.* After everything I've done to protect you, to get us this far, and you—" He stopped himself, his voice trembling with frustration. "Do you even understand what's at stake? Do you even care?"

"Let go of me."

I yanked myself out of his grip, but he shot out his hand and wrapped it around my forearm, tightening to the point of pain. When I winced, his eyes darkened, his voice dropping to a low, venomous whisper.

"You're supposed to be the one who's going to save us all." He snorted. "Except you're too much of a coward to use your power. You'd rather let Obsidians tear this place apart than admit what you really are."

I yanked on my arm, but he held fast. Fear and anger churned inside me, urging me to show him exactly what I really was. "I'm not the coward."

I felt the surge of power before I could stop it. My magic, dark and wild, lashed out like a storm, slamming into Callan with enough force to send him crashing into the far wall. He grunted in pain, his body slumping to the ground, glass shattering around him.

For a moment, he didn't move, his breath ragged as he lay there, stunned.

Then, slowly, he pushed himself up, his eyes gleaming. "Your magic is dark."

I stood frozen, my chest heaving, the remnants of my power crackling in the air between us. "You're mistaken."

"Am I? And what will you do to convince me of that, Princess?" His mouth twisted. "Will you make me forget again? Wipe my memory so I can't spill your secrets?"

I stared at him, recovering belatedly to shake my head. "Of course not. I don't know what you're—"

"Save it." He climbed to his feet, wiping blood from his lip. His eyes were colder now, darker. "Do your people know you have darkness inside you? Or did you wipe their memory too?"

"Of course not," I hissed. "And I didn't wipe yours."

"There's no use pretending anymore, Aurelia. It won't help you now."

"I could say the same of you, general. I saw you run from Heliconia that night. You're no warrior, Callan. You're a coward."

"And yet you accepted my proposal so easily."

I exhaled. "When did you know?"

"When the ward came down."

I stared at him. "That was before you proposed."

"I kept waiting for you to explain. To just be honest and tell me why you did it. But you never said a word. I gave you more than enough chances, and you lied every time."

I shook my head. "The Aine—"

"Enough!"

I flinched.

"I don't want to hear any more lies," he said.

I held his gaze, releasing any guilt I might have had for wiping his memory. "You can't tell anyone," I said firmly. "Especially your father. The fate of the realm depends on our alliance, Callan. You and me. That's how we destroy Heliconia."

"You should've thought about that before you lied. Maybe if you'd been honest, I would've been willing to help you." His voice was low, dangerous. "But now, you leave me no choice but to use you the way you used me."

My heart raced. "Callan—"

He raised a hand, silencing me. "Marry me and give me your magic willingly, or I'll let him drain you so thoroughly you won't have anything left."

"I'd burn this place to the ground before I let that happen."

"And then what?" he challenged. "Where will you go? Word is already spreading of the dark wielder with Hel's flames who took down that donation center. Once the people learn your magic is just like hers, they'll come for you. Not a single kingdom in the realm will save you. And you'll end up just like the cursed fae you left behind—alone and lost, forever."

His threats settled inside me like ice in my veins. I'd saved them by burning that place, but Callan was right; they might not see it that way.

Callan smiled, a cruel, twisted thing. "Get some rest, Princess. The king will want you at your best when he takes what's his."

THE
MOON

Chapter Forty
Aurelia

The moment the door slammed behind Callan, I went to the armoire and dug past the gowns Callan had bought for me until I found the bag I'd brought from home. Shoving it open, I inhaled the familiar scent of Aine leathers and felt something inside my chest unfurl. Sonoma might have been a formidable fighter, but she'd been wrong about one thing: I didn't need Callan's help to destroy Heliconia. The oracle had spoken true. I had always only been looking for myself. And as horrible as it'd been since coming here, I'd found her.

Shucking my dress off, I pulled on the warrior's clothing that I'd mistakenly thought had no place in my new life. I worked quickly, braiding my hair and strapping Dorcha and Latha, my swords, to my back. Finally, I pocketed the gold and jewels I'd taken from Sunspire. It felt all too familiar now, this hasty departure. I'd have to abandon my other plans. But I couldn't be here any longer. I'd have to find a way to help Autumn's citizens from the outside.

Crossing the room, I felt for the doorway to the passage I'd come through earlier. It was more difficult to access from this side, the seam hidden and the latch stubborn. My shaking fingers finally found it, though, and the panel slid open with a soft click.

Darkness yawned before me, cool air rushing out like a whisper of warning. The torch I'd left earlier was gone, which reminded me I wasn't the only one using this passage. But I had to risk it.

Staying would be a death sentence.

If not for me then for Callan. And if I slipped and used my magic on him again, I might not be in a position to escape the consequences.

Pulling my hood up, I stepped into the narrow passage. The stone walls pressed in close, and the only light came from the faint glow of a torch burning from a sconce farther up the path.

I forced myself to move, every step echoing in the silence as I descended deeper and deeper into the bowels of Grey Oak.

Focus.

But my mind wouldn't quiet. Callan's threats, Duron's betrayal, the prophecy—they all swirled like a storm in my head. My skin prickled with fear, my magic coiling inside me, restless and wild. What if they came after me? What if Callan had already told Duron I'd escaped? What if guards were waiting for me at the other end?

And beneath it all, I thought of Rydian.

Despite everything, I fought the urge to find him first. To make sure Duron hadn't hurt him like he'd done to Callan.

Stupid, I told myself. *He doesn't need you.*

I kept going.

My footsteps were soft but swift as I navigated the narrow twists and turns. Just like before, the passage descended lower and lower until I felt like I was being swallowed by the earth itself. My pulse roared in my ears, louder than the quiet shuffle of my cloak brushing the walls.

Suddenly, a noise echoed from up ahead. I froze, my heart slamming against my ribs. *Voices?*

Gods, no.

I pressed myself flat against the wall, holding my breath as the distant murmur of voices—servants, from the sound of it—drifted through the passage, barely audible but unmistakable. They were close. Too close. My fingers clenched into fists, the familiar tug of magic pulling at the edges of my mind, begging to be released.

I forced the magic back down, clenching my jaw as I waited. Seconds stretched into an eternity, the cold stone biting into my back as I stayed perfectly still. My breathing was shallow, quiet, but each exhale felt like it echoed off the walls.

Finally, the voices faded, drifting away into the distance.

Slowly, carefully, I started moving again. Every step felt like a gamble. Every moment, I expected to hear the clang of swords being drawn, the rush of footsteps coming for me.

But they didn't. And after what felt like forever, I found myself at the end of the passageway where Vanya and I had come through earlier. From here, I'd have to get to the exit using the main halls. My chest tightened at the thought of who else might be out there.

I listened intently before easing open the portrait. The door swung out, and I slipped through before gently clicking it back into place. Then, I waited, straining to listen.

Silence.

I crept around the furniture draped in cloth, careful not to disturb the dust. At the doorway to the storage room, I paused again.

Footsteps sounded faintly until they disappeared.

I didn't let myself second-guess it before slipping into the hall. With my hood pulled low, I strode confidently toward the back door. If anyone stopped me, all I had was royal arrogance. The absolute belief that I was allowed to go where I pleased.

I prayed to the Fates it wouldn't come to that.

The grand doors that led out of the castle were just ahead, and it took all I had not to break into a run before I reached them.

Even when I shoved them open and stepped outside, I braced for a guard to demand to know what I was doing. But the exit was empty. Overhead, a sliver of moonlight filtered through the clouds—just enough to see the path that led past the stables to the hillside Rydian and I had visited earlier—but mostly, the night was wreathed in shadows.

The Fates were smiling on me.

I didn't bother with a horse, despite wishing I could bring Shadow. Risking the stables would only get me caught. Maybe I could come back for him one day.

I kept moving, and when I got to the hillside, I nearly lost my footing, thanks to my harried pace. Every snap of a branch, every rustle of leaves felt like a threat. But I forced myself to slow, picking my way carefully down the rocky slope.

The trickle of the stream reached my ears.

Almost there.

At the bottom, I grabbed handfuls of my cloak, lifting it, and ran, my feet flying over the uneven ground, my heart thundering in my chest.

My legs burned as I pushed forward, stumbling over roots and rocks, my breath coming in short gasps. The cold bit at my cheeks, but I kept running, faster, harder. The river was close—I could hear it now, the water growing louder with each step. If I could just get across it and to the forest on the other side, I would be free.

Just a little farther. Just a little—

Suddenly, a figure loomed out of the darkness, grabbing me by the arm and yanking me to a stop. I gasped, instinctively reaching for the magic that simmered beneath my skin, ready to unleash it on whoever dared to—

"Hello, Furious."

One look at Rydian's expression and my hopes of escape came crashing down around me.

He stood between me and the river, blocking the way. His arms were crossed, his body taking up too much space even out here in the wide open. The light of the moon slashed across him, making him look more like a predator than a soldier.

I froze.

"Going somewhere?" His voice was low, calm. But the look in his eyes wasn't.

My pulse spiked, but I kept my expression neutral. If he was going to stop me, I wasn't going to make it easy. "Move," I said, my voice steady. "I'm leaving."

"You need to go back inside."

I clenched my fists. Magic built inside me, pushing against my skin, ready to explode if I let it. "You don't know anything about what I need."

He didn't flinch. He just stood there, watching me like he always did, like he was waiting for something. "You leave now, you're as good as dead. Do you really think there aren't more Obsidians out there waiting for us to let our guard down?"

"I can take care of myself," I snapped, stepping closer.

"And where do you intend to go?"

"The coast," I said, daring him to argue with my plan. "Even the Rada aren't as bad as this place."

His eyes darkened at that, but he didn't move out of my way. "You won't make it halfway. You know what's out there. What's waiting."

I took another step forward, close enough now to see the tension in his jaw, the tightness around his mouth. And the swollen bottom lip. Duron had gotten him too. "What's waiting out there is better than marrying your precious brother and being drained of my power until I'm one of the Withered."

The mention of Callan had rage flashing in his eyes, though I had no idea if it was meant for Callan or me. He shook his head, his expression hardening. "I told you, Furious. The next person who puts his hands on you dies. Or did you forget that part?"

I bit my lip, deciding to spare Callan's life by not mentioning the way my *ex*-fiancé had grabbed me earlier. Not to mention the kiss.

"Is there something you want to tell me?" His voice had gone low and full of violence.

Nope. Definitely not telling him. "I refuse to be a pawn— in the coming war or in your sibling rivalries. Now move."

For a split second, I thought he might. But then his eyes locked on mine, steady and unwavering. "I can't let you do that."

The words hit me harder than I wanted to admit. I'd thought—*hoped*—he might help me, that whatever strange connection we had might be enough to make him let me go. But no. He was still Duron's soldier—Callan had been right about that after all.

"I'm not your property," I said, feeling the magic flare hotter inside me, begging to be released. "You don't get to decide what I do."

"You think this is about me controlling you?" His voice sharpened, something cold slipping through his calm. "I'm trying to keep you alive. You leave now, and you won't make it a day."

The frustration, the fear, the pressure that had been building for weeks—months, years—all crashed into me at once, and I let the magic loose.

It burst out of me in a violent pulse, sending a wave of black flame surging toward him.

He grunted, stumbling back as it hit him. But he didn't fall. Or burn. He barely even flinched.

"Aurelia, stop," he warned, his voice tight.

The sound of my name on his lips shuddered through me.

I had no idea how he'd withstood what I'd just thrown at him, but my rage and desperation made it impossible to care. I gathered more magic, feeling it burn in my chest as I pushed it outward again, harder this time. Instead of flame, raw power burst from inside me.

The ground shuddered as the force slammed into him.

Rydian held his ground, growling as he braced himself against the impact. He was stronger than I'd realized—too strong. Before I could summon another burst, he moved, closing the distance between us in an instant. His hand wrapped around my waist, his grip firm and unyielding as he dragged me against him.

There was no malice behind the move.

It was the opposite.

In his eyes burned a flame that lit my core.

Then, with his other hand, he cupped my throat. His thumb brushed over my tattoo, and though his grip was firm, it wasn't painful. Being held like this, by him, was intoxicating.

My magic sputtered, fizzling out as his fingers tightened around me, sending a shockwave through my body that had nothing to do with power. I struggled against him, waiting for the moment when he'd tighten his grip and choke the air from my lungs. But instead of hurting me, he brushed his mouth over my throat, inhaling deeply.

I shuddered, hating myself for it.

"Let me go," I hissed, twisting in his grip, but he didn't. His body was too close, too warm, and I hated the way I could feel his strength—hated the way my heart reacted, pounding harder in my chest for reasons that had nothing to do with fear.

When he kissed me, I didn't fight it.

I melted instantly.

His mouth was greedy and hot, his tongue demanding—claiming. I whimpered, ready to beg for more if that was what it took.

But he pulled away, refusing to give me what I wanted.

"I'm not your enemy," he said. "But I can't let you leave."

I shoved at his chest, but it was like trying to move a stone wall. "You can't keep me here."

His grip loosened a fraction, but not enough to let me go. His voice was quieter now, softer. "I only want to keep you safe."

"*Safe*?" I spat, glaring up at him. "From what? Being used by your brother like some kind of hunting trophy? Or from your father draining me until I'm dead?"

He went still, his expression hardening. "I'm sorry," he said quietly. "But I can't let you go."

"You knew," I realized. "You knew all along what Duron was after. What he wanted me for."

When he answered, his voice was ragged. "Yes."

I sagged against him. Tears burned at the edges of my vision, but I swallowed them. I wouldn't cry. Not in front of him.

"Why do you hate me so much?" I whispered, utterly defeated.

His grip on me loosened, but he didn't let me pull away. His eyes held mine, filled with some emotion far more absolute than anything I'd been expecting.

"I could never hate you," he said softly, like a promise.

But it didn't feel like a promise. It felt like a lie.

THE
MOON

Chapter Forty-One
Rydian

I was weaker than I ought to be, which was why I ended up in the passageway outside her bedroom long after the castle had gone to sleep. Tomorrow, I would lose her forever. There was only tonight. And I'd be damned if I let it go to waste.

The secret doorway opened silently, thanks to my shadows.

I stepped into her bedroom, my eyes already adjusted to the darkness. Like a beacon calling to my soul, all my attention went to the slight frame tucked beneath the covers of her bed. Her back was to me, her golden hair splayed out on the pillow, just begging to be touched. I closed the distance, my heart pounding louder than it should, considering my training.

Not to mention my nature.

I was a walking nightmare. But when I closed my eyes, she was the one starring in every single one of my dreams.

Rounding the bed, I knelt beside her, studying the smooth lines of her face as she slept. In this state, her features were unmarred by worry—or ire for me. But behind those closed lids, there was more than fear or fury.

There was light.

Even as I thought it, her lids flew open. She looked at me with startled blue eyes, and then her hand whipped beneath her pillow, and she thrust a blade to my throat.

"Good girl," I told her, pride and lust coating my words.

Her eyes narrowed. "What the Hel are you doing in my room?"

"Saying goodbye."

"Have you changed your mind about letting me go?" she asked.

"Not tonight."

Tomorrow.

The unspoken word hung between us. She lowered the blade.

"If you put that away, I'm going to kiss you," I told her, my voice ragged. "And I'm not going to stop."

"You want me to slit your throat to keep you from kissing me?"

"I want you to tell me to stop right now so I can leave you alone like I should have done from the beginning."

She hesitated, her expression softening. The way she looked at me now was so inviting that I groaned.

"Stay."

My mouth crashed against hers, and at the first taste of her, I forgot my intention to be slow. Or gentle. She tasted like sunshine and warmth; an intoxicating relief against the frigid cold I'd lived inside for far too long.

"Rydian," she whispered against my lips, and I lost it.

Crawling into bed, I did the thing I'd fought against since the moment I met her and tangled my fingers in her soft, thick hair. Burying my face against her throat, I inhaled the scent of moonflower and roses. The way her scent infiltrated my senses reminded me of that rooftop party so long ago. The way I'd taunted her about pleasing her. The way I'd thought of doing nothing else since.

Pressing kisses to her throat, her cheek, her jaw, I made my way back to her mouth. Her lips parted willingly for me. Her arms wound around my neck, her hands roaming and pulling me in closer. Drunk on her, on this moment at last, I took exactly what she was offering, which was everything. With my tongue, I conquered her. With my hands, I begged for more.

She was sunshine incarnate.

And at least, for one night, I reveled in the light.

Aurelia

Rydian's kiss shattered me.

I had spent so long fighting him, denying the pull that had always drawn me toward him like a ship toward a deadly, beautiful shore. But tonight, there was no denying him. No denying myself. Even the secrets he still kept from me didn't matter because he was right. This was goodbye.

Rydian's hands tangled in my hair, his grip firm but reverent, as though he had spent an eternity imagining this moment. When he drew back, his dark eyes shone down at me as if I were the goddess and he the acolyte come to worship.

"You can't imagine how long I've wanted to do this."

I didn't have an answer for him except to reach up and press my lips to his in silent agreement.

His mouth was all heat and desperation, and I met him with the same reckless hunger, my fingers fisting in the fabric of his tunic to pull him closer. As if I could drag him into me, into my bones, and make him stay there.

The weight of his body settled over mine, the familiar scent of him—smoke and spice, shadow and danger—filling my senses as I arched into him. My heart pounded, my breath caught, and I knew, deep in my soul, that this was the first and last time I'd ever be with Rydian Nytherra.

Tomorrow, I would leave this place—and him—forever.

Tonight, I would give him every piece of me I had.

I squeezed my eyes shut, pushing the thought of tomorrow away, focusing only on the now. The way his lips moved against mine, the way his body trembled as though he, too, was holding on by a thread. I tugged on his tunic, and he lifted just long enough to peel it off. Even in the dark, I noted the symbols etched across nearly every inch of his bared skin. I had no idea what any of them meant, but they reminded me of the one the oracle had given me. The mark of a bargained favor.

Had Rydian promised favors to someone too?

When he lowered himself over me again, I ran my hands over the hardened planes of his chest and found more than a few slashes of raised scars. He shuddered at my touch and kissed me like I was the last breath he'd ever draw. I thrilled at holding such power.

His hand snaked up my thigh, shoving my nightgown to my hips. I tensed, need burning like furyfire inside me. He trailed his fingers across my inner thigh, higher and higher until his thumb brushed over my clit.

I arched my hips into his touch, breathless for more. Instead, he broke his kiss to look down at me with wild, fervent eyes.

"Where are your undergarments?" he whispered roughly.

My lips curved at the desperation in him. And the hardness that pressed against my leg. "They're uncomfortable to sleep in."

He barked out a laugh.

"You never cease to surprise me, Furious." He growled as he kissed me again, his tongue licking and stroking as his fingers slid through my folds. "So fucking wet for me already."

He pushed a finger inside me, and I whimpered.

Gods.

I was coming undone.

My nails raked across his back, and he groaned into my mouth, his fingers flexing at my waist as though he wanted to mark me, claim me, make me his. But we'd already been stolen from each other before I'd ever had a chance to belong to him.

Slowly, he drove his finger inside me. Then nearly out again.

I gasped, clinging to him. Kissing him. Opening for him.

"I asked you once how I could please you," he said against my mouth. "Do you remember?"

"I remember," I managed, tipping my head back as he trailed kisses along my jaw.

"Does this please you, Furious?" he whispered before taking my mouth again.

"Yes," I moaned.

He gave a dark, delicious sort of laugh as he increased his efforts.

With his fingers stroking me, his lips left mine, trailing fire down my throat, over my collarbone. "Beautiful," he whispered, his voice wrecked, reverent.

I shuddered as his breath warmed my skin, my hands slipping into the midnight strands of his hair.

The words were useless, but I couldn't stop them. "I don't want to lose you," I breathed.

Rydian's head snapped up, his storm-cloud eyes blazing as they met mine. "Then don't."

A plea. A demand. A promise.

The world outside these walls was already waiting to tear us apart. Duty would demand that I rise from this bed in the morning and walk toward a future that had never truly been mine. But tonight, in his arms, I was free.

I gripped his arms, pulling him back down to me, silencing any more words with my mouth. This time, it was my turn to take, to demand, to savor. His lips parted beneath mine, and I didn't hesitate. I kissed him with every ounce of the longing, the anger, the hunger I had been forced to lock away, and he responded in kind.

His hands roamed, mapping the curves of my waist, my hips, branding every inch of me with fire. His lips never stopped moving, trailing from my mouth to the sensitive skin just beneath my ear, down the column of my throat. He kissed me like I was something he had no right to touch, something he would be forced to let go of come dawn.

But I wasn't letting go.

Not tonight.

I surged up, wrapping my arms around his neck, pulling him down, deeper, closer. His pants came off. Then my nightgown. I wrapped my hand around his length, noting the sheer size of him with a thrill of anticipation. But he hesitated, his gaze holding mine even as he strained to keep himself still.

"Say you want this," he rasped against my skin. "Say you want *me*."

There was no hesitation. No doubt.

"I want you," I whispered, my voice raw, honest.

With a rumble from his throat, his lips found mine again, stealing my breath, stealing everything, and I let him take it.

Let him take all of me.

He slid inside me, and my mind blurred, lost in the sensation of him, in the way his hands traced fire across my skin, in the way our bodies tangled, moving together, chasing something we had spent too long denying. My magic thrummed beneath my skin, heating me from the inside out. Or maybe that was Rydian. I was lost to tell where I ended and he began.

The way he filled me, stretching me gloriously as he drove into me, ignited my soul.

I told myself it was desire, nothing more.

For so long, I had fought against this, against him, against the way he made me feel. But I was tired of fighting. Tired of pretending.

So I stopped.

I let go.

And I fell.

THE
MOON

Chapter Forty-Two
Aurelia

Beryl's hands moved deftly as she tightened the laces of my gown, her austere features set in concentration while she worked. Her demeanor was as cold and clinical as ever. I'd grown used to it in the past few days, but I couldn't shake the sense that her unfriendly manner hid more than just a rigid personality.

I glanced at Vanya, who stood by silently. The dark circles beneath her eyes were finally beginning to fade, but she hadn't been the same since her donation. Apparently, the building I'd burned had been one of three spread across the city. Vanya had reported to one of the two I'd left standing and paid her tax after all.

She met my eyes and nodded once before quickly looking away again. It was the confirmation I needed to know my message had been delivered. Now, I could only hope its recipients decided to accept my offer.

Beryl pulled again at the laces of my gown; this time so hard that I gasped. "I think that's tight enough," I croaked.

"The king wants everything perfect for the party, Your Highness. You'll barely notice the snug fit once you've worn it for a few minutes," Beryl said briskly, finishing with the final lace. "There. All done."

I met her gaze in the mirror, forcing a smile that felt more like a grimace. One more night in a gown was worth it if it meant I was free of this place. "Thank you."

Vanya gave me a pointed look as she stepped forward to adjust the folds of my gown. "Everything is ready," she whispered, her voice barely audible.

I gave her a small nod, my throat tightening with emotions I didn't dare show. Studying my reflection, I had to admit the dress was beautiful—a deep green, embroidered with silver vines, that hugged my figure at the top then flowed out in a wide skirt at my waist.

I could barely feel the thick velvet against my skin, not with my thoughts swirling. Callan's betrayal. Rydian's midnight visit. The passage in my room, locked when I'd woken up this morning. And my single scrap of a plan already set in motion.

A knock sounded at the door, and my heart squeezed.

It was now or never.

I knew it was Callan even before the door opened. Turning to face him, I fought the urge to strike out at him. It wouldn't do any good. Even if I ran for it, there were too many soldiers between me and freedom. Too many Autumn fae willing to drag me back to Duron and let him do whatever he wanted with me.

As if to prove it, I glimpsed Fletcher and a few other soldiers through the open door. Callan might've insisted on keeping up the illusion that I was here of my own free will, but it was a lie.

I was a prisoner.

And tonight, I was nothing more than a symbolic decoration on his arm. A tool to wield for his own gain.

A trophy, after all.

He entered expectantly, his gaze immediately locking onto me, and a smile—charming and practiced—spread across his lips. He looked every bit the prince tonight, his auburn hair swept back, his forest green tunic embroidered with gold thread that shimmered in the firelight.

His black eye had healed with no trace of injury.

"You look beautiful." He took my hand and raised it to his lips, brushing a kiss over my knuckles. "I know the past few days haven't been what we envisioned for our partnership, Aurelia. I hope that tonight we can start over." His voice was as smooth as the silk of my gown. "That we can forget everything else and just... begin again."

I stared at him, barely blinking.

Is he serious?

He thought we could wipe the slate clean, pretend he hadn't betrayed me, used me? I didn't answer, letting the silence stretch until it became uncomfortable.

Callan's smile fell.

Whatever happened, I wasn't going to let it be easy for them.

But then, behind him, I caught a glimpse of Rydian standing in the hallway with the others, his arms crossed, his expression as dark as ever. In another world, in a different life, Rydian and I would have had more than one night. But that was not the world we lived in.

He nodded at me as if urging me to play along.

Whatever harsh words I'd been about to unleash died on my lips. Instead, I smiled sweetly at Callan, as if nothing were wrong. "Of course," I said, my voice light, airy. "We're all adults here."

Callan's smile widened in relief, and I forced myself to focus. "Good," he said, oblivious to the bitter taste those words had left in my mouth. "I want us to be unified in front of our allies. Tonight is important."

I nodded. "Yes. Very important," I murmured, my own agenda simmering beneath the surface.

Callan gave my hand one last squeeze before offering his arm. "Ready?"

I took his arm.

"I'm ready," I said.

The ballroom shimmered, thanks to the chandeliers over-head. They reminded me of the lamplight party Sunspire threw every year for my birthday, which only made me think of my family—and home. Swallowing against the lump in my throat, I stopped beside Callan just outside the open doors, waiting to be announced, and my breath caught for a moment at the opulence of it all. Red roses and moonflowers—symbols of the Summer Court—twined in delicate clusters around glowing lanterns set as centerpieces on the tables scattered along the far edges of the room. The small nod to my home should've reassured me, but it only served to tighten the knot of anxiety in my chest. Because everywhere else I looked, there was only Autumn—opulently displayed.

Leaves the color of burnt orange and fiery gold wreathed the banquet tables. Vines made of gold crawled across the ceiling and down the walls. Alive somehow, despite the enchantments to make them gleam and glitter. Servers wore deep burgundy uniforms with crowns of ivy woven into their hair.

Duron wasn't leaving any doubt that his power was greater than the enemy's curse. Unfortunately, he'd all but killed his own people to do it.

My stomach roiled with the thought of how much magic he'd taken from them in order to make tonight possible.

Vanya's, for one.

The idea that her magic had gone to turning freshly grown vines into gold fueled my rage. I tamped it down, reminding myself of the task at hand.

Tonight was a performance, and I was the star of the show.

As if on cue, our arrival was announced.

"His Highness, Prince Callan of Grey Oak, and his betrothed, Princess Aurelia of Sevanwinds."

Every eye in the ballroom turned to stare.

Mostly at me.

I stiffened as the whispers began, but Callan seemed perfectly at ease under the scrutiny.

"You look breathtaking," he whispered, taking my hand and raising it to his lips. His touch was warm, his expression smooth—too smooth. I caught the calculated glint in his golden eyes, and it ignited a familiar flicker of anger in my chest as I thought of a party very similar to this one seven years ago.

One that had ended in him deserting me to save himself.

Heliconia had ruined the night. Would she try it again?

"And you look like the perfect son," I said with mock sweetness as he led us into the ballroom.

Out of the corner of my eye, I saw his brow twitch, but he said nothing. Instead, his grip on my hand tightened just enough to remind me what this was between us. I refused to give him the satisfaction of a reaction.

Across the room, I spotted Rydian standing in the shadows, his dark eyes following my every move. I could practically feel his hands on me all over again. The way he'd made me writhe for him last night. The way he'd broken me apart and put me back together with his body.

My smile slipped as I caught his gaze for a moment. The storm clouds in his eyes hadn't dimmed. If anything, they looked darker and more violent than ever. I should have been turned off by the possessiveness inside that storm. The way he honed in on how close Callan and I stood. Where our bodies brushed. Instead, it thrilled me. In that moment, it took every ounce of control I had not to cross the room and step right into his arms. Besides, there was more than a shared night in bed brewing behind that stormy look he wore. What was he planning?

"Care to rein in some of that darkness, my darling?" Callan's voice broke through my thoughts, and I realized with a jolt that I'd let my power seep far too close to the surface.

Biting back a scowl, I reeled it back in, steadying myself for what was to come.

"Good girl." Callan pressed his hand against the small of my back, guiding me toward the gathered guests.

I imagined cutting that hand off and shoving it up his ass.

Or casually mentioning to Rydian that Callan had done it. That probably made me evil, but something had shifted for me since last night. Or maybe it had changed the moment he'd dragged me into his kitchen and pinned me to his wall with his mouth. There were too many moments to know for sure. Maybe it had been a gradual slide. Maybe I'd fallen for him the night of the lamplight party. All I knew was, somewhere along the way, we'd stopped hating one another. Or I'd stopped caring that we did.

We moved together through the ballroom, Callan exchanging pleasantries with other court members while pretending this was the happiest day of his life. But I couldn't help noticing none of the other courts had come. As the night wore on, I sensed Callan's uneasiness at their absence. I wanted to be smug—but their refusal to show meant my chances of gaining their aid were basically zero.

When Duron finally arrived, Callan slipped away to speak with him, finally leaving me alone. I exhaled, relieved to have a moment to myself even if it happened to be in the center of a crowded ballroom.

"Princess Aurelia," a lilting voice greeted me.

I turned and found a stranger extending his hand. He wore the burnt bronze colors of Autumn, and the scent rolling off him was distinctly animal. Shifter then. But his green eyes sparkled with intrigue as he took my hand, his touch cool.

The moment our hands met, the glamour surrounding him dropped away. Before me stood a fae male, tall and graceful, his long golden hair cascading down his back. My surprise must have registered at the sudden reveal because he grinned, clearly entertained.

"A necessary trick tonight," he said simply.

"Have we met?" I asked, struggling to place his familiar face.

"Many years ago. I'm Talthis. Emissary to the king and queen of Lightshore."

"Of course. You visited Sevanwinds the year before—" I couldn't finish and instead said, "It's nice to see you again."

"Lightshore sends its regards to its neighbors," he said smoothly.

Spring, the court of eternal first blooms and last frosts. Neighbors felt accurate. Once, our kingdoms were even friends, in fact. But somewhere along the way, that had changed. And now, beneath his pleasant smile, there was something sharp enough to remind me that friendship wasn't something I could count on.

"Have you spoken to Callan or Duron?" I asked. "They'll be glad to know their invitation was answered."

"I haven't decided whether to do so." His gaze swept over me. "We all thought you were lost, Princess," he said quietly, his voice tinged with disbelief. "But it seems the Summer Court has managed to thwart Heliconia after all."

Just the sound of her name spoken aloud bothered me more than I wanted to admit. And I didn't dare tell him the rest of my kingdom still slept beneath Heliconia's magical grip.

"For seven years, I was lost," I admit quietly. "And now that I've returned, I want only to pay her back for what she took."

"You surprise us all by allying yourself with Autumn."

"And you disappoint me by not allying with anyone. Heliconia will come for us all. Alone, we suffer. Together, we stand a chance of defeating her."

His brow rose. "Is that what the Autumn king tells you? That Lightshore has no allies?"

My confusion was clear, but his gaze only sharpened as if it told him what he'd wanted to know.

"Duron is the one with no allies, Princess. Lightshore has friends willing to do what Duron will not."

Hope lifted inside me. "And what is that?"

He looked up to where the king stood, speaking with his advisors. It was clear from their flushed cheeks and the goblets they held that they were well on their way to inebriated. "We would put our people before all else," Talthis murmured. "Including our own ego."

When he looked back at me, I realized the truth with a jolt. "You know," I said. "You know what he's doing here—to his own people—and you do nothing to stop it?"

"We have our own kingdom's fate to worry about," Talthis said, eyes flashing at my accusation.

Yes, whatever friendship there might've been between our peoples before was long gone now.

"I don't believe we should have to choose between the two," I said coldly.

"Your naivete is endearing. But your father knew better."

"What do you mean?" I asked.

"Princess," someone called in a sing-song voice.

I glanced over to see a female headed our way, complete with an entourage at her heels. Talthis turned back to me, but his glamour had returned. It was clear I wasn't going to get an answer to my question—not now.

The fae emissary's expression softened, though his eyes remained unreadable. "I am glad you survived, Princess. We shall see how long you can keep that up," he murmured, bowing low before disappearing into the crowd.

THE
MOON

CHAPTER FORTY-THREE
AURELIA

The ominous tone of Talthis's parting words stayed with me even after he'd gone.

"Princess Aurelia," came a sultry, melodic voice that pulled my attention. A woman with iridescent scales glittering faintly against her pale skin approached with a predatory smile.

Her dark blue hair rippled like water down her back, and her eyes, sea-deep and shimmering, locked onto mine with unabashed admiration. "I am so thrilled to finally meet you, Your Highness. I'm Princess Naliadne, daughter of Patamoi, King of the Osphanis." She bent her head low, adding, "But don't tell any of them."

She jerked her head at the rest of the ballroom. Her flirty irreverence made me like her instantly. But I couldn't help registering my surprise. No one above surface had ever laid eyes on the king's only daughter. Until now.

"Your secret is safe, Your Highness."

But she waved away the title, saying, "No need for that. I'm incognito tonight. Just Nali."

"It's an honor to meet you."

The female naiad's lips curved into a sexy smile. "Believe me, the honor is mine. We thought it was a rumor that you'd somehow survived and returned. And then a worse one when we heard you'd allied yourself with Autumn."

One of the males in her entourage cleared his throat. The mer princess smirked. "My companions warn me against such comments while standing in the enemy's house."

Despite their warnings, she didn't look worried.

"I take it you're not here to accept Duron's offer of an alliance then?" I asked.

Naliadne made a face. "Ugh. Sea gods, no."

Another of her companions snickered.

"I don't understand. Why come at all?" I asked.

She winked. "I came to see you."

My pulse quickened. If the Osphanis people were offering an alliance, maybe they could help me get out of here.

"I'm glad you did," I said. "Sevanwinds has always considered the river people our friends."

"As do we," she said.

"Maybe there's a way to strengthen that friendship."

Her face fell. She looked almost apologetic as she said, "Unfortunately, I've been instructed to say that can't happen as long as you're aligned with these bottom feeders."

"Nali." The male who'd cleared his throat now hissed her name.

She rolled her eyes. "Respectfully," she added.

"What if I told you I was thinking of ending my alliance here?" I asked as quietly as I could.

Naliadne's eyes lit. "In that case, I'd be happy to extend our favor—"

"There you are." Callan's voice sliced through the conversation like a rusty blade.

I winced as the river heir's expression shuttered and her companions pressed in tightly as if they expected an ambush. Callan ignored them, shoving his way to my side. "And you made friends," he added, clearly angling for an introduction.

"Callan, this is Nali, a representative from King Palamoi's court," I said, offering her a wink of my own.

She smiled, but it fell away as she turned back to Callan.

"Ah, the king sent an emissary then," he said as he took her hand. But I could see the disappointment that the king himself hadn't come.

Nali pulled her hand back, her smile mostly a show of pointed teeth. "Charmed," she said with more sarcasm than could be ignored. "But we were just leaving."

"So soon? Aurelia and I haven't even taken our vow. Won't you stay for the celebration?"

Nali sighed but shot me a thoughtful glance. "If we must. But I'll need a beverage."

"Of course," Callan said, gesturing to a server. "Here we are."

The server veered toward us with a tray of full glasses. Callan passed them around with a friendly smile. When we all had a glass, he lifted his, saying, "A toast. To new friends."

Nali met my gaze and said, "To new friends." We all drank. Nali grinned at me then handed hers off to one of her friends. "Let's dance, boys."

They followed her to the dance floor without a goodbye.

When they were gone, Callan turned to me. Already, I could see the charm turning to irritation. "What the Hel did you say to her?"

"Nothing. She said the river people are impressed by the health and beauty of Autumn's lands."

"If they're so impressed, why did they run off the moment I walked up?"

"How should I know? I've been gone for seven years.

You're the one who's supposedly been trying to woo them to the alliance table."

He scowled. "Don't push me tonight, Aurelia. We need this to work. You have no idea how badly."

"I'm sure Daddy will punish us both if we don't deliver."

His lip curled. "You think this is a joke?"

"Of course not. No one is taking this more seriously than I am. But I can't force someone to change their opinion of you when you've apparently spent a lifetime convincing them you are what you are."

His eyes narrowed. "And what exactly am I?"

"Why don't you ask the river people? Since they're the only other court besides your own who deigned to show up tonight."

He snarled at me, drawing more than a few stares.

"Careful, darling. Your people are watching," I said.

Callan opened his mouth, clearly ready to blast me with some sharp threat, but he never got the chance. A second later, the music cut off, and the room buzzed with voices. I glanced at Callan and was surprised to see his expression flash with a look of sheer panic that mirrored my own. Then, he blinked, and it slid away.

His confidence—a thin veneer, I realized—returned.

"Come," he said, taking my hand and tugging me toward the center of the room. "It's time."

Standing in the middle of the now-empty dance floor, I forced myself to remain steady as the murmurs died down.

Duron strode out to join us. "Where are the other emissaries?" he hissed.

"I don't know, Father," Callan said quietly.

"They said they'd come," Duron grumbled. He turned to glare at Callan. "You said you'd convince them."

"As you know, I need to make physical contact with them for that to happen." Callan's tone had gone brittle.

Duron sneered at him. "Your gift is useless to me if you can't do what I asked."

Gift?

"I have done plenty," Callan said defensively. At Duron's lifted brow, Callan added, "I got her to Grey Oak, didn't I?"

I reared back, reeling.

"You were supposed to persuade her to give up her magic willingly," Duron snapped.

Wait. What? "You compelled me?" I demanded.

Every one of their heads swung to me. Duron sniffed dismissively. Callan's cheeks burned, whether with anger or embarrassment, I didn't know. Nor did I care.

"Persuasion," he corrected.

"Isn't that the same thing?" I shot back. "You convinced me against my will to come here. To agree to marry you."

Callan didn't answer.

My head spun as I thought back to all the casual touches between us. His hand on mine in the carriage. At dinner with his father that first night. The kiss he'd given me at Sunspire. Had all of those *touches* been to keep me under his thrall?

I hadn't even noticed.

Then again, compulsion—or persuasion as he insisted on calling it—hadn't been gifted by the gods in centuries.

One of the king's advisers strode up. Koraz. "Your Majesty, we can't wait any longer, or we'll lose the audience we already have." He eyed me, clearly still unhappy with the decision to bind me to the royal family.

That made two of us.

"Fine," Duron grumbled. He looked at me. "When this is over, there's work to be done, persuaded or not."

Callan didn't bother to contradict him.

Duron turned to face the crowd, his smile as radiant as it was fake. "We celebrate together tonight because my son and heir has finally chosen a mate," he said, his voice booming over the room. "Even more joyous is that his betrothed is none other than the lost princess of Summer, Aurelia of Sevanwinds."

The room clapped and cheered.

Nali whistled loudly from the back. I caught her eye, thrown off by her sudden change of heart about my engagement. Then I remembered. Callan had taken her hand in greeting. A new horror spread through me. The reason he'd been so confident the courts would ally with us tonight. He planned to compel them all. It had already begun to work on Nali.

And I had no way to warn her.

"My son and his betrothed stand before you, a symbol of hope and light against Heliconia's darkness." Murmurs rose at her name, but Duron spoke right over them. He looked out over the audience, fire burning in his eyes now. "You saw the richness of my lands as you arrived. Untouched by that bitch's curse." I flinched at the viciousness in his tone. "My power protects us all. United with Summer, we are made stronger. United all, we will defeat her forever."

Across the room, Talthis was glowering.

"I hope our friends from neighboring courts, if they are here tonight, will consider joining us in this fight," Duron went on. "Witness the binding of these two souls as a symbol of hope and a promise for our future. Let us begin."

My heart thudded.

"Hey," Callan whispered. "Just concentrate on me. We're almost there."

He flashed an encouraging smile, and I took a tiny step away from him, refusing to let him touch me again.

Duron turned to Callan and said, "My son and my heir, do you take Aurelia Valeen, daughter of Tyrion and Celeste Valeen, as your wedded mate and make a binding vow before this court and the world to wed her?"

The entire room seemed to hold its breath as I looked at Callan, waiting for him to utter the words that would bind us.

"Yes," Callan said. "I take Aurelia Valeen for my wedded mate."

"And Aurelia, do you take Callan Ashfall as your wedded—"

"No." My answer rang out loud and clear.

Beside me, Callan made a soft sound as if he'd been struck.

Murmurs began, but Duron's face flushed red. "Silence!" he screamed. "You will make your vow," he hissed at me. "Or you will—"

"I refuse Callan Ashfall," I said, louder this time.

Duron stared at me, clearly at a loss. After all his threats, he hadn't expected me to defy him. But I needed the courts to hear me reject him. The last thing I needed was for someone to drag me back here, thinking I'd defected from a marriage contract.

The quiet that followed my declaration was more shock than obedience to Duron, but it quickly deepened into something more.

Something wrong.

I prayed to the Fates and the Furiosities that my plan had worked.

A scream tore through the room, echoing off the walls. My head snapped toward the sound just as a rush of putrid magic washed over me, thick and nauseating. At the back, the doors that led to the patio and the gardens beyond flew open.

Rotting, waning magic poured inside.

Along with the Withered.

Some had cloaks pulled over their faces. Some had tossed their hoods back to reveal their wrinkled, sunken features. All of them wielded swords and wore looks of pure wrath.

The crowd scattered in panicked waves as they came— foul, twisted figures with hollow, black eyes and gnarled limbs.

I realized the Withered I'd seen in the street that day had been the healthier, stronger ones. Some of these were clearly much farther gone than the others. Outrage burned inside me at what their king had done to them.

The chaos heightened as the Withered surged closer. Duron was whisked away by a dozen armed guards. Gone in an instant.

Callan yelled for me to run.

But I only smiled grimly at the sight of my new friends joining the fray.

Callan drew his sword, an ornamental thing meant to match his royal wedding uniform, and pointed it at the Withered fighting to get past the line of guards who'd rushed forward to meet them. Well, that was new, at least.

I started for the back doors, aiming for the gardens where Vanya had promised to leave my leathers and swords.

Then I saw him—Rydian, shoving his way toward me through the chaos, his gaze locked on mine. Shadows poured out of him, punching out with fists of their own or shaping themselves into blades that cut a path through anyone in his way. Some of those shadows had eyes that glowed like a demon's. Every one of them was its own unique nightmare.

Most scurried away from the mere sight of the creatures he conjured. But I was drawn to the look he wore, the relentless and utter determination etched in every line of his brow and in the flex of his jaw.

He looked like a vengeful god cutting through his enemies. Untouchable. Unyielding. Mine.

The last thought clanged through me unexpectedly. I shook it off and started in the other direction, determined to slip past him while the Withered kept him busy.

When he reached the barricade of soldiers, his form flickered, becoming more shadow than flesh. And then he was through the lines of clanging swords, closing quickly on my heels.

I ran faster and made it all the way to the open back doors before his hand snagged mine.

"Come," he said, voice low and urgent. He took my hand with a grip that left no room for argument. "You must leave. Now."

One of the Withered careened toward us. Rydian held up a hand, and a bolt of power knocked it back.

"Stop it," I insisted, putting myself between him and the Withered. "They're with me."

Rydian looked at the cloaked figure with disbelief. The Withered raised its head, hesitating.

"Go," I insisted.

It turned away and aimed for a royal guard instead.

I tried to pull away from Rydian, but he tightened his grip.

"Let me go," I demanded.

"I can't." His gaze searched mine for a single second before he added almost pleadingly, "Trust me."

It was a horrible thing to ask of me now. And even more awful that I gave in.

We plunged into the mass of bodies, ducking and weaving as my mind spun with questions. The Withered were everywhere, screams tearing through the night as they attacked the soldiers in their path. And still, Rydian led me, his hand never leaving mine as he cut a path through the patio doors and down the terrace steps into the garden.

Freedom washed over me.

I'd made it out.

A few more steps and I'd be clear enough—

"And where exactly do you think you're going?"

The sound of the male's voice cut through my silent victory like a killing knife. Still, I might have taken my chances and kept running, but Rydian pulled us up short as Koraz stepped out ahead of us, blocking our escape.

"This is as far as you go, traitor," Koraz hissed at Rydian.

Rydian snarled at him and drew his sword. But the voice behind us spoke again, stilling Rydian's hand.

"My bastard son running off with his brother's bride. Now this is quite the entertainment."

With arms and legs full of lead, I turned to face the king.

THE
MOON

Chapter Forty-Four
Rydian

Aurelia's hand in mine went cold.

I swept my gaze over our surroundings in a quick assessment. Daegel and Slade had other orders, and the Withered were busy with Callan and whatever guests they'd managed to pin down. No one else was coming.

I turned to face Duron without fully taking my gaze off Koraz.

My father was as I'd always known him—cold, cruel, with eyes like frozen amber and a voice like a blade cutting through the air.

"I'm afraid your little tryst ends now," he said. "What a waste of fucking power too."

On my other side, Koraz grinned, shifting his grip on the wickedly curved blade in his hands. I would have preferred to kill him much more slowly than time would allow tonight. But his death would satisfy me nonetheless.

His red eyes gleamed with amusement as he looked at me. "I've been looking forward to this for a long time."

He took a step toward me.

"Rydian," Aurelia breathed.

She stood at my side, her chest rising and falling with quick breaths that gave away her fear, but I felt the power crackling beneath her skin. Furyfire licked at her fingertips—black, twisted flames that pulsed with unnatural heat. Power she barely understood. Power she might never be able to control unless she stopped fighting it and truly accepted what she was.

"If you touch her, I will peel your skin from your bones," I said.

Duron merely laughed, the sound cutting right through the sharpest edges of my threat. I tightened my grip on my sword, my heartbeat steady even as unease coiled in my gut.

I couldn't touch Duron.

Even if I wanted to, the blood vow wouldn't allow it.

Koraz saw it in my face before I could mask it. His grin sharpened. "Ah. There it is. That pathetic obedience. Like a dog trained to heel."

I ignored him and watched Duron instead. He hadn't moved toward us, nor had he interrupted Koraz's taunts, which told me he was going to let his advisor fight this one for him. Good. I'd been waiting for this chance. Now I just had to get Aurelia to leave me to it.

"Listen to me," I said in a low voice, uncaring that they could hear us. "I want you to run to the edge of the garden when I tell you. Don't stop, no matter what you hear—"

"No," she hissed, pulling her hand from mine. "I'm not leaving you."

"Furious."

"I'm done running," she said. "I choose to fight."

Hope wove through the violence in my veins, but I shoved it back. She was fighting for herself, and that was all I could ask of her now. All I needed.

Koraz tilted his head, watching me like a predator sizing up weak prey. "Tell me, does she know?" His voice dipped into something cruel. "Does she know you can't so much as lift a blade against your master?"

Aurelia stiffened beside me, her flames flickering with uncertainty.

I didn't look at her. Instead, I raised my sword, nodding toward Koraz. "Are we going to fight, or do you need to run your mouth a little longer?"

Koraz lunged first.

I met him mid-strike, the force of his attack rattling through my bones. He'd poured magic into the blow. And the next one, and the next.

The gardens blurred around us as we moved—strike, parry, counter—his vicious stabs meeting my speed. He fought like a battering ram, every thrust of his blade or his magic meant to break me in half. I dodged, spinning low to avoid the crushing weight of his blade, but my focus split the moment I heard Aurelia's sharp inhale behind me.

I turned, just for a second—

Pain tore through my side.

Koraz's blade bit deep, hot blood spilling down my ribs. I gritted my teeth, forcing myself to stay upright, to move before he could strike again. His magic infiltrated my flesh like a poison.

"Rydian!"

Aurelia's voice was raw with fear, but I had no time to reassure her. I had to finish this.

Koraz lifted his sword for the killing blow—

My shadows coiled around him, using his blind spots to tug on his momentum. To slow him just enough. In the moment of his hesitation, I twisted, driving my blade through his chest before he could land another strike. His eyes went wide as he staggered, a choking sound spilling from his lips. I ripped my sword free, and Koraz collapsed to his knees, blood blooming dark across his tunic. It was more than satisfying to watch.

But it wasn't over.

Duron remained, untouched, standing in the firelit garden like a ghost of every nightmare I'd ever had. I turned to him, blade slick with Koraz's blood—

And my body seized.

Pain. Deep, writhing, unnatural. My hands trembled as I tried to lift my sword, but the moment I so much as thought of striking him, the blood vow coiled around my bones like barbed wire, lashing deep.

I gasped, barely able to breathe.

Duron smiled. "I wondered when you'd try."

I could do nothing. Couldn't move, couldn't fight. I was utterly, uselessly *helpless*.

And Aurelia saw it all.

Her face was unreadable—shock, betrayal, fury all twisting into something I didn't have the words for. But there was no time to explain, no time to tell her I'd done this to *protect*.

Because the furyfire at her fingertips erupted into an inferno.

Duron's smirk vanished, and he threw his hands up to block it. A windstorm blew from his palms—the last dregs of his waning magic—and for a moment, I wondered if it would be enough to stop the furyfire, but it didn't last. The black flames overtook the wind, eating through whatever barrier it had provided. The moment those dark flames touched his flesh, Duron screamed.

But Aurelia's flame didn't stop.

Rather than lick at his clothing, it engulfed Duron's entire form. He staggered, his vain glamour peeling away, his wrinkled skin cracking like scorched parchment beneath the force of her magic. He opened his mouth—to speak, to scream— but the furyfire swallowed him whole.

I felt it like a weight being lifted off my skin. A pressure between my shoulder blades that had been there so long I'd forgotten what it felt like without it. But then it was gone. The blood in my veins answered to Duron no longer.

Instead, it sang only for her.

The flames winked out, and all that remained of the Autumn king was a pile of ash.

Trembling, Aurelia stared at Duron's ashes, her golden hair wild, her skin glowing as if she'd somehow taken power from the kill itself. Slowly, she turned to me, and I noted the power that still clung to her skin, still burned in her eyes. But it wasn't triumph in her expression. It was something darker. Something depthless and unending and fated. Something even the Fates and Furiosities hadn't seen coming.

I knew, in that moment, that I should be afraid.

Not of her.

For her.

For what she'd just done.

For what she'd become.

For what she'd do when she found out the truth. Not just what I'd planned for her tonight but the truth of her choices and who'd ordered me to let her make them. To do it all without telling her what had really brought me into her life. The truth of what she was capable of. What she'd just chosen. And what it would cost her in the end.

And how, no matter that I'd kept her safe—

She might never forgive me for any of it.

THE
MOON

CHAPTER FORTY-FIVE
AURELIA

Rydian stared at me like he'd seen a specter. The furyfire had cooled inside me, but my veins swam with the life force I'd taken from Duron just before he'd—

Before I'd ended him.

And whatever power I'd unleashed inside me went far beyond anything I'd ever wielded before. Maybe that was why Rydian looked so stricken.

"I'm sorry," I said.

"For what?"

"I didn't mean to use it... I just—"

"Furious, you have nothing to apologize for. That was incredible. *You* are incredible."

His gaze softened, and of all things, he cupped my cheek. Like I hadn't just committed the murder of a king. His own father. The way he looked at me now... the mask was gone. This was him. Vulnerable and real and...sad?

Nothing made sense.

Exhaustion tugged at me. I'd used more of my magic than I ever had, and apparently, that came with a price.

"Will you tell anyone?" I whispered. "About the furyfire?" Did he know about the death magic I'd used? The way I'd inhaled Duron's life force at the end?

"I've kept your secrets since long before you even knew them," he said and I could have sworn the ink on his skin writhed as he spoke.

Before I could ask what he meant, voices rang out somewhere else in the garden. Followed by the clang of swords. Reality crashed in around me. The Withered. My escape. I had to go now or risk being caught.

"We need to go," Rydian said, echoing my thoughts.

He wiped his sword clean on his pants then slid it back into its sheath. His hand slipped into mine, firm and sure as he tugged me toward the path we'd been on earlier. We'd have to step over Koraz to get there. I didn't let myself look down at the bloodied tunic or the frozen, unseeing eyes.

When we came to a fork in the path, Rydian pulled me to the left.

"Wrong way," I said, trying to yank him in the other direction. "My bag—"

"Vanya gave it to me," he said. "This way."

Uncertainty rippled through me. Vanya had betrayed me to Rydian? Considering what we'd just done, there was no time to argue it now.

We ran through a maze of hedges and came out at the edge of the gardens on a narrow walkway that led toward the road. A dark carriage waited, horses snorting, their eyes gleaming as though possessed. The driver wore black armor emblazoned with a silver sigil that caught the moonlight. A crescent moon with a sword through it. Recognition of the symbol chilled me to the core.

The Midnight Court.

Rydian tugged me toward it.

"What are you doing?" I hissed, trying to pull my hand

from his grip, but he wouldn't let go. His gaze was sharp, unrelenting.

"They won't hurt you," he said.

Bullshit.

The Midnight Court were notoriously savage with prisoners. They'd torture me to learn my secrets and relish the pain they'd cause while doing it. They'd make me beg for a swift death.

Rydian knew that. And he'd sold me out to them anyway.

Panic surged as he opened the carriage door and pulled me toward it.

"Please, no." I braced myself against the doorframe, twisting around to look at him. "Why are you doing this?"

His expression softened, a flicker of something that might've been regret crossing his features. "I'm keeping you safe."

My fingers dug into the wood, every instinct screaming at me to fight, but the commotion behind us grew closer. The castle guards were swarming, pushing through the courtyard with horrifying speed even as the Withered tried to fight them back.

"Furious," Rydian said, his tone low and almost pleading. "I can't let him have you."

Him. Callan.

He'd be made king now. And he'd know I killed his father.

I glanced back toward the fray where Callan and the guards fought against the Withered who'd come to my aid tonight. Autumn would win, I could see that now, and guilt tugged at me for the danger I'd caused the magicless fae. My choice pained me: Stay to fight alongside them and risk Callan's wrath for my crime or give myself over to the Midnight Court.

In the end, I never got to choose.

With a final push, Rydian forced me into the carriage. The

door slammed shut, locking me inside with some kind of spell I couldn't break. The horses lurched forward, their hooves pounding into the night.

The carriage rattled as we sped through the open front gates and away from Grey Oak.

My heart pounded against my ribs, the carriage walls closing in as I processed everything. Rydian hadn't saved me. He'd kidnapped me and delivered me to the enemy. Worse, he'd handed me over to the only court more cowardly than Callan himself. I would find no friends in Midnight's court. No allies or aid.

Rydian had made me a prisoner again. And he'd done it using my feelings for him as a distraction. Or as bait.

The hurt of his betrayal tore a hole through my heart. I gritted my teeth against the pain, crafting it into rage and resolve instead. As the carriage rolled on, I vowed to the Fates to make Rydian pay for what he'd done to me. For this, I would become my father's daughter. A Furiosity with Hel's fire in my veins. And before it was over, the entire realm would feel my flames.

Thank you for reading! Aurelia's story continues in Prince of Secrets & Shadows! Find out what secret Rydian has been keeping from Aurelia...

And if you enjoyed Kingdom of Briars & Roses and want more from this world, snag the prequel story called A GLAMOUR OF SMOKE & SHADOWS to find out how Sonoma ended up having a secret baby (Aurelia) with a demon king of Hel against the wishes of the Aine and why Heliconia is dead set on killing them all...

Want a completed ROMANTASY series while you wait for Prince of Secrets & Shadows? Don't miss the Accidental Alchemy Series, starting with the reader favorite, ONE DARK SPARK. Paige has always been clumsy but when she spills her pumpkin spice latte and accidentally conjures a naked dragon king from the pages of a book, the library—and Paige's mundane life—will never be the same again.

I appreciate your help spreading the word, including telling a friend. Reviews help readers find books! Please leave a review on your favorite book site. To keep in touch, you can join my Facebook group, Heather's Book Horde for exclusive giveaways & sneak peeks or join my newsletter to find out when I have new books.

Turn the page for a sneak peek of ONE DARK SPARK...

One Dark Spark
Paige

This particular Thursday starts out like every other. I'm early to rise, quick to coffee, and off to work. The fact that my workplace is the ancient and very secret library that exists one floor below my small Boston apartment is just a bonus that means I don't have to deal with rush hour traffic or, well, humans in general.

Then again, it's not my choice to remain separate from the humans, so I'm not sure that's actually what I'd call a *bonus*. But I've made my peace with it. There is—unfortunately—no other option. The work I do here is too important to risk creating any attachments *out there*.

As an intern for the Athenaeum, the creatures I interact with are few and far between—and rarely ever human. Trolls, giants, elves, fae, shifters—the clientele that come to study or search the library are diverse and strange. Have you ever met a banshee bookworm with a top-secret clearance? It's not a combination one might expect. Also, not to stereotype, but banshees are just weird in general.

With my earbuds streaming a spicy alien romance audiobook, I spend the morning patrolling the ogre section and watching for anything sneaky or out of place among the quiet stacks.

The Athenaeum has one purpose, and that is to contain the threats trapped among the pages of the volumes kept inside it. As the library's newest—and most hopeful—intern, my job is to make sure nothing inside the books contained here makes it out again.

Unfortunately for the Athenaeum, I kind of suck at it.

As if to prove my point, a large tome on the end of the shelf shakes ominously as I pass it. A single, gnarled green finger pries itself from between the pages, attempting to push the book open. I rush forward, adrenaline surging. With two hands, I grab the book and squeeze it shut again.

"Clauseruntque," I hiss and the green finger withdraws as the book seals itself shut at the command of the magic.

Exhaling, I re-shelve the book into its proper place then let go and back away, bumping into the shelf at my back. Several books vibrate with the impact, and I suck in a breath, jumping clear of them before my clumsy ass can do any more damage.

A moment passes, and the books fall silent again.

Damn, that was close.

It happens far more often than I care to admit. As though, for some reason, the books *enjoy* toying with me. Truthfully, I wonder if they can sense how afraid I am of screwing things up. They don't act like this for the full-fledged keepers, that's for sure.

I tune back in to the audiobook still playing in my ears and resume my patrol, fingers crossed the incident wasn't strong enough to raise any alarms with Hoc.

I can't really afford any more fuckups.

Not after I *barely* managed to avoid getting thrown out for the last one.

So, I keep strolling, putting one foot in front of the other while I imagine the hands of a deliciously muscled blue alien running all over my body.

A shifter—as evidenced by her golden gaze—steps into the aisle and looks up. She mouths something, but I can't hear her. She repeats—

"Sorry!" I pull one of my earbuds out.

"No biggie," she says easily. Her blonde hair is long and braided over her shoulder. When she smiles, I get the sense that she's new to the library. Mainly because the smile doesn't reach her eyes, and it's not hard to sense her uneasiness here. She's not the only one. Most of our guests don't realize how alive this place truly is until they experience it for themselves.

"Can I help you?" I ask.

"Yes. Please. I'm trying to find some history on shifters. Books detailing what comes first in terms of creation. A real chicken or the egg type of situation." She laughs.

I return her humor, deciding that, if I were going to make a friend outside of this place, she could be one of them. "Yes. We have quite a lot of reference material about shifters in the non-fiction section. Unless, of course, you want a spelled fictional story."

"No, thanks," she says with a shudder. "I've had enough dealings with spells to last a lifetime."

"Well—"

"Serenity," she offers.

"Serenity," I continue, "You can find the non-fiction down the hall and toward the back. There's a sign over it, though it might not be lit yet." *Damn gnomes. They had* one *job this morning.*

"Great. Thanks so much—"

"Paige," I say.

"Paige. Great name." She grins, but after so many years of jokes, the humor doesn't hit me in the same way anymore.

"Thanks, it's fitting, I suppose."

"Very. Have a great day!" She waves and turns. Normally, supernaturals are escorted through the more volatile sections of the library. The ones who need keeper or intern status to enter. For what Serenity is looking for, though, she shouldn't run into any issues.

Unless, of course, she tries to break into the restricted areas. But, as far as I know, that's never happened. The library's magic is too strong for that. It sees everything.

I continue my perusal, re-shelving books as needed and checking through the areas to make sure no one has wandered where they shouldn't be, and by the time I surface again, I realize that the entire morning has passed without much incident.

Winning! My stomach growls, and I become aware I've very nearly missed lunch, thanks to my audiobook as a pleasant distraction. The story is about a human woman who crash-lands on an alien planet only to be saved by a large, muscled creature with two dicks. *Two!* Her dream come true.

If only.

I snort, enjoying the spicy scenes and the fiction of it all. Humans write the best fairy tales. This place? It's full of stories that are much too real to be enjoyed.

On my way back to the break room, I reach the witch section. There's a title called Midnight Falls something-or-other, and my fingers brush over the spine as I try to imagine what a place like that would look like. The spine moves beneath my hands, and I jerk away again, scowling at how unsettled it leaves me.

A noise ahead snags my attention. Grunting. And then a heave of breath and a *crack!*

The sound of a weapon wielded has me running toward it.

Rounding the corner, I pull up short. Blossom, a female keeper not much older than me with stark white hair is standing over a body that's currently oozing blackened blood into the carpets. Blossom has a severed troll head clutched in one hand and a blood-tipped axe in the other.

She looks up at me, her sharp gaze mildly annoyed at seeing me here. "He a friend of yours?"

"What happened?" I ask, eyes wide.

"This asshole was shelved incorrectly." Her glare turns accusatory, and I jolt, realizing her meaning.

Interns are the only ones who shelve books. And I'm the only intern. Which makes that exclusively my problem. *Shit.*

"Does Hoc know?" I ask, keeping my voice a near whisper.

Before she can answer, a harsh blaring sounds overhead, and dread spears through me. Double shit.

Blossom gives me an apologetic look. "He does now."

Then she returns her attention to the decapitated troll and mutters a string of words in a language I've yet to learn. The language of the keepers. Magic sparks, engulfing the troll until its body and corresponding head are sucked into the open volume lying at her feet.

Blossom grabs the book and slams it shut with a muttered, "Clauseruntque," to cap it off.

The pages stick.

She hands the book to me.

"At least it wasn't the main character. Come find me when he's done yelling at you," she says, and I know she means Hoc. "You owe me a drink for that one. I got troll-blood on my new shoes."

I look down. Sure enough, bright blue troll blood coats her normally shiny Doc Martens. Great. "Add it to my tab."

DOWNLOAD ONE DARK SPARK >

About the Author

Heather Hildenbrand lives in coastal Virginia where she writes paranormal and fantasy romance with strong-willed heroines and dark, grumpy heroes who'll burn the world down for their mate. Her most frequent hobbies are cuddling with her giant goldendoodles, riding country roads on the back of her husband's motorcycle, and avoiding killer slugs.

You can find out more about Heather and her books at www. heatherhildenbrand.com.

Or find her here:

Online Store (get signed copies)
heatherhildenbrandbooks.com

A Witch's Soul

A Witch's Prophecy

A Witch's Hope

Twisted Tides

The Girl Who Cried Werewolf

The Girl Who Cried Captive

The Girl Who Cried War

The Girl Who Never Cried

The Winter Witch

The Spring Witch

The Witch's Heart

Midnight Mate

One Dark Spark

Two Blazing Hearts

Three Scorched Kingdoms

Goddess Ascending

Goddess Claiming

Goddess Forging

Kiss of Death

Knock Em Dead

Death's Door

Dead to Rights

Dead End

The Girl Who Called The Stars

The Girl Who Ruled The Stars

Alpha Games

Alpha Trials

Alpha Chosen

Dirty Blood

Cold Blood

Blood Bond

Blood Rule

Broken Blood

Imitation

Deviation

Generation

Heather also writes small town contemporary romance as Violet Stafford.

Stay For Summer